Praise for _The Prophecy of Zephyrus_

"A modern-day teenager is swept through time in Hesse's exhilarating fantasy tale of enchanted lands and rampaging monsters.

This gem of a well-plotted adventure tale is a worthwhile addition to the fantasy genre."

— Kirkus Discoveries

"Hesse has a definite talent as a storyteller and a true flair for description. The world she builds is varied and vibrant, and Obie's transformation from insecure, angry teenager to confident and competent warrior is believable . . .

. . .the story proves an appealing, inventive, and enjoyable read for young adults."

4-Star Review (out of 5)

—ForeWord CLARION Reviews

The
Prophecy
of
Zephyrus

G. A. Hesse

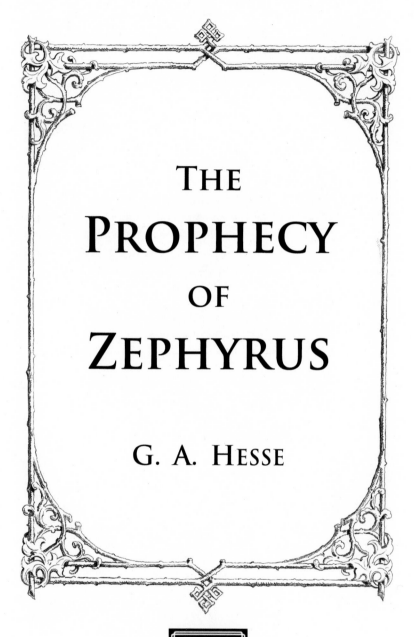

THE PROPHECY OF ZEPHYRUS

FIRST EDITION 2009

Library of Congress Control Number: 2009906847
The Writer's Guild of America, West, Registration Number 1332829

Cover art by Steve A. Roberts
Maps illustrated by T. Avery

AHAH Press Books
PO Box 7273
Laguna Niguel, CA 92607-7273

www.ahahpressbooks.com

ISBN 978-0-9824693-0-9

Printed in The United States of America

10 9 8 7 6 5 4 3 2 1

For my daughter Hilary,
the light of my life,
whose perceptive comments
and good suggestions early on
helped in shaping this tale,
and my dear sister Oma,
for believing in me.

ACKNOWLEDGMENTS

To the members of the Writers' Roundtable that has met at Barnes & Noble in Aliso Viejo, California for many years now, especially Casey, Bill, Kathy, and Shari. Others include Angela, Diana, Jacqui, Jan, Lee, Mary, Nanette, Paul, Phil, and Phoenix. Thank you all for your many good suggestions and for catching things I missed.

Also, special thanks to Bonnie Daybell for editing the book when I thought it was finished and then discovered it wasn't, and to Lou Kirk for helping with final edits.

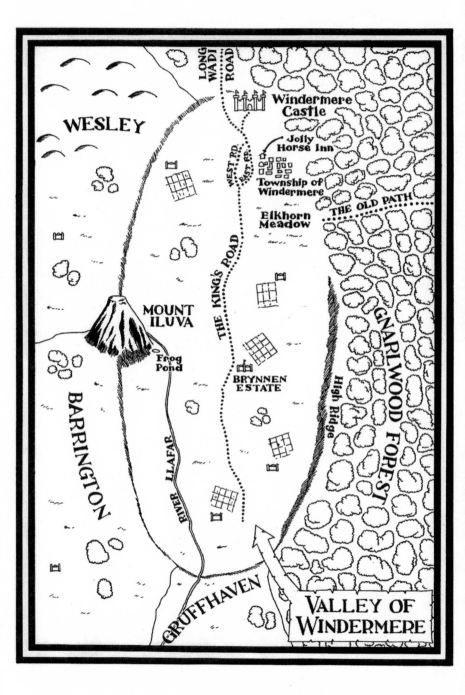

THE PROPHECY OF ZEPHYRUS

Star Crystal dark, Star Crystal light,
Bright jewels that crossed the void of night,
Streaked flaming o'er Earth's storm-worn seas,
White fire sent from yon Pleiades,
Brought unto dark, chaotic Earth
New Order, Action, Art, and Mirth.
Heavenly hand this gift did bring,
Entrusted to the Eagle Kings.

The Light Crystal the eagles kept
In mountains lonely and windswept;
The Dark Crystal by eagle's plume
They carried to Earth's infant Moon;
Forever parted must they stay,
Bright beacons that shall light the way,
Providing Man and Beast the key
To thrive in cosmic harmony.

But when black chaos doth arise
And from The Pit the Serpent flies,
Then forth six sorcerers shall come,
To hide the Moon and steal the Sun.
In darkest hour when hopes subside,
The Moonpath must the Guardians ride.
From Phoebe's hand for hearts aggrieved,
The Dark Crystal must be retrieved.

Then from afar 'neath orbs grown pale,
Seek him borne on the comet's tail,
For he with steadfast heart must dare,
Defend the task the Guardians bear.
When skies are dark and two is three,
And fiery breath burns frozen trees,
The battle for the Earth doth come,
With trampling boots and beat of drums.
Beware ye when the Serpent comes,
Beware ye, for the Serpent comes.

CONTENTS

THE
PROPHECY
OF ZEPHYRUS

CHAPTER ONE

THE SUMMONS

FEAR. TEETH-GNASHING, gut-wrenching fear ignited in him like a flash fire. He was exiled from the light to a place of black terror and godless emptiness, adrift in a soul annihilating void. His nerves stretched to the breaking point, his body jerked violently— and he awakened. He sat up, his heart pounding and his breath coming hard. Where was he? The face of his bedside clock glowed through the darkness like an old friend. It was a little after five a.m. He wasn't floating in space after all. As on all the other nights, Oberon Griffin, called *Obie* by most, was in his bed in his home-town of Garrett, Wyoming. He took a deep breath to calm himself. His body was clammy with sweat and his sheets were damp. Through his open window, he saw the stars still shining in the east. Was he going crazy? He needed to talk to the old man.

The old man was Will Gray Eagle, a Native American herbalist in his early fifties, who lived alone in his cabin a few miles outside of town. He had been more of a father than Obie's own dad, and his wisdom and candor had saved Obie, a junior at Garrett High School, on numerous occasions over the years. Now, Will was possibly the only person on earth who could help him. He should have gone to see him days ago. He'd stop by his cabin after his last class today.

Obie's left leg was aching again. The result of an old injury, it had left him with frequent pain and a bad limp. A warm shower would help. He pulled himself out of his childhood bed that at some indeterminate time during the past year had grown too

short for his six-foot-one frame. Slender of build and broad
shouldered, a Griffin trait, he wasn't bad looking at seventeen.
That fact might have been more gratifying if it wasn't for his limp.
Frequently, he had to remind himself that at a standstill his
disability didn't show. But would he ever be able to conquer his
inner demons, the ones that kept telling him he was a freak?

He switched his bedside lamp on and headed for the bathroom. While toweling off after showering, he glanced in the
bathroom mirror. His eyes were red from lack of sleep, but it was
useless to go back to bed. If he slept at all he'd probably have
the nightmare again. He slipped into a clean pair of blue jeans,
T-shirt, and tennies, then pulled his black ball cap on over his
sandy-blond hair and went downstairs to study for a math quiz.
Hopefully, he wouldn't run into Shannon at school today. She
wouldn't be impressed with his bedraggled appearance.

***

"The stars blink out like someone's turned the lights off, and then
something black, like a fungus, creeps over the moon and eats it
away until it disappears too," Obie said. "The valley's pitch-dark.
Then I'm suddenly up there floating in that black, empty sky. It
was the worst feeling I've ever had . . . like I'm lost in a place of
nothingness and I'll never find my way back. I felt like I was . . ."

"Yes?"

"About to be erased."

A look of compassion came over Will's face.

"You've got to help me, Will. I'm afraid to fall asleep. Every
time I do I have this dream again."

Will nodded. "Your dream is terrifying, yet it has a positive
side: it's trying to tell you something. The last part of it is a
warning."

Obie scowled. "A warning? What kind of warning?"

"I can't say, son. That's something you must discover. But I can tell you the warning is linked to the moon and stars. Is the moon full in your dream?"

"Yes."

Will got up and put another log on the fire, then leaned an arm against the stone mantle and stared into the flames, his brow furrowed in thought. Obie watched his mentor, respectful of his wrinkled face, his deep knowledge of things, and his presence that always filled the room. No one knew much about him except that he claimed to be a Sioux Indian. He had just shown up one day close to twenty years ago and built the cabin in the wilderness up against the hills. Living alone with his cat, his horse, and his books, he earned money by dispensing to locals the medicinal and culinary herbs he either grew or gathered in the hills.

"When did you start having this dream?" Will asked. He sat down again, cross-legged, opposite Obie.

"Just over a week ago, the same day I went to Ghostrise Valley with Josh. It was that night. But there's something else, something I need to show you." Obie reached into his leather ammo pouch and pulled out a large, gray, geode-like stone about the size of a baseball. He eyed the letters scratched on it that said,

Oberon,

then handed it to Will. Will held it up in the firelight and gazed at the inscription.

"So you found it," he said. Shadows from the flickering fire played over his face, and, for an instant, Obie saw a strange look in his eyes.

"Josh's dog ran into a hidden cave at Watcher Mountain, and we crawled in to get him out. I liked the feel of the rock's roundness when I touched it in the dark, so I put it in my pouch. I didn't even look at it until I got home. How did you know about it? Did you put it there for me to find?" Obie looked hopeful, half expecting him to confirm it.

Will was silent for a long moment. When he spoke his voice was deep and calming. "No. I knew about it, but I didn't put it there, son. I saw it in the cave long ago, but left it."

"Why?"

"Because it had your name on it; I couldn't interfere. Why didn't you come to me with it sooner?"

"You might have thought I was the one who wrote on it. I did wonder, though, if you were playing a joke on me."

"I would never play a joke like that, Oberon. This is no laughing matter—as your bad dreams have shown you. And by the way, you look like something the cat's been slapping around. It might help if you combed your hair."

"I *feel* like something the cat's slapped around, but I'm not in a mood to worry about my hair." Obie pulled his ball cap on to hide his hair, positioning the visor in back like he usually did. "What I want to know is, who wrote that on the rock, and why? Tell me what to do, Will. What's going on? How can I get rid of these bad dreams?"

"You should have guessed by now the rock and the dreams are linked. When I first saw the rock with your name on it, I knew it was a summons for you to come to the valley. Your dream is simply another part of the message."

"Well, what's the message?" Obie asked impatiently. Will's yellow cat, Buttercup, came over and lay down next to him.

"The moon in your dream is telling you *when* to come to the valley. It's summoning you there on the night of the full moon."

Obie's face paled. "You have to be kidding. I mean, what am I supposed to do when I get there . . . watch the moon and stars disappear? That's as crazy as the dream."

Will's eyes were dark and inscrutable as he stared at Obie.

Realizing he would get no answer, Obie drew a deep breath and exhaled quickly to calm himself. "So, what if I don't want to go?"

Bits and pieces of Ghostrise Valley's dark history flashed through his mind: unpredictable weather, strange lights circling over it on nights of the full moon, mysterious disappearances, insanity, and fatal accidents (if accidents they were) had all been linked to the valley over the years. He knew the old Indian legend that warned of spirits guarding the valley from intruders. There was also the issue of its namesake, *Ghostrise,* so-called for the ghost-like clouds that sometimes inexplicably rose up from the valley floor. No one knew what caused them. A couple of years ago, Obie saw them for himself as he stood on the edge of the mesa overlooking the valley. He had been looking through his field glasses when suddenly the clouds began rising from the valley floor like phantoms from the grave. Then a dust storm whipped down the valley and swallowed up the clouds. Watching them had been a chilling experience because the cloud shapes had been so human-like. A few people had tried to capture on film the ghost clouds and the strange lights that circled on nights when the moon was full, but the pictures never came out. Whatever was going on at Ghostrise, the townspeople wanted no part of it and kept away.

Not that any of this had discouraged Obie initially. In fact, the mystery surrounding Ghostrise had been his reason for going there. It was the only way he could be sure of getting the A he needed in history. He'd talked Josh into going with him, and early in the morning on a school holiday they had hiked around taking pictures and gathering rock samples. But they had left the valley by late afternoon, well before sunset. Spending a few hours there one day last week was one thing . . . spending the *night* in the valley was something else entirely. Two people had camped there for a couple of nights about three years ago. When they failed to return home a search party was sent out and brought back their mangled bodies. No one ever knew what killed them. And just last year, a man went there to prospect and came out a couple of days later believing he was Attila the Hun. His hair had turned from dark brown to pure white.

Will peered deeply into Obie's troubled eyes. "I can give you some herbs for tea that will help you sleep, but it won't take the dream away. Only you can stop the dreams by returning to the valley and facing your fears."

"That's easy for you to say," Obie grumbled. "You're friends with the spirits."

"Try looking beyond your nose, Oberon. Do you think it's only a coincidence that on your first trip to Ghostrise Valley you found a hidden cave and a rock with your name on it? And is it also a coincidence that you immediately began having the same bad dreams every night?"

"I'm not sure what I think," Obie said irritably.

"These are not coincidences. Something powerful is drawing you to the valley, son. Face it and trust your heart to guide you. Take Josh with you if you wish."

"Yeah . . . he'll be dying to go," Obie said dryly. He remembered how Josh had been spooked by their visit to the valley last week, and how he had jumped about six feet when he almost stepped on a sleeping rattlesnake.

Obie stroked the cat, curled up against his leg. She raised her head to look at him and her eyes slowly opened and closed affectionately. At least the cat made sense. He stared at the wood plank floor, considering Will's words. Nearly a minute passed before he raised his eyes to Will. "When's the next full moon?"

"Tomorrow night."

Obie was taken back. He hadn't realized it would be so soon. On the otherhand, the sooner he stopped having the bad dream the better. "All right. I'll go."

A look of approval came onto Will's face. "You've made the right choice, Oberon. Here, keep this with you—it may prove useful." He tossed the rock back to him.

Obie's hand trembled as he caught the stone and returned it to his leather pouch. The old man got up and went to the bookshelves opposite the hearth. The shelves were built around a window overlooking the downward slope of the low hill the cabin sat on. Beyond spread the grassland, bisected by a two-lane road leading into town. The room was sparsely furnished with a wooden sofa and chair for visitors who chose not to sit on the floor mats, a colorful, hand woven blanket that hung above the hearth, and many clay herb pots on the floor along the walls. Will removed one of the old coffee tins lined up next to his tattered bound volumes of *The Complete Works of Shakespeare*, took out a handful of dried herbs and dropped them into a small bag. Obie got up. Already, he stood a couple of inches taller than Will.

"Make tea from this before you go to bed tonight. You may sleep better." Will handed the bag to Obie.

If it had been anyone else telling Obie to spend the night in Ghostrise Valley, he would have scoffed it off as a bad joke. But he trusted the old man. Will knew more than anyone about the valley. In fact, he was the only one around who would even go there. But he was close-mouthed about the place, which made people suspicious. Some even claimed he had supernatural powers.

Although Obie refused to listen to the superstitious talk about Will, something occurred when he was ten that he'd always wondered about. He and his older brother, Scottie, had been hiking on the hill above Will's cabin and had seen him cutting wood below. It had seemed like only moments later when Obie looked up in horror to see a cougar crouching in the rocks just above, ready to leap down on them. Then Will was there. He'd pushed Obie and Scottie aside, yelling and waving a club at the big cat until he drove it away. How had Will known? And how had he gotten up the hill so fast? The old man only smiled when asked. It annoyed Obie that he never would answer his questions. Finally, he decided Will just enjoyed being mysterious.

When Obie left the cabin the old man called after him, "I'll pray to the spirits for your safe return."

Stopping abruptly, Obie spun around to face him. "Are you suggesting I might not come back?"

Will didn't answer. Exasperated by his silence, Obie stalked off.

"Remember to control your temper and you'll think more clearly," Will said.

"Yeah, thanks a lot," Obie said without turning. But he knew the old man was right. His temper had gotten him in a few fights over the years. Feeling Will's eyes on him as he limped down the hill, Obie remembered his words from a few years back, *You don't have to walk that way. You'll walk straight when you choose to.* Angry tears had come into Obie's eyes and he'd shot back, "Do you think I *like* this freakin' limp?"

Then Obie's memory snapped almost as far back as he could remember, to when he was just a little kid. It was the awful day of his third birthday, the day of the accident. Afterwards, he'd taken Scottie's baseball bat and beaten his teddy bears up and thrown them in the trash, crying all the while. That was the day he began to limp and suffer pain and stiffness in his left leg. His dad took him to several medical specialists over the years, but the doctors were unable to help. Current medical science could not explain his disability, they had all said.

After the accident, Will had taken Obie under his wing and treated him like a son. It had felt good to have a father who was always there. His real dad had to travel a lot on business, and spent little time at home. With Mom gone, he and Scottie, aka *The Scott*, were mostly on their own. Because Scottie was eighteen he was supposed to be in charge; but he wasn't all that responsible and sometimes seemed like the younger brother.

Obie sighed and breathed in the night air filled with the scent of cottonwoods.

The road was dappled with moon shadows cast through trees growing in dark thickets along the way. He listened to the wind murmuring over the grassland, and the crickets scrubbing out their washboard sonatas. The sounds of nature always had a calming effect on him. He'd thought for years about leaving, going off by himself and living in the mountains. Maybe he'd really do it someday. Rounding a bend he spotted his house a half mile down the road. The kitchen light was on, which meant Scottie was home. They lived almost two miles north of town and Will's cabin was a mile and a half farther out. Obie checked his watch. It was almost 7:00 p.m.

When he got home he'd call Josh and ask him to go with him tomorrow. Josh wouldn't like it one bit either. To stop the dreams, though, he'd go with or without his friend. Then, too, his pride was at stake. He didn't want Will thinking he was a wuss. But he had a sinking feeling, a foreboding that something was askew, out of balance, and he wasn't sure he wanted to know what it was.

***

Josh packed the last of the sandwiches and zipped their backpacks shut, then leaned against the kitchen counter and combed his fingers through his red hair. "I just hope you know what *we're* doing, Obie. I'm going with you, man, but I still think it's crazy."

Obie finished screwing the top on the last of four canteens he had just filled, two for each of them, and then pulled a small package wrapped in aluminum foil from the refrigerator. It was a steak bone he had saved for Josh's dog, Hudson. He lay by the back door thumping his tail on the floor, a blue bandana tied around his neck. Mutt or not, Josh thought his dog was just about perfect. He appeared to be a mixture of Labrador retriever and boxer, with a reddish-tan coat.

"I mean, I know it's only a small thing at stake here," Josh continued, "but I've grown sorta' attached to my life. And just so you know, I'm only going because I'd feel like a chump letting you go alone. But, dude, you're gonna owe me."

They had watched out for one another since forth grade when Josh was the new kid in town and two classmates started beating up on him. Obie had jumped into the fight and evened up the odds. They came out of it with a black eye each, a few bruises, and a lasting friendship. One of the things they shared in common was a love of sling shots. Soon after they became friends, Josh's dad, a slingshot aficionado with many trophies, had given them their first slingshots and some lessons. With a little time and practice, they became expert shots themselves, and when they were twelve, Josh's dad started entering them annually in the NWRST, the Northwestern Regional Slingshot Tournament. Both boys had taken top trophies several times in their age group. Then, without warning, Josh's dad was ripped from their lives when he died of a heart attack. Obie and Josh were fifteen when it happened. After that they had stopped attending the tournament. They might have continued going if Obie's dad could have taken them, but his work always seemed to get in the way. They still practiced, though, and respected the fact that their slingshots were deadly weapons.

Obie stuffed Hudson's steak bone into his pack and threw Josh a grin. "Yeah, I know I'll owe you. When I get my car I'll let you borrow it sometimes." He got his heavy hiking boots from their place by the back door and sat on a chair by the kitchen table to put them on.

"You mean after you raise your grades so your dad will let you get a job, and then after you *get* a job and save some money, right? I'll have my own car before then." Josh put a couple of filled water bottles inside the backpacks and attached the canteens to the outsides of each.

"Good point. My dad's making it a real pain."

"Awww, he just cares about you getting good grades."

"Sure," Obie said in a flat voice. *He's never around—that's how much he cares.* He finished tying his shoelaces and then got his Raptor slingshot from where it lay on the sideboard. It was his pride and joy, the weapon that made him feel like something. The Raptor's high-tech design made it function similar to a bow with a deadly projectile force of more than 200 miles per hour. Its long arm brace, held in place by a strap under the forearm, and adjustable ammo bands were characteristics that distinguished it from ordinary slingshots. He attached it to the front of his leather pouch with velcro straps and then opened the two exterior side pockets to check his ammo supply. Good. There was plenty of steel shot in several sizes. His mood improved, he gave Josh a glancing smile and pulled the long strap over his head and across his chest so the pouch rested at his right hip.

I'm glad you're bringing your Raptor. Do I get to use it?" Josh asked. "The one I ordered hasn't come in yet."

"Yeah, okay." Obie strapped his sleeping bag onto his backpack and pulled his fleece-lined jeans jacket through another strap. Sounds of cheering came from the living room where his brother, Scottie, was watching a Raiders game on the tube.

"Hey, what all did Will say when you went over there?"

"Not much more than I already told you. Just that the rock I found and the dream are linked, and I'm supposed to spend the night in Ghostrise Valley tonight."

"*Supposed to?* Why? You didn't mention anything on the phone about *supposed to.*"

"Because that's where I am in my dream. He doesn't think the dreams will stop until I go there and face my fears. It sounds sort of like the *coming to manhood* thing he's mentioned in the past." Even before he finished his sentence, Obie regretted giving Josh this last bit of information.

"Oh . . . well then, that's different," Josh said, sniggering. He pulled his ball cap on low over his eyes and raised his chin to see out from under the visor. "I mean uhhh, we wouldn't wanna interfere with your COMING TO MANHOOD."

Ignoring Josh's comment, Obie lifted his pack onto his back.

Josh looked thoughtful while he slipped his own backpack on. "Did, uhhh, did Will say anything about *my* manhood?" He peered out from under his visor again, daring Obie to answer.

"Nope. He just gave you his blessing to go with me."

"Oh, lucky me. I'll wanna thank him for that." Josh pantomimed a chokehold on Will. Obie grabbed his cap from the kitchen table and slung the strap of his .22 rifle over his shoulder. "Let's get out of here."

Josh pushed the screen door open and Hudson squeezed past with a yelp and ran down the stairs into the yard. At that instant they heard a thunderous belch and the door between the living room and kitchen swung open. Scottie, six-foot-three, the star running back on the Garrett High School Football Team, and a favorite among the cheerleaders, came in scratching his stomach through the tear in his T-shirt. He headed for the refrigerator.

"Nice one, dude," Josh said, lingering at the door.

Scottie grinned apologetically at Josh. "Awww, that was just a little one." He opened the refrigerator and pulled out a Pepsi, popped the top, then downed half of it and belched again.

"See you later, Scott." Hoping to escape before his brother asked where they were going, Obie half pushed Josh out the back door and was right behind him.

"Hey! Wait a minute. Where are you guys camping tonight?" He turned his full attention on Obie.

Obie threw a long-suffering glance at Josh, and they stepped back inside.

Josh shoved his hands into his jeans pockets and peered upward, grinning as he watched a fly walking on the ceiling.

"We're, uhhh, camping at Ghostrise Valley."

"Ghostrise?! Obie, I don't think you guys . . ."

"No sweat," Obie said, cutting him off. "We'll be okay."

"You know Dad wouldn't like it. And I'm the law when he's gone."

"I'm old enough to take care of myself."

"Yeah? So was that prospector who camped in the valley last year and came out a raving lunatic. Did you forget about *him*?"

"No, I haven't forgotten." Obie glared at his brother. He hated butting heads with Scottie, but, even more, he hated being treated like a kid when he was only a year younger. Anyway, his mind was already made up.

The two argued for several minutes and then Obie told him about his talk with Will. Scottie's stern expression softened. He crossed his arms and leaned against the kitchen counter staring out the window in thought. Obie silently waited. He knew Scottie had trusted and admired Will ever since the day the old man had saved them from the cougar.

Finally, Scottie pulled away from the counter, planted his feet wide apart, and looked Obie in the eye. "All right. If Will really thinks going there is gonna help with your nightmares, I'll go along with it. But I'm only agreeing to *one* night. I want to see you guys back here by noon tomorrow or I'm coming after you."

"We'll be here." The tension melted from Obie's face.

"And I want you to stay away from the mountain after dark. Camp at The Boulders and keep a fire going to keep the ghosts, rattlesnakes and whatever else is there away—and keep the rifle loaded. Got that?"

"Got it. See you tomorrow, Scott." Obie noticed the grimace on Josh's face. He wished his brother hadn't mentioned the ghosts and rattlesnakes.

It was almost ten in the morning when Obie, Josh and Hudson left the house and headed north along the two-lane road.

"You got lucky," Josh said in a low voice, "but I sure didn't."

Letting the comment pass, Obie pulled his cap on. The warm sun felt good on his face.

Josh glanced over. "Well, at least you're not as crabby as you were yesterday. You look a little better too. Your eyes aren't as bloodshot."

Obie laughed. "You really know how to cheer a guy up." When they weren't bloodshot, Obie's eyes were his best feature. Like his paternal grandfather's, his eyes were an unusual shade of deep blue that looked almost violet when the light hit them just right.

The noise of an approaching car came from behind. Josh glanced over his shoulder. "Uh-oh, trouble. Jabo and his posse."

Obie groaned. "Awesome."

"Hey, dude, I warned you."

Jabo was one of the jocks at school. He always had a nice car to drive because his dad owned a Ford dealership. Obie heard the engine decelerate close behind. Then he heard loud whispers mingled with hushed laughter. The voices stopped and there was only the low drone of the engine as the red mustang convertible began trailing them.

He and Josh kept walking.

Suddenly several male voices started chanting, "ba-dump, ba-dump, ba-dump, ba-dump," to the rhythm of Obie's limp. Pulling up alongside, Jabo was stepping on and off the gas pedal jerking the car to and fro in time while the guys bobbed their heads like ducks. Clenching his fists, Obie turned to face them. Jabo stopped the car and grinned.

"You guys constipated or something?" Obie yelled, his face contorted in rage. He quickly surveyed the occupants of the car. In the backseat a girl with bright pink hair was doubled over laughing. She sat between Dennis Murphy and Chad Pauley. Obie's eyes came to rest on a girl with long dark hair seated next to Jabo. She was bent over with her hands over her face. Then Shannon Piper lifted her pretty, unsmiling face towards Obie and their eyes met. His anger momentarily faded.

"Hey, Obie-Dobie, bummer about your leg. We'll miss you at football this year," Jabo said. "But, hey, I hear the water-boy position's still open."

"He'd make a better practice dummy," Dennis said.

"Dude, you're the one . . . you're . . . you're the big dummy around here," Josh blurted out. "Hey, are you guys drinking?" He was staring inquisitively at the pink-haired girl. Her head was thrown back as she swallowed something from a bottle covered almost to the lip by a brown paper bag.

"Cool it, man . . . it's only root beer," Jabo said.

The pink-haired girl exploded with laughter and sprayed her mouthful of drink all over Dennis. Scrunching his small eyes and nose so he resembled a dried prune, Dennis uttered something under his breath and wiped his face with his shirt.

Then Chad leaned close to Obie and confided, "I'll try and pull some strings for you on that water-boy position."

Something detonated in Obie's brain. He grabbed the front of Chad's shirt in one hand and his left arm with the other and half yanked him from the car. Dennis and the pink-haired girl grabbed hold of Chad's waist in a tug-of-war with Obie. Everyone was yelling and Hudson was barking when Josh finally pulled Obie back, forcing him to release his antagonist. Josh was shorter than Obie, but he was strong.

"Ignore those guys, Obie. They're just being morons."

"Alright, alright." Obie pulled free from Josh's grasp.

Red-faced, and veins popping out in his neck, Chad yelled, "If Scot weren't your brother, Obie, I'd get out of this car right now and beat the crap out of you."

"I'm ready for you anytime," Obie yelled back.

"You'd better muzzle it Griffin unless you want me to do it for you," Jabo snarled. He stepped on the gas and peeled rubber as he sped away.

"Dude, that was a dumb thing you just did," Josh said to Obie. "And I hate to rub it in, but didn't I warn you not to let Jabo catch you talking to Shannon? You know what a jerk he can be. I mean, I know you like Shannon and all, but how cool can she be hanging around with that guy?"

"I don't want to hear this, Josh, so just shut up, okay?" Obie felt sick.

"Okay, but don't let those guys get to you, 'cause they're a lot lamer than you are, dude."

"JOSH."

"Okay, okay, I'll shut up."

Obie's stomach had gone sour. He wished he hadn't tried out for football the previous week. He should have known better. Word had gotten around that the coach ordered him off the field and told him to take up golf. Coach Barnes had a reputation for speaking bluntly.

Obie and Josh continued north for another mile, then left the road and hiked west through the forest that bordered the east side of Ghostrise Valley. Obie managed to push the incident with Jabo from his mind. He had more immediate concerns, like what would happen tonight? Nothing, he hoped. Maybe when he saw the moon shining brightly, saw that everything was okay, the dream would stop and that would be that. But then, why did Will tell him he was being *called* to the valley? The same troubled feeling he'd had the night before came over him, the feeling that something was wrong . . . something was very, very wrong.

CHAPTER TWO

JOURNEY

OBIE AND JOSH stood at the top of the forested mesa overlooking Ghostrise Valley. A silent, empty land of cracked gray soil, relentless sun, and throat-parching dust stirred by erratic winds, it was the forsaken realm of rattlesnakes and vultures. Here and there a few weeds clung stubbornly to the earth, the last vestiges of plant life. What once were trees, time had stripped clean of bark and branches, leaving only broken spines dotting the flat landscape like fingers pointing skyward. Across the valley floor, six miles to the west, the dark rocky slopes of Watcher Mountain towered over all. It seemed more a brooding presence than a geological formation, for on a steep cliff face near its summit two light-colored mineral deposits stood out agaist the darker rock like large grey eyes watching the valley.

"Shall we take the trail down like last time?" Josh asked.

"Yeah. It's a little rough, but it's quicker than following the mesa north another eight miles until it sinks to the valley floor." Obie adjusted the straps on his backpack and took a drink from his canteen. "Ready?"

"Righto. I can hardly wait," Josh said despondently, then added in a muffled voice, "to go home."

Obie pretended not to hear, like he did with a lot of Josh's comments. A little ways down the trail Obie made a half turn and couldn't help but grin. Josh looked like a condemned prisoner dragging himself to the execution.

From the trailhead Ghostrise stretched seven miles south and fourteen miles north. The Boulders, where they would camp, lay a little south of the valley's center. It was a big granite formation surrounded by boulders and broken rocks covering an area equivalent to a large house, and rising twenty-one feet at its highest point. The wind began to whip along the mesa wall, blowing stinging sand in their faces. They stopped and tied bandanas over their noses, then positioned their ball cap visors low over their eyes and continued on, heads lowered against the wind. Running ahead, Hudson disappeared around a curve in the path and then started barking. Seconds later he raced back around the curve and rejoined them briefly before bounding off again.

Nearly half-way down the trail the wind died down and they pulled their bandanas down around their necks. Obie's bad leg had started bothering him. He tried not to show it, but he could never fool Josh. Maybe a small change in his gait was what tipped Josh off.

"Hey, I'm getting tired. Let's take a rest," Josh yelled.

Obie could feel the blood pulsing in his ears. He hated it when people accommodated him because of his limp. Josh had known him long enough to know better. Stopping, he turned and gave Josh an icy stare.

"What?" Josh said with a nervous laugh.

"Who are you trying to kid, man? I know you don't need a rest. You don't even sound tired. *You* just try and keep up with *me*, okay?" Obie clenched his teeth and bolted down the trail. A few yards farther on his foot caught under a root growing across the path and he fell on his face. Pushing himself to his knees, he struggled to contain his anger. His leg was aching now, which made it worse.

Hudson trotted over and licked Obie's face between yelps, in what is commonly taken for canine concern. *Sweet. Even the dog pities me.*

By that time Josh was there. "Here, take a hand," he said, offering to help Obie up.

"Just get away, Josh. I'm all right." Scowling, Obie pushed Hudson aside and got to his feet. Josh backed off and they continued on in silence. Trudging along the broken path allowed Obie to blow off steam, especially when his thoughts went to Shannon. She was always in the back of his mind lately. Did she think he was a fool? Jabo and his friends made him look pretty idiotic when they parodied his limp. Maybe they were right. He guessed he did look like a freakin' duck when he walked. Would Shannon want to be seen walking with him? But when he stood beside her he looked okay. And what did she think about him attacking Chad? Would she even look at him when they met at school? She'd probably already written him off. He had a sinking feeling in his gut. Then he remembered she hadn't laughed with the others, and how she made him feel when their eyes met. It lifted his spirits. He'd try and patch things up with her when he saw her at school.

When they reached the valley floor they dropped their gear. "Time to rest and have some grub," Obie said. He heard Josh's stomach rumbling like an ignored alarm clock advising that lunch was long overdue. It was late September and the temperature in the valley was still uncomfortably warm. Obie pulled his damp T-shirt off and laid it over his pack to dry. In the bright sunlight, the sweat glistening on his tanned skin accentuated the youthful curves of his back and shoulder muscles. He glanced at his arms and frowned. His tan was beginning to fade, making the birthmark on his left shoulder more visible. It was a small, round mark with four smaller round marks above it. He had been a little self-conscious about it since age nine, when Josh said he must have been slapped by a bear since the mark resembled a tiny paw print. Although Josh had stopped teasing him about it years ago, the *bear paw* tag stuck.

Josh gave Hudson some water and dog biscuits, then pulled a couple of sandwiches from his pack and tossed one at Obie. From the corner of his eye, Obie saw the foil wrapped package coming at him and grabbed it as it flew past his face.

"Good hands. Just testing you." Josh sat down and looked around sourly.

"Yeah, sure." Obie wanted to tell him the *real test* would be tonight, but thought better of it. Josh didn't want to be here in the first place, so no use stirring him up any more than he already was.

"See that ugly vulture sitting on that dumb excuse for a tree trunk?" Josh asked.

Obie turned his head and saw the black carrion bird perched on a tree trunk about thirty feet away. It was probably the biggest vulture he'd ever seen. It stood up and fanned its wings revealing one badly deformed leg, as if it had been broken and the bone healed crooked. "It's watching us," Obie said. "Maybe it's bored."

"Or hoping we'll die. It's creeping me out. As soon as I finish this here sandwich, I'm gonna shoot him."

Obie regarded Josh for a moment. "I think the sun's getting to you."

"It's this valley that's getting to me. It's bad enough those eyes on the mountain are always watching us, now we've got a hungry vulture staring at us too.

"Okay, shoot the thing if it makes you feel better. But if you kill it the carcass will just attract more vultures."

Josh eyed the bird again and frowned. "All right. Let's just eat and get over to The Boulders so we can settle in for the night. How soon in the morning can we start for home?"

"When it's light enough to see—if that's okay with you."

"Yeah, I guess," Josh said, then mumbled into his sandwich, "if we live that long."

It was a little past two o'clock when Obie slipped his T-shirt back on and they set out for The Boulders, a little over three miles away.

"Hudson doesn't like this place," Josh observed. "Look at him. He's slinking along with his tail tucked between his legs and his head down. He's usually running ahead of us exploring everything."

"I noticed. Looks like he doesn't like the vulture either."

They had walked a little over a mile when Obie began hearing barely audible sounds in the breeze, like moaning. Was it a trick of the wind? Soon the moaning stopped and he heard sounds like sad, lamenting voices whispering words he couldn't make out. *Am I imagining it?* A glance at Josh's worried face told him otherwise. *He hears it too.* He rubbed his hand over his sling-shot, hanging at his side. *Maybe talking will help.* "Josh, do you think we could still take top cups at the slingshot tournament?"

Josh seemed relieved, as if hearing a human voice helped dispel his fears. "You bet," he said, "if anything, we're probably . . ." He stopped mid-sentence at the sound of flapping wings coming from behind. It was the vulture. Hudson yelped in terror and leaped away with the huge bird in pursuit. Seconds later it buzzed his head. In a rage, Josh loaded his slingshot and chased after it yelling, "Stay off my dog, crapbag! I'm gonna kill you, you glorified chicken—think you can get my dog?"

Hudson made a quick turn, hightailed it back to Josh, and started running at his side, now in pursuit of the vulture. Obie tried to get the bird in his rifle sights, but it flew so low that Josh was in the way. Lowering the gun, he yelled, "Josh, you're wasting your energy. Come on back and we'll watch for the vulture." Josh ignored him. Obie thought their roles seemed oddly reversed. He was the one who usually needed to calm his anger, not Josh.

Realizing how really spooked his friend was, Obie felt a pang of guilt. He shouldn't have brought him back to Ghostrise. The

whole thing was probably a wild goose chase, anyway. ·He'd like
to tell him to go home, but he knew Josh wouldn't leave without
him. He should just go too and come back alone next month
when the moon was full again. But could he stand the bad dream
for another month? It was an agonizing thought, one he'd have
to figure out later. Right now, he needed to go after Josh. Obie
had only gone a few yards when he heard his friend scream for
help. "I'm coming, Josh, I'm coming!" He dropped his pack and
gripped the rifle. Where was he? He could see Hudson struggling
with something ahead. Josh had to be there with him—he just
couldn't see him.

Ignoring the stiffness and pain in his left leg he forced himself
to run, pushing off with his right leg, coming down softly on his
left, and pushing off again on his right in an awkward rhythm
that, oddly, began to smooth out as he ran. It was about another
two-hundred and fifty feet and every second counted. Obie was
on the verge of panic. He'd known for a long time he was bad
luck, a jinx for anyone to be with. It was probably inevitable that
he'd end up causing harm to Josh. If anything happened to him
he'd never forgive himself.

"Obie, hurry, I can't hold on much longer." Still struggling,
Hudson moved to the side. And then Obie spotted Josh. He had
fallen into a hole. Just above ground level, his frightened face
peered out from beneath his red cap. His arms were stretched
out in front of him, and he was holding on to a small clump of
weeds. Hudson had the neck of Josh's T-shirt in his teeth,
tugging at it in a vain effort to pull him up. When Obie drew
closer he saw the weeds pull slowly out of the cracked gray soil
and Josh's arms sliding backward. Obie dove for Josh's hands,
caught his fingers and watched them pull out of his grasp. The
T-shirt ripped from Hudson's mouth as Josh's face slipped below
ground level. Obie felt relieved when he heard Josh hit bottom;
he hadn't fallen far. The dog stood yelping at the brink of the golf

umbrella sized opening. Obie crawled to the edge and peaked over. He could just make out Josh's form moving in the dark cavern.

"Are you okay?"

"Yeah, I think so. I landed on my pack and I don't know what else—something soft and squishy. I've got my flashlight out." Josh snapped it on. "Awww, crap! Aaaahhhhh, aaaahhhhh, get out of here," he yelled. Hudson started barking.

Obie watched Josh kick and dance around like he was stepping on hot coals. Then he heard an unmistakable sound and knew what was down there. He grabbed Hudson to try and stop his barking.

"Snakes, stinkin' snakes! They're everywhere!" Josh was stomping the ground with his hiking boots. "I've fallen into a rattlesnake den. They were crawling over my feet, but I kicked 'um off. One bit me on the arm and it's stinging. I don't wanna die, Obie. You gotta get me outta here quick."

Sweat beaded on Obie's forehead. "I will, man. I'll get you out! But you've got to try and calm down so the venom doesn't move too fast, and so you don't stir the snakes up any more than they already are."

"Okay, okay, you're right. I'll make myself calm down."

"And please don't worry, Josh, you'll be out of there soon." He wished he was as sure about that as he sounded. The rifle wouldn't reach and they hadn't brought a rope. Josh's flashlight beam moved around the walls of the small cavern. From above it appeared approximately fifteen feet deep, twelve feet wide and fifteen feet long. Josh had broken through the thin ceiling.

"There must be over a hundred rattlers around the walls," Josh said, speaking in hushed tones now. "They're little ones, probably born during the last few weeks. They seem a little sleepy. Since I kicked them off my boots they're sorta staying away from me, but there's three or four big ones curled up in a corner. They look like they're asleep, though I don't know how they could be with all the noise I've made. Like you said, Obie, I don't want to disturb them anymore, so talk softly and pleeese keep Hudson quiet. And hurry and get me outta here. I don't feel so good."

"All right." Obie knew the snakes had to be Prairie Rattlers. Born live beginning in September, they had fangs and were capable of biting from birth. If the large snakes weren't in hibernation yet, they would awaken to feed in the cool of the night. And if Josh was still there they'd find him in the darkness by his body heat. He wouldn't be able to handle his slingshot and spot them with his flashlight at the same time. Obie had to get him out of there fast, then go for help and bring back some antivenin before the poison moved through his body. In the meantime Josh needed to remain still. Whatever demons awaited Obie in Ghostrise tonight would have to wait.

Hudson stopped barking so Obie released his hold on him. He scanned the area for something he could use to get Josh out. Except for the boulder pile a little over a mile away and an occasional tree trunk, the valley was empty. A sturdy tree branch would work if he could find one long enough. Will told him there were several fallen trees at The Boulders he could use for firewood. But it would take too much time to go there and drag one back—if he could even find one large enough. He might tear his sleeping bag apart and make a rope. That would also take time. His eyes locked on a bare tree trunk a few feet away and his hopes rose. It was long enough. If he could knock it down and lower it into the pit, Josh could climb out. It was old and dead, probably brittle, and possibly hollow inside. He prayed it wasn't too brittle to sustain Josh's weight for the minute it might take him to climb out.

"What are you doing up there, Obie?"

"I'm working on something, Josh. Hang in there and stay calm."

"Yeah, easy for you to say. Come on bro, get me out of here!"

Obie tested the tree by giving it a hard kick with his right leg. There was a small cracking noise. Then he was jarred by a loud screech. He turned. It was the vulture with the deformed leg barreling down on him, its eyes murderous. He ducked, but a wing brushed his head causing him to stumble. Recovering his balance, he grabbed the rifle and cocked it. A soul chilling scream came from behind. Wheeling around he saw the black feathered fury, the fiendish onslaught of wings, beak, and claws coming at his face. He fired. Then it was quiet. There was no sign of the vulture anywhere. Obie was stunned. Had it been some evil spirit, the thing he was sent to face in the valley? Maybe it was over now and the bad dreams would stop. Then he remembered the full-moon—it hadn't risen yet. Feeling a numbness in his limbs, he dropped the rifle. He wasn't off the hook.

"Obie, what happened? Why'd you fire the rifle? Obie?" Leaning over the edge of the cavern, Obie said in the calmest voice he could muster, "I shot the vulture." After a long moment of silence, he heard Josh's deep-throated chuckle.

"I have to get back to work. I may have you out in a few minutes."

"All right." Josh was still chuckling.

Obie moved back from the tree trunk to get a running start. He raced towards it, leaped up like a horizontal projectile, and rammed his booted feet into it as hard as he could. He hit the ground pretty hard. His bad leg smarted a lot, but the pain was worth it. The trunk had partially split at the bottom. On his next attempt the old trunk crashed to the ground.

"Obie, what's that noise?"

Obie went to the cavern opening and looked down with a grin. "Your lifeline."

Josh threw his pack up and then stood aside while Obie shoved an end of the trunk into the pit. It banged down at an angle on the cavern floor with the opposite end extending a couple of feet above ground. Then, Obie heard the hissing.

"Ohhh, crap, Obie, some of the big rattlers woke up and I think they're coming for me. I can hear'um."

"Stop talking and get out of there," Obie yelled. By the time he finished his sentence Josh had already shinnied halfway up the underside of the trunk. At the top he pulled himself around to the upper side and climbed onto solid ground.

"Thanks, man." Josh dropped down and stretched out on his back.

Squatting beside him, Obie examined his right forearm. Josh raised his head and watched him run his finger around the two puncture marks. "Are we gonna have time to get me to a doc?"

Obie gave him a sober look. "Did you get bit anywhere else?"

"No."

"Well, a doctor won't be able to do anything for you."

Josh's face fell. "So, you think I'm gonna die?"

"Yeah. When you're about a hundred and three—and probably not from rattlesnake poison." Obie grinned. "It was a dry bite, no venom."

He had learned from Will that adult rattlers deliver dry bites on defensive strikes about a third of the time, preferring to conserve their venom for prey. Baby rattlers weren't so discriminating, so were more dangerous. Josh had lucked out and won the dry snake bite lottery for baby rattlers.

A smile spread over Josh's face. He lay back down with a sigh and closed his eyes. "An angel must be watching over me."

The emergency over, Obie leaned forward and rested his arms on his drawn-up knees. He tried to relax, but the incident with the vulture haunted him. Where had it gone? And why had it attacked him? Vultures were scavengers and didn't normally attack live prey. It raised questions he had no answers for.

Josh opened his eyes. "I'm glad you got the vulture, Obie. I think it tried to kill me. It led me straight to the rattlesnake den." He raised his head, his eyes searching. "Where's the carcass?"

"I don't know. It just disappeared."

Josh scrunched his brow in disbelief, opened his mouth to speak, and then apparently changed his mind. Sighing, he dropped his head back down and closed his eyes again. Then Obie realized he had to offer to leave the valley with Josh. He couldn't continue endangering his best friend. He'd been lucky to get out of that snake den unharmed. What else might happen if they stayed? Glancing around, he noticed the shadow of the mountain had crept far over the valley, leaving them in deep shade. If they were going to leave, it had to be soon. "Josh, let's head for home. I'll come back next month. You've been through enough for one day, especially after falling in that snake den."

Josh looked over at Obie. "Naw. We've come this far, man. I'm gonna see it through with you tonight. I don't want you coming back here alone. Besides, the vulture's gone now."

Obie smiled. "Thanks for sticking with me. You know I appreciate it."

Josh smiled. "Yeah, I know."

"Why don't you rest a few more minutes and then we'll get my pack and head for The Bould . . ." A startled look came on Obie's face. "Josh, remember Will telling us a while back to take cover fast if we saw two dust devils in the valley because it meant a big dust storm was brewing?"

"Yeah, do you see two?" Josh was wide awake now.

"No."

"So what's the problem?"

"I see three." Obie was already on his feet and shouldering the rifle when Josh jumped up and grabbed his gear. They were big dust devils spinning north of The Boulders, two to the east and one to the west of it. Josh started towards the mountain but

Obie caught his arm. "We can't make it to the mountain in time. We'll have a better chance of reaching The Boulders. If you lose visibility on the way, keep going in the same direction. And don't wait for me—I'll be right behind you." They took off running. Reaching his pack, Obie stopped only long enough to lift it to his back and bolt off again. The sky to the north was darkening as the huge dust devils moved towards them, sucking dust up and blowing it everywhere.

Things worsened. It was as if someone had opened the doors to the underworld. On both sides of Obie, bluish-white clouds in ghostlike shapes whirled upward from the valley floor and the air filled with sounds like the agitated whispers of a thousand tortured souls. When one of the clouds moved overhead, Obie felt a sudden chill and his hair bristled. Josh was about a hundred feet ahead when he turned and saw Obie in trouble. He and Hudson made a quick turn.

"It's the Ghost Clouds," Obie yelled. "Keep running for The Boulders."

Josh ignored him. His face white and eyes fear-stricken, he reached Obie and turned to run at his side hollering, "Those creep clouds are behind you now. You've outrun them."

Obie looked over his shoulder. They were behind, all right, but were gathering and growing in number. Ahead the sky was nearly black with dust. "The storm might blow them away," he answered.

Josh glanced back and his face dropped. "Maybe. But right now they're coming after us, and they're coming fast."

His adrenalin rushing, Obie ran faster, but he knew it wasn't fast enough. The legion of voices returned in a frenzy with malicious, wrathful whispers, like demon utterances threatening mayhem and doom. Josh covered his ears with his hands and Hudson yelped pitifully. A long white cloud tendril crept around Obie's chest and an icy bolt shot through him. Panicking, Obie tried to push the tendril away but his hands passed right through it. He stumbled forward and fell, struggled to get up, but couldn't move. Something held him down. The voices invaded his mind and he felt the deep cold working its way to his very core. He tried to fight his way to his feet, but drowsiness was overtaking him. He felt his arms suddenly yanked forward. It was Josh, pulling him out from under the heavy Ghost Cloud that was sitting on his back.

"Obie, come on. Don't quit on me." Saucer-eyed, Josh pulled Obie to his feet. Then they were running again, fleeing for their lives. The Ghost Clouds flitted wildly on all sides. Then the dust storm hit. The Boulders were near now, but hidden behind the gray-brown curtain of dust. Josh pulled the blue bandana down over Hudson's eyes for protection. Almost instantly, something yanked it down on his nose, but Obie pulled it back up. He and Josh grasped Hudson's collar, partly to guide him, and partly to keep together in the near zero visibility.

Heads down and bandanas over their faces, they ran blind. Obie prayed they hadn't veered off course. If the Ghost Clouds were still around, he couldn't hear them. The only thing he could hear was the howling wind. He hoped the storm had blown the ghosts back to Hell where they belonged. Cupping his hand over his eyes, he raised his head slightly to look. All he could see was Josh's shadow on the other side of Hudson.

Josh tripped and went down. Stumbling to his feet, he said, "We should have reached The Boulders by now. Did we miss them?"

"No. We're there." Obie pointed off to their right, towards the dim outline of two large boulders.

They ran into a recessed area in the rocks, up against the granite formation. The spot offered some protection from wind and dust. After climbing into their sleeping bags they drew the strings tight over their heads to escape the choking dust and wait out the storm. Hudson yelped a couple of times inside Josh's bag

and then settled down. Obie lay wondering about the Ghost
Clouds. Was there a scientific explanation for them, or were they,
like Will said, really ghosts? Whatever they were, they were
dangerous. But at least they were gone—for now anyway.
Exhausted, he fell asleep.

He had the bad dream again, and when the moon was eaten
away a threatening black shape came at him in the darkness.
Gasping for breath, Obie pulled his sleeping bag open and sat up.
He remained still while the terror subsided. His throat felt
french-fried and sprinkled with dust. Reaching for his canteen,
he unscrewed the top and took a drink. Hudson trotted over and
licked his face. It was night and the storm was over.

Josh was putting wood in a fire pit he had dug just outside the
recessed area. He had evidently scouted out the branches among
the rocks, and piled up a large stack of wood near the pit. Looking over, he yelled, "After today, the rest of the night oughta' be
easy." He came over and dropped down beside Obie. "We'll just
sleep it off and first thing in the morning we're outta here."

It was the most cheerful Josh had been all day. The safety of
the Boulders and the calm night air must have made him think
the worst was past. "Morning can't come soon enough for me,"
Obie answered. He climbed out of his sleeping bag and sat down
on it next to Josh. For a moment, it almost seemed like an
ordinary camping trip. Then he raised his eyes and knew better.
The full moon had risen.

Josh pulled off his cap and tossed it aside as he combed his
fingers through his hair, then looked up at the sky. "Most of the
dust settled pretty fast and then the wind came up and blew the
rest away. No wind now though. Perfect night. What a crazy day,
though. My head's spinning."

It isn't over yet, Obie thought.

"I just hope those ghost . . . things don't come back tonight,"
Josh continued.

"The fire might keep 'um away," Obie offered. "Maybe they don't come out that often. Anyway we didn't see any last week."

"Yeah. But I get the feeling they definitely don't want us here."

Obie looked down and inspected his T-shirt and jeans. "I feel like I've been wallowing in a pig pen."

Josh gave Obie the up and down. "That'd be my guess."

Pulling off his boots, T-shirt, and jeans, Obie shook the dust out and then slipped them back on. It was getting cold so he put his jacket on too. Meanwhile, Josh pushed things along by shaking the dust from Obie's sleeping bag and laying it out near the foot of his own, next to the fire pit. The campsite location provided a good view of the valley and the mountain. From there, Obie thought, they could watch the ground and sky for anything that might approach during the night. When he deposited the rest of his gear beside his sleeping bag his eyes fell on the .22, lying next to Hudson at the foot of Josh's sleeping bag. It was as slick as an oiled water snake.

"Thanks for cleaning the rifle."

"Yep. I want it ready if we need it." Josh gazed out on the moonlit valley. "This is the creepiest place I've ever seen, especially at night. I don't ever want to come here again."

"Me either," Obie agreed. "How about getting the matches out so we can start the fire and keep those cloud things away?" He squatted next to the fire pit and began stuffing kindling between pieces of wood. "At least we've seen them and lived to tell about it."

Josh gave Obie a wry grin. "Yeah, you can tell Shannon how you were mowed down by the Ghost Clouds."

Obie scowled. "I don't think so."

Josh chuckled. "Well, I don't really wanna be a character in a ghost story that'll be told around town for the next hundred years. So, maybe we should keep our mouths shut." He sat down on his sleeping bag and wrapped an arm around Hudson.

"Good thinking. Now where are the matches?"

"In your pack I guess. Why are you asking me?"

"Why am I . . . you mean you don't remember where you put them?" Obie stood up slowly, staring hard at Josh. "You *did* hear me tell you to pack them back at the house, right?"

"Whoa, dude, I didn't hear you say that."

"Great. That's just great." Stuffing his hands in his jacket pockets, Obie kicked a small rock and stared thoughtfully at the ground. "Okay, we'll have to do it the hard way."

"Not *we* dude. *You.* And hurry up 'cause I'm starting to freeze my butt off."

"Fine." Obie searched the ground for another rock, then, remembering something, stopped. Opening his leather ammo pouch, he pulled out the round stone with his name on it and his utility knife; then he knelt beside the fire pit and started scraping the steel file component over the rock. Almost immediately he got some small sparks, and after a few more vigorous scrapes a large spark ignited the kindling.

"Right on, Obie. That's just what I would have done." Obie rolled his eyes in disbelief. Grinning, Josh got to his feet and gave Obie the jock's fist-tapping routine. "Hey, how'd you get the fire started so fast?"

"It was the rock I found. It looks like there's a lot of flint in it." While he built the fire up, Josh tended to Hudson's needs.

When the fire was blazing they climbed into their sleeping bags and got more sandwiches out. The peanut butter tasted amazingly good to Obie, but then peanut butter had that quality of making him feel like every sandwich was the best-tasting ever. After eating, he pulled his camera out and set it beside him, then leaned against his pack to keep watch until morning. Josh was stretched out on his back staring drowsily up at the stars, his eyelids beginning to droop.

Obie?"

"Yeah?"

"With all that happened today I almost forgot about those weird lights that circle the valley sometimes. Think we'll see any tonight?"

"I don't know. If we do, I'll try and get some pictures."

"Well, they better not come too close 'cause I'm keeping this rifle right here next to . . ." Josh's voice trailed off as he drifted into sleep.

The Milky Way was sprinkled across the night sky like field poppies reflected in a stupendous black mirror. It was a peaceful and reassuring sight after a tough day. Josh's light snoring made Obie smile. He looked so peaceful. Hudson lay in the sleeping bag next to him with only his black nose poking out.

Obie studied the mountain, standing dark and ominous against the night sky. The eyes, visible in the frosty moonlight, were still staring down at him. He shifted his gaze to the moon and remembered the dream. Then he realized something that made his flesh crawl: the only sounds he heard were their own. Josh had stopped snoring and at this moment all he heard was the crackle of burning wood and his own breathing. There was no sound of wind, animal, or insect. It seemed a tension lay over the land, as though the valley and the mountain were listening and waiting for something. What was out there in the darkness? Would the Ghost Clouds return to finish what they started? Or were the strange lights something even worse to fear, some special evil? His breath was coming in short bursts.

Unable to stand his growing panic, he got up and walked around to calm down. Then he put more wood on the fire. The physical activity helped push back his fears and he began to feel better. *Sure the valley's quiet: there's nothing here and the wind normally dies down at night. Josh and I have already experienced the worst the valley has to throw at us . . . haven't we? If the strange lights show up later, they could have some rational explanation. Most likely they're some odd weather phenomenon.* He crawled back into his sleeping bag. All he had needed to do was talk it out with himself. Tonight was simply another camp-out and before they knew it, it would be morning.

Soon he began to doze off but was startled awake when he thought he heard whispering voices again. He sat up straight and his eyes swept the area around them. There were no Ghost Clouds. No one was there except Josh, and he was asleep. He thought something moved in the sky and looked up. Was it a light he just saw disappear behind the mountain? He got out of his sleeping bag and stood up. Yes, there it was streaking out on the other side, moving counter-clockwise around the outer edge of the valley.

He hurriedly slipped into his boots and jacket, pulled his ammo pouch and camera straps over his head, and climbed to the top of the granite formation. On its return, the light passed in front of the mountain and began a second, smaller elliptical orbit around the valley. Obie strained to see what appeared to be two objects moving side-by-side with a comet-like tail streaming out behind. He tried snapping a couple of pictures, but the objects were moving too fast to focus on, so he set his camera down. He'd try again if the light slowed down. Again, it passed in front of the mountain and began a third smaller orbit around the valley. Then he remembered Josh and yelled down, "Josh, wake up! There's a light circling the valley."

"Wha...? Who's there? What'd I do?" Josh said, struggling out of his sleeping bag and getting to his feet. He shook his head and looked up. The light passed behind The Boulders and continued north until it curved around and headed back towards the mountain again.

"I see it Obie. What is it?"

"I'm not sure." Obie's voice trembled. Torn between an impulse to flee to safety and a desire to satisfy his curiosity, he stood fixed to the spot, his knees wobbling under him. When the light neared the mountain again it unexpectedly swerved and streaked towards the camp.

"Obie, get down from there, get down," Josh screamed.

A second later the light dipped low and Obie saw the spirit-like forms of an eagle and a winged horse about to pass directly over his head. Too late to run. His breath caught and he felt himself being swept up into the comet's tail. At the moment before he was whisked away, he glimpsed Josh staring up in disbelief, and Hudson howling.

CHAPTER THREE

WINDERMERE

WATCHER MOUNTAIN receded rapidly in the darkness below as Obie was pulled along head first and belly down on the tail of the steeply rising comet. The translucent white light beneath him felt something like a firm mattress that held him by some unknown force. At first he felt the rush of air pushing against his head and shoulders, but it subsided as they rose through the stratosphere and the ionosphere. He realized the comet must carry its own air, for his breathing was only slightly affected. He turned his face upward and froze: directly ahead in the cosmic night floated the barn-sized mouth of a vortex of blue and purple light emanating from a misty core. They closed on it fast. Within seconds the eagle and the winged horse disappeared into its swirling curtain, pulling Obie along with them. The comet's tail dissolved when his winged bearers faded into the mist ahead. Simultaneously, turbulent forces yanked him into a weightless, spiraling descent through bursts of white light exploding in the blue and purple roil.

Dizziness and nausea plagued Obie as the spinning increased. Pain stabbed through his bad leg and his chest was tight with fear. In a state of near panic, his mind exploded with terrifying thoughts. Was he dead? Was this purple whirlpool the tunnel to Hell? Had the ghost creatures been sent to fetch him? Will's face flashed before his mind and he grabbed at the image like a lifeline tossed out in a typhoon. "Pray for me old man," he implored. When a sharp pain shot through his leg again, he welcomed it as a good sign. If he could feel physical pain, maybe he wasn't dead. But if he was still alive, where was he? And what was this purple whirlpool? The word *wormhole* leaped into his consciousness. His science teacher had defined wormholes as tunnels created when black holes caused a rip in the fabric of space. Theoretically, they could be used like time machines. Was it possible he was in a wormhole? If so, where would he end up? He hoped he wouldn't spin forever. *Forever* lingered in his mind until he realized he had no perception of the passage of time.

Seconds or centuries could have passed—he couldn't tell which—and then the white bursts of light and the swirling blue and purple mist vanished. He had exited the vortex and was again riding the comet's tail. Ahead he saw the diaphanous forms of the eagle and the winged horse transporting him through a gray-white sky above the Earth. Swiftly they descended and then, in the midst of a blinding flash of light, Obie dropped. A jolting cold enveloped his body a second before he thudded onto solid ground. He gasped and liquid poured into his nose and mouth and he realized he was lying face down under water. Scrambling to his knees he thrust his head and shoulders above the surface, choking and sucking in air in the thin sunlight.

When he opened his eyes he found himself face-to-face with a large blue-eyed creature with flaring black nostrils.

"Auuugh," he cried out, pushing backwards a foot or two at the same time the great white horse whinnied, reared, and spread its wings. Obie stared at the animal in disbelief. *What the . . . another horse with wings? Where am I?* Well at least he was *somewhere*, which was far better than where he had just been, which had seemed to be *nowhere*. The thought had a calming effect. Obie breathed a sigh of relief when the horse settled down and stood staring at him. Did he see amusement in its intelligent eyes? And if that wasn't disconcerting enough, he thought he heard the horse laughing, although his ears perceived no sound. *Has Ghostrise Valley driven me mad . . . like it did that guy last year? Is any of this really happening? Yeah. It's happening all right. Have to get a handle on myself. Stop panicking.*

It was not until he stood up that he spotted the slender, buckskin-clothed rider astride the winged horse. The rider's bow was drawn and an arrow pointed at his heart. Obie sneezed mud from his mouth and nose. The dangerous expression on the rider's face softened and the hand holding the bowstring relaxed. The rider's pale blue eyes shone with the hint of a smile, though the face betrayed no sign of humor. When a moment later the rider's cap came off revealing long wheat-colored braids wrapped neatly around her head, Obie realized it wasn't a male as he had thought, but a young woman of about nineteen or twenty years of age.

"Are you beast or man who rises from the floor of the pond?" she asked.

Reaching up he felt the stringy vegetation and pond debris hanging from the top of his head down past his shoulders. His cheeks grew hot beneath the muck on his face. *Great! Now I've turned into Frankenvine.* He began yanking the vegetation off. "Very funny," he said, scowling up at her.

"No offense intended. You just look very strange—though I suspect there's a young man in there somewhere under the plants and mud."

"Well I happen to *feel* very strange at the moment, so excuse me if I don't laugh at your joke. Something bizarre just happened to me." As he pulled the last of the vegetation off his legs felt weak and he began to tremble convulsively, as often occurs on the heels of traumatic experiences.

"Bizarre? Yes, I would agree with that," the young woman said absently, returning the arrow to her quiver and slinging her bow over her back.

"Where am I?" Obie muttered to himself. *Thanks, Will.* He felt like yelling at the top of his lungs, but decided to restrain himself and keep the last shreds of his dignity. Besides, he needed the young woman's help and hadn't exactly gotten off to a good start with her. He noticed her eyeing something at his side and realized it was his Raptor, still attached to his leather pouch. He was thankful he'd secured the pouch strap across his chest before the wild ride. Having some means of protection in this strange place helped him breathe a little easier.

"You can wash off over there." The young woman pointed to a waterfall cascading down a rocky outcropping of a mountain slope about twenty feet away.

"Thanks." For the first time, he took in his surroundings. The pond was a water-lily laden frog haven bordered by fir and deciduous trees growing just beyond the narrow rocky shore. As he waded to the waterfall he spotted his ball cap floating nearby and picked it up. Worried that the young woman might leave, Obie rinsed off quickly under the falls, then pulled his wet cap on and waded to shore. "What place is this?" he asked, stepping from the water. He felt her eyes on him as he limped to a nearby boulder. He just wanted to sit down and rub his aching leg. The girl and her winged horse remained in the water a couple of feet from shore.

"You're in the Kingdom of Windermere. I'm Gabrielle of the House of Brynnen and this is Mara," she said nodding down at the winged horse. "Who are you and what is your business here?" Her voice sounded more demanding than Obie liked.

His face skewed into an oddly contorted grin and he replied in a slightly mocking tone, "I'm Oberon of the House of Griffin, but people call me Obie."

Gabrielle raised an eyebrow.

"I'm from Garrett, Wyoming," he continued, wondering if he should tell her how he got there. She'd probably laugh at him again, but he had to risk it—she might know something. "I know this sounds crazy, but a ghost comet brought me here—at least that's what it looked like to me."

Gabrielle appeared startled. "These are indeed strange times."

Relieved that she hadn't laughed, Obie's mind raced with questions he wanted to ask, but he cautiously held back. She wasn't all that friendly. In fact she seemed almost haughty sitting up there looking down at him from her winged horse. Although he'd never met one before, he guessed from her manner and the way she sat her steed that she was an aristocrat. And not an overly feminine one, either. Obie watched Mara wade to the waterfall where Gabrielle began filling her water bag. He had learned a lot about horses the past few years while tending Will's mare, Daybreak. His eyes moved along Mara's strong, well-proportioned body and great folded wings to her long, silky mane and tail that gleamed like ice crystals against her snowy white coat, then to her contrasting blue eyes and dark, velvety nostrils. With head and tail held high, she stood tall and noble. For a few moments he forgot everything else. Never had he seen such a beautiful animal.

When Mara moved closer to the shore he feared she and Gabrielle were going to abandon him. He needed to say something fast, anything to delay their departure. "Mara's really special. I've never seen a horse with wings before. We don't have them where I come from."

"I'm sorry to hear that," Gabrielle said. "Yes, she *is* special. But she's not really a horse, although she and her kind are descended from horses. Mara's a windlord."

"Windlord." The name seemed perfect when he repeated it. "Will you think I'm strange if I tell you I keep imagining she's speaking to me telepathically?"

"Telepathically? What is that?"

"Well, where I come from it means talking mentally to someone."

Gabrielle remained silent for a moment and then responded, "*Mentally* is easier to say."

"Hmmm. I never thought of that. Okay, *mentally*."

A smile crept into Gabrielle's eyes. "To answer your question, why would I think you're strange? Mara probably *was* talking to you. She and her race are among those who retain the ancient power to communicate mentally with other creatures that also have the ability."

"With other creatures that *also* . . ." Obie repeated, considering her words. "Are you implying *I* can communicate mentally?"

"You must be able to—otherwise, you wouldn't hear her. Didn't you know you had the power?"

Her words startled him. "No, I didn't. Can she hear everything I'm thinking?"

"No, you have to be directing your thoughts to her. She also understands when you speak aloud. Learning to use your ability should be easy enough. It only takes a little concentration to project or guard your thoughts. As you practice and learn, you may experience more—some do."

Obie was so focused on the possibility of communicating with a windlord that he barely heard Gabrielle's last sentence. "So, you think I can speak mentally to Mara?"

"Why don't you try?"

"All right." He asked Mara if she had been laughing at him earlier.

Yes, I confess, your appearance made me laugh. I apologize if it caused you distress, she said.

Whoa! This is amazing!

I think it's even more amazing that you rode a comet to Windermere, she replied.

Her words jarred Obie into visualizing himself riding the comet, like some comic strip character. He pictured the grimace on Scottie's face when he got home again, his hair turned white and standing on end as he told his brother about his comet ride to Windermere, and how he carried on a conversation with a telepathic horse with wings. Then Scottie would be on the phone calling the men with the strait jackets. It was too much. His laughter started quietly and grew steadily louder until he was doubled over with tears streaming down his cheeks. At last he sighed and sat up, wiping his face with his hands.

Mara stepped from the water onto the shore. Gabrielle dismounted and sat down on a small boulder across from him. "Are you all right?"

"Yeah, I guess I needed a good laugh. From now on, though, I don't think anything will ever surprise me again."

Gabrielle stared briefly at him and then replied, "I wouldn't be too sure of that. The universe is full of unimagined possibilities for those willing to accept its gifts. Maybe what happened to you was such a gift."

Obie barked a quick laugh. "Well, if it's a gift, I wish it had come with a set of instructions, because I don't know what I'm doing here. What I'd really like to do is go home." Gabrielle looked puzzled. *Oh well, at least she's not rushing off before I get around to asking for help.* When she gave him a knowing smile, an alarm sounded in his head. "No, don't tell me. Can you hear my thoughts too?"

Gabrielle nodded. *Yes, the members of my family also have the power of mental speech.*

"Now you tell me. Why didn't you say so sooner instead of letting me make a bigger fool of myself?" He started shivering in his wet clothes.

"I guess you didn't realize you were projecting your thoughts to me," she said. She got up and pulled a blanket from Mara's back and tossed it to him. "Wrap up in the blanket before you get sick."

He threw it around his shoulders. He'd have to guard his thoughts more closely and not inadvertently direct them to her. At least she knew now that he wanted help. Attempting to make some pleasant conversation, he ventured, "It's pretty cool for a sunny day." He saw Gabrielle's pained expression. She turned her head for a moment and it seemed to him that some quick communication passed between her and Mara before she turned back to him.

"You don't even know what's going on, do you?"

Obie could feel the blood rushing to his face. "Well, I *used* to think I knew some things, but I'm not sure anymore. In fact I have no idea what you're even talking about. What I'd really like is a lot less mystery and a little more help from you, that is, if you can spare it."

Gabrielle flinched. "All right. Mara and I have been trying to decide what to do with you. We can't allow you to wander alone in our land. Your life would be in danger. And your ignorance tells us you have either come from very far, or else you have long been sleeping and need to be awakened. Open your eyes and look at the sun," she said, pointing to the sky.

Obie looked up and his jaw dropped. The sun appeared strangely cold and small, like some pale-green, alien orb afloat in the grayish-white sky. "What . . . what's happened to it? Why does it look so strange?" Filled with a sense of foreboding, he feared hearing the answer.

"The sun, moon and stars are fading out. Our people call it *The Celestial Dimming.*"

It's happening, then. My nightmare is coming true. Obie felt weak as he stared at the dying sun.

"We don't know what's causing the dimming, but we think black sorcery is behind it." Gabrielle's eyes flashed with anger when she spoke. "Already the stars have faded from sight unless one flies high in the night sky to see them. But, even up there, they're fading. In another month the stars may disappear entirely." Gabrielle turned her head away for several moments, and when she turned back all emotion was wiped from her face. "I'm sorry to be the bearer of such bleak news, but you may as well know everything. Our royal astronomer warns us that if the sun continues to fade, it will disappear within a year, maybe sooner. And when the Earth is left in total darkness, it will freeze into a ball of ice. Unless we find a way to reverse the dimming, it's doubtful anything will survive for very long."

Obie leaned his elbows on his knees and buried his face in his hands. After a few moments he raised his head and asked, "Does anyone have any ideas about how to solve the problem?"

"Not yet. But there is someone who may be able to help us." Gabrielle stood up and Mara trotted over. "We must leave the pond now. We've lingered too long already. I'll take you to Grandfather. He should be home from the keep soon. If anyone can help you get back to your home, it will be him." Grasping the pommel, Gabrielle pulled herself up onto Mara's saddle. "You may climb up behind me, Obie. Mara will carry us both. But I warn you to mind your manners—Mara and I are in control in the sky."

"Got it," he answered half-amused by her words; yet he respected her need to make the comment. He handed Gabrielle the blanket while he climbed up behind her, then took it back again and wrapped it around him. "What did you mean when you said we've lingered here too long?" he asked.

"King Torolf, a black sorcerer, sends frequent raiding parties to our borders and they've even entered our land of late. We think he's planning war against us."

Obie looked around nervously. *No dull moments around this place.*

"Hold on to me if you need to, and don't worry, we won't let you fall."

Mara stepped forward and, gently flapping her great white wings, lifted effortlessly into the air. Butterflies fluttered in Obie's chest as he watched the pond and trees grow smaller. Flying northward, the shape of the valley reminded him of Ghostrise, but the similarity ended there. Unlike the dead and barren terrain of Ghostrise, this valley was green and alive with rich farmlands, pastures, wooded areas, streams, ponds, and a river near the mountain that flowed from north to south. He fixed his eyes on the mountain bordering the west side of the valley. Was it mere coincidence that its shape and position resembled Watcher Mountain, though this one appeared a little higher and was clothed in a pine forest? He noted another difference: this mountain had no visible eyes. Were they there, hidden under the trees, or beneath rock that had not yet eroded away? Had he been brought back in time to a world where winged horses and sorcerers existed? He could vouch for at least one winged horse and a young woman who spoke with a Gaelic accent. His stomach began to churn dangerously. No. Not now. He had to control himself, shove his worrying to the back of his mental drawer until he could be alone to think. Breathing deeply, he lifted his face to the cool wind and the sick feeling passed. He forced his thoughts to the sights below. There were a few roads paved with stones, three small stone castles, and farmhouses with thatched roofs sprinkled through the valley and far into the west beyond the mountain.

"What's the mountain called?" he asked.

"Mount Iluva," Gabrielle answered. "It means *the fair mountain.*"

He was about to ask what language *Iluva* came from, but was distracted when Mara flew into a cloud and they were enveloped in the quietude of cool white vapor. Then, as suddenly as they had entered, they burst back out into the gray daylight. Briefly forgetting his cares as the thrill of flight overtook him, he pulled his cap off and let the wind blow through his hair. *This is awesome . . . riding on the wings of a windlord.*

Thank you, Mara responded.

Obie smiled. He hadn't realized he was projecting his thoughts.

At the northern end of the valley he spotted a town with two and three-story masonry buildings and houses with high angled roofs, many gables, and tall chimneys. A little farther north, where the forest bordered the valley, stood a great castle. He watched a silver windlord and rider descend within its high walls. "What castle is that?"

"Windermere Castle, the keep of our good Queen Olwen of the House of Gruffydd," Gabrielle said.

"It looks almost new."

"I suppose it is *almost* new. It was built a little over fifty years ago to replace the old timber keep. The stone provides greater defense against enemies. We learned of stone castles from the eagles. They had seen them in far off lands beyond the Great Western Sea."

"Did they bring back plans to build them?"

"No. After hearing of them our royal architects rode windlords to the lands of the almond eyed people and beyond, to see for themselves. They befriended the citizens, who then shared with them the secrets of building stone castles and many other things. It is said our architects brought back the best of what they saw and then added their own improvements when they drew the plans for Windermere Castle."

Without warning, something big swooped down on their left. Startled, Obie jerked his head around to see. A very large eagle, possibly large enough to carry a man, flew alongside them. Its feathers were brown and black, its wings powerful. Obie knew

Gabrielle had to be aware of its presence, though she didn't seem surprised and didn't even turn her head to look.

After a few moments she said, "Hello, Andor. I wondered if we'd see you today."

"Greetings to you, Gabrielle and Mara." Andor's voice was deep and resonant.

"My companion is Oberon of Griffin, or *Obie* as he prefers. Obie, this is Prince Andor, though he prefers to be called *Andor*."

"I'm glad to meet you, Andor," Obie said, still recovering from his astonishment at hearing an eagle speak. "I've never met an eagle prince before. In fact I've, uhhh . . . never actually met an eagle before."

The prince's intelligent eyes registered mild amusement as he scanned Obie. "Greetings, Obie."

"The Spirit Comet brought him to Windermere from a distant land," Gabrielle said. "While Mara was drinking at the Old Frog Pond we saw a burst of light, and then he appeared."

Andor squawked and turned a piercing eye towards Obie. "I have never heard of Haldor and Allegra bringing anyone to this valley before."

"Nor have I," Gabrielle said gravely.

"And yet I believe there is a prophecy of such an event."

"Now that you mention it, I remember hearing of such a prophecy. Grandfather Andras would know its contents. I'm glad you reminded me of it."

"I would advise taking Obie to your grandfather with all haste, Gabrielle. The old prophecies are not to be taken lightly, especially during such times as these. There may be an important message in it."

"I will. Grandfather should be home soon."

Obie wondered what they were talking about.

The eagle prince screeched and banked to the left. "Fair winds," he called and spiraled upward in an arc over their heads.

"Fair winds to you, Andor," Gabrielle called back.

"Fair winds," Obie called out.

"Prince Andor is a renowned warrior and a remarkably dependable friend to have," she said.

"And he sure can fly." Obie watched him diminish to a speck above them.

"Yes, flying is a great joy to his life."

"Gabrielle, I'm not trying to be nosy, but what did he mean when he said Haldor and Allegra brought me here? Who are they? And what's the *prophecy* you're anxious to find out about?"

"Yes, of course you wouldn't know about those things. Let's stop down there." Gabrielle pointed to a meadow that lay a little way inside an oak forest bordering the Valley of Windermere on the east. "I'll explain while Mara treats herself to some sweet clover. It's a special variety she enjoys and it grows only there." Mara landed near the western edge of the clearing and they dismounted. "This is Gnarlwood Forest, and it's not a friendly place."

Obie made a quick sweep of his surroundings and agreed. It was an old, dim forest, and its very atmosphere felt hostile. The oaks were tall and dark with low reaching branches and lichen covered trunks, some of such girth it would take three or four men to reach around one. From the base of the oldest trees, great gnarled roots rose as much as five feet in height before snaking back into the ground. Peering into the shadows he saw rich hues of purple, brown, sienna, black, and grey amidst the foliage and bracken; and he wondered what secrets this forest guarded.

"I think we'll be safe here for a few minutes, and then we must go. Just keep your eyes open."

"For what?"

She gave Obie a hard look. "Goblins and trolls, of course."

"Goblins and trolls, of course, of course," Obie repeated to himself. He unfastened his Raptor and slipped it onto his left arm.

"Good," Gabrielle said, observing his movements. "It's wise to be ready for possible attack. Are you a warrior in your land? I noticed your leg injury."

"No, that happened when I was a little kid. I'm not quite old enough to go into the military. But I can take care of myself with my Raptor."

"Yes, I noticed your weapon also. I've never seen anything like it before—is it a powerful?"

"It can stun or kill a large animal. At home we use them mostly in competitions and for hunting small animals."

"Hmmm."

Obie watched Gabrielle's eyes move past the trees on the far side of the meadow, and he wondered if she was even listening. She didn't seem all that impressed with his Raptor. He'd have to give her a demonstration later. Right now, though, he had other things on his mind. "What about the ghost comet, and who are Haldor and Allegra?"

"Haldor and Allegra *are* the comet, the *Spirit Comet*." Gabrielle nocked an arrow as she spoke and held her bow in readiness at her side. "On nights when the moon is full we see them flying over the Valley of Windermere. This valley was their home and their spirits have remained here. Haldor was the last and, it is said, the greatest of the eagle wizards, while Allegra is the mother of the race of windlords."

"An eagle wizard?"

"The eagles have always been a powerful race. Long ago, there were eagle wizards, but that time has passed and they're all gone now. The legend goes that Haldor could assume the physical shape of any creature. He admired the noble race of horses so much he sometimes transformed himself into a horse so he could run with them. But when he did, he kept his eagle wings. He became smitten with Allegra, a beautiful horse maiden, and they took one another as life companions. He used his magic to give her the gift of wings so they could soar high above the Earth together. All of their descendents were born with wings, and he called them *windlords*." From where she nibbled clover nearby, Mara neighed softly, as if giving her seal of approval to the story.

"Why do their spirits remain in the valley?" Obie asked. Gabrielle appeared increasingly uneasy. He began to feel it too. It seemed too quiet.

"I'll tell you quickly, and then we must go." While she talked Obie noticed a small golden pendant in the shape of a triangle hanging from a golden chain around her neck. In the center, two crystals were embedded, one light and the other dark. "We believe Haldor and Allegra are still helping to guard the Star Cryst . . ." Gabrielle's words were abruptly cut off by a sudden commotion coming from the far side of the meadow.

"Eyaaaa, eyaaaahaaahaaa," rang the battle cries of the large grotesque creatures that streamed from the trees with clubs and spears held high.

"Trolls," Gabrielle yelled.

CHAPTER FOUR

THE GUARDIANS

OBIE WAS HORRIFIED to see twelve, shrieking and grunting warriors racing towards them. The only thing he could compare them to was huge, upright toads with thick gray skin. Two fang-like lower teeth protruded upward from each side of their frog-like mouths, and knobby arms and legs were attached to barrel trunks. This last assault on his nervous system was too much. Obie stood frozen to the spot while two trolls came at him.

"Defend yourself! Use your weapon!" Gabrielle yelled, as she loosed her arrows at the oncoming trolls. But the first troll was almost upon him—too late to use his Raptor. Then something swished past his ear, and the troll's eyes bulged. Gabrielle's arrow was lodged in the soft spot of its throat just above its metal breastplate. The warrior fell at Obie's feet, but an instant later the second troll grabbed his arms and held him like a shield against Gabrielle's arrows.

"Run," Obie yelled. She didn't see the warrior coming up behind her. It grabbed her bow arm and she turned and bit the troll's wrist. It bellowed, loosening its grip slightly. She wrenched free and kicked it hard in the knee. As the troll buckled, Gabrielle backed up and drew her bow. Maddened, it came at her again, but she stopped it with an arrow between its eyes. Twirling, she shot a large troll as it leaped at her. It crumpled mid-air and hit the ground face down.

Obie struggled in vain to free himself from the brute's vice-like grasp. He felt its hot, rancid breath on the back of his neck. It grunted something in troll language and pushed down on his shoulders, as if telling him to stay put. The troll released its hold on him and fumbled at its belt for a rope. Seizing the opportunity, Obie threw his shoulder as hard as he could into its chest. Crashing to the ground atop the troll, he rolled to the side and scrambled to his feet. *Maybe I can outrun him.* But before he could take a step, the surprisingly agile troll leaped up and lunged at him. Its clammy hand tightened around Obie's throat and squeezed as it raised its club arm. Choking, Obie saw the blunt weapon begin its descent towards his head, but before the motion was completed the arm went limp and the troll sank to the ground, an arrow through its neck.

"Thanks," Obie yelled at Gabrielle. His blood was racing. When he saw how many trolls she'd slain, he was shamed that he'd done nothing to help. His unused Raptor was still positioned on his left arm.

"No time for niceties, we have to save Mara."

The remaining five trolls were pulling the windlord away. Two warriors at her sides had bound her wings with leather straps while the other three tugged at the ropes thrown around her neck. Mara neighed and snorted, defiantly resisting their efforts to draw her into the shadows of the forest, but she was losing the tug-of-war. One of the trolls lifted a horn to its mouth and blew three long, low, wails.

"You've got to help," Gabrielle cried. "They're calling their friends—the meadow will soon be overrun by trolls."

With the flurry of movement the trolls were making around Mara, Obie knew Gabrielle couldn't risk using her bow for fear of hitting the windlord. As he watched the hideous creatures pull Mara away, rage erupted from deep within him; a burst of heat ignited in the crown of his head and moved swiftly through his body. In that instant it didn't matter that he was a green youth pitted against several large, battle-seasoned trolls, for his own safety was not a concern. Only one thought burned through him: he must stop the trolls. With quick, sure movements and a mental clarity that amazed the observer part of his mind, he inserted a supply of large steel shot into his mouth, loaded his Raptor, and sprang towards Mara and the trolls. Gabrielle blinked when she saw this change came over him; then she too leaped to action.

At sight of the two humans barreling down on them, four of the trolls abandoned Mara and ran for the clubs and spears they had left lying on the ground near-by. Only one troll remained to hold Mara's rope. Parted now from the windlord, the four were clear shots. Obie ducked sideways to escape an oncoming spear, then stood and sent two trolls tumbling to the meadow floor with quick shots to their heads. He glanced towards Gabrielle and saw she was doing just fine. She had felled the other two warriors and stood watching Mara. The windlord's punishing hooves stabbed down at her troll captor again and again until it released the rope. Separated from its weapons by the two humans, the last troll turned and fled into the forest.

Mara's eyes were half wild and her nostrils flaring as she galloped towards Gabrielle and Obie. *No time to bask in victory,* she said, coming to a quick halt. *Unbind my wings. We must be gone!*

Before she even finished speaking, Obie and Gabrielle were unfastening the straps and flinging them to the ground. Seconds later, the windlord's wings were freed. Gabrielle pulled herself onto the saddle as Obie slid several ropes from Mara's neck. As he reached for the last one, more trolls issued from the trees from two directions.

"Leave the rope—let's get out of here," Gabrielle yelled, extending her arm to him.

Her arm was stronger than he would have guessed when he took hold of it and swung up behind her. Mara unfolded her wings for flight, but the first warrior reached them and grabbed Obie's leg, trying to pull him down.

"Get away," Obie yelled, shoving his foot hard into the troll's face. It fell backwards and Mara lifted from the ground just as two more arriving trolls jumped up and grabbed her hind legs. Obie shot one and it fell to the ground, but he could not get a good shot at the other. It dangled below, refusing to let go. Straining her wings against the added weight, the windlord slowly gained altitude. When she reached the treetops, she flew low over them and brushed the troll into the upper branches as easily as scraping mud from a boot. Then up she soared above the clearing while below thirty trolls screamed insults and shook their weapons.

"Close call." Obie's heart was pounding like a bass drum against his chest wall. "Thanks again, Gabrielle, for helping me out. I know it took me a while to get moving."

"Helping one another is what warriors do. Be thankful you survived to fight another day. From your actions and what you've told me about yourself, I'm guessing this was your first battle."

"Yeah."

"Then I'm glad to have fought at your side. You won't hesitate in battle again. I see now your Raptor truly is a weapon. You use it well—when you use it."

"Thanks." It was a half-compliment, but he'd take it. He could hardly expect more after his initial performance."

You indeed have skill with your weapon, Mara added.

"Thanks Mara, you weren't bad yourself. But, why didn't they try harder to kill us? Only one threw a spear, and that was when *we* attacked *them*. They seemed to hold back."

"They were trying to capture us," Gabrielle answered. "They highly prize windlords."

"I can understand that, but what about you and me? Why would they want us alive?"

"Perhaps they had eaten already. Trolls keep captives. They like their meat fresh."

Obie grimaced. It was a gruesome thought. "Well, I'll say one thing for them, they'd win an ugly contest hands down."

It's a fact that I have never yet seen a pretty troll, Mara put in.

The excitement left Obie feeling a little shaky. His upper arms were sore where the troll grabbed him and he had a scratch on his left leg above his boot that had bled slightly, but it was minor.

"We're going to my home now," Gabrielle said. "Grandfather Andras may be there."

"So, do you think he'll help me get back home?"

"You'll have to talk with him about it."

As they neared Gabrielle's family estate, located just south of the center of the valley, Obie saw horses grazing in the pasture to the north, and to the east and south lay rich farmlands. Mara landed in the cobblestone courtyard before a large, gray stone manor house. Green vines covered much of the nine-foot stone wall that surrounded the main house, carriage house, and other buildings; and two large maple trees grew beside an arched gateway that was large enough to allow the passage of horse and wagon. A second gate on the east wall also provided egress and ingress for ranching and farming activities. The three-story house resembled a small castle.

A pretty woman stood waiting on the doorstep. Her softly curled honey-colored hair was pulled back from her face, and her long forest-green dress seemed befitting to the lady of a great house. He wasn't surprised when she gave him a curious look.

"Mother, I'd like you to meet Oberon, or *Obie* as he is called, of the House of Griffin. He'll be staying for dinner." When she raised an eyebrow, Gabriel added, "I've brought him home to speak with Grandfather."

He smiled politely and removed his cap. "I'm pleased to meet you Mrs. Brynnen."

The proper way to address her is Lady Brynnen, Gabrielle corrected mentally.

"I mean, Lady Brynnen."

Her face relaxed into a smile and she curtsied. "We are pleased to have you join us for our evening meal, Obie."

He bowed awkwardly in return.

"Your grandfather has been detained at the keep, Gabrielle, and your father is meeting with a neighbor. So they won't be joining us until later tonight. In the meantime, we can offer our guest a bath and some fresh, dry clothing before dinner. Talbot, will you show him to the bathing room?"

A young house servant, about Obie's age, stepped from the shadows near the door. "This way, Obie," he said with a smile.

A warm bath and some clean clothes sounded good to Obie. Aside from looking soiled and disheveled, he strongly suspected he reeked of rotten pond vegetation. He followed Talbot through the great room and down a hallway, turning in at the last door-way on the left. The bathing room appeared Roman, with a white marble floor and a sunken marble pool filled with water. Obie realized his surprise must have shown on his face when Talbot asked, "What did you expect?"

"I don't know . . . maybe a wooden tub with buckets of hot water poured in?"

Talbot grinned. "Where have you been?"

"I came from a long way off." He dropped his jacket and pouch on the floor and started pulling off his boots.

"Apparently so," Talbot said with a quick laugh, "because the big houses have had these baths for well on fifty-years. Some of the smaller houses have them too, but usually not so grand. This house has two bathing rooms. The water's warmed in a vat in the next room and then piped in and out. I light the fires beneath the vats in the early afternoon to ready the pools for the evening baths. It's an improvement the architects in my grandfather's day brought back to us when they traveled across the sea to the Isle of Crete."

"It's impressive," Obie said, pulling his T-shirt off.

Glimpsing Obie's upper arms, Talbot whistled softly. "Those are serious looking bruises you've got there, Obie."

Obie's sore arms had turned black and blue. "It's nothing," he said, not in the mood for explanations. He finished stripping down and stepped into the bath. The warm water caused the scratches on his lower right leg to sting at first, but he sat down and the feeling began to subside.

"I'll take your damp clothing and boots and clean them," Talbot said. Gathering them up, he hesitated, staring curiously at the Raptor. He lifted the leather pouch and gave Obie a questioning look.

"Leave it. I'll tend to that."

"As you wish." Talbot set it back down, and started to leave, but stopped at the door and turned around. "Begging your pardon, Obie, but do you like to fish?"

"Fish? Sure."

"Well, the river's not far from here and I know the best spots to go catfishing. I would be pleased to have you join me—I like to go at night when they bite best."

Obie smiled. It would be nice to do something normal for a change. "Sounds great. I may take you up on that. I noticed a river on my way here. Are you talking about the one that runs down from Mt. Iluva and veers south?"

"That's the one. It's the River Llafar."

"What does it mean?"

"*Llafar* means *babbling,* or *vocal.* It babbles as it comes down from the mountain, but quiets down in stretches when it turns and flows down the valley."

"I'll look forward to seeing it."

Talbot flashed white teeth and disappeared around the door. Obie reclined his head against the edge of the tub and expelled a sigh as he began to relax in the water. He must have dozed after that because the next thing he knew Talbot was whistling a happy tune and laying out clean clothing and shoes.

"Here ya go." Talbot laid a bath sheet at the edge of the pool, next to Obie.

After Obie dried off and dressed, Talbot showed him to the great room where he joined Gabrielle and Lady Brynnen. Together, they went to the dining room for the evening meal. Gabrielle had changed into a long and shapeless, gray dress, and her hair was still tightly braided around her head. Obie thought she blended in nicely with the furniture, and resembled a cinder maid more than the daughter of a noble family. Most girls he knew cared about their appearance. Why didn't Gabrielle, especially when she had the means to dress well? In contrast, her mother was attired for entertaining in a stylish looking yellow silk dress with an amber pendant at her throat. Soft curls hung to her shoulders, and when she smiled at him he noticed that her face was flawless.

The rich color of the light oak walls, floor, and open-beam ceiling gave the dining room a warm atmosphere. The furnishings, though elegant, were few: a long, well-crafted oak table and twelve chairs with upholstered seats and backs, a sideboard, candles in glass lamps on the walls, a few tapestries, and silky yellow and green striped draperies at the tall windows. From the center ceiling beam, a large candelabrum hung over the table. The table was set with white candles on silver bases, fine white dishes, and silver goblets. Many of the fine things, Obie would learn, were purchased from the friendly goblin traders that traveled in caravans from far off lands and occasionally stopped in Windermere.

They sat at one end of the long table, with Lady Brynnen at the head, and the meal arrived almost immediately. A pleasant looking serving woman smiled kindly at Obie and heaped healthy portions of roast duckling and potato-onion pie onto his plate.

While they ate, Gabrielle told her mother about the Spirit Comet bringing Obie to Windermere and of his desire to find a way home. Lady Brynnen looked greatly surprised as she quietly listened. When her daughter finished, she said, "I've never heard of such a thing, yet it must be a good omen. You've come to the right place, Obie. Lord Brynnen, who is Gabrielle's Grandfather Andras, is the best person in the kingdom you could consult with. He's our Royal Historian and Lore Master, and he will know more than anyone about the Spirit Comet."

"That's encouraging, Lady Brynnen. Thank you for telling me."

"You're welcome, Obie. Please call me *Annwyl*." She talked so much that Obie was unable to get a word in, so he merely smiled and nodded.

"Lord Brynnen is also on the Council of Elders, which means he's close to Queen Olwen. She may be willing to help you, too— though it's a busy time for her. She and the Elders met with High Elf Envoys from the Isles of Eluthien just two days ago."

Elves? Obie thought. Why should that surprise him?

"The elves rarely come to Windermere. It's the fearful times that brought them. I wish I could have been there to see them, but there was no time. Andras said they came and went quickly in the night."

He laid his fork down, forgetting for the moment the succulent duck on his plate. "I'd like to see some elves. Where I come from we think the little people exist only in fantasy tales."

Annwyl raised her brow and looked surprised. "Oh, my goodness no. The elves are as real as you and me. And the High Elves are the most wonderful sight you'll ever behold. But, Obie, they're not *little people*, the High Elves. Tall and graceful they are, with such a light shining in their eyes as you'll never see in another creature. It's the magic in them they say. Long ago, a great clan of them came here from the Isles of Albion.

The same land our own people came from, though we also call our homeland *The Misty Isles*. But we came here much later. Like the High Elves, we sought out and found the Land of the Windlords. We came to escape the barbarian hordes that kept invading our lands, plundering, and savagely murdering our people."

Annwyl's words left Obie in mild shock, for she had more or less confirmed what he already suspected: the Spirit Comet had brought him far back in time. He'd had a poetry book in his English class last year titled *The Songs of Albion*. *Albion*, he had learned, was the ancient name for the British Isles before it became a Roman Province. The name was believed to be Celtic in origin. He swallowed hard. He was truly far from home.

He glanced at Gabrielle and saw that she was absorbed in her own thoughts. After her initial explanation regarding Obie's arrival in Windermere, she had remained silent and eaten very little. Obie responded to Annwyl's questions about his own family, and then she told him a little about hers. Among other things, he learned that her husband, the younger Lord Brynnen, managed the farming activities and the horses for his father, who was generally tending to business at Windermere Castle.

When the meal ended they retired to the comfort of plush, high-backed chairs in front of a large hearth in the great room. The room was illuminated only by the fire and a few candles. Obie noticed a couple of tapestries on the walls of battle scenes depicting windlords, men, eagles, trolls and some other strange creatures in mortal combat. He'd have a closer look at them later. Gabrielle remained quiet while Annwyl talked on about local people and events.

As Obie sat listening, his mind strayed to thoughts of home. He wondered if Josh thought he'd been burned up by a weird comet, or abducted by a UFO. He felt bad about leaving him and his dog alone in the valley. Was he safe? Had the ghost clouds returned to plague him during the night? He hoped Josh and Hudson made it home okay. And what about Scottie and Dad? Scottie would be worried sick. He wasn't sure about dad. His thoughts were interrupted by the sound of the front door opening, followed by deep voices and heavy footsteps.

Gabrielle, Annwyl, and Obie stood up as two men entered the room wearing hooded cloaks and leather riding boots. They pushed their hoods back and in the dim firelight Obie could see the older man had a strong, handsome face with salt and pepper hair and a well-groomed beard. The younger man resembled the other, though his hair was dark brown.

"Father, Grandfather, you've arrived home together." Gabrielle kissed them both on the cheek.

"Yes, he keeps following me around," her grandfather said jokingly as they removed their cloaks and handed them to Talbot.

Her father's conservative brown jacket contrasted to her grandfather's lime-green, velvet tabard with gold trim. Grandfather wore several long gold chains around his neck attached to large pendants encrusted with rubies, emeralds, and diamonds, and five large gemstone rings bedecked his fingers.

Obie suppressed a grin. *He looks like a peacock.*

A second later, Grandfather Andras locked eyes with him and mentally said, *But not a peacock to be trifled with.*

Obie's face flushed as he realized he'd unconsciously directed his thoughts to Andras.

"We've been waiting for you," Gabrielle said to her grandfather.

"Yes, I noticed our guest."

"A guest you'll want to speak with Grandfather—and he has the gift of mental speech."

A wry grin came onto his face. "Yes, I know."

Surprise flickered in Gabrielle's eyes. Then she turned to Obie and mentally instructed him, *Please call Father and*

Grandfather *"Lord Brynnen."* When she introduced him as *Oberon of Griffin*, he felt her eyes watching him. Groaning inwardly, he realized he'd just have to live with this *Oberon of Griffin* thing he'd started. And judging by the look on her face he was sure she sensed his discomfort with it. When the two men bowed politely he imitated their movement and said, "Please, call me *Obie*."

"As you prefer, Obie," the younger Lord Brynnen said. He looked Obie up and down with a critical eye, and added, "My clothing fits you fine."

"Oh, yes, thanks Lord Brynnen. Mine were wet so Lady Brynnen let me borrow them."

"I shall look forward to hearing the story as to why you were wet. In the meantime, since my good wife would think it scandalous to have a soggy guest running about the house getting the furniture wet, I suppose I can live with it, lad." He winked at his father.

"They look better on him than on you anyway," the elder Lord Brynnen said.

"I've been looking forward to talking with you, sir," Obie said to Gabrielle's grandfather.

"Yes, yes. Let's all sit down and relax a bit first." He waved Obie to a chair. "No doubt you're seeking a position at Windermere Castle or some such thing. Well, I'm going to get comfortable by the fire and light my pipe, and then I suppose I must lend you an ear."

"No sir, I . . ." Obie began, but was stopped when Gabrielle shook her head and made a silencing gesture.

Everyone sat down and the two men settled back in their chairs and lit their pipes. Obie waited quietly as the elder Lord Brynnen took periodic puffs and blew curls of white smoke that floated up into the shadowy recesses of the ceiling beams. Finally, he pulled his pipe from his mouth and said, "Well, Obie, since my granddaughter brought you home to me, the matter must be of some importance to you." Grinning roguishly, he continued, "How may this *peacock* be of service to you?"

Feeling like a turtle stripped of its shell, Obie swallowed hard and began his account of the Spirit Comet bringing him to Windermere. When he finished, he asked, "Sir, can you help send me home again?" He hoped he hadn't totally alienated Gabrielle's grandfather.

Lord Brynnen looked gravely at Obie and pulled his pipe from his mouth. "This is a very serious matter, lad. Gabrielle, my dear, you did the right thing in bringing him to me."

Obie was relieved. Apparently, her grandfather believed him.

Talbot and the woman who served him dinner brought in cups of mead and a tray of small cakes. The mead was fermented from honey and had a pleasantly sweet flavor. As Obie drank it he felt a warm sensation.

"Where exactly did the comet set you down, Obie?" Lord Brynnen continued.

"It dropped me face down in the mud in the Old Frog Pond. When I stood up I must have frightened Gabrielle and Mara. I was covered with pond muck and plants."

Lord Brynnen chuckled quietly. "Forgive me lad. I'm not laughing at you. I doubt that Haldor and Allegra intended to treat you so roughly. My guess is they wished to drop you off near Gabrielle and Mara. Perhaps they wanted you to be in our care. Unfortunately for you, Mara was standing in the pond at the time. Did you injure your leg when they dropped you? I notice you have a limp."

"No, Lord Brynnen, it happened when I was small."

"I see," he said softly. "Now, regarding the spirits, did you happen to see them?"

"I saw an eagle and a windlord just before the comet swooped down to pick me up, and then I could see them pulling me behind them."

"And, Grandfather," Gabrielle interrupted, "Mara and I saw a bright flash of light just a few seconds before Obie stood up in the water."

"Hmmm, yes, that supports Obie's story. But I'm a little mystified by all of this because Haldor and Allegra do not bring people to Windermere. Not until now, anyway."

"But, Grandfather," Gabrielle put in, "isn't there an old prophecy about . . ."

Lord Brynnen gave her a sharp look and she stopped mid-sentence. Obie wondered if her grandfather had mentally silenced her. And if so, why?

Perhaps catching the concerned look on Obie's face, Lord Brynnen explained, "Obie, I don't want to worry you about a prophecy at this point, at least not before I've had time to find it in the library at Windermere Castle. I'll do that in the morning. I won't mislead you, lad."

"Thank you, Lord Brynnen." Obie hoped he was as sincere as he sounded.

Lord Brynnen sat back and furrowed his brow in thought for a few moments, then asked, "Tell me, Obie, how did the sun, moon, and stars appear before the comet picked you up?"

"The sun was bright during the day, and that night there was a full-moon and the stars were shining."

"Then there is no Celestial Dimming in your homeland?"

"No, sir. I saw it for the first time after I arrived here. It's an awful thing."

Lord Brynnen frowned. "Yes, awful, to say the least." He looked at Gabrielle and the tension on his face relaxed. "But all is not lost yet. There is still hope."

Obie wondered if the *hope* involved his granddaughter.

"And I believe it was no accident that the Spirit Comet brought you here during this time of peril to the world. Obie, we would like you to be our guest while you're in Windermere. Will you stay with us?"

"Thanks for the invitation, sir. I'd like to stay here with your family. After the run-in we had with those trolls in Gnarlwood today, I'd hate to be . . ."

"Run-in with trolls in Gnarlwood?!" Lord Brynnen cut in, turning a stern eye to Gabrielle.

"Trolls? You were in Gnarlwood?" the younger Lord Brynnen repeated, with a shocked look at his daughter.

Annwyl gasped and clasped both her hands over her heart. "Oh, Gabrielle."

Obie caught the *Obie you idiot* look on Gabrielle's face. He would have kicked his own butt if his foot could have reached.

Gabrielle explained what had happened earlier, and how Obie stopped several trolls with his Raptor, adding that they should see him use it. He was glad she hadn't mentioned his initial poor performance.

"If it's that odd looking contraption projecting from his bag, I have already taken note of it, though I don't know why he's carrying it around in the house," her grandfather said, glancing at Obie. "And yes, I would be very interested in seeing him demonstrate his weapon tomorrow. But at the moment, I'm concerned about your poor judgment, Gabrielle. Aside from Queen Olwen herself, it's you and Mara whom King Torolf would most wish to capture. You know that. It's imperative that you stay away from Gnarlwood Forest."

"Yes, Grandfather."

Apparently satisfied with the scolding he had given his granddaughter, his composure grew calmer and his voice mellowed. "Will you promise?"

"Yes, I promise, Grandfather."

"Thank you, my dear." He smiled at Gabrielle and then turned to Obie. "I can see this conversation is confusing you, lad. There's much to tell and much we wish to learn about you in the next few days. But I know you must have some questions you would like answered before you close your eyes in slumber this night, so I'll do my best to answer them."

"Thank you, Lord Brynnen, sir. I do."

"I think we can dispense with you calling me *Lord Brynnen, sir*. We are not so formal—not in this house at least. You may call me *Andras*, and if the younger Lord Brynnen agrees, you may call him *Ilar*." Andras glanced at his son who nodded his assent.

"Thanks, Andras, Ilar."

"Now, what would you like to know?"

First, I'm wondering why King Torolf would like to capture Gabrielle and Mara. And second, I noticed Gabrielle wears a golden pendant with two crystals on it, and all of you wear the same pendant, but without the crystals. May I ask why?"

"You're very perceptive, Obie, for these two questions go to the very heart of things. You'll want to listen carefully to what I am about to tell you. Gabrielle and Mara are the Moonpath Riders, the new Guardians of two very powerful crystals called the Star Crystals. One of them is the Light Crystal. It's hidden away somewhere in the Kingdom of Windermere and only Gabrielle, Mara and one of the elders in the queen's court know its location. The other is the Dark Crystal. It's kept on the moon and guarded by Phoebe, the Moon Maiden."

"The *moon*?"

"Yes, the moon. I see that surprises you. It's kept there under Phoebe's protection until the time comes for the Moonpath Riders to retrieve it and bring it back to Earth to be joined with the Light Crystal. Only Phoebe knows the power of these crystals when they are joined. Until now, there has never been a need to retrieve the Dark Crystal."

A doubtful look crossed Obie's face. Was Andrus serious?

"As to the reason King Torolf would like to capture Gabrielle and Mara, it's because above all, he lusts for power. If he can obtain even one of the Star Crystals from them, he will be in possession of what may be our only hope against the Celestial Dimming.

Obie slid from his chair and hit the floor. He had been sitting on the edge of the overstuffed chair, so immersed in Andras' story that he hadn't noticed he was slowing sliding off. It had happened so quietly that no one took much notice. But Obie could tell from a sidelong glance at Gabrielle that she was staring directly at him, and she wasn't smiling. It annoyed him. He'd survived a killer vulture, ghosts, a wild ride through space and time, and trolls. Why should he now allow himself to be annihilated by her eyes? Avoiding her gaze, he reseated himself as if sliding off a chair was the most ordinary of experiences. Of course if he didn't look at her, he'd never know for sure what was in her eyes. It was a sacrifice he was happy to make.

"Now, what was your other question, Obie?" Andras asked.

"I asked about the pendants, sir."

"Oh, yes." Andrus examined the golden pendant on the chain around his neck as he spoke. "The three points of the triangle symbolize the Triple Alliance among the Windermerians, the Windlords, and the Eagles. Generations ago, King Cyneric the Great formed the Alliance with the eagle king and the windlord king to mutually defend each others homelands should the need arise. The need did arise, there was a war, and the Alliance won. A story for another time. By now, you have no doubt realized that the crystals embedded in Gabrielle's pendant symbolize that she and Mara are the Guardians of the Star Crystals."

"Yes, that part is clear to me," Obie said. "But, when you said Gabrielle and Mara are the Moonpath Riders, do you mean they actually ride a path to the moon?"

"Yes, indeed. The Moonpath opens up once every month on the night of the full-moon. As with the location of the Light Crystal, only The Guardians and one elder know where the Moonpath entrance lies."

A path to the moon. Obie turned an astonished look towards Gabrielle. "May I ask what it's like riding the Moonpath?"

"Mara and I have only recently been given the Guardianship, and we haven't actually ridden the path yet. We'll ride it at the next full moon, a few days after the Festival of the Harvest. We're going to seek Phoebe's counsel to learn whether anything can be done to stop the Celestial Dimming. Although we don't know the power of the Dark Crystal, it's our hope that it can help, and that she'll send it back with us."

Obie stared at Gabrielle, unable to look away. He hadn't guessed this aloof and plain looking young woman would hold such high status among her people.

"We have great hope in Gabrielle and Mara," Annwyl put in.

Then Andras said, "Legend tells us, lad, that the Moonpath is fraught with peril. Because of that, few Moonpath Riders have ever attempted to ride it. The Guardians are selected for their strength of will and purity of heart as well as for their great riding and flying skills. It is said that only such riders can successfully navigate the Moonpath."

"What if the *wrong* sort of person tried riding it?" Obie asked.

Andras puffed on his pipe and then said, "According to legend, a person or creature of ill spirit attempting to ride the Moonpath will meet their doom, for it will dissolve beneath them once they leave the Earth's atmosphere. But we believe Gabrielle and Mara possess the qualities needed to survive the ride. It's a journey we never make light of." Andras laid his pipe down and stood up. It seemed to be a signal to all that it was time to retire, for the others rose too. "Oh, Gabrielle, will you bring Obie to Windermere Castle in the morning and show him around? You needn't go as early as I will." Judging by the movement of his eyes, it seemed to Obie that Andras communicated something mentally to Gabrielle, and he saw her nod slightly to her grandfather. Oh well, it was probably none of his business.

Annwyl leaned over and whispered something in Ilar's ear.

"Oh, yes," Ilar said. "Before I forget, Gabrielle, so that you and Obie don't have to double up on Mara again, you may pair him with the horse of his choosing in the morning." He turned to Obie. "We'd pair you with a windlord if we could, lad, but there are so few of them in Windermere that none are available."

"That's all right, Ilar," Obie said, feeling a little light-headed from the mead. "I'll be happy to be paired with a horse."

Annwyl got a lamp and showed Obie to a guestroom with a large comfortable looking bed. The covers were pulled down and a nightshirt had been laid out. She lit a candle on a small table and wished him pleasant dreams as she left the room. When he climbed into bed, the worries he had been pushing back all afternoon returned. He wondered what Scottie and Josh were doing right now, and if Will was praying for his safe return. And what would Shannon think when he didn't show up at school? Would she care? Dad probably didn't even know he was gone. He had a heavy feeling in his chest.

While he lay in the dark room, near exhaustion from all that had happened, the softly glowing candlelight brought back the memory of the night-light in his room so many years ago. An angelic woman with light hair was tucking him into bed and singing softly. That was when the world had been a safe place filled with warmth and love. Then the old haunting memory came back. He was strapped in his car seat in the backseat of the car and his mother was driving. It was just the two of them, laughing happily, and he saw his teddy bear come flying towards him. They were playing the teddy bear game. He caught it and threw it back, but something went horribly wrong. Everything was spinning around and the world turned upside down and then all went black. He'd awakened to Will's strong hands pulling him from the car just before it exploded in flames. Obie sat up in bed and leaned forward, burying his wet face in his hands.

CHAPTER FIVE

WINDERMERE CASTLE

WHITE PATCHES of early morning mist obscured Obie's vision as he walked through the pasture. He was wearing his own clothing and boots that had been cleaned during the night and left just inside his door, and over his shoulder he carried one of Ilar's saddles. Gabrielle rode beside him on Mara as they searched for the horses. He heard a snort off to the left and then a soft nicker to the right, but couldn't see anything. Then he stepped out of a fog patch and found himself among at least twenty horses. Gabrielle waited while he moved through the group looking them over and finally settled on a chestnut stallion. He looked around for Gabrielle, but the fog had rolled between them. Oh, well. She'd know soon enough which one he'd chosen.

The stallion stood perfectly still while Obie threw the saddle over his back, tightened the girth strap and slid the bridle over his head. Then, putting his foot in the stirrup and his hands on the pommel, he pulled himself up and was swinging his right leg over the saddle when he heard a telepathic voice say, *Bad choice. I'd try another if I were you.*

The suggestion came too late. As soon as Obie was in the saddle the chestnut danced about uncontrollably, then leaped straight up in the air with back bowed and head down. When his front hooves touched ground again, his back legs kicked out with a jolt that sent Obie flying forward. He hit the ground and lay there groaning.

Told you so, came the mental voice again. *He isn't called Cyclone for nothing.*

"Yeah?" Obie said with a groan, rising up slowly on his elbows. "Maybe somebody ought to hang his name around his neck." He turned to see who spoke to him. A powerful looking brownish-black stallion with a black mane and tail and dark glistening eyes stood in the mist a few feet away. "Are you the one who was talking to me? Naw, couldn't be." Obie stood up and brushed himself off, still looking around for the speaker.

Why not? The dark stallion was staring at him.

It was you. I didn't know horses here could speak mentally.

They don't. Only me. I'm one of a very few left among my kind who has retained the old power of mental speech. I'm called Shadow.

I'm glad to meet you, Shadow. I'm Oberon Griffin, but call me Obie.

Shadow snorted. *I like a human I can talk to—so few can speak mentally.*

Although he'd been careful not to show it, Obie had been disappointed at not being paired with a windlord. But the possibility of riding a horse like Shadow while in Windermere hadn't occurred to him. It was more than he could have hoped for. Not only could they communicate, which in itself made him extremely desirable, but this was a strong looking and exceptionally beautiful animal. The question was, if Shadow agreed to a pairing, would Ilar allow it? Had the mead last evening made him forget about Shadow? It was worth a try, anyway.

I'm glad we ran into each other. Do you think you could help me select another horse? Obie asked, not wanting to appear overly anxious.

I might. What qualities would you like in the horse you pair with?

Hmmmm, well I'd want him to be strong, spirited, courageous, yet wise and even-tempered, and I'd want him to be a friend and confidante.   Of course he'd also be a horse that expected to be treated well by a human who has his best interests at heart because he really likes horses. This horse would expect to be an equal and a partner to the human. And it wouldn't hurt if he was also as fine a looking animal as you are. So, uhhh, what do you think?

That sounds a lot like sweet talk to me.

Okay, it may sound that way, but I meant every word of it. And you <u>did</u> ask me what qualities I would want.   Besides, wouldn't it be nice to get out of this boring pasture?

True. I'm too young to be grazing—that's for old timers. I would like some excitement in my life. But there are worse things than living in a pasture—like bearing a human on my back that I have no rapport with. That I will not do. But I like you. You're young and energetic like me, and I can tell you like horses. I think we might become good friends, especially since you mental speak.

Thanks for saying so, Shadow. I feel the same way.   Then, grinning, Obie added, *By the way, I like your term <u>mental speak</u>. I haven't heard anyone use it before.*

Of course not. I just made it up.

Shadow, you're amazing! A horse that can coin a term. Do you have any other talents?

Only that I once tried wooing the females around here with some poetry. But they didn't appreciate it very much.

Obie laughed. *Shadow, you're definitely my kind of horse. So, we're a team?*

All right. I'm willing to bear you on my back.

Great.

Now let's get out of here. Time is on the hoof.

You got it. Do you mind if I use a saddle?

No, I don't mind, as long as you don't fasten the girth strap too tight.

How about a bridle?

No bridle. I won't tolerate having a bit in my mouth. A halter is all right, but when you tell me where we're going you won't even need that. You can grab hold of my mane if you need to—I'm tough skinned.

Thank you, my friend. I'll honor your wishes. He could hardly believe his good fortune. On the other hand, there was a lot that he could hardly believe. Today was, without a doubt, starting out better than yesterday.

Cyclone neighed and shook his head unhappily a couple of times, but behaved while the saddle and bridle were removed. Afterwards, he immediately ran off. Obie saddled Shadow and mounted. When the dark horse shot forward, Obie could feel the power of the stallion beneath him and the motion of his sturdy legs moving in long graceful strides over the pasture. Then Gabrielle and Mara came out of the fog and were galloping alongside him. He looked over and saw a spark of amusement flickering in Gabrielle's eyes.

"I see you and Shadow have found each other," she said. "But father *did* say you could have your pick of the horses, and I know he meant it."

"I hope Ilar doesn't mind," Obie said. "I know Shadow's special." Shadow acknowledged Obie's compliment with a low whinny as he and Mara slowed to a trot.

"If he does you'll never know it," Gabrielle said. "He's a man of his word."

They left the pasture and slowed to a walk as they entered the cobblestone road and headed north towards the keep. Gabrielle told him it was called *The King's Road*. A lone meadowlark's song pierced the air and was answered by another in the distance. The pale sun had risen in the grayish-green sky over the forest, revealing the effects of the Celestial Dimming on vegetation bordering the road. Morning glory vines, instead of being lush and full of blooms, were stunted and stringy with few blossoms; the wildflowers, too, were scant. But the stubborn, undiscouraged honeybees buzzed about the hardier jasmine blossoms, tirelessly harvesting the sweet nectar.

Though sore from being thrown by Cyclone, Obie felt more rested this morning than he had in over a week. When he finally fell asleep during the night, he hadn't had the nightmare. Coming to Windermere must have been the cure. But what now? Was he naïve to think he could just go home again? He sighed and glanced over at Gabrielle. She was so quiet. Was she thinking about riding the Moonpath? He would be if he were in her shoes. But he had enough to worry about just being in his own shoes. Like, how successfully was he guarding his thoughts? Maybe he was starting to get the hang of it. He'd had no indication of anyone hearing him this morning. He'd have to practice on Shadow. Right now, though, there was something he wanted to find out.

"Gabrielle?"

"Yes?"

"I've been wondering. Since I wasn't able to communicate mentally before I came to Windermere, where did this ability come from?"

"Perhaps you've always had the ability and didn't know it, or possibly Haldor somehow gave you the power when he and Allegra brought you here."

"A gift from Haldor would explain it. But if it wasn't, and if I've always had this ability, why didn't I know it?"

"You *wouldn't* know unless you used it towards someone else with the same power, or unless that person initiated mental contact with you."

"Hmmm," Obie said, thinking it over. "That makes sense." It occurred to him that the few people back home who had the power would probably discover it accidentally. "How many others in Windermere can speak mentally?"

"Only those of the House of Gruffydd bloodline and four other family bloodlines within the kingdom. But the royal family's mental speech is not a remnant of the ancient power the others have retained. The House of Gruffydd powers come from their elven blood."

"The queen's an elf?"

"No, the elven blood came from the king's side of the family. Many generations ago, his ancestor King Cyneric the Great wed Gwendina, an elf princess from the Isles of Eluthien. It's said that when he gazed into her beautiful eyes he fell hopelessly in love with her. Their marriage brought the elven blood into the House of Gruffydd.

"May I ask how many children the king has?"

"Our king was killed during a goblin skirmish when I was a child. But to answer your question, he had three sons. The eldest was murdered and the second left the kingdom after that."

Obie watched her draw a deep breath. "Then the youngest son is here in Windermere?" he asked.

"No." Her voice had changed to a monotone.

"Where is he?"

"He also left the kingdom, to travel for a while, and has never returned." Gabrielle bit her bottom lip and turned away. When she turned back he could see that her eyes were moist with tears. An instant later Mara leaped forward into a gallop. Shadow sprang after her and Obie slid sideways on his saddle. He grabbed hold of the saddle horn and, with his right foot braced in the stirrup, used his leg muscles to push himself back onto the saddle.

Sorry about that, Shadow—you caught me off guard.

My fault. I'll warn you next time.

Why is Gabrielle upset? Did I miss something? He could hear Shadow chuckling mentally.

I daresay you missed something. Where females are concerned, you would be wise to watch their body language. It will often warn you of their mood changes.

Thanks, I'll try and remember that. Is there anything else you can tell me about what just happened?

No.

Racing along the road seemed to lift Gabrielle's spirits. She was one of the best riders he had ever seen. She rode as if she had been born on a horse—or a windlord. He recalled Andras saying great riding skills were a necessary quality for a Moonpath Rider.

When a couple of miles along the road they slowed to a trot, she brushed some loose strands of hair from her face and called, "We're not far from the keep now."

She seemed to have thrown off whatever was bothering her, so Obie ventured to ask how she and Mara usually spent their time.

"We teach riding and flying. We had just dismissed two students yesterday shortly before you appeared. I also spend a few afternoons each week with Queen Olwen."

"You're friends with the queen?"

"Yes, she's like a second mother to me. I make a point to be with her often now that she's alone."

They came to a fork in the road and Gabrielle motioned towards the left branch. "We can save time by taking this road and bypassing the town of Windermere." A couple of miles farther up the road they rounded a curve and just beyond a meadow loomed Windermere Castle. Obie's first close-up view of it was awe inspiring. A windlord and rider glided in and disappeared behind the great front wall, and moments later another flew out. The castle was as large as a small city. As they rode Obie's eyes moved along the high gray stone walls with battlements, its towers with banners flying atop, and the gatehouse with arrow slits for the archers.

They stopped at the gate and waited while two men on horseback entered. The horsemen wore chain mail under leather jerkins, dark britches, boots, and each had a longbow across his back with a quiver and arrows. Both nodded respectfully and smiled at Gabrielle when they passed. She whispered to Obie that these were two of the queen's best archers. Then thirty horsemen exited the keep wearing metal breastplates and swords at their sides.

"Who are they?" Obie whispered.

"New recruits. It looks like they're going to the North Field for battle practice. Would you like a quick look?"

"Now?" A smile spread over Obie's face.

"Yes, now."

At a brisk trot they followed the soldiers around the outer wall to the North Field. Obie and Gabrielle stopped at the edge of a gentle slope and watched the recruits continue down a few yards to a huge grassy field where battle sounds shocked the quiet morning air. In one area swordsmen clashed blades, in another, sword wielding warriors astride galloping war horses struck down wooden enemies, and elsewhere archers with longbows shot into haystack targets.

"Our men are well-trained," Gabrielle said. "They fight fiercely and, when they must, die bravely in battle. Our people revere their courage. See the bowman over there approaching the wooden target on his horse?" She pointed towards the north side of the field where a man was riding with his bow drawn. "His name is Gaylen. He is one of many who can hit center target at fifty feet while riding his horse at full gallop. They make the feat look easy, but it isn't. Notice their bows. They're made from the yew tree for greatest strength. Those trees don't grow here, so we buy the wood from the friendly goblin caravans, though, oddly, we have not seen them this year." Turning in her saddle, she pointed to the far western side of the training field where men practiced kneeling in close ranks with shields raised above them to form a single huge barrier. The men on the outer edges held their shields in front of them, extending the barrier to the ground. "Do you see the men over there, huddling beneath their shields?   It's called *the tortoise formation.*"   In this exercise, they're awaiting an imaginary rain of enemy arrows.   They're trained to think of them as harmless toys."

"Some toys."   Obie wished Scottie was there to see the battle training. His brother would be impressed. He could almost imagine him down on the field training with the men, like he'd seen him so many times on the football field. Only this game was for real, and it was deadly. "Are all the men in the kingdom trained here?"

"No, only the men of Gruffhaven train at Windermere Castle. Gruffhaven comprises the eastern sector of the kingdom and includes the Valley of Windermere and lands to the south. There's also the northwestern sector of Wesley, and the south-western sector of Barrington.   Lord Cadwallen of Wesley and Lord Gerallt of Barrington train their own men."

Obie noticed an anxious look come over Gabrielle's face when she finished speaking. "Time to go?" he asked, a hint of disappointment in his voice.

"Grandfather will be waiting for us."

They rode through the gate into the noisy courtyard where craftsmen and merchant vendors, castle workers and attendants, soldiers and others were going about their daily activities. When Obie and Gabrielle dismounted, Mara and Shadow turned and started trotting back through the gate.

We're going to the West Meadow to graze on the sweet grass growing there, Shadow said.

Enjoy your lunch, Obie responded.

Gabrielle waved at a man across the way and called out to him to wait while she and Obie hurried over. The man had just mounted a silver windlord and was about to depart.

"Greetings, Ivor."

"Greetings, Lady Brynnen." His voice was deep and his smile broad. The windlord turned around to get a better look at Gabrielle's companion. After Gabrielle introduced Obie as a friend of the family, he learned that this man was the royal bow master, and the windlord was called *Rune.* Ivor, a large muscular man with long, fair hair looked every inch a seasoned warrior. He was steady of eye, strong of face, and had a confident bearing. Like the two riders at the gate, he wore chain mail under his leather jerkin, dark britches and boots, with a longbow across his back and knife at his belt.

While Gabrielle and Ivor exchanged a few words, Obie turned his attention to the windlord. *I'm pleased to meet you, Rune.*

The pleasure is mine, Oberon. I am happy to meet a human whose thoughts so clearly reveal his appreciation for my kind.

Obie admired Rune's high spirit as the windlord danced around in a state of excitement, visibly anxious to be gone.

"Rune and I must be off now, my lady," Ivor said. "There's been a troll sighting a flight hour to the north."

After Ivor and Rune departed Gabrielle identified a few of the buildings within sight. These included the armory and stables, the Chapel of the Earth Mother, whose blessings assured good crops, Gabrielle explained, and the Chapel of Phoebe, the Moon Maiden, who blessed warriors and the hunt; there was also the Great Hall, an important meeting and dining place. It was attached to the Queen's Building where the queen resided.

"When we have more time I'll take you on a tour of the keep," Gabrielle said. They hurried towards the Queen's Building which stood directly across the courtyard from the gate. Obie wondered if they were rushing because Andras wanted to show him around. He was about to ask when a messenger stopped them. They were to come immediately to the throne room as Queen Olwen desired an audience with Obie.

"Now?" He was startled by the idea of meeting the queen. When he saw the smile in Gabrielle's eyes, he realized his nervousness showed.

"Don't worry, Obie, Queen Olwen probably isn't biting people today. We'll sit with Grandfather, and when she calls you, just stand up and bow and address her as *Your Majesty.*"

Obie drew a deep breath. "Okay," he said, trying to appear calm. "Let's go."

They walked briskly through the long hallway towards the Throne Room, and Gabrielle pointed out the library and the entrance to the Queen's Garden. She told him the queen resided on the third floor, and that there was a large kitchen, bathing rooms, and guest rooms in this building. He figured she was trying to put him at ease before his audience with the queen.

The great doors of the Throne Room were shut when they arrived, but the guards quickly opened them for the two latecomers. When they swung open Obie saw a couple of hundred well-dressed people sitting in partially upholstered wooden chairs three rows deep along the two side walls. The high walls that reached to the great beam ceiling were of dark oak with raised panels. Light entered through tall, narrow windows where red velvet drapes were pulled to the sides and fastened with sashes. At the far end of the room the silver-haired queen sat atop a three-tiered dais on a red velvet throne with arms and legs of intricately carved oak. On the wall behind her hung a golden tapestry with a large red and white shield in the center that bore the heraldic designs of the Royal House of Gruffydd. The red and white sections were separated by a diagonal golden stripe. In the upper red section was the sigil of a golden lion wearing a crown, while the sigil in the lower white section was a golden sword.

Obie heard their names announced as he limped forward beside Gabrielle. Andras was sitting on the right side of the room in a front row chair near the queen. He motioned them to two empty chairs beside his. Obie pulled his ball cap off when he sat down and laid it on his lap. Then he noticed the two small white dogs curled up at the queen's feet. Their little gold and white jackets matched Queen Olwen's gold and white gown. He smiled to himself. *Look-alikes.* Queen Olwen turned her head towards him, her golden crown catching the light. Obie saw her stern eyes survey him, and his heart beat faster. Then the hint of a smile formed at the corners of her mouth, and her eyes seemed to soften.

"Welcome to the Court of the House of Gruffydd, young man."

Obie stood up so quickly he forgot his cap and it tumbled from his lap onto the floor. Fumbling to catch it, he missed and stumbled, but recovered his balance. The queen's ladies in waiting tittered at his awkwardness. Queen Olwen smiled at them and lifted her hand in a small silencing gesture. Obie leaned over and grabbed his cap, then stood up straight and tucked it into his jacket pocket.

"Thank you, Your Majesty."

"Come, let us have a better look at you." She motioned him to draw near.

He limped forward to the bottom of the dais and bowed. When he stood up tall before her he felt like he was in a spotlight, for a ray of light was shining on him from one of the tall windows. The queen stared silently at him and he thought he saw her flinch slightly.

"Tell us your name."

"Oberon Griffin, Your Majesty."

"Oberon of Griffin is it. A good name. And where might you have gotten it?"

It's been in my family for a long time, Your Majesty." Immediately, he regretted his inane answer.

Again, the ladies in waiting giggled, but this time the queen seemed not to hear them.

"What we mean, Oberon, is what land does your family hail from?"

"Garrett, Wyoming, Your Majesty. But my family is originally from the British Isles."

"British Isles?"

Unsure of his situation, his good sense told him not to reveal his belief, in front of so many people at least, that he came from the future. "Yes, Your Majesty. I think it might be the same place as the Isles of Albion, where I was told your people came from. In my land our name for Albion is *the British Isles*."

Queen Olwen raised her brow in a look of wonder as she listened. "That is a curious thing," she said, "for there are kingdoms of Brettas still living in our homeland, just as we are Brettas. But, we have never heard Albion called the British Isles." Her gaze lingered on him a few moments longer and then she changed the subject. "Your attire is rather odd, Oberon." He noticed her eyes lingering momentarily on his Raptor. Beckoning with her fingers she said, "Come and sit by us on the step here, next to Rae and Asta."

Ascending the dais, he seated himself on the top stair next to the dogs. When they abruptly raised their heads to look at him, he couldn't help but smile. This wasn't what he had expected. It was far less formal. The queen's invitation to sit next to her and the presence of the dogs helped put him at ease.

Queen Olwen leaned forward and began speaking in a confidential tone, out of hearing of the others. "I would like you to tell me how you came here. Andras already informed me, but I wish to hear it in your own words."

Obie told the queen about being picked up by the Spirit Comet back home in Ghostrise Valley, and that he had ridden on its tail to Windermere. As she listened, her face took on a strained appearance. "I see," she said quietly when he finished talking. "This is very unusual, and yet, as Andras has suggested, the Spirits of Haldor and Allegra must have some purpose in bringing you to us. Have you told anyone other than Andras' family about your ride on the comet?"

"No, Your Majesty."

"Good. It would be best for now if we simply tell others you're visiting from a distant land. My people have more than enough to consume their thoughts at present."

"Yes, Your Majesty, I can appreciate that," he said sincerely. He knew she was referring to the Celestial Dimming. Although he had been in Windermere only a day, he was experiencing the sense of helplessness in the face of impending disaster that he supposed the people must feel pretty intensely by now.

"Well, you don't look like much, Oberon," she continued, "but I suppose we'll just have to wait and see what you're about. In the meantime, we shall be pleased to have you as our royal guest in Windermere."

"Thank you, Your Majesty."

"Andras informed us you have a weapon that Gabrielle thinks is impressive."

"Yes, here it is, Your Majesty, my Raptor slingshot." He detached it from his pouch and handed it to her.

"Hmmm, we have never seen anything quite like this." She turned it over, examining it. "Will you demonstrate it for us?"

Obie smiled up at the queen as he stroked Asta's head. "Anytime you'd like, Your Majesty."

"I would like to see it now." She handed the Raptor back to him and stood to make the announcement. "Our young guest is going to demonstrate a new weapon. All who wish to watch may accompany us to the East Meadow."

Queen Olwen descended the dais with Obie and gestured for Gabrielle and Andras to join them. Sword Master Ull and three of his swordsmen who were posted nearby moved in quickly behind and alongside them, while all others in the room followed. Meanwhile, the queen's two little white dogs, resembling white fluff balls with beady black eyes more than canines, ran excitedly towards the great doors which were now open. Queen Olwen's energy level had apparently not declined with her age, for she walked swiftly and most had to hasten to keep up. The procession moved out of the building and through the front gate, then turned left towards the East Meadow.

CHAPTER SIX

PROPHECY

RAE AND ASTA BOUNDED far out on the turf, chasing one another and leaping lightheartedly at butterflies and moths. The target covered hay bales used for archery training were already in place. Obie planned to demonstrate his Raptor up to a hundred and fifty feet, a reasonable range for slingshots. He took his position on the rocky soil bordering the turf, kicking at the hard dry shale with one foot and digging in with the other. The crowd spread out behind and on each side of him to watch. Had he been a novice he might have been nervous, but he was used to shooting in front of crowds at the regional tournaments. Then again, those crowds consisted of soccer moms in tennis shoes and suburban dads in double knit pullovers. Obie peered over his shoulder and spotted leather jerkins, lambskin vests, intricately patterned broadcloths draped over chain mail, silk and satin dresses, and velvet tabbards. He grinned as he slipped his Raptor over his arm and took some steel shot from his ammo pouch. Stragglers kept arriving. Apparently word of the young stranger with a new weapon had spread. The growing crowd quietly watched while he loaded his slingshot. The familiar burn in his muscles felt good as he pulled back on the band and eyed the target. The steel pellet streaked forward and Obie knew his aim was true.

The score keeper ran to the fifty foot target, inspected it, then turned to the crowd, and yelled, "Bull's eye."

Mild applause came from the gathering. Again Obie loaded and drew back on the band, this time for a shot at the hundred foot target. But just when he released, a sharp pain jolted his right arm and threw his aim off. His arms still ached where the troll had grabbed him the day before. He quietly berated himself, but refrained from throwing his Raptor to the ground in frustration. That wouldn't do here.

Again, the score keeper ran over and peered at the target, hesitated a few moments, then turned to the crowd and announced, "Missed."

The silence of the crowd hurt more than the isolated jeers that rang in Obie's ears. He needed to make a good showing. On the next shot he'd grit his teeth and be prepared for the pain. If he could win the queen's approval, maybe she would help him to go home. But for the moment that wasn't what he cared about. A fierce determination took hold. He would not miss again. He reloaded and felt the pain again when he drew back on the band, though it was not so intense this time. Every eye watched when he shot.

"Bull's eye," the score keeper yelled.

A more impressive shot at this greater distance, the applause was a little louder this time and a quiet murmur of approval passed through the crowd. Even so, Obie could tell he wasn't exactly bowling anyone over with his demonstration, including the queen. How exciting could a slingshot be compared to swords and longbows? His weapon had to seem pretty lightweight to these people.

He loaded again, took a deep breath, and fixed his aim on the hundred and fifty-foot target. Just after he shot, a large gray wolf streaked from the forest and darted towards Rae and Asta, romping far from the spectators.

The dogs spotted the wolf and took off racing across the wide meadow towards Queen Olwen as fast as their short legs could move. Cries of alarm went through the crowd. Obie started out across the field towards the fleeing pets and was joined by two of the queen's bowmen. Seconds later the wolf reached the slower dog, snapped up the white fluff-ball in its teeth, then turned sharply and raced back towards the forest with its prize. Obie shot at the retreating beast, but missed. In the heat of the moment it didn't occur to him that he was pacing a healthy gray wolf. He reloaded when the bowmen shot. Even as their arrows left the bowstrings Obie knew both shots were off the mark. One arrow zipped over the wolf's head and the other passed to its right. Picking up speed, Obie left the heavier bodied bowmen behind and shot a second time. This time the steel pellet found its mark. The wolf staggered sideways, but regained its footing and kept running with the dog still clenched in its teeth. The shadowy refuge of the forest was only seconds away now and Obie knew this might be his last shot. He drew back hard, released, and hit the beast in the head. Stunned, the wolf hit the ground and relaxed its jaws. Suddenly freed, the little dog looked like a white streak shooting across the field towards Queen Olwen. The crowd cheered wildly when the queen leaned down and Rae leapt into her protective arms. The dog's thick fur was damp and matted from the wolf's mouth and she shook violently. But she suffered no apparent wounds. At the queen's feet Asta yelped and leaped up and down. Out on the field the two bowmen tethered the wolf's legs and muzzle to carry the dazed animal into the keep for display. Obie limped briskly towards the crowd to check on Rae, cuddled in the queen's arms.

"Oberon, I'm very grateful to you for saving Rae," she said.

He could see she held back tears. "I'm glad she's all right, Your Majesty. She just seems a little shaken." He gently stroked Rae's trembling head, then reached down and lifted Asta into his arms.

The queen smiled approvingly. "You seem to have a natural affection for animals."

"Yes, Ma'am." Asta leaned into Obie's fingers as he scratched behind her ears.

"I think this calls for a celebration." The queen turned to the crowd and announced: "This night we shall have a banquet in the Great Hall, and young Oberon will be our honored guest. You are all invited. The invitation will be formally posted within the hour."

The people cheered and began talking excitedly among themselves.

"It is our wish that you sit beside me at my table, Oberon."

"Thank you, Your Majesty, I'm honored." Even though he had not performed at the targets as well as he might have, he was happy that Rae had been spared.

One of the attendants whispered a message to Queen Olwen. Giving Obie a quick smile, she turned to the crowd. "I have just been advised that the third and final target was a bull's eye. Well done, Oberon." Cheers and applause went up at this news, and many people gave him approving smiles.

"And now, there's much to be done before nightfall." The queen motioned a couple of attendants over and gave instructions for the kitchen master regarding food and drink for the evening's festivities. The attendants set out on a dead run.

Obie put Asta on the ground and when he stood up Gabrielle was at his side. It took him by surprise when she reached out and hugged him and kissed his cheek. Her hair smelled like wild flowers and her eyes were luminous when she pulled back and gazed into his face.

"Thank you for saving Rae, Obie. It means a lot to me that Queen Olwen was spared the grief of losing one of her pets today. You were quite remarkable out there."

"Thanks, Gabrielle, but someone else could have done just as well."

Andras cut in. "Oh no, Oberon. I agree with Gabrielle. You performed quite amazingly. When you feared for the lives of the dogs you stopped limping—did you realize that?"

Obie was startled. "No, I didn't." He'd been too busy to reflect on what had happened. His full attention had been on saving Rae, but now he remembered—he *did* run without limping. While he was running he had taken mental note of that fact in some recess of his mind. The limp only returned when the wolf was no longer a threat. Will's words came rushing back to him: *You will walk straight when you choose to.* What was this? What was going on?

"You look surprised," Gabrielle said. "Yet you ran without limping yesterday, too, when the trolls tried to take Mara away. Don't you remember?"

Obie stared blankly at her for a moment before answering. "This may sound strange, but there was so much going on that I didn't think about it. The only thing on my mind was saving Mara."

He was glad when Andras pulled him away from the crowd. "Where are we going?" he asked.

"To the library. I have something important to show you."

Andras smiled and placed his hand on Obie's shoulder as they walked quietly through the hallway of the Queen's Building towards the library. "Well Oberon, you certainly distinguished yourself today."

"I'm glad I was able to help. But the queen's bowmen would have stopped the wolf if I hadn't. I probably got in their way."

A low-pitched laugh rumbled from deep within Andras' chest. "Those bowmen couldn't keep up with the wolf, Oberon. If it weren't for you the queen would now be minus one little dog. I was amazed at your speed. It seemed like you'd been running all your life. I don't know what it is, lad, but considering the way you overcame your limp out there, I'd say something significant is going on inside you."

Frowning, Obie stuffed his trembling hands into his jacket pockets. "I wish I knew," he said softly.

Their footsteps fell across the cold stone floor of the library. The air was heavy with the musty odor of old books that lined the walls. Through a tall stained glass window feeble rays of early afternoon sunlight cast pale spots of vermillion and yellow light over the dark oak tables where lay a few parchments and books. From narrow alcoves between the bookcases, grim-faced statues of past kings peered down on all who approached.

Andras motioned for Obie to sit beside him at a table before a very old looking black book. He opened it to a page held by a red ribbon marker.

"This page contains the prophecy Gabrielle mentioned last night," Andras said. "*The Prophecy of Zephyrus* it's called. It was translated into the common language generations ago from a stone tablet inscribed in ancient eagle runes by the eagle wizard, King Zephyrus. The first stanza tells us the guardianship of the Star Crystals was originally entrusted to the eagle kings. Haldor, who, with Allegra, brought you here, was the last eagle guardian. After him the guardianship went to the windlords. Later, it passed to the windlords and Windermerians jointly, and recently to Gabrielle and Mara. Read the entire poem and tell me what you think about it."

THE PROPHECY OF ZEPHYRUS

Star Crystal dark, Star Crystal light,
Bright jewels that crossed the void of night,
Streaked flaming o'er Earth's storm-worn seas,
White fire sent from yon Pleiades,
Brought unto dark, chaotic Earth
New Order, Action, Art, and Mirth.
Heavenly hand this gift did bring,
Entrusted to the Eagle Kings.

The Light Crystal the eagles kept
In mountains lonely and windswept;
The Dark Crystal by eagle's plume
They carried to Earth's infant Moon;
Forever parted must they stay,
Bright beacons that shall light the way,
Providing Man and Beast the key
To thrive in cosmic harmony.

But when black chaos doth arise
And from The Pit the Serpent flies,
Then forth six sorcerers shall come,
To hide the Moon and steal the Sun.
In darkest hour when hopes subside,
The Moonpath must the Guardians ride.
From Phoebe's hand for hearts aggrieved,
The Dark Crystal must be retrieved.

Then from afar 'neath orbs grown pale,
Seek him borne on the comet's tail,
For he with steadfast heart must dare,
Defend the task the Guardians bear.
When skies are dark and two is three,
And fiery breath burns frozen trees,
The battle for the Earth doth come,
With trampling boots and beat of drums.
Beware ye when the Serpent comes,
Beware ye, for the Serpent comes.

Obie read the poem and then reread the last stanza. Frowning, he leaned back in his chair and stared at the page. "The ending sounds bleak."

"To say the least," Andras said solemnly. He waited for Obie to continue.

"I guess you think I'm the person in the poem because the comet brought me to Windermere." He looked at Andras. "And the words, *neath orbs grown pale* sound like the Celestial Dimming."

"Yes, to both of your statements."

"What about *the six sorcerers who hide the Moon and steal the Sun*?"

Andras' expression now turned grave. "The eagles have brought word from around the world that black sorcerers have gained control of four kingdoms, and a fifth kingdom may soon fall to another. If so, King Torolf would be the sixth black sorcerer king."

"And these six sorcerer kings are causing the Celestial Dimming?"

"According to the prophecy, yes."

Obie nodded. "It all seems to fit . . . but . . . I don't understand what part I could play in all of this. I don't have any military training. I'm just a seventeen-year-old with a slingshot, and I can't even walk right. Andras, do you think Haldor and Allegra brought the wrong person? Maybe my brother, Scottie, was supposed to come here. I'm nobody special. My brother's the *special* one. Could it have been *him* they meant to bring?"

A fatherly expression came into the older man's eyes. "No, Oberon, I don't think so. I have long thought that Haldor and Allegra are time travelers. If this is true, they see and know things that we cannot. They wouldn't be likely to make a mistake. And as to your participation, who of us can know what parts we'll play in the unfolding events of this life?"

Obie stood up and almost knocked his chair over. "It's hot in here—I need some air." He pulled his jacket off.

"Let's go outside. Fresh air is what you need."

In the courtyard he lifted his face to the cool breeze and breathed deeply. "Everything's jumbled in my mind right now. I need some time to clear my head and sort things out."

"Fair enough. And while you're doing that, Oberon, I hope you'll also consider staying with us in Windermere for a while."

Stay in Windermere? The thought jolted him. Would Andras try to prevent him from going back? Maybe the longer he remained here, the less likely his chances were of returning home.

Andras must have seen his discomfort, for he quickly added, "Of course if you wish to leave us I'll not try and stop you. I'll send you home if I can—if Haldor and Allegra are willing to take you when they return at the next full-moon. But you don't have to make a decision now."

Andras' words were reassuring. Obie didn't want to be pressured into making any decisions at the moment. "Thanks, Andras."

"Well now, it's hours yet before the banquet. How would you like to practice flying on a windlord? Riding the sky and getting away from everything for a while will do you good. It's a great way to clear your mind—I've done it many times. You haven't had a chance to ride by yourself yet, have you?"

"No. I'd like that."

"Good. You can ride my windlord, Magnus. He's out on the West Meadow right now. You'll see him, the big golden stallion. Oh, and Gabrielle often goes to the Queen's Garden to read. If she's there she may wish to go flying with you. Would you like some company?"

It was a cheering thought. "Yes, I'd enjoy riding with Gabrielle. I'll look for her."

"And don't worry about anything. Magnus will take good care of you. Come back by sundown and you'll find me in the library. Then we'll bathe and dress for the banquet."

Obie entered the Queen's Garden and hurried along the smooth stone walk-way looking for Gabrielle. Winding through the trees and open areas of lush green grass and flowers, he passed over two footbridges that spanned a meandering brook and continued around a pond of water lilies partially shaded by weeping willow trees. Here the walkway began snaking slowly back to the entrance. The gardeners must have worked extra hard this year to keep the grass green and the flowers blooming, Obie thought, for unlike the lands beyond the castle walls, this garden showed little sign of the Celestial Dimming.

Obie sat on a garden bench to rest his bad leg. Today it wasn't bothering him much, not even after all the running. Yeah—the running. He reflected on the new oddity of his limp. Why had it disappeared at crucial moments over the last couple of days? It had begun in Ghostrise Valley when he had raced to Josh's aid at the pit. His gait had smoothed out some. But the change had not been as pronounced on that day as it was after he arrived in Windermere.

A small movement off to the right drew his attention. A startled squirrel with a tail that appeared electrically charged stared at him from its frozen stance on a tree trunk a few feet away. Obie smiled and got to his feet, peering up the cobblestone walk. Gabrielle was nowhere to be seen. He'd like to take a flying lesson from a Moonpath Rider. Not many people ever got to do that. His smile faded as two lines from the last stanza of the prophecy came back to him:

> For he with steadfast heart must dare,
> Defend the task the Guardians bear.

How was he supposed to defend the Moonpath Riders against anything when he couldn't even protect his own family? He was no hero—he'd proven that. Disgusted with himself, he picked up a small rock and threw it down the walkway as hard as he could. He stared glumly after it. With the next full moon, he'd just go home. Then the real person in the prophecy would come along to defend the Guardians. The mistake would be rectified. In the meantime, he'd just take each day as it came. The banquet tonight would be a good distraction. Andras and the queen were treating him well, obviously because they thought he was the one in the prophecy. Sure, he had saved Rae from the wolf. He could understand the queen's gratitude for that. But honoring him with a banquet seemed extreme. And could he trust that Andras really wouldn't try and keep him in Windermere against his will? He seemed honest. But, even so, did Andras have any influence on whether Haldor and Allegra would take him home at the next full moon? His head began to swim with too many unanswered questions. This was no good—worrying was no good. About all he could do was keep his eyes and ears open until the Spirit Comet returned. But that was almost a month off. In the mean-time, Windermere did have an allure. He'd try and make the most of his time here. And right now, it was time to go flying.

Leaving the garden, he exited the Queen's Building and passed through the great gate, returning a nod to the gatekeeper as he passed by. Outside the keep he turned right towards the West Meadow and walked along the gray stone wall. Upon rounding the southwest tower, he saw Shadow and Mara grazing on the meadow among a group of windlords. When he drew near, a tall, golden windlord stallion about nineteen hands high, as tall as a Clydesdale, trotted forward. Obie was struck by his noble bearing and intelligent gray eyes.

Greetings, Oberon, I'm Magnus. Andras said you might wish to fly with me.

Hello, Magnus. Yes, I would— if it's okay with you.

My pleasure. Climb aboard. After Obie mounted Magnus added, *Since I don't wear a bridle, you can hold onto my mane if you like, just try not to yank it.*

Thanks, Magnus, I'll do my best not to. Obie grasped a piece of the windlord's gleaming golden mane in his left hand. It was long and full like his tail and felt like spun silk.

A fluttering sound and the light movement of air caused Obie to glance upward. It was a bay windlord mare passing overhead as she glided to a landing. When Magnus unfolded his wings and stepped forward, Obie felt a powerhouse of controlled muscle and energy moving beneath him. It felt like riding atop a gently moving locomotive. Then they were airborne. The cool air rushed past his face and he heard the rhythmic sound of wind-lord wings rising and falling on the wind. Below, Shadow raised his head and said, *Hold on.*

Obie smiled down at him. *Right now that's my highest priority. See you in a while.*

They circled high over Windermere Castle and then flew southwest towards Mount Iluva.

You take naturally to flying, Magnus said. *You lean into my turns and anticipate my movements so we don't work against one another. But may I suggest you relax your legs a little? You're digging your boots into my sides.*

Sorry, Magnus. Obie loosened his leg pressure.

Don't worry, I won't let you fall. Even if you did, I could catch you before you hit the ground.

That's reassuring, Obie said, *but, uhhh, I think I'll just try not to fall.* Even if he did take to flying, it had seemed easier when riding behind Gabrielle. Riding alone seemed a little more challenging.

You might have cause to worry if you were riding one of the fledglings, but you're safe enough with me. When you want me to turn, just press your heel lightly into my side and I'll turn in that direction until you release the pressure.

Okay, like this? Obie pressed his right heel lightly into Magnus' side.

Yes, that's fine. Magnus turned to the right and continued turning until he had made a complete circle and then began another.

Finally noticing, Obie released his heel pressure. *Sorry about that.*

Instantly, Magnus stopped circling. *I felt confident you'd remember before I made too many circles.*

The windlord flew over the mountain and along its western slopes, and Obie started feeling more at ease. They had left behind the wheat fields and pastures. Below lay a wild, broken land of crags and crevices where granite spires towered over rushing mountain watercourses and aqua pools half hidden in shadowy canyons.

After a while they found a grassy area next to a stream and landed. Magnus was already drinking when Obie slid from his back and knelt to drink beside him.

Smart choice, Magnus said. *The water in Andras' water bag tastes musty. It's old and should have been replaced years ago, but he refuses to get a new one. He says he likes the old bag just fine.*

Obie grinned. *Thanks for the warning.* When they finished drinking, Magnus nibbled a patch of clover and Obie sat down and leaned against a willow tree growing next to the stream. *Magnus, why did some of the windlords give up their freedom to come live with the Windermerians? Do you mind my asking?*

Magnus raised his head, as though considering the question. *No, Oberon, I'm glad you're interested enough to ask. The union came about a long time ago, before the reign of the present windlord ruler, King Ymir. My race befriended the Windermerians shortly after they arrived in the valley. After a while, our king at that time, King Vidar, allowed a few windlords to pair with them as a gesture of the friendship between us. Our race had also made pairings with the High Elves when they migrated to our land long ago. I was born in Windermere, and Andras and I bonded when we were young. We regard each other as brothers, though we've long disputed who is the better looking.*

Obie grinned. *I'd vote for you, Magnus.*

Thank you, Oberon— just don't tell Andras.

Obie smiled inwardly and leaned forward with his arms wrapped around his knees. *Do you ever wish you could live with the windlords who follow King Ymir?*

Most of us admire the nomadic life of our kin, but our home has always been in Windermere. We love being part of the busy lifestyle humans seem to thrive on, and those of us who have paired for life cherish the close relationships the pairings bring. That's why we would choose no other life. But from time to time I visit my kin, and I've felt the joy of flying among them.

You're an admirable race.

Thank you for saying so, Oberon.

Obie didn't have the heart to tell this noble creature there were no windlords in the world he came from.

When they again took flight, Magnus showed Obie a secret forest glen on Mount Iluva where a stream flowed down granite rocks into a cool, blue-black pool, and the water was the sweetest and purest Obie had ever tasted. The trees, moss, ferns and vines surrounding the pool ranged from shades of lime greens and emeralds to dark greens, deep purples and rich umbers. In days when the sun had been bright, Magnus said, these woodland colors had been even more vivid. Obie was sorry to leave this beautiful place, but there was more to see. They spent an hour flying over the forested hills and dales to the west of Mount Iluva. The woods had been cleared here and there for farms and houses with thatched roofs where smoke curled up from the chimneys and men were plowing fields.

When the gray daylight began to fade, Obie looked at the pale greenish sun sinking ominously towards the western horizon.

Soon it would disappear and the starless sky would be black and empty except for the pale, sickly moon. A shiver passed through him. It was time to return to the keep. Magnus must have caught Obie's open thoughts, for he turned and flew towards Windermere Castle.

***

After sending Obie to his rendezvous with Magnus, Andras went to his small office behind the library to work, but was interrupted when an attendant brought a summons from the queen. When the messenger left, Andras stood before the tall mirror hanging on the wall beside his desk and adjusted his jacket, then checked his teeth. Using the hand-mirror and comb he took from a desk drawer, he combed his hair over the small bald spot on the back of his head, his routine practice before paying a visit to the queen.

Hurrying to his meeting, he saw the hunched over form of the old wizard Marduk ahead. He was slowly making his way along the corridor, his walking stick clicking rhythmically on the stone floor with each step. Just before Andras overtook him, the old man turned into a short hallway leading to the kitchen. The clanking of pans and the kitchen master's loud voice barking orders to helpers signified much activity was afoot in preparation for the banquet. At the end of the corridor Andras ascended the stairway to Queen Olwen's private sitting room on the third floor. One of the kitchen master's assistants was just leaving with what appeared to be a list, while several other servants waited outside to see her. The guard at the door immediately admitted Andras. The queen was seated at a small table writing a note. As he entered she glanced up and then laid down her pen. "Greetings, Andras," she said pleasantly. "Please sit down."

"Your Majesty." He bowed deeply and seated himself in the chair opposite her.

She smiled sheepishly at him. "It's been a long while since the servants have had to put a feast together on such short notice."

Andras laughed softly. "I think they're up to it, Madame. I just saw old Marduk going into the kitchen. He should be able to lend some help."

"Yes, hopefully. He remembers so little now of the old magic. But I still like to call on him to do small tasks, and he helps my gardeners keep things blooming. It makes him feel useful."

"I imagine he can conjure up a few roast pigs, at the least. And I think the kitchen master and his help love the excitement. It must feel like the old days to them."

"No doubt." She smiled as though basking briefly in memories of past feasts and happier times. Then her smile faded. She got up and went to the window and gazed beyond the East Meadow towards Gnarlwood Forest. "Has Oberon seen the prophecy yet?"

"Yes, a little while ago."

She turned to face Andras. "How did he respond?"

"Naturally, he's a bit confused. He doesn't want to believe he's the one in the prophecy. I think he just needs time to think about it. The lad doesn't know his own potential."

"That isn't surprising in one so young." A look of concern came over the queen's face. "Is he willing to stay in Windermere with us?"

"I'm not sure. He misses his home. At this point, I think we can only hope. On the other hand, whether he leaves or stays may have already been decided."

The queen raised an eyebrow. "How so?"

"Because, Your Majesty, if Haldor and Allegra brought him here for a purpose, it's unlikely they'll return him to his world until that purpose is realized."

A look of hope came over Queen Olwen's face. "Does he know this?"

"I only told him that if he wished it, I would try and send him home when the moon is full again. But Haldor and Allegra would have to be willing to take him."

"Good. I'm glad he knows the issue may be beyond our control." Queen Olwen sat down at her table again and her face softened almost to a smile. "Oberon performed extremely well on the East Meadow today. For a while I wasn't sure these old eyes were seeing what they saw. Did you notice he wasn't limping when he ran after the wolf?"

"Yes . . . an odd thing, but maybe a good sign. Who knows what he carries with him from his world." Andras fell silent for a moment, then continued, "I believe he has a good mind and heart and, as we saw, the makings of a warrior. But there's something else about him . . ."

Queen Olwen smiled sweetly. "You noticed too?"

"Yes."

"Well, old friend, we'll just have to wait this one out—though the time grows short."

A worried look came on Andras' face. "Short, indeed."

CHAPTER SEVEN

GIFTS

ANDRAS RAISED HIS HEAD and smiled when Obie entered the library. "How was your ride?" He closed the book he had been perusing.

"Great. Magnus is really something."

Andras' eyes flashed. "I know, but don't tell him I said so. Did Gabrielle go with you?"

"No, I tried to find her in the garden, but she wasn't there."

Andras knitted his brow. "Hmmm, that's too bad. Be sure and ask her to ride with you sometime soon. She's an excellent teacher. I'm sure the two of you will have an enjoyable time. You can ride Magnus again."

"Thanks, Andras. I'll be sure and ask her."

Andras stood up. "We had better bathe and dress for the banquet. The honored guest cannot arrive late."

The air grew humid as Obie followed Andras down a stairway and into a room with a large, marble pool. Andras explained how the water was heated in vats in a room below and that the warm water rose naturally through pipes into the pools.

Several of the male bathers on the other side of the pool called friendly greetings to Andras and he returned them as he disrobed and stepped into the water. The pool was shallow at this end and he sat down. This being a new experience for Obie, he hesitated. He was used to stripping for gym class, but at least he knew the guys there. Glancing up at Obie, Andras said laughingly, "Don't be shy, lad, it's our custom to bathe together like this. Come in, you'll find it relaxing. The ladies have their bathing rooms too."

Reassured, Obie tossed his robe onto a nearby bench. "How's the water?" he asked just before stepping in.

"You'll find it quite wet," Andras said with a chuckle as he reclined his head against the side of the pool and closed his eyes. "I think we still have a little time to soak."

Obie entered the water and found it pleasantly warm. He sat down against the side of the pool, but his mind was too active to do much relaxing. He began cupping water over his chest. "Andras?"

"Hmmm?"

"On the ride to the castle, Gabrielle mentioned Queen Olwen's three sons."

Andras opened his eyes and looked at Obie. "What did she say about them?"

"Only that one was murdered, and two are gone. She didn't seem to want to talk about it."

"I'm not surprised. Gabrielle is troubled by what befell them. The entire kingdom was hurt by it. I didn't want to go into it last night, but I'll tell you now." Lowering his voice, he spoke in a confidential tone. "King Torolf, the dreaded black sorcerer I've spoken of, is the second-born son of the queen."

Abruptly, Obie stopped sloshing water on himself. "Why did he become a black sorcerer?"

"He probably wouldn't have if he could have become King of Windermere. That's what he really wanted, but his older brother was next in line to the throne. There had always been something unwholesome about Torolf, a malevolent streak that surfaced occasionally. Even in childhood, he enjoyed some perverse diversions, one of which was killing the castle cats. He got into trouble over it more than once, especially when he got caught throttling the master cook's best mouser. We should have seen it coming. Now, it appears he's in league with the Dark Presence."

"The Dark Presence?" Obie sat up straight and turned to face Andrus.

"Yes. No one knows for sure what it is or where it came from. We only know that it's evil and it's been in the world for as long as anyone can remember."

"I think I know what you're talking about, they call it *Satan*, or *the devil* where I come from."

"Yes, different peoples call it by different names." Andras submerged his head, then reemerged with a splash and shook the water from his face. "Regarding the three princes," he continued, "Queen Olwen's first-born son was Prince Urien, and her third and youngest son is Prince Ulrik. After their father was killed fighting goblins some years back, Prince Urien was crowned King of Windermere. Torolf couldn't hide his jealousy. His contempt for his older brother was apparent for all to see. It was unfortunate that King Urien chose to ignore it. Within a month of the coronation, Torolf left the kingdom on Arend, his black windlord. They crossed over the Great Eastern Sea where Torolf, we later learned, took up with a black sorcerer who began teaching him the dark arts. Torolf's desire to be king must have eaten at him during that time, while his jealousy of his older brother festered.

"To make matters worse, Prince Ulrik left the kingdom soon after that. Being young and curious about the world, he wanted to visit lands far beyond our borders. He hasn't returned or been heard of since. The queen sent scouts out in all four directions searching for him, but he was never found. It's been especially hard on Gabrielle."

"Gabrielle? Why?"

"Because she's been betrothed to him since childhood." He turned to Obie. "Of course he was older than her, and it would be

years before she was of marriageable age. But they used to love
playing together when I brought her with me to the keep. I'd
often see them dancing around and laughing, and he'd make
garlands of flowers for her hair. She was such a happy child—
had a fairylike quality about her."

"She still does." Obie was surprised at his own words.

Andras smiled appreciatively. "You're right, she hasn't lost
it, and, I daresay, young Prince Ulrik was captivated by her. Anyway, shortly after Ulrik set out to see the world, Prince Torolf
returned and murdered King Urien with the aid of a deadly
potion he'd brought back with him. Afterwards, he proclaimed
himself King. He tried to cover up the murder, but with the
wizard Marduk's help it was only a matter of days before the
Council of Elders found him out and informed the people.
Torolf's black sorcery was not so strong then, and when the
people rose up against him he fled on Arend.

"We received news he returned to his old teacher and
immersed himself harder than ever in studying the black arts.
We think, at this time, he may have made a pact with the Dark
Presence or, as the prophecy names it, the *Serpent from the Pit*.
Later he traveled to Targus Dol in the north and used his sorcery
to build himself a kingdom there. It's said that when his windlord, Arend, rebelled, Torolf turned him into a huge hawk. The
will of a windlord isn't easy to overpower, even for a black
sorcerer it seems. Turning Arend into a hawk enabled him to
gain control of his mind. Some claim they've seen Torolf riding a
great black hawk with blood-red eyes and claws like knives.

"Many believe Torolf also murdered Prince Ulrik to prevent
him from ascending to the throne. If that's true, then only Queen
Olwen is left to rule—and she's growing older. We shall deeply
mourn the passing away of the Royal House of Gruffydd, for with
Prince Ulrik gone, no more children will be born to it and the
elven bloodline will be lost to us."

"For the sake of your kingdom, Andras, I hope Prince Ulrik returns someday."

"Thank you, Oberon. I hope we'll *have* a someday." Obie saw the pain in Andrus' eyes and something stirred deep inside him.

After bathing, the attendants dressed them in stylish white silk shirts, long sleeved velvet jerkins, gathered at the shoulders, light blue for Obie, and dark blue for Andras, with matching velvet breeches. Over these the attendants attached short matching cloaks lined in gold colored satin, and fitted them in polished black shoes befitting two gentlemen attending a royal banquet. Obie was amused at his fine appearance, yet glad it would allow him to blend in with everyone else.

On the way to the banquet hall Andras confided, "You may notice something different about Gabrielle tonight, Obie, something it apparently takes a special occasion or the queen's wishes to bring out in her."

"What's that?"

"Well, you've no doubt noticed, she does not take to dressing, shall we say, *properly* for a young woman? It distresses her mother to see her daughter, of marriageable age, looking so unfeminine. But there doesn't seem to be much any of us can do about it. She's strong-willed and continues to dress as she pleases most of the time." Andras lowered his voice to a whisper as they neared the hall. "I had better say no more."

Approaching the great open doors of the banquet hall, Obie saw a tall, slender, young woman standing nearby. In the space of a moment he observed how the stylishly low cut, burgundy-colored gown accentuated the fullness of her youthful bosom and clung to her small waist before sliding like water over her narrow hips to the floor. Was it . . . ? Yes, it was *Gabrielle*. Andras was right. Obie hadn't realized how truly beautiful she was. How well she had hidden it. Or maybe he hadn't looked closely enough at her. Tonight her wheat-colored hair was not tightly braided on her head, but fell luxuriously over her shoulders and far down her back. She was smiling when they reached her.

"You look wonderful tonight, my dear," Andras said, his pride apparent.

"Thank you, grandfather."

"You look great, Gabrielle," Obie added, hardly aware he was speaking as he gazed into the blue ether of her eyes and breathed her fresh scent. She was intoxicating.

"And you look like a gentleman, Obie," he heard her voice say. "But, we must hurry. The queen will arrive soon."

"May I, my dear?" Andras held his arm out for her to take.

Obie felt light-headed when she took his arm also, and he had to glance at his feet to make sure they were still in contact with the floor. Arm-in-arm the three entered the banquet hall and ascended the stairs to the royal table, elevated on a dais a few feet above the others.

Andras motioned for Obie to be seated directly to the left of Queen Olwen's royal chair, which had a higher back than the others and was ornately carved and upholstered in red velvet. Gabrielle sat next to Obie with her grandfather to her left. Several other well-dressed, dignified appearing guests seated themselves to the right of the queen's chair. After they exchanged greetings with Andras and Gabrielle, Andras introduced Obie to Lord and Lady Brighton, and Lord Hastings and his sister, Lady Heatherwood. Lord Hastings was asking Obie if he was enjoying his visit to Windermere when the trumpets blew signifying Queen Olwen's arrival. The guests stood. Obie watched in awe as the queen entered and crossed the floor accompanied by six attendants and six guards. She wore a red velvet gown and red cloak trimmed in gold brocade, and her golden crown glittered in the torchlight. Rae and Asta trailed behind in matching red and gold coats. At the stairway to the royal table the attendants left her and found their places at lower tables.

Two of the guards followed her up the stairs and stood at attention nearby, and the other four took their stations along the walls.

Queen Olwen seated herself and smiled warmly at her many guests. "Greetings, and welcome to you, my good friends and subjects. There is food and drink in abundance tonight, so let the festivities begin." Her words cued the musicians who began playing, and as everyone sat down a stream of servers came forth bearing the feast. To the tables they brought platters of capons with walnut and cranberry stuffing, suckling pig with apple, roast beef with suet pudding, salmon in wine sauce, venison with onions, barley, and herbs, also turnip and new pea casseroles, potato pie, greens with pears, walnuts, and grape dressing, several varieties of cheese, loaves of warm breads with honey-pecan butter, fried tarts, raisin and rice pudding, blackberries in clotted cream, honey cakes with sweet cream, platters of fruit, and silver pitchers of mead and wine to fill their goblets.

In the background stringed instruments and flutes played merry rhythms while the guests partook of the feast and the hall echoed with laughter. It was an opportunity for the people to forget, at least for the space of an evening, their growing fear of the Celestial Dimming, a fear that, Obie knew, stalked their thoughts by day and their dreams by night.

He had hoped to spend some time talking with Gabrielle, but Queen Olwen drew him into such engaging talk that it was impossible to turn away. He found her a delightful conversationalist who had the ability to draw him out and make him relax. He hadn't expected to enjoy himself so much.

Midway through the meal, Andras leaned over and whispered in Gabrielle's ear, "The queen seems happier and more youthful tonight than I've seen her in years."

Nodding in agreement, Gabrielle smiled and whispered back, "Despite all of her worries, she still loves being a mother."

"Yes, Oberon does appear to bring out those instincts in her."

Then Gabrielle's voice took on a more serious tone. "Did you find the prophecy, Grandfather?"

"Yes. It appears that Oberon is the one it speaks of. It says we should look for the one who rides the comet's tail to Windermere, as he will be the Protector of the Guardians when they must ride the Moonpath."

Gabrielle stared wide-eyed at Andras for a moment, as though digesting the significance of his words. "That fills me with both dread and hope for what lies ahead."

"I share your feelings." Andras said gravely. He glanced over at his sovereign just as she threw her head back in laughter.

"That's a good story, Oberon," the queen said. "Josh must be a loyal friend, indeed. Oh, and before I forget, our Festival of the Harvest is going to be held at the end of the month. Our best archers and swordsmen will be there, and we would like you to join them and demonstrate your Raptor."

"I'd be honored, Your Majesty."

"We're pleased to hear that. Sword Master Ull is setting up the event. He'll make arrangements with you." Then the queen leaned close. "Tell me, do you have skill with a sword?"

"No, m'am, I've never used one."

"As I thought." The queen looked towards the end of the table and, catching Ull's eye, nodded slightly. He immediately got up and left the room. Then she motioned for some servants to clear the dishes in front of her and Obie. Obie wondered what was going on as they continued in light conversation. A couple of minutes later Ull returned bearing a long bundle which he deposited on the table before the queen. It appeared to be a rich garment of some kind wrapped around something. Queen Olwen stood and tapped a knife against her silver goblet. As soon as the hall quieted she looked at Obie and spoke for all to hear.

"As a reward to you, Oberon, for saving our beloved pet Rae from the jaws of the wolf today, we wish to honor you with some gifts. First, Sword Master Ull will instruct you in the art of swordsmanship. It is a noble and necessary art that every young gentleman must learn."

"Thank you, Your Majesty." Obie watched her unwrap the package.

Using both hands, she lifted a sword and held it out to him. His eyes moved along the black scabbard to the golden hilt etched with an intricate floral design, then to the magnificent golden pommel crafted in the shape of a lion's head.

"Oberon of Griffin, we have seen today that you have the makings of a warrior, and it is our pleasure that you become one."

Speechless, Obie stood up, his eyes fixed on the beautiful weapon. Moments passed and then he heard Gabrielle whispering to him, "Obie, take the sword."

He watched his hands reach out and take hold of it. Then, raising his eyes to the queen, he spoke in little more than a whisper, "I don't know what to say, Your Majesty, but I don't think . . ."

The queen looked amused. "It's probably best you *don't think*, Oberon. Just accept these gifts." He was vaguely aware of the friendly laughter nearby.

"Yes, Your Majesty." A light moved in the depths of his eyes when he grasped the scabbard in his left hand and the hilt in his right. He drew the sword and laid the scabbard on the table, then gripped the golden hilt with both hands and held up the bright blade. Although he knew almost nothing about swords, the weight and balance felt right. It was like a physical extension of his arms, as though they and the sword were one. Moving backward a few steps, he swished it back and forth while the guests clapped in approval of his obvious pleasure in the gift.

He saw the queen's eyes glittering while she watched his movements, but when he glanced at her again he caught a fleeting look of sadness pass through them. Was she remembering her sons? If so, she quickly masked it.

"This sword from the House of Gruffydd was crafted by the finest swordsmith in the realm, Oberon. What will you name it?"

Obie smiled at the queen as his mind raced, searching for an appropriate name. He looked along the length of the blade to the hilt, and then at the golden pommel shaped into a lion's head. In a flash it came to him. "I name it *Roar*, Your Majesty."

Queen Olwen smiled warmly. "A fitting name for the sword of a warrior, Oberon. May Roar serve you well."

The people clapped and cheered.

While he carefully sheathed the sword and laid it on the table, she unfolded the garment it had been wrapped in and held it up. "And this will preserve you in the deep chill of winter." It was a long cloak made of brown wool on one side and white sable on the other, made reversible so it could be worn with either the wool or fur side outwards. Queen Olwen placed the cloak around his shoulders and fastened it at the neck. A stir of approval came from the guests. Then the queen sat back in her chair and smiled up at the tall young man standing before her. "It suits you well, Oberon." The fabric side of the cloak was turned outward and the white sable underside made a border of fur several inches wide down the front opening.

He didn't believe himself deserving of such wonderful gifts, but he knew refusing them would offend the queen. Maybe it wasn't unusual for royalty to honor someone with lavish presents, he reasoned.

"We have one more gift," she said. "Tomorrow morning you will visit our royal tailor. He will fit you with some new clothing. Immediately after that you are to begin your lessons with Ull." She caught Ull's eye and he nodded in confirmation.

"I'll be here early, Your Majesty," Obie said.

When he later reflected on the queen's desire that he be trained as a warrior, he was surprised at his excitement. Her words ignited something in him he hadn't known existed, some part of him that was eager for the training, and it had nothing to do with the pleasant effects of the small amount of mead he had consumed during the evening.

The next morning at the Brynnen manor, Obie went to the dining room and was disappointed when Annwyl told him Gabrielle had gone early to the keep to breakfast with Queen Olwen, as she always did on this day of the week. After a quick breakfast of porridge with cream and blackberries, and some fried bacon, he went to the barn and saddled Shadow for the ride to Windermere Castle.

Between his visit to the tailor and his first swordsmanship lesson, it would be a full morning. Thinking about the lesson filled him with nervous energy as he and Shadow passed along the cobblestone road. Before long his thoughts drifted to the previous night and how beautiful Gabrielle had been. Maybe he'd run into her at the keep today and they could find some time to . . . No, he needed to put that out of his head. What was he thinking? He probably wouldn't be in Windermere very long. So even if she was interested in him, which he seriously doubted, he had no right to monopolize her time. Besides, she could have her pick of any number of noblemen if she wanted, so how could he think she'd give him a second thought? He controlled a sudden impulse to ask Shadow for advice. Nothing worse than having your horse laugh at you. The truth was, Gabrielle was way out of his league.

After arriving at Windermere Castle, Obie left Shadow at the stable and took off for the tailor's shop. As he entered he heard heated words passing between two of the assistants. A moment later one of them flew at the other in a rage. They tumbled to the floor, punching, kicking, and rolling over. The tailor ran in from an adjoining room and separated the angry, red-faced young men. He gave them stern reprimands and sent them back to work in different rooms. When they were gone he turned a concerned face to Obie.

"Please excuse the fracas, sir. This sort of thing never used to happen. It's the Celestial Dimming causing it. It's got us all edgy these days."

Obie nodded. "You don't have to apologize. I think people are holding up pretty well for the most part. A few flare-ups here and there are bound to happen."

The tailor smiled gratefully. "Thank you, sir—you're most gracious."

Obie was measured for breeches, shirts, jerkins and tabards, and then the shoemaker came in and took measurements for several pairs of boots and shoes. He saw sketches of the clothing that would be made for him. The drawing he liked best was the hunter's outfit, a long sleeved jerkin and close fitting breeches to be made from soft, dark-brown leather, and a white cotton shirt. The clothing would be ready in a few days. Obie was surprised it could be done so quickly, but he noticed there were many helpers to do the work. And since the order came from the queen, he suspected it took priority over other work. Finally the tailor handed him two gray quilted tabards with gray pants to wear for his swordsmanship lessons. He used the fitting room to change into his training clothes, buckled on his belt with his sword attached, and went in search of the sword master.

Obie found him at the back of the armory inspecting the blades of a new batch of swords sent over by the blacksmith. Ull was a tall man, wide of shoulder and narrow of hip, who moved with an easy, confident stride. His dark brown hair was shoulder-length, and his beard closely cut. Judging by the lines in his weatherworn face, Obie guessed him to be in his mid-thirties, and not given to much laughter.

The sword master gave him a wry grin and laid down the blade he was examining. "Ready for your lesson, are you?"

"Yes, sir." Obie noticed some hostility in his manner and tone.

"For starters, you need a proper belt for your sword. Are you right handed?"

"Yes, sir."

Ull grunted and selected a leather belt from a supply shelf. He attached Obie's sheathed sword and then, none to gently, fastened the belt around Obie's waist so the weapon hung at his left hip. "This is how to wear your sword at your side. When you ride, and at other times, you will want to carry it on your back." Unbuckle your sword belt and I'll show you. He pulled another, longer belt from the supply shelf. Removing Obie's sheathed sword from his waist belt, he reattached it and then lifted the strap over Obie's head, positioning the sheath at an angle across his back. Then they went to the training room.

"Remove your weapon and lay it to the side," Ull said as he took two training swords from hooks on the wall. "We'll use these wasters for your initial training."

Obie did as he was told and the sword master tossed him one of the wasters, which was a wooden sword.

"All right, we've seen you can stop limping long enough to impress us with your running. Now let's see if you can stand and fight."

Ull wielded his waster aggressively at his new student, forcing him to fight. His first hard blow sent Obie's weapon flying across the room. "Grasp it firmly with both your hands like this," the sword master commanded, demonstrating the proper way to hold his sword. "Your enemy will not coddle you, and neither will I."

Obie retrieved his wooden sword and held it as he was shown and the lesson continued. Next, he found himself being backed in circles. He fended off and blocked the master swordsman's hard blows as best he could. But soon he was trapped against the wall with the point of Ull's sword at his throat. When Obie's eyes dropped down to the wooden blade, Ull grinned and backed off. Fending off his teacher's relentless barrage of blows began to take its toll. Several times, Obie lost his balance and fell; but, angered at what he perceived as excessive force by Ull, he refused to quit. Once, he fought on his back from the floor, spinning himself around until he could scramble to his feet again. Early on, two of the sword master's men came in and stood to the side watching.

Awst shook his head. "What's gotten into Ull? He's working him too hard."

"That he is, and the lad doesn't seem to know when to quit," Eren said.

"Well, he's got heart, I'll giv'em that."

Obie was wet with sweat and barely able to lift his sword from sheer exhaustion, when Ull finally lowered his weapon. "There's more mettle under your skin than I thought, lad. Even with your limp, your movements are quick and you can think on your feet, important qualities in a swordsman."

His face flushed and legs wobbly from the ordeal, Obie was relieved the trial was over. "Thanks, sir," he said with a scowl. He did not try to hide the anger in his voice.

"I go by *Ull*." Although the sword master was not smiling, there was surprising warmth in his voice and eyes. "Tomorrow we'll start in earnest, same time. If you're prepared to work hard, Oberon, I'll make a swordsman of you."

"Tomorrow then." Obie went to retrieve his sword and clothing by the wall.

"You can wash up in the room behind the barracks, across the way," Ull called after him. "The men have already had their midday meal, but if you go to the mess hall next door you can still get a plate of food if you tell them I sent you. Look for Wud, a bald, heavy-set man. He's one of the cooks."

No one was in the wash room when Obie got there, but he found a bar of soap and a drying sheet on the supply shelf. Along the opposite wall was a long trough of clean water and pails the men used for dipping and splashing themselves. The water was cool, but invigorating. The planks on the floor were spaced a little apart so the water drained through. Where the water went after that, Obie didn't know. After washing, he dressed and positioned his sword on his back as Ull had shown him. Then, with his training clothes neatly bundled and tucked under his arm, he headed for the mess hall.

A man who turned out to be Wud was whistling as he wiped off one of the long dining tables. A good-natured man with a large scar on the left side of his face, he brought Obie a plate piled high with pork pie, roast yams, dark bread and butter, and a mug of cider. He told Obie he could come everyday at this time if he wished as there would still be plenty of food for him. And tomorrow roast beef was on the menu. Obie thanked him and after finishing his meal returned to the stable and saddled Shadow for the ride back to the Brynnen Estate.

Each morning Obie rode to the keep for his lesson and returned by the end of the day to share the evening meal with the family. Taking an after dinner walk with Andras became a regular activity. The fact that the Brynnens treated him like one of the family was comforting. If only his life at home could be as good. If only mom could . . . As always, he pushed the torturing thought from his mind. What right did he have to wish for a good home life anyway?

At dinner one evening, Andras announced he was too tired to take his nightly walk and suggested to his granddaughter, "Gabrielle, why don't you walk with Obie tonight? It will do you good."

"All right, Grandfather, if you wish."

"Just don't go far, and keep a sharp eye and ear. We must always be vigilant."

It was dusk when they set out walking north along the road. They went a short way and then turned left onto a path and passed over a wooden footbridge. The path followed a creek into a beech, oak and elm forest. It was the same path Obie and Andras usually took on their walks.

"Look, the crescent moon is rising to light our way." Gabrielle pointed at the pale orb moving up the darkening starless sky.

Obie frowned. "In a month or two it'll be too dim to light anyone's way." As soon as he said the words, he regretted it.

"You of all people shouldn't despair, Obie, since you'll probably not be here when that occurs."

"I'm sorry, Gabrielle," he said, putting his hand on her shoulder and stopping her. "I shouldn't have said that. Will you forgive me?"

"What you said is true, so there's nothing to forgive," she answered coolly and walked on. He skipped a few awkward steps to catch up. His leg felt stiff tonight, though he was doing his best to ignore it. He changed the subject to the coming festival. During their conversation Gabrielle mentioned she would be helping with the Windlord Races on that afternoon. The races were an opportunity for the young windlords and their youthful riders to demonstrate their skills. Obie confirmed that Ull had included him in the weapons demonstrations using his Raptor. He was glad when she said she would find some time to attend. Soon they reached the end of the path and started back.

The thin moonlight cast a dull phosphorescent glow on the trees. The forest was still except for the sounds of water gurgling in the creek and wind in the treetops. Low fog patches over the creek sent long, misty tendrils inching up the bank and snaking across the path.

"It's getting cold," Gabrielle said glancing up at the moon and pulling her cloak close around her. "The days are cooling off earlier this year."

"I've noticed the cold," Obie said softly. He looked down at her frowning face. She was beautiful even when she was unhappy. She turned her face up at him and he was struck by the unguarded expression of sorrow she wore. She looked away. He wondered if she was thinking about riding the Moonpath. Was she afraid of failure? Who wouldn't be? But there was something more he saw in her face. Was it fear of having her life ripped away from her before she could ever fully experience it . . . before she could fulfill whatever hopes and dreams she might have? He was careful not to let her hear his thoughts.

A dark form, low to the ground and half-hidden by the mist started across their path only inches in front of them. "Watch out," Obie yelled, grabbing her arms.

She yelped in alarm as he pulled her back. His movement was so quick and unexpected that she lost her balance and ended up pushing him down with her. Obie pulled her close to break her fall and they hit the ground together. Then they were laughing. It was the first time he'd seen her like that. She was radiant when she laughed.

"You almost stepped on it," he said.

"What was it?"

"A raccoon. It's in the bushes over there watching us—see its eyes?"

His arm was still around her as they lay in the middle of the path laughing. Looking into her face he saw the soft glow in her eyes and looked down at her full, pink lips. He stopped laughing and reached up and smoothed some loose strands of hair back from the side of her face. Then their eyes met. A wave of euphoria ran through him and he leaned close and felt her warm lips touch his. He felt like he was floating. Suddenly she pulled away and sat up, a pained expression on her face.

"I can't do this." She drew her cloak together and lowered her head. "I didn't mean for that to happen."

Shaken back to reality, Obie sat up. How could he have been so stupid? He knew better than to try that with her. He gazed at Gabrielle, trying to figure her out. She was a puzzle to him. "I'm sorry, Gabrielle. I'd never do anything to hurt you. I hope you'll believe that."

"We'd better get back before my family starts worrying about us." He stood up and pulled her to her feet.

"Still friends?" he asked sheepishly. She didn't answer and they started walking.

"Will you at least spend some time with me at the festival? It may be my last day here."

She gave him a half smile and said, "Yes, if you'll help me evade a certain Squire Bigam, who's pursuing my affections."

"You've got a deal."

***

Gabrielle and Andras always flew the windlords to the keep, so Obie had to ride the road alone. Still, he had Shadow to talk to and they carried on some interesting conversations. When they weren't conversing, he'd often think about home, or his swordsmanship lessons. Despite his efforts not to think about Gabrielle, he sometimes did. She wasn't like any girl he'd ever known, and he knew it wasn't just her physical beauty that attracted him. Though he had to admit, it had stopped him in his tracks when he saw her at the queen's banquet. He admired the way she faced the world on her own terms, although he suspected she paid a price for it. She was tough on the exterior, but he sensed a deep loneliness in her that she hid from others. Loneliness was something he knew about.

CHAPTER EIGHT

THE CHALLENGE

UNDER ULL'S TUTELAGE, Obie's swordsmanship skills improved rapidly. He learned to compensate for his limp by making swift evades, and each day his skills increased. The sword master's growing respect for his student was apparent. Queen Olwen also seemed pleased with his progress when she and Gabrielle stopped by to observe one of his early lessons.

At the queen's request, Obie gave some of Ull's men Raptor slingshot lessons in the afternoons, for which he was compensated from the royal coffer. Stunning an enemy with such a weapon would prove useful for taking captives, the queen had told him at the banquet. To this end, a few days later she asked Obie to direct a craftsman in making up fifty Raptors. Since plastic and rubber were modern materials, unavailable in this time period, boiled leather, the hard leather used in making saddles, was substituted for the body of the Raptor. Where the leather worked well, reproducing the thick rubber band was more challenging. They had to ask old Marduk to use his magic to produce some rubber-like bands. Marduk's first two attempts failed, for they either stretched too much or too little. But on his third try, he succeeded in creating bands that were a good match to Obie's prototype.

When the lessons began, Obie was disappointed at the lack of commitment among his students who were all skilled swordsmen and archers. Some arrived late for practice while others failed to show up at all, and a few seemed resentful about taking instruction from a youth. He overheard one man refer to the lessons as "little more than child's play." During Obie's third lesson, Ull stopped by and observed the problem himself. The next morning he ordered the men to attend. After that they all showed up and participated, some grudgingly.

The following day, after his swordsmanship session with Ull, Obie was leaving the armory when he accidentally overheard three of the men talking about him. As he listened his jaw tightened and his pulse quickened.

"I, for one, will be glad when he's gone and this Raptor nonsense is done with," Jasper said and spat on the dirt floor.

"Aye. The queen's taken a fancy to spoiling Obie, and we're expected to humor him," Elwan said.

"Lads, now aren't ya being a bit hard on'em? After all, he did show some skill in that business with the wolf," Awst said.

"Awww, it was just luck if ya ask me," Elwan said.

On the verge of exploding, Obie's eyes searched for an object to smash, instead of someone's face. Deciding on the wall, he drew his arm back ready to punch it, but hesitated as he recalled Will's words, "Remember to control your temper and you'll think more clearly." Ull had given him the same advice. After taking a few deep breaths he unclenched his fist and left quietly. At least Awst had put in a good word for him. Maybe he'd saved his hand, too. Stone walls could be brutal. He'd let it go for now, but he'd have to deal with the problem soon. It wasn't likely to go away by itself. He got his chance that afternoon during his Raptor class on the East Meadow when he again heard grumbling. Some of the men could hit the target at fifty or a hundred feet, but others were still having difficulty. Obie worked with each man to improve his aim and offer whatever assistance was needed. But Jasper refused help, cursing every time he missed the target, which was most of the time. In a sudden fit of temper, he threw his Raptor down.

"I say it's no more than a boy's toy and a waste of time," he yelled. "It can't compare with a bow."

Obie seized the opportunity to throw down the gauntlet. "You're right, Jasper," he said. He turned away from the man he was working with and approached Jasper. "In some ways a Raptor can't compare with a bow—it's a different weaon. But that doesn't mean it isn't valuable."

"Hah! Different is right. Too different if ya ask me." Standing with his legs planted wide apart, Jasper crossed his arms, squared his jaw, and spat on the ground.

The men crowded around them, some grinning.

"Okay, I'll pit my Raptor against your bow at up to a hundred paces. What do you say?"

Obie's challenge created a wave of excitement among the men and some egged Jasper on. "A hundred paces for a Raptor? Hah! I'd accept that challenge Jasper. He don't have a chance," Eren advised with a devilish grin.

"Yep, you'd best be acceptin' his challenge," Awst urged.

"Aye, unless ya want a boy showing ya up," Dylan added in his baritone voice.

"Well if it's a beating ya want, I'll accommodate ya. You're on," Jasper said.

Dylan slapped Jasper on the back. "Hey now, that's the spirit, man."

They were all betting men who loved a good contest, and now that the tension was broken they began wagering with one another.

Obie felt a hand on his shoulder and turned. "That's showing the spirit lad," Awst said in a quiet voice. "Don't let Jasper get the best 'a ya."

Obie wasn't sure he could beat Jasper, but he might at least gain some respect for Raptor slingshots by making a good show-ing. He knew he couldn't outshoot a long bow at a hundred paces with a normal slingshot, but it might be possible with his Raptor, and a little skill.

The men set five targets out, evenly spaced at increasing distances up to the hundred paces agreed upon. The contest began and Jasper shot first. He made a bull's eye on the nearest target and some of the men cheered. Then it was Obie's turn. The high thrill he always felt when competing rushed through him as he drew back on his Raptor, eyed the target, and aimed. When he heard the forward snap of the band he knew his shot was good. It hit center, next to the arrow. He smiled inwardly when some cheers went up for him and ignored the boos and jeers from Jasper's friends. When his next turn came, several men tried distracting him by making high-pitched "whup" sounds, laughing at their own foolishness as they did it. A few choice words hurled at them from two other men silenced them. The score remained close as the tally went back and forth like a ping pong ball. Some onlookers nodded their heads knowingly, others whispered, or chuckled and poked each other. It was time for their last shot at a hundred paces, and the score was tied. Frowning, Jasper drew back on his bow and released the arrow. The score keeper ran over and reported: the arrow struck three inches from center target. Jasper's frown deepened. Obie loaded his largest steel shot. Dead silence followed. He braced his feet, pulled the band taut, eyed center target, and released. The score keeper reported, "Obie's shot hit two inches from center, an inch closer than Jasper's arrow."

Jasper stood motionless, staring at the target while some of the men cheered. But the cheering quickly died out and all eyes focused on Jasper, waiting to see what he would do next. Moments of awkward silence passed, and then Jasper turned and stalked off.

"Bad temper," Awst said, keeping his voice low.

"Poor sport," Dylan added.

A few others made quiet comments about Jasper being a sore loser.

"It was a close match, maybe I should go after him and try to smooth things out," Obie said to Awst, a note of uncertainly in his voice.

"No, no. Let him be, lad," Awst cautioned. "He's too upset now, but he'll get over it. He's not a bad sort underneath. His pride's just bruised a bit."

The men congratulated Obie, and Awst and Dylan slapped him on the back and invited him to join them for ale at the Jolly Horse Inn. Although some of Jasper's friends were a little stand-offish, they were in good enough spirits to join the others at the pub. So, in the late afternoon, after sending the stable boy with a note to Andrus that he might be late getting home that night, Obie and the men rode to the pub at the edge of town.

Have a jolly time, Shadow said as Obie followed the others into the pub. Obie glanced back over his shoulder and grinned. The semi-dark room was illuminated only by the fire in the hearth and a few candles along the walls. This was Obie's first time in a pub, but the innkeeper's wife helped to ease his nervousness. She came over with a big friendly smile that exposed two front teeth with a gaping space between them. "What's yer pleasure, lad?"

"I'm buying a round of ale for these gentlemen." Obie pulled his earnings from his pocket and handed a silver coin to the round-faced woman.

The woman looked around at his companions and grinned. "And when will these gentlemen be arriving? 'Cause I don't see no gentlemen in *this* room."

Some of the men laughed good naturedly at her cheeky comment. Then Dylan said, "Awww now, Molly, don't be telling on us. We've got our young friend believing we're capital fellows."

"Well, he appears to be a good lad," Molly said. "Don't you be teaching him any 'a yer bad habits."

"We're hurt, Molly. Would we do a thing like that?" Awst said, clutching his chest in mock despair.

She put her hands on her plump hips and looked squarely at Awst. "That ya would," she bellowed.

Several men guffawed, and one said, "We love ya, Molly."

With a quick laugh that sounded more like a snort, she left to draw the ale. Before long she and a helper returned carrying trays of foaming mugs.

When everyone had taken one, Awst held his up. "Here's to Obie—a good sport 'an a regular fellow."

"Aye, I'll drink to that," one of the men chimed in, raising his mug.

"Aye," the others jovially put in.

Smiling, Obie raised his mug and drank long and deep with the queen's men, dribbling some of the ale down his chin. After that, everyone took turns buying rounds. The men drank and sang and made merry that night, and Obie listened to their stories, basking in the warmth of their friendship and the flowing ale.

Later that evening Andrus and Ull stopped by the pub and found Obie sleeping on a bench in a corner. He wore a silly smile on his face, and someone had thrown a blanket over him.

"Is he all right?" Ull asked a burly man named Thorkil.

"The lad's all right in my book," Thorkil answered in a mellow voice and winked. "Just a little under the weather, I'd say."

Andras lifted one of Obie's eyelids and let it drop shut. "He's gone," he said glancing up at Ull.

"I'll put him on his horse," Thorkil said. He carried Obie outside and laid him over Shadow's back.

After thanking Thorkil and bidding Ull good-night, Andras took Obie home and, with Ilar's help, put him to bed.

Obie awoke the next morning with a headache and a queasy stomach. The last thing he remembered was his knees buckling under him while Thorkil was telling about a goblin chase. Everything had gone black after that. He dragged himself out of bed and went to the kitchen to find something that might agree with his stomach. Knowing how bad he must look, he was glad most everyone was gone. Breakfast was long since over, but the kindly cook prepared him a special egg recipe and black tea with honey, saying they were guaranteed to improve his condition. He felt a little better after eating, so he went to the barn and sheepishly asked Shadow how he had gotten home.

Over my back, in a very undignified position. Andras and Ull came to fetch you.

***

When next he saw the two men he could see they were suppressing grins, but neither man ever commented on the incident.

Obie welcomed the quiet evenings with the Brynnens, where spirits remained relatively good, for elsewhere tension was mounting. Obie witnessed fights between shopkeepers, stable boys, noblemen, and warriors alike. People observing on the sidelines would often jump in and turn a small fracas into an all-out brawl. And how many times had Obie observed people staring up bleakly at the dying sun? Some handled the stress better than others.

Talbot was one who managed to maintain an even temper. On a couple of occasions, Obie went catfishing with him at a quiet spot along the River Llafar late at night when they were known to bite best. During these outings they kept watchful eyes for possible marauding goblins or stealthy bands of trolls.

On the day before the festival, the valley was filled with activity and, surprisingly, there was little bickering to be heard. Actors and musicians readied their costumes, rehearsed, and loaded their wagons.   Merchants, tradesmen, craftsmen, and land-owners busied themselves packing their carts with textiles and leather goods, candles, pewter dishes and mugs, jewelry, weap-onry, saddles and bridles, nuts and grains, baked goods and anything else that could be sold.

It was tradition to hold the festival at Elkhorn Meadow, a handful of miles south of town, where the task of setting up tents and booths would continue through the night and into the early morning.   Recently, there had been talk of relocating the festival to one of the meadows adjacent to Windermere Castle. Despite the greater protection afforded by such a move, a lingering dispute between the tradesmen and craftsmen guilds as to which meadow was best suited prevented the change from taking place.

Obie and the queen's best archers and swordsmen partici-pated in last-minute practice before their demonstrations. Young windlords and their riders perfected their flying skills while Gabrielle helped with preparations for the races. At home, Annwyl oversaw the making of breads and cakes to enter in the baking contest, and Ilar assisted some of his farm hands in loading the wagons. Few got to bed early that night.

The next morning dawned cool and misty. Andras and Ilar departed for the festival grounds earlier than the rest of the family. Ilar drove a wagon filled with bags of the family's best grains, and Andras rode alongside on Magnus. The previous day, Ilar had supervised the setting up of their green and yellow tent with the House of Brynnen banner flying atop. It bore the family crest, a white owl in flight with a dark green background. This morning he and Andras would oversee the setting up of tables within the tent and the placement of the grain bags. It was also an excuse to socialize with neighboring landowners who found time between their own activities to visit one another's tents and booths. Meanwhile, dancers, actors, musicians, jugglers and puppeteers arrived in colorful costumes.

A little before midmorning, Gabrielle astride Mara, and Obie riding Shadow arrived at Elkhorn Meadow. Behind them, Annwyl and two servants rode in a wagon partially filled with baked goods. Most everyone dressed warmly for the cool weather. At Ull's suggestion, Obie wore his hunter's clothing, brown leather boots, and long cloak for the demonstration.

***

Ull and the queen's men rode across the courtyard towards the castle gate. They were enroute to the festival when an eagle screeched close overhead and drew their attention.

"Errrickkk," he screeched, fluttering to a landing atop a near-by cart. "I bring news."

"Greetings, Silverclaw. What news?" Ull asked, drawing rein on his horse.

"I have spotted a band of goblins, fifty or sixty in number, less than two hours to the north by land. They speed on horseback towards Windermere by way of the Long Wadi Road."

"Thank you for your vigilance, Silverclaw. I'll give your report to the queen at once."

Minutes later, upon delivering the message to Queen Olwen, Ull added, "It's odd, Your Majesty, that they boldly ride the road in daylight instead of concealing their approach beneath the trees as they have done in the past."

"Odd, indeed," the queen said with a troubled look. "But we have no time now to spend wondering." She paced back and forth in thought, then stopped and said, "I must speak to my captains at once."

"I've anticipated your wishes, Majesty, and sent one of my men to summon them. They will arrive outside your door momentarily for your instructions."

"Well done. Tell them to come in when they get here."

Within minutes, twenty sober-faced captains began filing into the room. Wasting no words, the queen apprised the men of the threat and then selected four among them to ride north with a hundred horse soldiers to intercept the goblins. As a pre-cautionary measure, she dispatched a fifth captain and his forty men to the festival grounds to protect the people.

"All others are to remain here on temporary alert," Queen Olwen said.

CHAPTER NINE

PURSUIT

DESPITE THE INCREASING ANXIETY, squabbles, and fights the Celestial Dimming was engendering among the Windermerians, they were a hardy folk who welcomed the chance the festival gave to forget their cares for a while. Whatever calamity the future might hold, today they would celebrate the fruitfulness of the land as they had always done. It would be a day of merriment.

The dread Obie felt was mostly for the Windermerians, for the moon would be full in two nights and, if all went well, he would be going home again. He would be safe—maybe. Yet, how could he leave his new friends if there was some way he could help them? What kind of help he could provide was a question that gnawed at him. Well, he wouldn't dwell on it today. Today he was going to enjoy the festival with Gabrielle.

The aroma of warm bread and sizzling meats titillated his nostrils. Succulent game birds and beef and pork quarters turned on open spits. And at the booths one could buy such tasties as fried sausages, warm meat and potato pies, bowls of corn chowder, roasted corn, fresh baked breads and sweet rolls, fried tarts, spiced apples on sticks, roasted chestnuts, pumpkin and mincemeat pies, fruit puddings, cakes and pastries, and many other delectable treats. To wash it all down, some booths sold horns of ale, mead, and apple cider.

"Mmmmm, just smell those hot spiced rolls," Gabrielle said as she and Obie strolled among the tents and booths. He liked the way she scrunched her nose while sniffing the air. "I'll get us a couple if you'll find a place to sit," he said smiling at her.

"I'll wait over there." She pointed to an empty bench nearby.

Obie soon returned with the hot rolls and cider and they sat enjoying the treats and watching the people pass by.

"Do you have any sisters or brothers, Obie?" Gabrielle asked.

"Yeah, I have a brother. His name's *Scottie*. There's a guy over there at the cider booth who reminds me of him."

"What does Scottie look like?"

Obie crossed his eyes and sucked his cheeks in.

Gabrielle started laughing. "You're being mean."

Her laughter reminded him of a soft summer breeze. He was glad she appreciated his humor, and gladder yet that she wasn't still upset with him for kissing her a few nights ago. "Okay, I'm kidding," he said. He only looks that way when he wakes up in the morning."

She looked him in the eye and raised her brow, waiting for him to get serious.

"All right. The truth is he's the handsome one in the family. He's eighteen, a couple of inches taller than me, and has dark brown hair and eyes. And he's fun to be around—most of the time anyway."

"You miss him, don't you."

"Yeah, I do."

A troupe of musicians playing woodwinds and lutes passed by. When they were gone, Gabrielle turned to Obie. She wore the same soft-eyed look as that night on their walk, when, after laughing at the raccoon watching them from the bushes, their eyes had met. There was passion behind those eyes, a passion he knew she guarded closely. "Grandfather told me about the prophecy," she said.

"Did he?" Gazing at her, he became aware of the delicate white flower garland crowning her head, and he noticed her eyes were the same pale shade of blue as her dress. "I wasn't sure how much you knew."

"If you could believe you're the one it speaks of, would you stay in Windermere?"

He didn't want to tell her he was torn between his desire to go home and his growing sense that he should remain there. He was spared having to answer when Talbot appeared.

"Obie, I've been looking for you. Hey now . . . you wore your fine fur cloak and . . ." He suddenly noticed Gabrielle's presence and his cheeks turned rosy pink. "Oh, Mistress Brynnen. I'm sorry, I don't know how I could have missed seeing you sitting there," he stammered. "I don't mean to interrupt—I'll just excuse myself." He turned to go.

Obie was about to tell Talbot he'd catch up with him later when Gabrielle spoke up.

"Nonsense, Talbot." She grabbed his hand before he could escape and pulled him back. "You'll do no such thing. We're all here to enjoy ourselves today and you're welcome to join us. Besides, I'll be leaving soon to attend to my duties at the Wind-lord Races. Then you two can pal around if you like."

"I was just going to say I'd be, uhhh, pleased if you'd join us, Talbot," Obie said. He was touched by Gabrielle's kindness in asking Talbot to join them.

"Well, I guess a fellow can't refuse nice invitations like these," he replied with a bright smile. "I have to do some errands for my father soon, but I'll join the two of you for a while. Obie, you'll be giving your Raptor demonstration, right?"

"Right. Are you coming?"

"I wouldn't miss it."

The three strolled through the festival grounds talking and laughing. When they stopped to watch a jester juggling colored balls, something caught Gabrielle's attention and she stiffened.

"Quick, we have to go."

"What?" Obie asked.

"Squire Bigam is coming," she said with an anxious look. The three hurried behind the nearest tent and waited for him to pass by.

"What does he look like?" Obie asked.

"He has black hair with a round, pink face, and he's wearing a dark green cap and cloak."

Obie peaked around the edge of the tent and immediately pulled back. "The squire's looking at some jewelry at the front of this tent," he said with a grin. Gabrielle covered her mouth to muffle her laughter. They waited a couple of minutes and then sent Talbot out to check on the squire's whereabouts.

"Back in a jiffy," Talbot said, grinning at his co-conspirators. He walked to the front of the tent and peeked around, then rejoined Obie and Gabrielle. "I think we're safe m'Lady. He's joined up with some chaps and gone off that way." Talbot pointed back the way they had come.

"Close call," Gabrielle said with a laugh of relief. "I dislike hiding out like this, but I dislike his company even more. He would have insisted on joining us. Thanks for helping out, Talbot."

"Glad to be of service, m'Lady," Talbot replied with a mischievous smile.

Obie was also relieved. This was *his* time to spend with Gabrielle. Having Talbot along was one thing, but he didn't want to share this time with any would-be suitors.

Talbot soon left to do his errands, and shortly after that it came time for Gabrielle to help with the Windlord Races. Obie accompanied her to the racing area beyond the north end of the festival grounds.

Until now, the view to the east had been blocked by the numerous craftsmen's booths and multi-colored artisans' tents. When Obie and Gabrielle left the main festival area they noticed, for the first time, Jasper and some of the queen's horse soldiers posted along the border of the meadow and Gnarlwood Forest. They wore metal battle helms and breastplates, and were armed with swords and bows.

"I haven't heard anything about horse soldiers being sent here, have you, Obie?"

"No. The queen must have just decided to send them— otherwise, I'm sure Ull would have mentioned it." Something didn't seem right.

"There must be a goblin or troll alert," Gabrielle said. "Well, whatever it is, I'm sure it's being handled and we'll all be safe enough with the horse soldiers here."

"Ull and his men will arrive soon, so we should be okay." Obie suddenly felt protective. Skilled bow-maiden or not, she still seemed vulnerable. He heard hoof beats and turned to see Jasper galloping over on his battle-ready warhorse.

Jasper gave Obie only a curt nod and reined his stallion to a dancing halt alongside Gabrielle. "Good morning, Lady Brynnen."

"Good morning, Jasper." Gabrielle gave Obie a concerned glance, apparently sensing some friction between the two.

"There's no need to worry about the men and me patrolling the border here. A little earlier we had a goblin sighting a ways to the north, but a patrol was sent out and likely has intercepted them by now. We're here merely as a precautionary measure."

"I thought that might be the case. Thank you for the information, Jasper."

"My pleasure, m'lady." With a parting nod, Jasper wheeled his horse around and sped back to his post.

Gabrielle gazed towards the forest, as though listening to the faint droning sound that Obie had also heard off and on for the past ten minutes. Its volume fluctuated from a low pitch to barely audible before it disappeared from one direction and reemerged in another. The sound stopped again. "Probably a swarm of bees," Obie said.

"Yes, maybe." She glanced towards the racing area. "I'd better be going. Good luck with your demonstration, Obie—though you'll hardly need it. I'll come later to watch."

He watched her walk away. She had an energetic, athletic stride he'd always liked in girls. Mara was waiting next to the starting line and whinnied a greeting when Gabrielle approached. Then the two began welcoming the jittery young riders who were arriving on their young windlords. Obie lingered a while, observing the youthful contestants. And then it happened.

As if someone turned on a switch, the droning sound re-emerged so loudly that people searched the sky for its source. It came. A great black, pulsating cloud appeared over the trees of Gnarlwood Forest. It changed shape slightly and moved over the festival grounds where it hovered menacingly, expanding and contracting like a huge, black lung. Within seconds, it ballooned gigantically and swooped down on the horrified onlookers. Bats, hundreds of thousands of them, fluttered through the crowd blinding everyone. Panic-stricken people scurried for cover or sank to their knees, slapping the bats away from their heads. Women and children screamed while men shouted and fell over one another trying to grab their children. Obie thrashed in vain at the bats, trying to knock them away. Then he heard hissing and clicking sounds and saw something large and dark moving towards him through the dense cloud of bats. Something hard hit him in the head. Sinking to his knees in a daze, he was pushed backwards and pinned against the ground. Everything was fuzzy for a few seconds and something told him he was about to meet his worst nightmare.

He blinked, and when he could see again he gasped: he was peering into the bright yellow eyes of a huge black spider. Green saliva dripped from its beak-like mouth onto Obie's chest. Then he realized the creature was something more than a giant spider.

It appeared to be part spider and part man. Except for the beaky mouth and yellow eye-color, his eyes, face, and stringy black hair seemed human, and he had two hairy, human-like legs with booted feet. But his upper appendages consisted of six long spider arms with claw-like hands. His attire told Obie he was a soldier, for he wore a black leather breastplate with metal studs, and carried a sword at his belt. Four of his hairy black arms held Obie down while two other arms prodded his neck and cheeks. A nasty sounding laugh rumbled from deep within the great arachnid chest.

"Aaaaaah, haaaaa, haaaaa. I could kill you now, human, hssssst, but I have to leave so soon, I'll save you for another meal, another day, hssssst. And I do hope we meet again so we can . . . dine together. Look for me in your dreams. Aaaaaah, haaaaa, haaaaa." The spider-man belched an odor that reeked of putre-fying meat.

Obie let out a convulsive yell. He was close to vomiting from the stench as the spider-man held him down, laughing hid-eously. Obie wondered what was so funny.

The bats were regrouping over the meadow to fly away when the creature glanced over his shoulder at his comrades heading back into the forest. With a final laugh he released his hold on Obie and, utilizing all eight arms and legs, sprang away at amaz-ing speed to join his companions.

Obie bolted up and drew his sword, but the spider-man soldiers had already departed from the festival grounds. His gaze swept the racing area and fixed upon a white flower garland lying on the grass. It was Gabrielle's. Next to the forest he saw several of the queen's men lying where they fell during the attack. A little to the left of them, spider-men were busying themselves with something. He spotted a flash of light blue between their dark forms and then some of them moved aside. It was Gabrielle in her light blue dress, hands bound in front of her, being lifted like a doll onto a horse. A rider grabbed the reins and pulled her mount behind him into the ranks of the swiftly retreating spider-men. A fat soldier rode Mara into line behind Gabrielle's horse. Heavy leather straps bound Mara's wings tightly. Gabrielle turned towards Obie and, for a moment, he felt her eyes meet his across the distance. Then she was gone, and seconds later the forest swallowed up the last spider-man.

As Obie helplessly watched, his vision blurred again and his ears rang. Images flashed through his mind of Dad, Will, Scottie, Josh, the dying sun and moon, and Gabrielle being whisked into the darkness by the loathsome black spider creatures. Clenching his fists he threw back his head and from far-off he heard a long drawn-out cry of anger and anguish. It grew steadily louder until he finally realized the voice was his own. His sight cleared and he turned and ran for all he was worth, cloak flowing out behind, towards the far western side of the meadow where Shadow waited in the corral with the other horses.

***

At first sight of the bat cloud above the festival grounds, the horses started mulling nervously around the corral. Something was clearly wrong. Then the cloud descended. Screams of shock and fear could be heard to the far ends of the meadow. Had the horses been outside the corral some might have raced to the aid of their keepers. But penned within, they were helpless to act.

Shadow snorted and pushed his way through the other horses. At the fence he saw the bat cloud rise into the sky again and regroup. Then he saw the strange black creatures on the festival grounds, also retreating towards the forest. He reared up and pounded his hooves on the top railing, trying to bring it down. It did not budge. Lifting his head, Shadow gave a loud whinny. Instantly, the horses parted, allowing him clear passage across the corral. He ran through the newly formed corridor, turned at the far side and started back, picking up speed. When he reached the fence he leaped high over the railing. As his hooves touched down he saw Obie approaching at a dead run and heard his unmistakable whistle. Shadow raced forward with his black mane and tail streaming behind. When they met, he came to a lively stop and Obie swung into the saddle.

"Shadow, we have to hurry.   Something terrible has just happened."

Shadow leaped forward again.

What has happened, Oberon?

Spider-men took Gabrielle and Mara into Gnarlwood. I want to go after them. Obie was breathing hard.

Then I will bear you, my friend.

At the festival grounds, Shadow halted long enough for Obie to slide down and grab two loaves of bread and a hunk of cheese. He stuffed them into his saddlebags and they were off again.

The grounds were a shambles with tables overturned, food and goods strewn everywhere, tents knocked down and trampled along with their contents; and the fine clothing people wore was torn and soiled. A few mothers comforted crying children while dazed men and women saw to the needs of others and tended to the injured and dead horse soldiers.

Shadow raced along the narrow strip between the field and festival grounds, towards the place where the spider-men had entered the forest with Gabrielle and Mara. Jasper, badly stung by spider poison, was being lifted into a cart by two of the townspeople. As the sound of galloping hooves approached, he opened his eyes just in time to see Obie and Shadow pass into the gloom of Gnarlwood Forest.

***

Andras helped his family and servants into a wagon and sent them home, then went in search of Gabrielle, Mara, and Obie. He learned from a young windlord rider that Gabrielle and Mara had been taken by the spider-men, and Obie followed them into the forest soon afterwards. Immediately, he and Magnus flew to the keep. When the windlord touched down, Andras found Queen Olwen in the courtyard where many horse soldiers were assembling. Ull stood beside the grave-faced queen.

"Your Majesty, I came as quickly as I could," Andras said, bowing. His eyes were red rimmed and his face drawn. "I see you've already received the bad news."

"The eagle Silverclaw saw the raid from above and came to me at once."

"I regret that I have more ill news, Madame. Gabrielle and Mara were abducted. Oberon rode into the forest in pursuit of them."

"No . . ." The queen's face went white.

Ull, too, looked shocked by the news and asked, "Who were the attackers? Was it the black trolls?"

"No, I've never seen anything like these creatures, large man-like spiders camouflaged at first by a dense cloud of bats. We didn't see them until they were on top of us."

"This is Torolf's work," the queen said, clenching her fists at her sides. "Woe that I ever bore him whom I no longer call *son*."

The others silently watched their sovereign pace heatedly back and forth, her dark blue high-necked dress rustling with each turn. At last she stopped and wheeled round to face Andras. "Silverclaw reported fifty dark soldiers. He said they came by way of the Old Path."

"I will confirm the path. As to the number, Silverclaw was in a better place to see than I. I'm sure he is correct, Majesty. With so few they will travel swiftly."

"Your Majesty," Ull said, "Prince Andor and Silverclaw are flying over the forest now looking for any signs of movement below, though the trees are so dense there may be little chance of seeing anything. The spider-men could turn off on any of the numerous paths that branch out from the Old Path. I'm sending our two best trackers with the men."

"How soon will they ride?"

"Momentarily. Forty bowmen and forty swordsmen."

"Good." She turned to Andras. "I don't think their lives will be in danger, at least not immediately. It's the Star Crystals Torolf wants. His lackeys will not dare harm Gabrielle or Mara."

"I pray that is true," Andras said.

"As to Oberon, that is something else. He doesn't know the great dangers he'll face in Gnarlwood, even were there no spider creatures."

"Aye," Ull said solemnly.

Andras shook his head in agreement.

"I wonder if he'll try to rescue Gabrielle and Mara on his own," Queen Olwen said.

"I hope the lad won't be that foolish," Andras put in.

"Ull, what do you think?" the queen asked.

"I'm not sure whether he'll try a rescue on his own. But I believe he'll keep his wits about him and avoid being seen. If he's spotted, he's got his sword and Raptor to defend with. At the least, he'll put up a good fight."

Just then Gaylen, the strike leader, hurried over and reported the men were assembled and ready to ride. Queen Olwen gave him the new information regarding Gabrielle, Mara and Obie, and instructed him to bring them back safely.

"We'll bring them back, Your Majesty." He bowed and turned to go.

"Wait, Gaylen, I'll speak with you also," Ull said, and then turned to the queen, "By your leave, Majesty."

"Yes, go now, Ull, but come to my map room in half an hour. Bring Ivor, and pass the word to all my captains at the keep to attend. Andras and I will meet you there. We must plan."

"Your Majesty," Ull said with a bow, and then departed to give the strike leader final instructions. Minutes later, Gaylen mounted his horse and eighty grim-faced soldiers, bearing the red, white and gold banners of the queen, thundered through the castle gate heading for the Old Path in Gnarlwood Forest.

The great gate closed behind the last horsemen as Andras and Queen Olwen stood watching. "Come, Andras." The queen put her hand on his shoulder as they turned to enter the building. "What are your thoughts?"

"I think it has begun."

***

Obie sped along the Old Path. The trees formed a shadowy archway with an occasional ray of gray light filtering through the thick, intertwining branches. Soon, the forest canopy rose higher and denser as the younger oaks bordering the forest gave way to the ancient oaks with their great gnarled roots. The farther Obie rode, the gloomier and quieter it became. The echo of Shadow's hooves pounding the ground bounced from tree to tree. After riding nearly an hour he stopped and put his ear to the ground to listen. He could hear something—was it hoof beats?

I feel vibrations in the earth of many horses ahead, Shadow offered. *They're still on this path.*

Obie gave Shadow an approving look. *Thanks, Shadow, this talent of yours will come in handy.* He mounted, drew his sword, and marked a tree trunk for the queen's soldiers to see when they followed, as he knew they would. Gnarlwood was a gloomy place, but they wouldn't miss the mark. Would Ull be among them?

Shadow had taken only a couple of steps when a long, low, wailing sound came from deep in the trees ahead and off to their right. The hair on Obie's neck bristled and Shadow fidgeted nervously. Obie thought he saw a dark form move in the distance. Was it a trick of his vision? Whatever it was had seemed to dart off the path and into the shadows.

Did you see that?

Yes, but I couldn't tell what it was. We must leave the path. We're easily seen here and my hooves make too much noise on this hard surface.

Agreed.

They turned left into the trees, where the forest floor rose and fell in long undulations. The low hills and oak trees made them less conspicuous to hostile eyes, and the softer ground helped muffle Shadow's hoof beats. Following the path at a distance, they occasionally returned to it to mark another tree. After a while they came to a stream and Obie dismounted. *Take a long drink, Shadow. You've earned it.*

Did I once say I needed excitement in my life? Shadow lowered his head to lap the stream water.

It may be a while before either of us will complain that life is dull. Obie knelt next to Shadow and drank his fill at the stream, then refilled his nearly empty water bag. He knew they had only a few hours of murky light left. When night came the forest would be pitch-black, and he dared not light a fire. He'd have to find a place to camp before then. The spider-men soldiers were moving fast, but they would also need to stop and rest at night. Could they have stopped already?

Shadow, what do you hear now?

I still feel vibrations of the spider soldiers, but now a sound is coming from behind us. I would say it's the queen's horse soldiers. They're riding fast, but they're still a long ways off.

Thank God they're on the way. I wish we had time to wait for them, but I want to stick to the spider-men's trail so we don't lose them. Obie mounted.

That is wise. If they move too far away I will no longer be able to feel their vibrations. And if they were to then leave the path and strike out through the forest, we would lose them.

I'm hoping they don't decide to split up and go in different directions. He drew his cloak close around him in the chilly autumn air and they hurried on.

I know you're worried about Gabrielle and Mara, Shadow said after a time. *Do you want to talk about it?*

Thanks, maybe it would help. I keep thinking about them in the hands of those spider thugs. From what I've heard about Torolf, I'm sure he sent them.

I agree. But if the spider soldiers serve Torolf, then Gabrielle and Mara are precious cargo. The soldiers would likely fear his anger if they mistreat his captives.

I needed to hear that, Shadow. I pray you're right.

Moving up and down the dim, silent terrain of tree trunk after tree trunk grew monotonous, though they had to keep alert. When they came to the top of a small rise Shadow stopped abruptly and started edging backward down the hill. *Danger.*

I saw it, Obie said. Ahead and to the right, two dark spider-man shapes moved stealthily through the trees near the path. Obie and Shadow retreated farther from the path and down a gully where they waited and listened. When it seemed the danger was gone they moved on and Shadow increased his pace to an easy gallop.

The gloom deepened around them. *We need to make camp soon,* Obie said.

A prudent observation.

Can you feel the spider soldiers?

Let me check. Shadow stopped and stood motionless a few moments. *No. They have most likely made camp. I can feel the queen's horse soldiers much closer now, but night will soon stop them too.*

They found a spot under a massive oak tree overhanging a stream. Shadow drank at the water's edge while Obie removed his sword and Raptor and set them against one of the great gnarled roots of the oak. He pulled Shadow's saddle off and rubbed his coat with dry leaves to soak up the sweat, then got a brush from his saddlebag and quickly curried the stallion. Afterwards, Shadow grazed nearby while Obie reclined against a tree root and drank from his water bag. Pulling a small piece off the end of a loaf of bread, he halfheartedly tried to eat it. What kind of disgusting food were the spider soldiers giving Gabrielle? His appetite lost, he tossed the bread in the stream and watched it float away on the dark water.

Shadow had followed the bank around a low hill. Obie knew he was searching for the thick patches of green clover that grew in moist soil. Darkness was only minutes away when he went to fetch him. As he started up the hill he heard several high-pitched neighs. Hurrying to the top, he spotted Shadow below, barely visible in the failing light, struggling oddly between two trees.

"What the . . . ? I'm coming, Shadow." He started down the hill. Without warning, he hit something that attached itself to his body and began bouncing him back and forth. Thrashing about to free himself, he realized the more he fought the more hopelessly stuck he became. He raised his head, and in the last moments of light saw the faint glitter of crisscrossing silky strands above him. *Nooo . . . this can't be happening.* Caught fast in a giant spider web, he strained to see into the darkness. At first, he couldn't see or hear anything. Shadow stopped struggling and made a low neigh.

Shadow, don't worry. The queen's soldiers will find us soon and cut us free. Obie wasn't entirely sure they would come tonight. But for Shadow's sake, he needed to remain calm.

I hope you're right. If the spider soldiers find us first we're in deep manure.

All they could do was wait and hope the queen's trackers found them before the spider-men did. Shadow was apparently too miserable to be social, so Obie let him be. As a matter of fact, he didn't feel so red-hot either. How could he have been so careless? This was the logical place for hungry spider-men to build webs: next to a stream where animals came to drink. If he had his sword, he could cut himself free, but he'd left it and everything else next to the tree. He promised himself that if he got out of this mess alive he'd never go anywhere in the forest again without his weapons. *It'll be just my luck if that creep who belched on me this morning shows up. Will, I hope you're praying real hard right now.*

Hours passed and Obie realized to his dismay that the queen's horse soldiers weren't coming. No one could track in pitch darkness—no human anyway. He shivered at the implication. Looking up, he saw black shapes writhing in the twisted branches. Then his eyes caught another movement. Something was creeping along a limb. Hardly daring to breathe, he waited. Whatever it was, it drew no nearer. Then bright eyes blinked at him and the creature hooted. He relaxed. It was only an owl. It must have been around midnight when he heard a hissing sound close by. *Are the spider soldiers coming?* He shuddered convulsively and his mouth went dry. A minute passed and nothing happened. *Must have been the wind rustling the leaves.* He fell in and out of troubled sleep, and once was awakened to some commotion in the distance. Was it a pack of wolves? The faint sounds died out quickly, leaving only the lonely stirring of the wind whispering secrets to the trees.

CHAPTER TEN

TAU

A LOW-PITCHED LAUGH drifted through the misty veils of sleep awakening Obie with a start. A few feet away, silhouetted against the gray light of early morning, a large figure stood shaking its head back and forth. Obie's vision cleared and he saw a strange creature staring at him. It had the appearance of a lion, but the build of a powerful man, standing six-foot-five. Curling his claw-fingers threateningly, he raised his arms and roared. Obie's face whitened as he jerked back, setting the web in motion. Bouncing back and forth, he was convinced he was about to draw his last breath. The lion-man lowered his arms and said in a deep pitched voice, "Did I scare you?"

Surprised and somewhat hopeful now, Obie managed to say, "Well, yeah, I . . ."

"You *should* be scared." The lion-man folded his arms across his broad chest and planted his feet wide apart. "Don't you know these woods are dangerous? What are you doing here?"

"At the moment, I'm just hanging around waiting for some-one to help me out of this spider web."

"No need to tell me you're fodder for the raks, boy."

"Raks?"

"That's what I said, Raks. That's what they're called."

"I didn't . . ."

"Never mind what you didn't know. Those who can't take care of themselves have no business wandering around in this forest." His yellow-green eyes glowed now. "Hrrrmmph," he growled, and drew his sword from the sheath on his back. He hacked at the web strands, snapping them away one-by-one. While he worked, Obie observed the bushy, golden-brown mane that flowed over his shoulders, the short, honey-colored fur covering his body, and the retractable claws on his fingers and toes. He wore a buckskin vest revealing muscular arms, buckskin pants, and he was barefoot. He projected a powerful, untamed image, yet there was something fine and noble in his face. A harmonious blend of lion and human features softened the savage effect, allowing his face to show human emotion. Obie sensed that emotions burned strong in this creature. The lion-man worked swiftly and soon he was freed.

"Thanks a lot," Obie said.

"Don't mention it," the lion-man grunted.

Shadow nickered from the trees below.

"Hold on, Shadow, I'll get my sword." Obie turned and started down the other side of the hill. "Back in minute," he called over his shoulder to the lion-man. When he returned, the creature was already at the base of the hill hacking away at Shadow's bonds. Obie noticed the lion-man glancing at his Raptor, and the golden lion's head pommel on his sword, Roar. He appeared somewhat surprised, but said nothing and continued working.

How are you feeling, Shadow? Obie asked as he slashed through the web strands alongside the lion-man.

You'll like my answer better if you ask again after I'm freed.

Understood, my friend. Did you hear the lion-man call the spider men "raks?"

Yes.

Obie decided it was best to keep silent until Shadow's mood improved.

When the last strand snapped the stallion gave a spirited snort and bolted away.

Yeah, you're welcome, Obie said.   He and the lion-man sheathed their blades and watched Shadow gallop up the stream and back again, stopping nearby to drink.   Scowling, the lion-man turned to Obie.

"Now, boy, go back where you came from.   Take your horse and leave this forest."

Disliking the lion-man's tone, Obie squared his jaw and said to him mentally, *Why don't you take your high-horse and jump over the moon?*   When the lion-man did not respond, Obie was disappointed over the wasted insult.   But it wasn't entirely wasted.   At least he knew the creature wasn't telepathic.   And there seemed to be enough humanity in him that Obie doubted he ate people.   Besides, he had two rabbits dangling from his belt.

"Go *now*, boy, before you get in trouble again," the lion-man ordered, then turned and strode off.

Obie watched him disappear into the greenish gloom of the forest.   "Yeah, thanks for the advice," he said quietly.

Shadow was in a better mood as they hurried back to the oak tree to get the saddle and be on their way.   *The raks left before dawn,* he said.   *Their sounds are growing fainter.*

Obie was shocked at the news.   They were on the verge of losing the trail.   Had he blown it?   His thoughts were interrupted by a loud rumbling in his stomach.   He hadn't eaten in almost twenty-four hours.   *Give me a minute to make a plan, Shadow.*   Obie squatted down to think.   *Make up time . . . ride faster on Old Path . . . meet queen's horse soldiers . . . eat while riding.*   He got up and started to saddle Shadow when he heard a yell and a roar coming from the direction the lion-man had taken.   *What now?*

Annoyed at the further delay, he limped hurriedly through the trees towards the commotion.   When he circled the wide girth of an oak tree, he found the lion-man on the other side.   He was upside down and ten feet off the ground, hanging from a tree.   A rope, which appeared to originate from somewhere high in the tree, was looped around his feet. He had been swooped into some long-forgotten hunter's trap. On the ground below lay his sword and knife, where they had fallen when he was ripped off his feet. The lion-man saw Obie coming and folded his arms across his chest.

This moment was sweet, so sweet, in fact, that Obie wanted to savor it. Grinning, he walked around the dangling body.

"Well?" the lion-man snapped.

Scrunching his face up, Obie roared, simultaneously raising his arms and wriggling his curled fingers in a clawing gesture at the lion-man. "Phsssst, phsssst," he said, slapping the air like a house cat and laughing. The lion-man did not look amused as Obie continued his taunting.

"You were saying, O Wise One?"

The lion-man's nostrils flared as he glared at Obie.

"Hrrrmmmph. How about less fooling around, boy, and more action. Cut me down or so help me I'll . . ."

"All right. Hang on a minute. No sense of humor," Obie muttered. Leaping up, he grabbed a branch to pull himself into the tree. Then he froze. Something large and black was moving through the trees towards the lion-man. Obie could hear the blood pumping fast in his ears. He dropped to the ground and loaded his Raptor.

"Hey, stupid! Over here. Hey, puke-breath, I'm over here." Obie waved vigorously at the rak soldier, trying to draw him away from the lion-man. Even though this was not the rak that had attacked him at the festival, having a score to settle stoked his courage.

Hissing and waving his black hairy arms in the air, the rak turned towards Obie. An instant later, he drew two swords and scraped the blades together in a sharpening motion while his deadly beak clicked open and shut repeatedly. He lunged forward and Obie shot him just above his armor, in the soft spot between his neck and chest. Green blood spurted from the wound.

"Arrrghh," the rak choked out, stopped only momentarily. Then he came after Obie with a vengeance, chasing him in a circle and grabbing at him with his four free arms.

"Stupid human boy, I'll get you. Stand still," he gurgled. He lunged again, but Obie leaped aside and shot him in the head. The spider fell back, his six long, hairy arms quivering in pain. Maddened, his eyes turned bright yellow. He hissed and sprang. Mid-air, Obie shot him in the eye and jumped aside, barely escaping. The raging spider spun around and was nearly on top of him when Obie drew his sword. But the last shot had done its job, and the rak fell in a crumpled heap at Obie's feet. It writhed for a few seconds and then lay still.

The lion-man made a low, throaty chuckle. "Well done, boy. Now hurry and cut me down. That sorry bag of rat dung might have friends on the way."

Pulling himself into the tree, Obie crawled out on the limb, sliced through the rope with his sword and watched the creature hit the ground with a thud. When Obie dropped down, the lion-man was rubbing the knot forming on top of his head. The creature got to his feet and retrieved his weapons. He prodded the spider-man with the tip of his sword. He lay motionless. "This brute is wolf meat. Uggghh, there's nothing worse than an uppity spider." Then the lion-man tossed his weapons and his rabbits aside and glared at Obie from beneath his lowered brow. "And now there's another matter," he growled.

The gleam in the lion-man's eyes caused something to snap in Obie's mind, and he had an overwhelming desire to punch the creature in the face. He knew his opponent was bigger, but his blood was boiling now. He'd do at least a little damage before it was over. He unbuckled his sword and tossed it aside with his Raptor and cloak, and stood facing his challenger.

"It's time you learn respect, boy," the lion-man growled. Crouching in attack mode, he retracted his claws and leaped at Obie, knocking him to the ground.

They rolled over and over like a spindle. Obie had the lion-man in a headlock; then the lion-man threw Obie over and twisted his arm behind him; Obie kicked the lion-man in the shin and when he grabbed his leg in pain, Obie twisted his other leg. The lion-man got Obie in a headlock, forcing him to release his leg, but Obie punched him hard in the stomach and his opponent let go. They both jumped up. Hunching down a few inches, the lion-man stood face to face with the youth. Fire burned in their eyes as they glared at each other. Obie butted his opponent's head, but it hurt him more than it hurt the lion-man and he fell back slightly dazed. Then the lion-man reached his two paw-hands out and grabbed his young opponent under his arms, lifted him off the ground and flopped him back and forth like a rag doll. Obie kicked and flailed until his face turned scarlet, and the lion-man burst into laughter.

Realizing how ridiculous he must appear, Obie started laughing too. The lion-man shook so hard with laughter that he dropped Obie to the ground and sank down beside him.

"You're a sorry sight, boy, ahhh hah hah, hanging around the, yahhh hah hah, way you do, ahhh hah hah. You looked, yahhh hah hah, pretty silly." The lion-man was doubled over with tears streaming down his furry face.

"Yeah?" Arms wrapped around his stomach, Obie was bouncing up and down laughing. "Well, you're better looking upside down," he managed to get out before bursting into another fit of laughter. Leaning forward and extending his forefinger, he pushed the lion-man over on his side where he lay bouncing in mirth. Finally they quieted. Obie expelled a deep sigh and wiped his tear-streaked cheeks.

The lion-man sat up and looked at Obie. "I am called Tau."

"I'm Oberon Griffin, but 'Obie' for short." Grinning, he extended his hand. Tau stared quizzically at Obie's hand and then hesitatingly extended his own.

"This is the way my people greet one another." Taking hold of Tau's hand, that felt more like a big paw, Obie shook it.

They got up and retrieved their weapons. Obie was anxious to be on his way as time was precious. He hoped Shadow could track the raks if they were out of range. But he needed to get some information from Tau. Maybe he'd seen Gabrielle and Mara. "I'm on business for Queen Olwen of Windermere," he offered, trying to draw Tau into conversation. "I'm chasing a group of raks, have you seen them?"

Tau seemed uncomfortable. "So that is it," he said, not answering the question.

Obie could tell he knew something. He had to find out *what*.

"I require food," Tau said, "and the rumblings from your stomach tell me you also do. When did you last eat?"

"Yesterday."

"We will eat and talk. I will share these with you." He held up the rabbits.

"Thanks for the offer, but I don't eat raw rabbit and I don't have time to wait while they cook."

"I can eat them either way, and I know how to cook them quickly if you wish. We shall eat, and then I will show you a short cut that will enable you to catch up with the raks."

"You're on." The offer lifted Obie's spirits. It meant he was still in the game. They returned to the tree next to the stream where Shadow was nibbling a patch of grass near the water's edge.

Tau instructed Obie to fetch three large, smooth rocks from the shoreline and build a fire around them. A small fire built beneath the branches of the great oak tree during the day was safe enough, as it would not be seen by any of Torolf's winged messengers that might pass over the forest. After getting the rocks and setting them in place, Obie found some dry wood and tinder nearby and laid it around them, then scraped his utility knife against the rock he carried in his ammo pouch and kindled the fire. Meanwhile, Tau skinned the rabbits and sliced the meat for fast cooking. He laid the rabbit parts on the heated rocks and sat down cross-legged, turning them as needed with the tip of his sword. While the rabbit cooked Obie saddled Shadow.

I'm glad this lion-man returned with you because I can no longer feel the vibrations of the raks or the queen's soldiers, and I will have difficulty trying to follow them, Shadow said as Obie fastened the girth strap. *Do you think he can help us?*

I'm counting on it. He's going to show us a shortcut to catch up with the raks. We'll be on our way soon. When he had Shadow ready to go, he took bread from the saddlebag and joined Tau by the fire.

The rabbit was done. Tau skewered the sizzling pieces with his sword and pulled them from the fire, piling them on another smooth stone Obie had brought from the stream's edge to serve as a platter. Obie pulled the bread apart and handed half to Tau. While they ate, Tau asked why he was chasing the raks. Obie hesitated, unsure how much he should tell. Yet, something told him this creature was trustworthy. After all, he'd rescued him and Shadow from the spider webs. That rak soldier he'd just encountered must have been on his way back to check the webs. He told Tau about the rak raid on the festival in Windermere and the abduction of Gabrielle and the windlord, Mara, and how he was trying to help rescue them. He held off telling him that Gabrielle and Mara were the Moonpath Riders.

"Do you know who King Torolf is?" Obie asked.

Tau's eyes flashed with anger. "Shhhh, speak quietly of him in this forest—his spies could be listening." While he spoke, Tau's eyes scanned the tree branches around them.

Obie lowered his voice to a whisper. "Who are his spies?"

"Be wary of crows, vultures, and hawks. Though not all of their kind serves him, you can usually tell which do by observing them. If one appears to be listening, it likely is. And there is something else you should know. You have seen the half-man, half-spider creatures of Torolf's creation that he calls *raks,* but have you seen the half-man, half-ant creatures he has named muks?"

Obie's mouth dropped open. "No . . . and I don't think I'm looking forward to it, either."

"Then I must warn you to keep your eyes open for them along the way. They are powerful warriors." Tau began licking the fur of his paw-hands clean of all trace of rabbit.

"I will." Obie's eyes darted from tree to tree, and when he was satisfied they were alone he quietly said, "I'm guessing Torolf is responsible for the abduction."

Tau stopped washing and gave Obie a hard look. "A good guess," he said sarcastically, lowering his paw-hand. "So you, all by yourself, are going to rescue the girl and the windlord from the black sorcerer king? He whose power is so great that he may be robbing the heavens of its lights?"

"Not exactly." Obie was nettled by his tone. "I've been waiting for Queen Olwen's horse soldiers to catch up with me. I've marked the trail for them. They must have already passed by on the Old Path, though. They'll probably beat me to the raks."

Frowning, Tau gazed into the fire and changed the subject. "I saw the marks you made on the trees, and so did two rak scouts. They tracked you for a long time, but you were fortunate. For some reason, they returned to their camp just before catching up with you."

Obie grimaced at the revelation. "Okay, so you did see them."

"Yes, they broke camp before dawn. I watched them move out and pursued them until they started following the River Weir that flows down from Lake Auber in the north. It was predictable. They have a poor sense of direction in the forest and prefer to follow main waterways or paths. As to the Windermerian soldiers, I can say nothing."

"And here I sit, not even knowing if the queen's soldiers are still on the trail." Obie got up. "I have to get going. What about the short-cut you mentioned?"

"From the place the raks started following the Weir the river veers northwestward in a great arc before straightening out and flowing due north again. Following the river creates extra leagues for the raks to travel. You can head them off if you cut across the arc the river makes. Also, their supply wagons will slow them some. You should reach the Weir again a half-day ahead of them, at the place called "Two Rivers," where the River Weir flows close to the waters of Witch River. How is your sense of direction?"

"Pretty good if I have some landmarks to go by."

"In this forest, as you have seen, there is nothing but endless trees, and each looks like the other. Without the Old Path to follow you will easily become disoriented and lost. I will go with you and show you the way. My sense of direction is keen, and should they leave the river I can follow their scent trail. Better yet," Tau's eyes flashed, "I know where they're going."

"You *know* where they're going?" A surge of excitement shot through Obie.

"Yes. Keep your voice down," he cautioned again as he glanced around, then quietly continued, "Yesterday when I followed the two scouts who were tracking you, I overheard them talking. One of them said their captain was anxious to get the human female and the windlord to the Necromancer. That is the name the goblins and others use for Torolf because they believe he communicates with the dead. You guessed rightly. The raks are taking their captives to him. They are going to his stronghold in Targus Dol, called *The Serpent's Tower*."

Shadow nickered and kicked the ground sharply with a front hoof.

"Targus Dol," Obie repeated, glancing at Shadow nervously.

"The tower is a dark and dangerous place with many winding passageways and caverns beneath it that house loathsome creatures. I hope we will not have to go that far, for even the land there festers as if infected with some leprous disease."

Obie's skin prickled. "How far is it?"

Tau thought for a moment. "Under cover of the forest it could take fifteen days."

"The queen's horse soldiers should rescue Gabrielle and Mara long before the raks reach Targus Dol," Obie said.

Abruptly, Tau stood up and started scooping dirt over the fire. "We should go now."

Obie nodded and pitched in. After erasing all signs of the fire he mounted Shadow and Tau swung up behind him.

"We will first take the Old Path to where it crosses the Weir," Tau said. Shadow headed through the trees towards the path.

"Thanks for helping," Obie said.

"I have my own reasons for helping you," Tau said quietly. Obie took mental note of the comment, but said nothing. He'd wait until Tau was ready to talk about it.

The ride up the Old Path to the Weir was not far. After crossing the wooden bridge, they spotted hoof prints and wheel marks from the supply wagons where the raks turned off the path to follow the river. "We will follow in their tracks until the river turns, and then we will cut across country. From here I will no longer burden your horse with my added weight as I prefer to run." Tau dismounted and bounded ahead while Obie followed on Shadow.

Minutes later, Tau stopped and stared towards a thorn bush. Obie saw it too. He dismounted and carefully removed the piece of light blue fabric from a thorny branch. "It's from Gabrielle's dress," he said, frowning down at it. Tau acknowledged with a low grunt. Obie put it in his ammo pouch and they moved on.

Before midday they reached the place where the stream began its journey northwest in the great arc around a slow rise in the land. Tau stopped and, with a troubled look, inspected the ground off to his right.

Obie dismounted. "What is it?" he said joining Tau.

"The raks split up here. Many set off to the east with the wagons, and a smaller group, unencumbered by wagons, continued along the river. Wait." Tau ran upstream and returned minutes later. "I have picked up the scent of the human female and the windlord. Just as I thought, they are with the faster group following the river." Obie read the frown on Tau's face to mean they might not beat the raks to the Two Rivers area with as much time to spare as he'd thought. "We cut across country from here," Tau said.

"How long will it take to catch up with the raks?"

"Three days."

Unable to bear watching Tau loping easily ahead while he rode, Obie took up running behind the lion-man. Bringing up the rear, Shadow did not appear entirely unhappy with the new arrangement. At first Obie's limp was troublesome, making it difficult to keep up with his furry companion; but soon the stiffness in his leg began to diminish until his limp finally disappeared. In days to come, this would continue to be the case whenever Obie ran. And although he would not understand what caused the improvement, he would have no complaints.

CHAPTER ELEVEN

BAD NEWS

GNARLWOOD FOREST continued to be a silent expanse of endless trees fading off in the gloomy distance, a place where little or no vegetation grew. Only where they encountered an occasional brook or stream that forced apart the dense forest canopy was sunlight able to reach the ground enabling ferns, grass, climbing vines, and flowers to grow. In normal times the flora thrived in such places, but in these days of dim sunlight, plant life was noticeably subdued. Yet, in the damp places beneath the trees, moss, mushrooms, and other plants requiring little light still flourished.

In late morning they came to such a place, and Obie spotted ivory colored mushrooms growing in the shade of a tree beside a brook. Tau warned him not to eat them but, thinking they were like the mushrooms he'd eaten at home, he tossed one in his mouth anyway. Tau leaped at him and slapped his back so hard the mushroom flew from his mouth. The blow knocked the wind out of Obie and he hunched over gasping for air until his lungs began to work again.

"When I tell you something it is for a reason," Tau scolded. "These mushrooms cause madness in those who eat them—and there are worse things in this wood."

Tau had made his point. "All right, next time I'll listen."

They followed the stream and in the early afternoon approached a meadow where they stopped for a brief rest just within the shadows of the trees. While there, Obie spotted an eagle flying high in the sky. Hoping it was Prince Andor looking for them, he hurried into the meadow waving his arms. But apparently the eagle did not see him, for it passed by and flew out of sight.

That night they camped along the stream in an open place under the black sky. They ate the last of the bread, some of the cheese Obie brought, and a few wild blackberries they had found growing nearby. When the air grew cooler Obie wrapped up in his cloak and settled back to rest. The forest was quiet except for the sound of water flowing over rocks. Tau had seemed withdrawn tonight, but after a while he began talking in a low voice.

"There is ill news I must tell you."

His muscles tensing, Obie turned to meet the gaze of Tau's yellow-green eyes glowing through the darkness. "What is it?" he asked softly, fearing what would come next.

"You have been waiting for the soldiers of the queen, but they will not come."

"Why? How do you know that?" Obie said angrily.

"They were following the raks, but, unluckily for them, they did not catch up with them before nightfall. They made camp under the trees. I had been watching the spider camp and did not know about the man soldiers pursuing them. If I had, I would have tried to warn them."

Obie felt a hot jolt in the pit of his stomach.

"Most of the raks crept silently out of their camp during the wee hours of the morning. I followed to see what they were up to. The queen's soldiers were sleeping and their guards could not see into the dark branches overhead. Perhaps they did not expect an attack from above. There was no time for me to help them. The raks dropped swiftly from the trees over the camp of men. They had no chance. It ended quickly. I am sorry, Oberon."

"We have to go back." Obie jumped up. "Maybe some of the men are still alive."

Tau sat up. "I wish it were so. When the raks left I went to check, but none were alive. The raks are swift and deadly when they drop from the trees at night, and they were hungry for meat. It would be better if you did not see it. The forest will quickly claim what little remains of the men."

Obie stumbled to the stream and dropped to his knees, craning his neck over the water. Tau watched, frequently glancing up at the nearby treetops. Obie retched until there was nothing left to bring up. Afterwards, he splashed the cold water on his face and in his mouth. He returned and lay silently on his back, his eyes red and swollen. After a long while, he quietly asked, "Why didn't you tell me before now?"

"I did not tell you this morning because I thought it best to get you away from there. Also, you needed food to keep up your strength and I guessed you would have no appetite after hearing of the attack."

"You should have told me anyway."

Tau turned his eyes away and did not respond. Obie tried pushing the thought from his mind that Ull might have been among the horse soldiers. But it wasn't just Ull. He had become friends with many of the men.

"I saw the girl Gabrielle and the windlord in the rak soldier's camp," Tau said after several minutes.

"You did? When?" Obie bolted to a sitting position.

"Early this morning just after the raks left to attack. Only a few soldiers remained and the captives were being held near the center of the camp. I saw them only briefly as I was hurrying to follow the raks."

"How did they look?"

"Not happy, but I saw no physical harm."

Obie heaved a sigh as he lay back down. He felt exhausted. Shadow's soft nose touched his forehead. *This is encouraging news about Gabrielle and Mara, Oberon. But I'm sorry about the queen's soldiers. I can feel your grief.*

Thanks, Shadow. He reached up and put his hand on the dark stallion's muzzle. As Obie was dozing off, the pale moon climbed into view overhead in the slate black sky and he was aware that it was full. He knew the full moon was important, but in his deep state of drowsiness he couldn't remember why. An instant later he sank into restless sleep.

They rose early and set out again at first light, running all through the morning hours with little rest. Obie seemed to be operating on sheer adrenalin. Around midday they stopped and Obie again made a small fire beneath an oak tree while Tau fished for their meal. He had already caught two large brook trout when Obie joined him with his Raptor.

"Shhhh," Tau whispered, "and don't cast your shadow over the fish or it will dart away." Then, lightning fast, Tau slapped his paw-hand into the water and knocked the fish onto the bank.

"Three. Not bad," Obie said unenthusiastically. Adjusting his Raptor on his arm, he moved quietly down the stream a few yards where he could see the dark outlines of several fish next to a mossy rock jutting out from the bank. Kneeling down, he took aim and shot. A moment later a speckled fish floated to the surface and turned on its silvery side. As Obie reached for it Tau came up behind.

"Hmmmm," Tau said, "it seems your weapon has several uses."

"Yeah, this works sometimes," Obie answered half-heartedly.

The four fish roasted quickly. Tau rationed out one apiece for the meal, reserving the other two for that night.

His thoughts far away, Obie picked disinterestedly at his food. After a time he said, "I'm still going after Gabrielle and Mara, even if it means going all the way to Targus Dol."

Tau looked up from the fish he was chewing on and set it down. "I know. And I have not changed my mind about going with you."

"Thanks."

"The raks may believe they are no longer being pursued. That is good for us. But still, they will have scouts out. We must always watch the trees for attack from above."

Obie nodded and took a small bite as his appetite started to return. They ate in silence. By the time Obie swallowed the last morsel Tau was busy washing himself.

"Tau?"

"Yes?" He spread his fingers apart to lick in between.

"When we catch up with the raks I think we should sneak into their camp while they're sleeping and free Gabrielle and Mara. Once we remove the straps from Mara's wings they can just fly away."

Tau stopped washing. "An adequate plan. We'll watch and wait for our chance. How well can you use that fancy sword of yours?"

"Well enough to fight off some raks, I think."

"Good, because we may have to fight our way out of their camp."

Shadow stopped nibbling grass. *I admire your courage, Obie.*

Thanks, Shadow, but I wouldn't exactly call it "courage." I'm running on anger—that and fear for Gabrielle and Mara.

Anger and fear are strong motivators. Courage often comes from those strong emotions. I see that in you.

Obie noticed Tau's eyes darting back and forth between him and Shadow, and turned a questioning look at him.

Tau responded with a knowing smile. "You and Shadow share the gift of mental speech."

"Finally caught, huh? Are we that obvious?"

"I have watched the two of you talking before and guessed it by your facial expressions. Shadow is not so obvious, but the fact that you reveal yourself so easily tells me you are not very experienced at it."

"You're right. I only recently discovered I had the gift."

"It is good that you do, for it may prove useful to us. But you should work at not giving yourself away."

They pressed on for the rest of that day and the night passed quietly. When they set out again at dawn on the third day, Obie's excitement level was high. They were nearing the Weir and soon they would rescue Gabrielle and Mara. They ran all day until darkness stopped them, and when they lay down to rest that night, Tau estimated the River Weir was no more than three hours away and they should reach it by mid morning. They would wait at the Weir for the raks to arrive, sometime in the afternoon, and then they would follow them until they made camp. While the rak soldiers slept, they would carry out their plan.

Obie's mind was filled with thoughts of Gabrielle as he lay awake, unable to sleep. When he saw Tau's eyes piercing the darkness, he asked in a low voice, "Can't sleep either?"

"No."

Obie had wondered what Tau's life had been like and where he came from. Now seemed like a good time to ask him. "Tau," he whispered, propping up on an elbow, "have you always lived in Gnarlwood Forest?"

"No, I have not been here long, only a few months." He remained silent for a time and Obie was about to lie back down when Tau said in a quiet voice, "This man body I live in is foreign to me, but I have learned to make the most of it. Torolf used his black sorcery to turn me into this half-lion, half-man creature to serve his purposes."

"I've wondered whether you had been a man or a lion to begin with. I'm sorry. It must be hard."

"Hard? Yes. So much has happened since I was a cub roaming freely in the grasslands and jungles of my homeland. I sometimes dream of that place across the Great Eastern Sea, and of the pride I once belonged to." Tau sighed, and continued, "It is good to have someone to listen." He lay back, apparently collecting his thoughts for a few moments, and then began again.

"I remember the day my mother taught my siblings and me to hunt. I can still smell the sweet morning air as the sun began its journey over that great grassy plain. It was exciting to run with her and the other females pursuing the antelope. Among lions it is the females who hunt for the pride and teach the cubs, though my father waited in the background ready to help if the females called. There were many mornings like that. It was the happiest time of my life. Then one day goblin raiders came.

"Their people prize my kind and many take young cubs for pets. We are a status symbol and bring a high price among them. My siblings and I were taken and my mother was killed trying to protect us. I do not know my father's fate, or what happened to my siblings, as we were separated. In a far off market place I was sold to a goblin family. I grew up with them."

"You lived with goblins?" Obie asked in a startled whisper. "What are they like?"

"They are noisy and quarrelsome creatures, yet they treated me well. It was they who named me *Tau*. It means *lion*. You would be unable to pronounce the name my mother gave me. My goblin family often took me out with them, walking me at the end of a chain. I hated the chain. All of my kind, large or small, hate it. But it was goblin law that lions must be chained in public, so I tolerated it though it was difficult. A little more than a year ago I went with them to the auction to see the new shipment of lion cubs. As it happened, King Torolf also attended that auction. His appearance was dreadful. His eyes burned from beneath the hood of his black and golden cloak, and he was surrounded by black troll guards. When he passed by, the goblins trembled in fear and shrank back. He was not looking for cubs. When he laid eyes on me, now full grown, he told my goblin family he wished to purchase me. I knew they did not wish to sell me, but they had no choice, for they feared the Necromancer. So I was sold and sent to Targus Dol by way of a goblin caravan over sea and land."

"Did he want you for a pet?"

"No, Torolf had decided he wanted lions for his personal guards instead of trolls. I was one of many he purchased, and they became my new brothers. But Torolf could not bend us to his will, though he tried for a time. Finally he cast spells changing us into lion-man creatures. The spell enables him to control our minds. It is the same spell he uses on spiders and ants. That is how he is building his army, an army of highly formidable creatures, half-man, half-spider or ant. It is already in the blood of muks to blindly follow orders, and they will kill for that reason. The raks are different. They enjoy killing. But Torolf under-estimated the heart of this lion." As if remembering, Tau's nostrils flared and his eyes glowed angrily.

"Even under his black spell I resisted surrendering my mind to him. But he did not know this. I was submissive and pre-tended to be under his control while I awaited my chance to escape. When he flew away one night on his great black hawk, I ran off. Since that time I have wandered the southern forests alone while my brothers still serve as the Necromancer's guards."

"And that's why you're helping me . . . because of what Torolf did to you and other lions?"

"Yes. I would gladly give my life fighting his evil. My brothers and I wish to be free of his spell, but I do not know if that is possible."

Looking into Tau's pain-ridden eyes Obie felt a growing admiration for him. "Thanks for sharing that with me, Tau. I'm glad we've teamed up." Obie hesitated a moment, then added, "Now, it's my turn to share something with you."

"Yes?"

"It's about Gabrielle and Mara. They're the Moonpath Riders. Have you heard of them?"

"Yes, I have heard the Moonpath Riders guard two crystals of power. But I know little more than that."

"They might be able to help stop the Celestial Dimming. That's the main reason we have to get them back."

"If that is true, and if Torolf is causing the lights of the heavens to fade, then he would indeed want them. The Moonpath Riders must be rescued." Obie could hear the controlled excitement in Tau's voice, as if new hope had awakened in him. They talked a while longer and then Tau suggested they get some sleep for they would be leaving before dawn and moving fast.

The next morning they set out immediately upon awakening. Before long the forest floor began a long and steady rise northward. In mid-morning they stopped to rest under the trees at the edge of a large meadow. "We have reached the Two Rivers area," Tau announced. "I can smell the waters of the River Weir and Witch River, for each has its own fragrance. After we rest we will go to the Weir. It is very close."

"At last," Obie said. Barely able to contain himself, he sank down in the grass. *Control, got to control myself. Just rest for a few minutes and try to relax. We're almost there, Gabrielle. Hold on, girl. You and Mara won't be captives much longer.*

Lying on his back in the grass, Obie's eyes were drawn to the pale specter-like sun floating westward in the gray-green sky. Though not a welcome sight, after the long, gloomy days beneath the trees it was good to see the sky again—even if it wasn't the right color. His eyes caught movement high up and he scrambled to his feet.

"Tau, there's a large bird flying by. I'm sure it's an eagle. It may be searching for me." Knowing it was risky, Obie ran into the meadow waving his arms with Shadow trotting behind. But like before, the bird had already passed overhead and continued on. Was it Prince Andor? Obie stared after it, disappointed at not getting its attention. But he had gotten the *full* attention of a large cavalry patrol of muk soldiers now bursting from the trees on the far side of the meadow and heading straight towards him. The soldiers were more like huge upright insects than humans. As their horses thundered forward the muk soldiers made a loud hissing sound. Their drawn scimitars and metal breastplates flashed dimly in the thin daylight, and their leader bore two curved horns atop his helm.

"Tau," Obie yelled again.

"I feared this," he hollered as he ran towards Obie and Shadow.

Oberon, I think we should be going now, Shadow nervously said.

Righto. Obie grabbed the pommel with one hand and threw himself onto the saddle. Upon reaching them, Tau took Obie's arm and swung up behind him. They rode back towards the forest, but more muk cavalrymen came through the trees, cutting off their retreat. Shadow wheeled around and headed east over the meadow with their pursuers not far behind.

Tau glanced over his shoulder. "They're gaining on us."

Obie darted a look back. "We can't outrun them—our weight's slowing Shadow.

"If they send any arrows our way, dodge them as best you can—Muks often use poison on their arrow tips."

"Awesome."

Shadow came to a sliding halt at the brink of a deep chasm and the two riders jumped down. Obie took a quick glimpse over the edge and saw a river flowing at the bottom. "Shadow, run for it!"

No. I'll stay with you, Oberon.

"No. Go, go, go! We'll catch up with you later." The dark stallion shot off to the right along the cliff edge and several muks veered away from the main patrol in pursuit. One glance at the flashing cold steel of the scimitars the muks were waving was enough for Obie. Like one who'd rather jump from a burning building than be charred to death, Obie decided he'd rather take his chances with the river than be hacked to pieces by the muks.

"Tau, c'mon!"

Tau's jaw dropped in a look of disbelief as he watched Obie charge towards the advancing muks. Then Obie turned and streaked back towards the cliff's edge, gathering speed. When he passed Tau he threw him an anxious look. "C'mon," he yelled, motioning towards the chasm. The menacing horde was almost upon them. The big muk leader shrieked a high-pitched death cry, leaned to the side of his warhorse, and lowered his head until the two long horns of his helm pointed directly at Tau's chest. Without further ado, Tau turned and made a running leap off the cliff behind Obie.

"Aaaahhhh," Tau bellowed, his arms and legs flailing in mid-air.

The river was far below—too far, Obie realized. Leaping from the cliff had bought them only a few more precious seconds of life. The world around him went briefly into slow motion. *Gabrielle, Gabrielle.* His heart grieved for all that might have been and all that was now lost.

At the chasm edge, the muks laughed and hooted as the pair began their death plunge. Then from seemingly nowhere, Obie heard the sound of wind beating beneath great wings and felt large talons close around his body. Looking up, he saw the underside of a great brown and black eagle that had swooped down and caught him. Then he heard Tau laughing and knew his friend was riding on the eagle's back. Muk bows zipped into action sending black-tipped arrows at the threesome. Andor took evasive action, tipping his body from side to side, but an arrow found its target in his left wing. Poison on the arrow tip worked an instant paralysis so that, able to move but one wing, the eagle prince spiraled slowly down, down towards the treacherous river with Obie dangling below and Tau hanging on for dear life.

CHAPTER TWELVE

WITCH RIVER

THE RUSHING CURRENT pushed and spun them around mercilessly. Obie tried to grab hold of something, anything, but the torrent was too strong and the vertical rock too slippery to grasp. He heard a roaring above the sound of the river and seconds later his body was jerked sideways and around. In horror he realized he was being pulled down the funnel of a giant whirlpool. The others spun helplessly below, moving farther and farther downward until Andor, and then Tau disappeared into the seething bottom of the maelstrom. Were they crushed? He'd soon find out. Lower and lower he descended towards the churning froth. He shut his eyes and braced himself as he, too, was sucked into the bottom. The weight of the water pressed hard against every inch of his body and he knew he was about to be crushed. Then the torrent released him into a strong current and he felt a spark of hope. Dragged along underwater, he held his breath until it felt like his lungs would explode. When he could stand it no longer he breathed in and the cold water surged into his lungs. Everything went black.

***

Obie opened his eyes and realized he wasn't dead. He was in a subterranean cavern with shimmering blue-green walls illuminated by flickering torchlight. Someone had laid him on a grass pallet and covered him with a blanket. He tried moving his fingers and toes and was relieved to find they still worked and he was in once piece, just bruised and achy. Raising his head a little, he was glad to see Tau's big furry feet sticking out of a blanket. He lay on a pallet nearby with a bandage around his head. One of his ankles was manacled and chained to the rock wall. Startled, Obie lifted his left leg. He felt the weight of the manacle around his ankle and heard the clank of a chain. So they were prisoners. Lifting his blanket, he also discovered he was naked. "Great." Too groggy to deal with it now, he laid his head down with a groan and drifted back to sleep. Sometime later he was awakened by a long, skinny finger prodding his cheek. A bald, nervous little gnome-like creature, approximately three and a half feet tall with large eyes, stood over him. Though his skin was flesh-colored, patches of iridescent blue-green scales grew below his cheekbones and were visible on his chest at the opening of his sea-green velvet jacket. If they existed elsewhere on his body they were covered by his jacket, pale-green leggings, and maroon booties. When he opened his mouth to speak Obie noticed small, widely spaced teeth.

"Dear me, dear me, the human boy is finally awake, yes he is." The creature spoke in a high-pitched voice and kept shifting his weight from one foot to the other, rocking his body and fidgeting with his hands. "You have slept long, yes long, I can assure you, since yesterday when you and the other one, and Prince Andor were pulled from the water."

"The water?" Obie was still in a fog. "Ohhhh, yeah, I remember . . . we were caught in a whirlpool in the river."

"Yes, yes." The creature clapped his hands together and jumped up and down. "*Witch River* is its name. Yes indeed, that is its name, and it belongs to Zelda, the River Witch. She brought you to her grotto, she did, yes she did. The meenie weavers saw you float to the top of her pool and they pulled you out." He grew increasingly excited as he spoke, causing him to rock even faster on his feet.

"What are the *meenie weavers*? And who and what are you?" Obie rose up on his elbows. "Hey! Would you slow down a minute, you're making me dizzy. Why'd you chain us to the wall? And what'd you do with my clothes?"

The creature jumped back in alarm at Obie's outburst and stood very still. "Too many questions, yes, too many questions. And you are rude, too, yes, yes very rude. But, I am a polite host, yes, yes I am." He began to rock again, but more slowly. "So I will tell you. I am a river sprite and a servant of Zelda, yes, Zelda's happy servant."

"Okay. Sorry I was rude. What about the meenie weavers?"

"They are fearsome creatures, yes, fearsome they are, and they help to guard these caverns." The river sprite stopped moving again and leaned close, his eyes narrowed. "And you would not want to incur their wrath . . . no you would not."

"Got it. Don't incur the meenie weavers' wrath." Obie was annoyed at feeling bullied. "How about my clothes?"

The river sprite resumed rocking and pointed across the cavern. "Your clothing is over there. They were wet and stunk, yes, so we cleaned them, we did."

"May I please have them?"

"No. No clothing for you, not yet, not yet." Once again, the river sprite grew still and a stern look came onto his face. "We chained you to the wall we did, yes, because we are friends of the eagles, yes we are. And we think you and the beast over there may have shot Prince Andor with the poison arrow. Yes indeed, that is what we think."

Obie's face melted into concern as the memory of events returned. "How . . . how is Prince Andor? Is he okay?"

"We know not. We are tending his wound as best we can, as best we can, but it is difficult even for Zelda. As you should know, the poison is very strong, yes very strong, and runs deep in his body. Most would be dead by now, yes very, very dead."

Obie wondered if there was a difference between being *merely* dead and being *very, very* dead.

"Maybe by tomorrow we will know, maybe we will know if he will live or he will die. His fever draws near the crisis point, it does. If he dies, it may go badly for you and the other one; yes, it may go very, very badly."

"I'd like to see him. He's a friend," Obie protested.

"You claim he is a friend, yes you do. But we do not know that, most assuredly, we do not. I must ask Zelda, yes. I must ask if she will allow you to see the prince."

Obie started to feel dizzy and lay back down.

"I will go now, yes I will, for the healing herbs we gave you are still pulling you into sleep, into sleep. Rest and we will speak again, oh yes, we will." He wheeled round, scowled at Tau, and darted out.

Awakened by the conversation, Tau sat up with a cranky look on his face. A good sign, Obie thought. He couldn't be ailing too much. "Tau, my furry friend. I'm glad you weren't crushed in the whirlpool."

"Not half as glad as I."

"How are you feeling?"

"I could have slept more if that river sprite had not chattered so much."

"Yeah, he's a hyper little guy." Obie's eyelids drooped and his speech slowed. "We need to get out of here tonight, Tau. Gotta catch up with the raks."

"We will go soon. Leave it to me."

That's the ole spirit, Tau. We'll just rip these chains out of the walls and be on our way. Sleep overtook Obie, but he was soon awakened to the sounds of clanking metal and breaking rock. Tau had ripped his chain from the wall and, eyes ablaze, dragged it behind him as he approached. He took hold of Obie's chain and stood over him with one foot braced against the wall. In the blink of an eye, rock and iron exploded from the wall as the chain wrenched free.

"I cannot abide chains," Tau said in a low voice.

Obie let out a muffled hoot of joy. "May I never doubt you, Tau. You da lion-man."

Tau's great nostrils flared in acknowledgment of that fact.

Grinning, Obie sat up and held his palm out. "Here, gimme five."

"Five?"

"It's a custom we have back home when you greet a friend you haven't seen in a while, or when you're sharing some kind of victory, like now. You're supposed to slap your hand, er, paw across mine."

"Okay, I give you five." Tau smacked his paw-hand across Obie's palm. Obie's hand smarted a bit afterwards, but it was worth the moment of camaraderie they shared. Tau glanced towards the cavern entrance. "We must go."

They began to dress, but were unable to slip their pant legs on over the manacles at their ankles. Obie spotted a key on the wall near the door and tried it. In moments the manacles came off and they pulled their pants on. The elation Obie felt at being free faded somethat as he reflected, "We've lost our weapons."

"We will find new ones."

Knowing he could never replace Roar or his Raptor, Obie kept silent on the issue. He fastened his cloak at the neck and glanced at Tau. "I want to find Prince Andor before we leave. He's the eagle who saved us."

Tau nodded. "Yes, I heard you and the river sprite speak of him. We will take a little time to look for the eagle prince. We owe him that much and more."

They crept out into a winding tunnel. Here, too, the walls shimmered in the torchlight in shades of blue and green. Moving stealthily through the passageways they made quick searches of the empty caverns they passed. They had to keep a sharp eye and dodge several sprites coming down the corridor. They also had to steal past two rooms of busy workers, but the worker sprites seemed well-focused and did not look away from their tasks.

As the two hurried along a passageway streaked with layers of rich green crystals, a golden glow appeared on the outer wall at a curve a little way ahead. Obie saw it first and grabbed Tau's arm. "Wait, something's coming." Each second the glow grew brighter until they began to hear a droning sound.

Exchanging looks of alarm they turned and fled back along the passageway and into a dim cavern they'd passed a few seconds before. Standing motionless with backs pressed against the wall near the entrance, they listened to the approaching sound. The opposite wall of the cavern glowed brighter and brighter as the droning grew louder. Whatever it was passed by, and the light and sound faded when the threat rounded a bend and continued on.

Tau peeked into the passageway. "That was close."

"Shhhh." Obie pointed towards a corridor on the other side of the cavern from whence a small noise was coming. Crossing over, they crept a few steps into the passageway and found the entrance to a second small cavern.

Tau darted a look inside and whispered, "He's here."

Obie took a quick peek. Prince Andor lay unconscious on a pallet within the chamber. A female sprite with long dark hair stood at his side with her back to the entrance. She appeared to be applying medication to his wound while she hummed softly, something Obie was thankful for since it helped mask their whispering.

Jerking back against the tunnel wall he turned a troubled eye to Tau. "Andor doesn't look good."

"I noticed. We must not be here if he dies."

Obie's heart was heavy at the thought of leaving Prince Andor. He'd risked his life to save them. But regardless of how bad he felt, he knew Tau was right. It was urgent for them to move on and he knew Andor would expect them to. The prince could be in no better hands. If he survived, Obie hoped he'd get a chance to thank him.

Tau's eyes were fixed on Obie, awaiting his response. "Okay, let's go." *Andor, my friend, get well*, Obie said mentally as he took one last look.

Retracing their steps, they found a larger passageway that wound upward and appeared promising. The air grew fresher as they ascended. Far behind them a horn sounded and then another and another until it seemed the whole network of subterranean tunnels resounded with the deep pitched calls.

Jolted by fear, Obie's eyes met Tau's. No words were necessary. Tau grunted and bounded ahead at full speed as Obie followed behind with his limping run, the stiffness in his leg not yet worked out. Less than a minute later Tau called over his shoulder, "I think I see a door ahead."

"I hope so because, you know that strange light we saw earlier?"

"Yes?"

"It's coming after us."

Between horn blasts Obie could hear the droning sound. They reached a heavy wooden door at the end of the tunnel.

"Where's the latch?" Tau vigorously ran his hand over the surface of the wood.

"Must be here somewhere," Obie responded. Sweat streamed down the sides of his face and his hands shook as he felt the wall around the door for some way to open it.

The droning grew louder behind them and the door began to glow brightly with reflected light. In a panic they kicked and pounded at the door, but it held fast. Realizing they were caught, they turned to face the menace and were engulfed in golden light. To Obie's surprise it was not a single light, but thousands of small lights swarming round them, a multitude of tiny flying sprites, no larger than bees, with wings that glowed like fire. Calling out excitedly to one another, the sprites loosed long golden strands, flying round and round at dizzying speed, binding Obie and Tau fast with the bright bonds.

"The meenie weavers," Obie said. "These must . . ." His words were cut short when his mouth was covered by the threads. In a matter of seconds the two resembled golden mummies, with only their eyes and nostrils left uncovered. Then the meenie weavers lowered them to the ground and flew away as fast as they had come.

What now? Obie wondered as he lay on the cold tunnel floor. *Are they just going to leave us here?* He could hear Tau struggling against his bindings. *He can't abide restraints—this has to be making him crazy.* Managing to roll himself over on his side, Obie saw Tau's angry eyes glaring out through the eyeholes of his bonds. Then he heard the sounds of many soft-shoed feet pitter-pattering towards them. *I never thought I'd want to be captured, but anything's better than lying here like this.*

The river sprites carried them back down the tunnel to another small cavern and then cut them free. This time they were not chained to the wall, but two guards, three and a half to four feet tall and armed with bows stood watch at the entrance. These younger river sprites were fair of face and had long, brown hair tied with a cord at the nape of their necks. They also had patches of iridescent scales below their cheekbones, and on their chests. Maybe their race had evolved from some underwater creature, Obie thought. Their sleeveless, brown jackets revealed muscular arms, and they wore brown leggings and booties. Except for their high-pitched voices and the fact that they were only three and a half to four feet tall, they might be considered handsome by human standards.

Soon the river sprite Obie had talked with earlier flitted in.

"So, you found the meenie weavers." He stood, hands on his hips, scolding them. "Perhaps you will not be so anxious, no not so anxious, to escape again."

"Please, listen to me," Obie pleaded. "Tau and I are on an urgent mission and Prince Andor was helping us. Time is important, and we're wasting too much of it here."

The river sprite laughed merrily and started rocking and fidgeting again. "Maybe yes and maybe no, too bad I cannot let you go, too bad, too bad."

"How can I convince you?"

"Dear me, dear me, it is Zelda you must convince, yes, yes it is. Otherwise we must wait, yes, must wait, to see if Prince Andor regains consciousness. If you speak the truth he will confirm what you say, yes he will, though that could take time, it could, for even if he lives he may not grow conscious for a while, no, no, he may not."

"Then I have to speak with Zelda. We don't have time to waste."

"As you wish. But I must warn you: you must submit yourself to Zelda's scrutiny, yes oh yes, and that could be perilous to you, yes most perilous indeed."

"How is it perilous?"

"You must take her hand in the water, you must, and allow her to enter your mind. Those who have failed to open themselves to her mind have lost their hand, yes, lost their hand."

Obie cringed at the thought of losing a hand, but if all she wanted was to see into his mind he'd let her. His imperfections wouldn't cause him to lose his hand, only refusing to let her see them would. His voice was shaky as he said, "Okay, I'll submit to her scrutiny."

"He wants to submit, yes he does," the old river sprite said, looking down and rubbing his hands together. When he looked up again Obie thought he saw a hint of sympathy in his old eyes. "I will have nourishing food brought, yes, very nourishing, and when you have eaten, I will take you to Zelda, I will, yes. I am Kort."

"I'm Obie, and my friend's name is Tau."

Kort nodded at his two captives, and then zipped out of the cavern.

Large gourd bowls filled with steaming potato, river leek, and truffle stew were brought in with wooden spoons, acorn bread, and water. Obie and Tau ate hungrily and felt energized almost at once. Soon afterwards, Kort returned and escorted them to Zelda's Grotto. They passed down a narrow tunnel and through two dim caverns with blue rock pools that glowed in the torch-light. Ahead, there was a green glow and, rounding a corner, they stepped into a dazzling cavern. The floor was polished rose quartz, and the rock walls were streaked with layer upon layer of wide emerald veins. The rock surrounding the veins was chiseled back revealing gemstones cut into many facets and polished so that the torchlight played through them like green flames. This, Kort told them, was the gift of the river sprites to Zelda. In the center of the grotto, Zelda's Pool shone with a soft light emanating from somewhere beneath the surface.

Kort motioned for Tau to wait a few yards back. "Only the human youth will approach Zelda, yes, yes." He beckoned Obie to the pool. "You must kneel and look into the water, yes, look into the water."

On hands and knees at the edge of the pool, Obie peered down and saw his own reflection. Within moments, the surface of the water began to tremble, then to bubble and froth, and finally to swirl round and round. He gazed deeply into the water as the swirling slowed and the face of an old, white-haired woman appeared. Her lips moved and she beckoned him closer. Lowering his face near the surface, he listened to the voice that mingled with the sound of flowing water.

"I am Zelda. I am she who is old yet young, she who is ever changing yet unchanged. I am Zelda the River Witch, I am the River. If you dare speak with me you must speak with your heart, otherwise I will not hear and you will suffer greatly. Do you wish to speak to me?"

"Y . . . Yes," Obie said.

"Then take my hand and look into my eyes," Zelda said, extending her hand towards him.

Trembling, Obie reached into the water and took it. He felt a tingling sensation envelope his body, and as he peered deeply into Zelda's eyes he knew a part of him had always known her. Then the hand and face he beheld was that of a lovely young woman with long red hair adorned with water lilies. He easily let her into the secrets of his heart and all that had happened. Finally, she smiled and released his hand.

"I know who you are now, Oberon. I will give you counsel and provisions, and you may continue on your way at first light. Listen carefully to my words. The raks have already passed north along the River Weir, and are too far ahead of you now. If you wish to rescue the Moonpath Riders you must travel to Targus Dol and find a way into the Serpent's Tower, for that is where Gabrielle and Mara will be. Travel north along my river at first. Keep watch for Torolf's soldiers who patrol my banks, and watch the sky for his messengers. In two day's time you will reach the Vale of Nepenthe bordering my waters. Do not enter that place, for evil and mischief lurk within. But when you approach the Vale, look for Mole. He will be nearby. He will prove most valuable to you. A day's journey beyond the Vale, where the river veers east, is an old wooden bridge you must cross. Then go upriver, just beyond the bridge, where you will find a path leading up the cliff wall. Take the path to the top and continue north through the forest. Avoid traveling the Long Wadi Road to the west, for though it is faster, it is heavily traveled by Torolf's soldiers and you would likely be captured. Beware the coming of winter, for it will arrive even before the trees have shed their leaves this year. Already it begins to chill the air. Try to reach the Hundred Valleys Region before winter's icy cloak descends upon you, as you may find help there from the Shadow People. You can trust them. Beyond that region is Targus Dol. Sleep well tonight, and remember: look for Mole."

"But, how will I know him?"

A smile crept over Zelda's face and her voice began to fade. "You will know him," she said as the water churned lightly over her.

"Thank you, Zelda."

Kort knelt next to the pool to receive Zelda's final instructions. When he arose he bowed to Obie. Then he skipped towards the passageway, motioning for Obie and Tau to follow. "I have a surprise for you, yes a surprise. Prince Andor has awakened, has very much awakened, and is asking for you, Obie. He will survive, he will, yes."

Obie was joyous. The eagle prince appeared to be asleep when they entered his chamber, so they waited quietly at his side. After a minute, one of Andor's eyes blinked open, then the other. "Greetings, Obie." His voice was deep and calm. "I'm glad you and your friend survived."

Obie smiled at the prince. "The feeling's mutual, Andor. And we're happy to see you awake. My friend here is Tau."

The eagle and the lion-man exchanged courteous nods.

"For a while there, we weren't sure you were going to make it," Obie said with concern.

The glint of a smile came into Andor's eyes. "I am not an easy bird to kill."

Obie smiled at Andor's toughness. "We saw an eagle fly over the meadow and I hoped it was you, but I didn't think you saw us."

"It was Silverclaw you saw. I passed him from the opposite direction and spotted you fleeing from the muk soldiers. Queen Olwen has learned of Torolf's new creations of muks and raks."

"We've had run-ins with both," Obie said with a sober look. "It was a good thing for us you showed up when you did. The river was a long ways down."

"My thanks to you," Tau added. "Even with your wounded wing, you saved our lives by slowing our fall into the river."

Andor's eyes closed and his voice dropped to a whisper. "Someday you may return the favor." Within moments his eyes opened again and he continued, "There are important matters we must . . ." but his voice trailed off as sleep overtook him.

The attendant whispered to Obie and Tau that Andor was weak and would fade in and out of sleep for a day or two before fully waking, but he had survived the poison. They remained by his side and when Andor awoke a little later he told them Queen Olwen had sent eighty men in pursuit of the raks, and asked if they had seen them. Obie and Tau exchanged uneasy glances, and then, in a solemn voice, Tau told Andor of the fatal rak attack on the men.

A sad look came into the prince's eyes. "We feared the worst when they did not return or send word. They will be mourned."

Obie nodded. They were silent for a while, and then Obie asked, "Andor, do you know whether Ull was with them?"

"He was not among them."

Obie breathed a quiet sigh of relief.

"When last I saw him he was helping the queen prepare for war. She put him in command of her army."

Obie was cheered at the news.

"Will you still pursue the raks?"

"We're going after Gabrielle and Mara. Tau overheard two raks saying they were taking them to Torolf's tower in Targus Dol. We'd have caught up with them by now if the muks hadn't chased us off the cliff."

"Do you think it wise for only two of you to attempt the rescue?"

"We think we'll be able to slip through quietly where a group of soldiers couldn't."

"That might work." Andor switched to mental speech. *And, you trust Tau?*

Yes, like a brother I guess, Obie responded, a flicker of surprise in his eyes. He hadn't known Andor was a telepath, though he should have guessed it. He wondered if the prince was a descendant of Haldor, though he did not project the question to him.

That is good. Andor switched back to spoken language. "When I am stronger I will fly north and give you what help I can."

"We'll be watching the sky for you," Obie said.

Andor dropped into sleep again, and pallets with blankets were brought into the room so Obie and Tau could remain with him. Early in the morning, the attendant awakened them with fruit, bread and honey. They dressed and ate quietly, trying not to awaken Andor, and then Kort came for them. He was cheerful, and Obie noticed that today he wore bright yellow bootees. When they were ready to leave, Andor awoke and bid them speed of the gods.

Kort looked back and smiled as he bounced along the passageway in front of Obie and Tau. "We have something that will please you, yes, will please you very much."

They followed him into a small chamber where he pointed towards two large packages on the floor, wrapped in brown cloth. "The one on the left belongs, I believe, yes I do believe, to Obie, and the other to Tau, yes, that is what I think."

Kneeling down, Obie opened his package and found his sword, his Raptor, and leather pouch. Then he wondered, *Will it still be there?* His hand trembled as he felt inside his pouch until his fingers found what they were looking for. He withdrew the small piece of blue fabric from Gabrielle's dress and breathed a quiet sigh of relief. The river hadn't damaged it. Carefully, he replaced it and then lifted his sword. He drew Roar from its black and gold scabbard and inspected the blade. It was in perfect condition and the golden lion's head pommel gleamed. Resheathing it, he lifted it to his back with the strap across his chest. Then he examined his Raptor and cloak. They were also in fine condition. He slid his ammo pouch strap over his head and threw his cloak around his shoulders, the hilt of his sword projecting above the back neckline. The old sprite had a delighted expression on his face as he rocked back and forth fidgeting with his hands. "We found your things in Zelda's Pool, we did, yes."

Tau uttered something between a low-pitched laugh and a pleased growl when he examined his sword. He lifted it to his back in readiness to go.

Kort then motioned for two attendants who brought packs for Obie and Tau. "Zelda said, yes she said, you will need these things, especially when the bitter snows come, yes, especially then."

Tall, fur lined boots and gloves hung from a strap on the outside of Obie's pack, and when he checked inside he found warm clothing, a lightweight blanket, flat bread, nuts, dried fruit, a water bag, and coils of rope.

Obie stood up and smiled. "Thank you, Kort. Will you thank Zelda for me?"

"You are welcome, yes, most welcome you are. Thank Zelda I will. Yes, I will." Kort nodded his head rapidly up and down.

Tau's pack contained the same items; but he received an additional gift: a long, fur-lined cloak. His eyes shone as he turned to Kort. "I am honored that the lady should think of me. I have never owned such fine gifts as these boots and cloak. Will you give her my thanks as well?"

"Thanks, yes, yes, I will thank her for you too," Kort said, bouncing up and down merrily.

Tau threw the cloak around his shoulders and strutted about, turning and swishing it several times.

"Tau, you look regal." Obie was glad to see him so pleased.

They shouldered the packs and discovered something else they appreciated. Although many supplies were contained within, the packs were neither heavy nor bulky. The river sprites appeared to be masters at making items not only excellent in quality, but also compact and lightweight for travel.

They passed silently up the winding tunnels until they reached the door they could not open the previous day. Kort uttered a few words and grinned at their surprised faces when the door swung open. After saying their good-byes, Obie and Tau stepped outside onto the east riverbank. A moment later the door swung shut behind them.

CHAPTER THIRTEEN

THE CHASE

OBIE STOOD WATCHING the gray-white mist billow over the Witch and roll against the high cliff walls. It was a welcome sight, for it would enable them to pass invisibly along the riverbank.

Tau took a few steps forward, then stopped and made a half-turn. "Coming?"

"Yeah, coming," Obie said, jarred from his thoughts. He slipped his Raptor on his arm, in case they encountered enemies, and they headed upriver. His bad leg was more troublesome than usual this morning. It helped that Tau always started out at a trot. Tau had said he needed time to wake up and get his blood flowing before accelerating to a run; but Obie suspected the lion-man was giving his leg time to limber up. Refusing to dwell on the puzzle of his on-again, off-again limp, he focused instead on watching and listening for signs of danger. They must not be captured. They'd find a way to rescue Gabrielle and Mara from Targus Dol. Before long, his gait smoothed out and he and Tau began running.

The riverbank was narrow and rocky, but widened here and there where the vine-covered cliff wall receded to form small coves. A few willow trees shared the gorge floor with stately boulders that, in eons past, had rested in high places on the canyon wall. The pale sun illuminated the river only briefly at midday; the rest of the time the Witch lay in shadow.

In the late morning the mist lifted. The deep shade in the gorge helped to conceal them, but occasional hawk sightings

high above sent them into hiding. If there was no cover they
stood motionless against the dark cliff wall, or lay on the ground
camouflaged under their cloaks until the hawks passed. Shortly
before noon they heard the sound of tramping boots coming up
from behind.

They stopped and Tau looked back. "Two soldiers tracking
us, but they haven't spotted us yet."

They scrambled to the top of a nearby boulder, partially
hidden by a willow tree. Tau drew his sword and Obie readied
his Raptor. Then they lay flat, waiting. Soon they heard whispering voices. The muks had stopped in front of the boulder and
seemed confused at the abrupt ending of the trail they had been
following. When they began circling the boulder in opposite
directions, Obie and Tau knew the game was up. Obie caught
Tau's eye and pointed towards the seven-foot-tall muk circling
on his side. The lion-man nodded his shaggy head in response.
Obie stood up and shot the muk on the side of his head as Tau
roared and leaped down on the other. They hit the ground and
rolled apart. An instant later they were on their feet again and the
muk drew his sword. Obie hoped Tau would make short work of
the muk because the sound of clashing blades could draw
unwanted attention.

The other soldier lay unconscious, slumped against the rock.
Obie noticed the muk's brown, leathery skin as he pulled him
behind the boulder and began binding his several sets of hands
and his feet with his own rope. He had a long, slim torso, and his
long limbs had both human and ant qualities. Obie could not see
his feet, which were booted, but he had scaly hands with skinny
fingers. His face was triangular with the narrow end at his chin.
On the sides of his mouth were short pinchers, and he had two
feelers above his round, human looking eyes. Satisfied that the
muk was secured, Obie went to watch the fight. He figured Tau
was enjoying it and didn't want to interfere unless he had to . . .

but why was he taking so long to finish off his opponent? This was getting serious. They were in danger of being seen and needed to move on quickly. Tau stumbled over a large rock and fell backwards to the ground, dropping his sword. Obie jumped into action with his Raptor and was about to disarm the muk with a shot to his sword hand, but he hesitated. The muk had thrown his sword aside and leaped at Tau. Obie lowered his weapon. He'd let Tau have his fun a little while longer. A creature who could pull chains from rock, as the lion-man had done, was surely more than a match for a muk. This was a lot quieter than sword play. The two rolled on the ground, kicking and punching.

Obie surveyed the narrow band of sky above the cliffs. "Hurry it up, Tau, we might be seen," he said impatiently, failing to notice Tau's eyes rolling back in his head and his tongue lolling out due to the stranglehold the muk had on him.

"How . . . hgggg . . . 'bout . . . guuurg . . . some hel . . ." Tau gasped, trying unsuccessfully to loosen the muk's hands from his throat.

Suddenly aware that Tau was in trouble, Obie made a quick shot with his Raptor and hit the muk soldier between the eyes. With a hiss, he dropped face down on top of Tau and lay still.

"Hawks," Tau yelled, shoving the muk off of him. Two hawks were approaching from down river.

"Let's get this guy out of sight," Obie said, grabbing one of the muk's feet. Tau grasped the other foot and they dragged him behind the boulder next to his comrade. While Tau peered out from their hiding place, Obie started binding the second muk's hands and feet.

"They are gone. I am not sure whether they saw us."

"We'll know soon," Obie said with a worried look as he tied a knot. "I guess we'll just leave these guys tied up, huh?"

"They will work free from their ropes in a day or two, but we shall be far from here by then."

"Tau, why did this guy throw his sword down when he had you?" Obie finished tying the last knot.

"For the sheer joy of physical combat. Although their ant natures make them well disciplined, the muks love to brawl whenever they get a chance, and at such times, anything goes with them. Maybe it's the strict discipline that brings this other side out in them. But at least they don't eat their victims like the raks do.

"Do muks ever travel with raks?"

"Only when they have to. Muks do not like raks because they know the raks would eat them if they were permitted to. I heard that it happened once, but Torolf put a quick stop to it." While he spoke Tau took a knife from one of the soldiers and attached it to his belt, then started rifling through his pack. He pulled out some small wafers and sniffed them. "Try this." Smiling oddly, he handed one to Obie. "It will give you great energy."

Obie tossed it in his mouth and began chewing. A moment later his mouth stopped moving and dropped open exposing the crushed wafer. His face contorted into a twisted knot of pain and disbelief as he dropped to his knees to spit it out. Afterwards, he ran to the river and washed his mouth out. Tau watched, chuckling the whole time.

When Obie returned, he glared daggers at the lion-man. "Very funny. Aaaaghhh . . . that was putrid. What was it made of?"

"Sanitized rat excrement."

Obie felt his face grow hot. He wanted to shove some of the rat excrement down Tau's throat. Then their eyes met, and he knew why Tau played the trick on him. "Alright," he said grudgingly, "I guess we're even." He realized his mistake. He had thought Tau just about invincible after seeing him pull chains from the rock wall in Zelda's caverns. Now he knew Tau wasn't invincible. It was an important lesson.

Tau had a devilish glint in his eyes. "Next time, I know you won't wait so long to help me out. Muks are exceptionally strong."

The thin sunlight crawled slowly down the west cliff face until, at midday, the ghostly greenish orb slid over the east canyon rim, driving all shadow from the gorge floor. Knowing they could now be easily spotted from above, Obie and Tau took refuge beneath a weeping willow tree and used the time to eat and rest. While Tau dozed, Obie lay on his back peering up through the tree branches. He thought about Shadow and was saddened at losing him. He'd been a good companion. Where was he now? Had he gotten away from the muk soldiers? He hoped he'd find his way back to Windermere. The sun moved into his line of vision behind the long, lacey, green fronds of the willow. He watched it move over the gorge until it disappeared beyond the west rim. Immediately, the west cliff wall was enveloped in deep shadow that moved rapidly across the bottom of the gorge, leaving the river in semi-darkness again. Obie shook Tau's shoulder. "Time to go."

They set out at a steady run and had just passed a cove when Tau's ears pricked up and he came to a stop. "Enemy approaching ahead," he growled. They fled back past the cove and around a bend searching for cover, but there was none. Tau's eyes darted everywhere at once and stopped at the river's edge. "Quick, under that rock." He pointed to a great flat rock overhanging the water. Racing over, they jumped into the cold river and moved beneath the overhang. Obie's cloak streamed out into the current, but Tau pulled it under the rock just before a patrol of twenty muks came round the bend in a heavy-footed run. They headed straight for the rock.

The patrol leader called a halt. Some of the soldiers wandered out to the edge of the overhang and knelt next to the river, splashing water on their faces and drinking. Two of the muks pulled their boots off and sat talking while dangling their large smelly feet in the water only inches from Obie's face. Obie scrunched his nose up ready to sneeze, and Tau pushed his head under the water to muffle the sound. After the muks filled their water bags and downed some rations, their patrol leader called them into formation again and they tramped off. When Tau could not suppress his urge to expel a low roar, Obie was alarmed. He was sure they were caught. They'd have to swim for it, try and cross the swift river. A few tense seconds passed, but nothing happened. Tau peeked out from under the rock and his smile told Obie they were safe.

When the last muk soldiers disappeared around a bend they climbed ashore. "How about controlling yourself in the future," Obie growled.

Tau grinned sheepishly. "It is difficult sometimes, but I will try."

Obie's cloak felt like a fifty-pound weight. He started squeezing the water from it, then switched to Tau's faster, easier method of rolling up his cloak and walking on it to force out the water. When they had removed as much water as possible, they shook their cloaks out and put them back on, fur side out, to dry in the air while they continued running upriver.

As black night settled in the gorge, they were lucky enough to find a small cave in a shallow cove at the base of the cliff. It was hidden from view by large boulders near its entrance, so Obie felt safe building a small fire inside. Tau disappeared for a while, and when he returned Obie had their damp cloaks laid out near the fire to finish drying.

"Here is our meal," Tao said. He held up two good-sized trout and a couple of long sticks to skewer them over the fire.

"That makes up for a tough day," Obie said. Grinning slightly, he asked, "Don't like the River Sprite food?"

"Not when we can get better. Besides, the food the sprites gave us will remain fresh. We must conserve it as much as possible for tougher times than these—and they will soon come."

Obie knew that, as usual, Tau was right. Once the snows started, food would be scarce. Hopefully they could make it to Targus Dol before the first winter storm came, though the odds were against it. They would need to keep their strength up to rescue Gabrielle and Mara. He'd eat tree bark if he had to. What was Gabrielle doing at that moment, and where was she? Was she warm enough tonight? From the corner of his eye he saw Tau observing him. "Okay, let's get these fish cooking," he said, rousing himself from his thoughts.

After their meal Obie removed the bandage from Tau's head to examine the wound he had gotten from the whirlpool. It was healing well, so Tau decided to leave it open to the air.

Later that night, Obie had the same bad dream he had had off and on for years, though each time it was a little different. He was laughing and riding in the backseat of his mother's car. And again, as he had done so many times before, he threw his teddy bear to her and she turned her head and gave him a loving smile. An instant later, he was rolling over and over in the car, down the steep hill and then, somehow, he was standing outside the car watching it tumble down the slope. When it stopped, he ran to it and tried to pull the door open, but the car exploded in flames. He was screaming, but no sound came out.

Then his dream changed. He was limping badly while running from something terrible, something large and black shrouded in an impenetrable dark haze. A little way ahead he saw Gabrielle. She was stuck in the center of a great spider web strung between two dead trees near the entrance to a huge dark tower. She called to him. Mara guarded her, but it wasn't Mara. This creature had Mara's head, wings, and hind legs, but it had a human body and arms. Thunder sounded in the jet black sky, and the only light came from molten rock exploding upward from fissures in the frozen Earth. The light cast an eerie crimson glow on Gabrielle, rocking back and forth in the huge black web. He looked up, but the tower was so high he couldn't see the top of it. He drew his sword and ran towards her, hoping to hack through the web and free her before he was caught by the terrible black thing that chased him. But when he approached, Mara brandished a silver scimitar and barred his way. Then he saw the huge amoeba-like form of his dark pursuer hovering above. He watched long black tentacles shoot out from its body and reach towards Gabrielle. Then he understood. It was Gabrielle it wanted. Suddenly, it was no longer her face he was looking at, but the face he had seen in his dreams for so many years. "Mother," he tried to call out, but he was paralyzed and no sound came forth. Anguish and fear stabbed him. When the black tentacles began to curl around her, he summoned every spark of energy he possessed to yell, "Noooooo."

Startled awake, he bolted up. Tau was still asleep, and Obie realized he'd only shouted in his dream. He was covered in sweat and his shirt was sticking to him. He pulled it off and went to the river and splashed himself with the cold water. A wolf wailed long and mournfully from high up on the canyon rim. A shiver ran down Obie's spine. He tried to see the strip of sky above the gorge, but he couldn't, for the pitch-black sky blended perfectly with the black canyon walls. He began to feel disoriented, as though he was lost in a black void where there was no up or down. It reminded him of the nightmares he'd had back home after finding the rock in Ghostrise Valley. Then he spotted the dim glow of the campfire reflecting onto a small portion of the canyon wall outside the cave. Relieved, he headed towards it, but was jarred by a new fear that the glow might be seen from above. Rushing into the cave, he scooped handfuls of sand over the low flames, leaving only a couple of small embers as a point of reference in the dark. The temperature dropped almost immediately. Obie reached for the cloaks. They were dry. He gently laid Tau's cloak over him. Then he pulled a dry shirt from his pack, slipped it over his head, and curled up in his cloak listening to the river sounds. Tau started purring in his sleep. Was he dreaming of his homeland? Obie wondered.

Later, he awoke to the feel of Tau's hand lightly touching his shoulder. "It is time," Tau said quietly as he squatted down beside him. "The fog will hide us well this morning, but we must make haste. We have far yet to go."

As they started upriver the sky began to lighten through the heavy bank of mist. When Tau turned his head, Obie knew he was checking on him. He was bounding along easily now and motioned for Tau to speed up.

The changes taking place within Obie continued to be a mystery. Although he knew the brain produced endorphins that created a high in runners, that didn't explain why his limp went away soon after he started running, or why it disappeared almost instantly when he had focused on rescuing Mara, Rae and Asta. It was more than that, though. As the days passed, he had also felt a heightening of his physical strength and endurance. The puzzle gnawed at him. But, whatever was happening to him, it came at a time when he sorely needed it, and he was glad it enabled him to keep up with Tau.

They covered many miles of river that day and passed unseen until late afternoon when they were startled by a red hawk that fluttered out from a dark ledge above their heads. Squawking loudly, it streaked off downstream. Obie and Tau exchanged worried glances and speeded up.

The gloom of the gorge had deepened almost to night when Tau pointed ahead to a patch of green jutting out from the cliff wall a little farther up the river. Obie understood: they would stop there for the night. Then Tau's face froze. "Red muks behind us! Speed up—they're the worst," he yelled.

Obie glanced over his shoulder. They were big brutes, and moving fast. Being captured by them wasn't an option he wanted to consider, so he picked up his speed.

The muks shouted and hissed at their fleeing quarry. It was pitch dark in the gorge now. Unable to see well, Obie stumbled and fell over something just before they reached the trees. Scrambling to his feet, he saw a pair of yellow eyes peering at him. Then the eyes blinked out. Tau ran back and grabbed Obie's hand. "Hold on, I'll guide you through the dark."

The muk soldiers had gained on them. They entered the trees on a dead run and bounded through the darkness while the shouts of the muks grew louder behind them.

"Tau, I don't think this is just a clump of trees. I think it's . . ."

"Just keep running. Trust me. You don't want to be taken by red muks. Low branch, duck!"

Obie ducked just in time. "How are they worse than other muks?"

"Bad stingers. If they don't kill you, you'll wish they had. Your body will feel like it's on fire and your head will swell up like a watermelon."

Running blindly through the darkness was like passing through a dream, and Obie lost track of time while deeper and deeper into the woodland they went. After a while, he didn't know how long, his mind snapped into a state of unusual clarity. His feet seemed to hardly touch the ground, as if they had sprouted wings, so light did he feel, while his vision and other senses grew keener. No longer running blindly through the darkness, he released Tau's hand. The lion-man grunted approvingly. Trees were now visible everywhere, and Obie began to hear sounds of small animals, insects, and the faint groaning of the Earth itself. It was like a journey into that primitive, hidden place within where senses and instincts rule. Tau's yellow-green eyes glowing through the darkness made Obie think of William Blake's poem about tigers, though he paraphrased it to: *Lion, lion, burning bright, in the forests of the night.* Drawn into what seemed the very essence of this nocturnal forest realm, he felt a deep kinship with the lion-man.

The waning moon lifted over the forest, silhouetting the treetops against the sky and casting dappled shadows on the woodland floor. Obie looked back and again spotted the small yellow eyes, following them. And again, they disappeared. On and on through the night Obie and Tau ran until the shouts of their cruel pursuers grew faint and disappeared.

"I think we've outrun them," Obie said as they finally slowed to an easy lope.

Tau grunted doubtfully. "Maybe. Or maybe they don't like this forest." They stopped to listen.

Obie noticed the trees and bushes in this part of the forest were much larger. "I don't hear them anymore, but I do hear running water."

They followed the sound to a large pond fed by a waterfall on the far side of its dimly moonlit surface. Lily pads with large flowers floated on the water, and frogs were croaking everywhere. Obie breathed in the sweet scent of lilies and he no longer felt concerned about muks or raks. Nor did Tau appear worried about attack from the trees, as he selected a place to sleep under a large tree beside the pond. Yawning, he unfastened his cloak and lay down on it. He had hardly closed his eyes, Obie noticed, before he was sound asleep. Obie curled up against one of the big tree roots. Oddly, it wasn't cold here. It felt like a summer's night. He thought about Zelda's warning not to enter the Vale of Nepenthe. That was exactly where they must be. On the other hand, it seemed a better choice to take one's chances in this wood than be caught by the red muks. It would be all right. Early in the morning they would leave the vale and return to the river. His eyelids grew heavy as his mind drifted to thoughts of home. Josh would think this place was a frog-hunting paradise. Soon the waterfall sounds and croaking frogs lulled him to sleep. Nearby, the two yellow eyes peered out of the darkness, watching, growing ever larger while the youth and the lion-man slept.

Obie opened his eyes and stared at the sky for a few moments trying to remember where he was. A cacophony of woodland sounds: frogs ribbiting, birds chirping, and insects buzzing, came from every direction. He jumped up. *The Vale of Nepenthe. It's mid-morning.*

"Tau, wake up."

"Uuuuhhhh?"

"Wake up. It's late." Obie pulled his leather pouch strap over his head and then lifted his sword onto his back in readiness to depart.

Groaning as if jarred from deep sleep, Tau sat up and blinked, then took a sweeping gaze around. Obie also surveyed their surroundings. They had not slept next to a pond as they had thought, but on the edge of a large lake where the water lilies and the forest around them were gigantic. It seemed odd that he didn't remember everything being so large last night. Perhaps he'd been too exhausted to notice. "I think we need to get out of here right away," he said with a worried look. "Zelda warned us about this place."

Tau eyed the lily pads. His nose began to twitch and a gleam came into his eyes. "Yes, we should leave very soon, but not before we eat. I have a taste for frog—I dreamed of them all night."

"Who wouldn't with all this croaking going on around us. Okay, go catch some frogs, but make it quick. This place is giving me the jitters."

Following Tau to the water's edge, Obie watched him place one foot on a lily pad to test its stability. Then Tau stepped onto it with both feet. It held firm. Satisfied that it was safe, Obie also stepped aboard and moved to the third pad out to get a better look at the lake. His limp made it hard to step lightly on the pads, but they were thick and sturdy underfoot and he managed. Tau joined him.

"See any frogs yet?" Obie whispered.

"No, but they're hiding all around us. Listen to them."

"It's impossible not to." Obie wanted to tell him that having frog legs for breakfast would be nice, but getting back to the river would be even nicer. He held his tongue.

Tau crouched and peered over the edge of the rubbery green lily pad into the water. Two huge, staring eyes broke the glassy surface and Tau shrank back in alarm.

"I think we found one," Obie whispered, frozen to the spot.

"Don't . . . move . . . a muscle," Tau cautioned.

Then, as quietly as they had appeared the eyes slipped below the surface again.

"Let's get out of here before it comes back," Obie said.

An instant later two huge frog heads popped up from the water. Then a third, larger frog leaped from the lake onto the lily pad beside Obie and Tau and sat staring down at them with a hungry looking glint in its eyes. They drew their swords and stood their ground.

"I hate the way it's looking at us," Obie whispered.

"It thinks we're bugs."

"Bugs with stingers." Obie raised Roar defiantly, ready to battle the monster frog if necessary.

Tau grinned and raised his blade. "I shall teach it who is breakfast around here and who is not."

The huge frog blasted them with a "RIBBET" and leaped back into the lake to attack the two smaller frogs that were getting too close. The great splash drenched Obie and Tau and shook the lily pad so violently they had to grab hold of a pink lily to keep from being washed off. Green frog bodies and webbed feet appeared and disappeared as they rolled over and over in the water. Finally, the two smaller frogs swam off in different directions, their wakes trailing behind.

"We're outta here," Obie yelled.

He followed close behind Tau who was bounding towards the shore. Tau was about to jump ashore when the giant frog leaped from the water again and sat blocking his way, its great bulbous eyes fixed on him. In a flash, the frog's sticky red tongue darted from its cavernous mouth, wrapped around the lion-man, darted back again, and the frog's mouth snapped shut. Tau was gone.

"Release him slime ball, or I'll slice you into sandwich meat," Obie screamed, his face crimson with rage. He held his sword up with both hands and waited for the creature to open its mouth again so he could whack off its tongue. The frog only blinked its eyes innocently and, as if dismissing Obie for a future meal, turned and hopped up the bank.

"Stop, wait—I'm not kidding," Obie shouted, in hot pursuit of the giant amphibian. He doubted the frog understood his words, but communicating with it was worth a try. The frog had almost reached the forest when it turned and started back towards the water.

Oh no, going to lake . . . can't lose Tau. Obie tackled and locked onto a big green hind leg, but the frog kept hopping, dragging him after it. *Let go . . . use Raptor . . . too risky . . . lose him . . . hang on in water . . . stab leg.* "Alright croaker, this is your last chance—I mean it," Obie yelled, his voice going hoarse. The water was only a few hops away.

CHAPTER FOURTEEN

THE
FURRY BROWN FURY

A GIANT BROWN MISSILE shot from the trees and down the bank and leaped on the frog's back, sinking its sharp teeth and claws into the amphibious neck. Obie released the frog's leg and backed off to watch the furry brown beast lift the green bulk off the ground and shake it violently in its teeth, growling all the while. The green legs wriggled and convulsed and when they went limp the brown beast dropped the motionless frog on its back. The beast grew calm then, almost peaceful, and did not appear threatening. It wiggled its nose and squeaked while prodding the lifeless carcass with the claws of one paw. Obie raised his sword and edged nearer, looking for an opening to rush over and cut the frog open. He was ready to yell and charge the brown creature to try and drive it off when the frog's belly began to contort oddly. It rose and fell in lumps, and Obie heard muffled shouts. Then the point of a sword stabbed through from inside the frog and began sawing a large circular hole.

Obie's face lit up. "Tau, you're alive," he said, choking out the last word.

He and the brown giant watched Tau's arms emerge through the hole. Then his head poked through and he started climbing out, eyes ablaze and nostrils flaring.

"Aaarrrggghhh, let me out of this stinking, suffocating slime-hopper," he bellowed at the top of his lungs as he came out. Tau did not appear to be in a good mood. Wary of possible attack by the brown beast, now sitting on its haunches looking down at them, Obie moved cautiously towards Tau.

"I've got you covered, Tau," Obie said, not taking his eyes off the beast.

"Don't worry. I won't eat you," the brown beast calmly announced. It sank down on all fours with its chin resting on its curled in paws.

Obie was a little taken back to hear the beast speak. "Who or what are you?" he asked. Then it registered. "No, don't tell me . . . you're Mole," he said with a laugh.

"Yes, I'm Mole. How did you know?"

Grinning, Obie lowered his blade. "The name suits you. Besides, Zelda the River Witch told me about you."

Mole lifted his head attentively for a moment then lowered it back onto his paws and sighed. "You know Zelda? That's good. And who are you?"

"Oberon Griffin, or Obie, and my friend here is Tau."

Tau had climbed out and was standing atop the frog examining himself with a frown. He was covered in green slime so thick it made his whiskers droop. Without a word he leaped down from the frog carcass and submerged himself in the lake, then stood up and began vigorously scrubbing himself. Normally, washing with water was not his way. But this was a heavy duty job. Two bullfrogs watched from distant lily pads, apparently keeping their distance while Mole was present. Soon the lion-man waded from the lake, sopping wet, but clean.

"I did not wish to be rude before," he said to Mole, "but my appearance was unseemly for introductions."

"I took no offense," Mole said.

"I am Tau. It appears I owe you my life."

"Your friend, Obie, helped also."

"I thought as much." Tau nodded his thanks to Obie. "You are one up on me, Oberon."

"You'll have time to catch up."

Tau's eyes flashed and then he turned back to Mole. "Come, Mole, and join us for a meal before we depart—such as it will be."

"I'll join you, but I won't eat. I've already dined on insects this morning."

"I have lost my appetite for frog," Tau confided quietly to Obie as they walked back to the tree they had slept under. "Today we will eat the river sprite food."

Obie suppressed a grin as Tau squatted and began pulling food from one of the packs. Sitting cross-legged, they dined on flat bread, nuts, and dried fruit. Mole lay near them quietly observing Obie while he ate. When he finished, Obie turned to Mole. "Zelda told us to look for you at the mouth of this vale. It was dark when we got there, though, and we didn't realize where we were until later."

Mole raised his head. "Indeed, you *did* find me at the mouth of the vale, in fact, you fell over me."

"That was you? Sorry. I thought it was a log or something. Must have been your foot or tail, huh?"

Mole's eyes flickered, but he made no reply.

"So the yellow eyes I saw following us in the dark . . . that was you too?" Obie noticed that Mole's eyes were gray in the daylight.

"Yes. I followed behind and watched over you all night."

"A good thing for us," Tau said. "We did not know we were in a giant forest with giant creatures."

Mole's eyes opened wider. "But, this is *not* a giant forest."

Obie and Tau exchanged alarmed looks, visibly shaken at the revelation.

"Well, if this *isn't* a giant forest," Obie began slowly, "does that mean, uhhh, you're not *really* a giant mole?"

"That's absolutely right. Although I'm considered large among my kind, I am far from being a giant."

The blood drained from Obie's face and his heart started thumping so hard against his chest he had to take a deep breath to try and calm down and find his voice again. "Zelda . . . Zelda warned us about this vale. But, she didn't say we'd shrink to the bottom of the food chain." Just then a huge dragonfly with blue wings buzzed their heads as if confirming his words. Obie and Tau jumped to their feet and metal rang as they unsheathed their swords. But the disinterested dragonfly merely continued on its way.

"Please, sit down while I explain some things to you," Mole said. An anxious glance passed between Obie and Tau. They sheathed their weapons and sat down a little closer to Mole.

"It's true that humans who enter the Vale of Nepenthe grow slowly smaller—like you did during the night. And if you stay here another day the spell will also make you forget who you are. I fear that your inclination to linger by the pond to hunt frogs rather than leave the vale in all haste may mean the early stages of forgetfulness are beginning to set in. But I can assure you the spell reverses itself the farther you get from this pond. And once you leave the vale you'll quickly return to your normal size. You *must* leave today, but there is still plenty of time."

Were he and Tau already beginning to lose their memories, Obie wondered? It suddenly hit him how unusual it was that he hadn't thought about Gabrielle since he'd awoken. Normally, she was always in his thoughts. And Tau's desire to stay and hunt frogs when they should have hurried back to the river had also seemed odd. Well, he would have to fight forgetfulness and remain focused on their mission. And they could spare Mole only a few more minutes of their time. Then he and Tau would hurry back to the Witch. They'd have to run all the way.

"I am glad to know we will regain our normal size when we leave this place," Tau said anxiously, then turning to Obie, "I am ready to go when you are."

"*If* we go," Obie muttered. He had just caught sight of a big sparrow eyeing them from a nearby tree.

"Because you are smaller now the journey back will be much farther for you than when you entered the vale, and as you have seen, fraught with peril," Mole said. "I know of one who came here before you and didn't make it back to the river before losing his memory."

"What happened to him?" Obie asked, his voice trembling.

"I was elsewhere in the forest and didn't witness it. But a mole living at the far end of the pond told me frogs got him. Don't worry, though. I'll bear you on my back to the Witch. It will be much faster."

Obie was elated at the offer, but wondered why Mole was helping them. Was it simply his friendship with Zelda? "Thanks, Mole. I should have guessed that any friend of Zelda's . . ."

"It's my pleasure to be of service," Mole interrupted. "Earlier you mentioned that Zelda told you to look for me. May I ask why?"

"She said you might be able to help us."

"Hmmmm, I sense you have a story to tell."

Anxious to leave soon, Obie quickly told his story beginning with his ride to Windermere on the spirit comet and ending with Torolf's red muks chasing them into the vale. Obie noticed the surprised look on Tau's face and realized he had never told him about the spirit comet. Mole seemed transfixed throughout the recitation. When it was finished he looked thoughtful for a few moments and then began speaking solemnly.

"As you both know, there's much at stake. The River Witch was right in sending you to me. She is of the Earth and does not take kindly to the evil Torolf is spreading, for she is also affected by it. Only the darkest power would conceive of stealing all light from the sky. I have watched the stars disappear from the night sky, and now I watch the sun and moon slowly dying. *You* see how sickly they are, as though infected by some black disease that is slowly consuming them." Mole gazed at the gray-green sky over the pond and mumbled something that Obie couldn't make out. Then with a pained look he turned back to Obie and Tau and continued. "I know of the Moonpath Riders, Guardians of the Star Crystals. They must be rescued at all costs." Mole rose tall on his haunches, anger shining in his eyes. "I'll go with you to Targus Dol. The black sorcerer must be stopped. My small size may enable me to slip undetected into Torolf's stronghold to locate the Moonpath Riders. Will you allow me to join you?"

"I'll be glad to have you join us, Mole," Obie said. "You'll be a valuable member of our rescue party, in your large and small size."

"I, too, welcome you, Mole," Tau added. "Your courage in rescuing me from the frog speaks well of you. You will need such courage in days to come."

The pallid sun was high over the pond when they climbed onto Mole's back and set out for Witch River, Obie in front and Tau behind. Hours passed as Mole ran through the towering trees past giant ferns where lordly butterflies with vibrant blue and yellow wings fanned the air above. Over dark Earth and deep carpets of moss, up low rises and down again, past decaying logs and deep piles of orange and yellow leaves they moved. With their swords in hand, Obie and Tau drove away occasional dive-bombing birds. They were midway up a low rise when Obie spotted something large and black crawling over the crest of the hill. "Mole," he whispered, "something's moving towards us."

Mole stopped and squinted up the hill. "Yes, I see it. It's as big as you, but not nearly as big as me. It might be a snack. Don't worry." Mole continued up the slope of the hill.

In the shadows it was hard to tell what the black creature was as it continued creeping down the hill towards them. When they drew nearer, it abruptly darted under a leafy bush. Mole scurried up to the bush and waited motionless for the creature to exit. With a rustling of dry leaves it soon came out, but froze when it spotted Mole. Then it spun around and raised its hind end high in the air in attack mode.

"Run, Mole," Tau yelled, staring incredulously at the creature's hind end.

"Mole, go, go, go," Obie shouted.

Mole jumped to the side, but not fast enough to escape the stinkbug's odious spray. For a while, sounds like "Awwwww," "Aaaarrrrg," "Eyaaaah," and "Squeeeeak" could be heard trailing off in the distance. Obie pulled his shirt up over his nose, but it didn't help. Tau held his arm over his nostrils, which also didn't help. Meanwhile, Mole raced down the hill and over another to a stream where Obie and Tau climbed down and washed the offensive essence off themselves and Mole. Obie was glad the stinkbug hadn't been a skunk. They decided to take a short rest there among a group of huge mushrooms growing near the water.

Obie knew he would never get another chance to sit on a toadstool. After Tau confirmed they were not poisonous, Obie climbed to the rounded top of a speckled one. He lay back and ran his hands over the velvety surface. The toadstool was comfortable. He wished he had his camera. It was probably still on the boulder back home where he'd left it. His thoughts went to Josh and he wondered, as he frequently did, if he and Hudson had made it out of the valley okay. Soon, his feet were dangling off the edge of the mushroom cap and he was elated to realize that he was slowly growing larger.

When he and Tau climbed onto Mole's back again, their legs hung a little lower down Mole's sides. On and on they went and as the afternoon waned, Mole's breathing became more and more labored. Obie whispered something to Tau, then leaned close to Mole's head and quietly said, "Pull up."

Mole squeaked and stopped. He was panting a little. His riders dismounted and Tau poured water from his water bag into Mole's mouth and over his head.

"Thank you, I needed that," Mole said.

"We have grown too large for you to carry," Tau said.

"We'll run along beside you," Obie added. "Tau gets fat and lazy if he doesn't get regular exercise." Tau's nostrils flared momentarily, but he let the comment pass.

They reached the Witch at dusk and found a place to sleep for the night behind a cluster of boulders near the cliff face. By this time Obie and Tau were half their normal size, and Mole told them they would be full-size by morning.

When the first dim light appeared in the dawn sky, Obie lingered for a time between sleep and wakefulness, and it seemed he could hear a woman's voice singing sweetly far off down the river. It was a haunting melody that lulled him back to sleep. When he opened his eyes again the first thing he saw was Mole's black nose and brown furry face. He was curled up in the crook of Obie's arm with his small head resting on his chest. Obie moved a little and Mole woke up with a squeak followed by a yawn.

"I trust you slept well, Mr. Mole?" Obie said, scratching Mole's head.

"Quite well, thank you." Mole shifted his head slightly so that Obie's fingers were scratching behind the place where his ears would be if moles had ears. Obie guessed this was his favorite spot.

"You're lucky I like moles."

"Shut up and keep scratching." Mole rolled over on his back and stretched out so Obie could scratch his rounded belly.

"If you're going to snooze next to me you better not have fleas."

"I do." Mole closed his eyes pleasurably. "But my sweet disposition makes up for it."

When Obie glanced at Tau, he was sitting up surveying himself and his surroundings. "Judging by Mole's size, Tau, I'd say the spell has worn off completely." Mole's sturdy cylindrical body looked about eight inches long, about as large as moles ever get, Obie thought.

"Ahhh, so I see," Tau said with a smile. "Thank you, little friend, for bringing us back to the river so quickly. May we put great distance between ourselves and this accursed vale today."

The three were soon on their way again. They hoped to reach the old wooden bridge and climb the path up the cliff wall before nightfall. Tau led the way and Obie and Mole followed side-by-side behind. While they ran slowly Mole was able to keep up. But as soon as Obie's limp smoothed out and they picked up speed, Mole fell behind. Each time Obie looked Mole lagged farther behind. Finally, Obie stopped and whistled ahead to Tau. Tau turned and saw Obie pointing towards Mole, far down the riverbank laboring slowly upstream. They hurried back.

"Sorry, Mole, I guess we weren't thinking about your short legs," Obie said.

"I was sure you'd miss me eventually. But, all the same, don't underestimate the value of my short legs," Mole said with dignity.

Tau opened his paw-hand and reached down. "Hop on, little one. It is my turn now to carry you. I promise, I won't eat you."

Mole's eyes glittered in appreciation of Tau's echoing words. "Well said, my friend." He climbed on and Tau lifted him to his shoulder where Mole positioned himself to ride facing their rear. "I'll make myself useful by riding lookout so I can watch for hawks or others approaching from behind." And this is the way Mole rode on many days after that. Tau's graceful, feline gait made it easy for Mole to hang on, and the view could not be better.

The journey grew more difficult the farther north they traveled. Not only did the threat of discovery by hawks and attack by

Torolf's patrols increase, but the weather grew colder with each passing day. As Zelda had counseled, and they well knew, winter would be a bitter enemy if it descended on them before they found help among the people in the Hundred Valleys Region. And there was no guarantee they would even find those people once they arrived there.

Later that morning they were startled by noises across the river. Before they could find cover a red muk patrol marched around a bend and spotted them. The muks drew their bows and sent a flurry of arrows towards them, though they fell short of their mark and landed harmlessly in the river.

Obie drew Roar. "Eeeeyyyyyaaaa," he yelled, jumping up and down and waving the blade high, challenging the muks.

"Rrrrraaaawwww," Tau roared, and began dancing around, clawing at the air and leaping back and forth along the river. When he tired of this he drew his sword and also waved it in the air shouting challenges. Mole joined in by racing back and forth along the riverbank baring his teeth and growling as ferociously as a mole is able. Across the river the red muks put on a similar display, jumping up and down while waving their weapons and shouting challenges and insulting epithets. But it was all for show. Everyone knew the river was too treacherous to cross. Before long the game wound down and both sides continued on their way in opposite directions. Although the incident had been a good release for pent-up tension, Obie knew it would have been better if they hadn't been seen. From now on they'd have to be extra careful.

"Boys will always be boys," Mole said to Tau as they continued upriver.

"Well, I noticed *you* joined in the excitement."

"Wouldn't have missed it!"

During the afternoon they hid several times when groups of hawks flew along the gorge, seemingly in search of something.

And Obie knew what that something was. The red muks had alerted the hawks and most likely another patrol was already racing towards them. It was now imperative they reach the bridge and climb the cliff wall before nightfall, for they could be easily captured in the gorge. They picked up their pace, but dusk came a little before they reached the crook in the Witch where the bridge was. Rounding the bend in the deepening gloom they spotted its dark outline, no more than two minutes away.

Obie reached it first and started across, the old boards creaking beneath each step. He saw Tau stop at the entrance to the bridge and look back downriver. He was frowning as he watched and listened. Seconds later, a large patrol of red muks came around the bend behind them. They were running hard.

"Enemy behind," Tau yelled.

"I see them," Obie yelled back as he neared the far side of the bridge.

Tau raced across while Mole watched the advancing muks from his shoulder. Suddenly Mole took a few quick steps down the lion-man's back, leaped down, and darted back towards the center of the bridge. The first red muk reached it and entered a little ahead of his comrades. Obie exited the bridge and stopped in alarm. Why was Mole running the wrong way? Had he lost his senses? "What's Mole *doing*?" he asked as Tau approached.

"Beats me. He just said to keep running." Unable to do anything, they watched Mole stop near the center of the bridge while the red muk leader bore down on him.

Then Mole stood up on his haunches and yelled out at the river, "Zelda, Zelda, squeak, help us! Help us Zeld . . ." In the midst of his plea the soldier reached Mole and kicked him like a football into the upriver current.

Obie and Tau saw the small dark form fly from the bridge with a "Squeeeeaaak . . ." followed by a small splash.

"Nooooo," Obie yelled, heartbroken at the sight.

"Mole, Mole," Tau called.

They strained their eyes hoping to see Mole bobbing in the torrent. Seeing nothing, they raced down river watching the water for him while the red muks sped across the bridge after them.

CHAPTER FIFTEEN

ELF RUNE

THE LAST OF FIFTY heavy-booted red muk soldiers tromped onto the bridge as the first neared the far side. Abruptly, the boot sounds stopped and cries of terror ripped through the gorge. Obie and Tau turned and saw the muks cowering below the angry onslaught of the Witch, its waters swollen into a dark mountain above them. The huge wave crashed over the bridge and when the deluge receded the old wooden boards were washed clean. Now there was only the sound of the river flowing. Stunned, Obie and Tau stared at the empty bridge.

"That was no accident," Obie said. "Mole summoned Zelda."

"Yes, I heard him calling her."

"And did you notice something in the wave just before it crashed?"

"I . . . thought I imagined the face of a woman."

"You didn't imagine it. It was Zelda's face." Obie's voice was sorrowful as he added, "Mole sacrificed himself for us. I'll never forget him."

Tau turned a solemn gaze towards the Witch. "The little fellow died well. I would like to find his body so we can bury him honorably."

A small wave crashed gently on the shore thrusting something limp and soggy at their feet. "Mole," Obie exclaimed joyfully as he looked down, "Zelda sent you back to us."

"Hey, little fellow . . . it is *you*." Tau lifted Mole, but his arms and legs hung limp. "Mole," he said, shaking him gently. It was to no avail. Mole did not move.

"Give him to me, Tau. He wasn't in the water all that long, maybe . . ." Obie had learned in CPR class that one of the uses of the Heimlich Maneuver was to clear water from the air passageways of near-downed victims, and that it could also be used on dogs or cats. Hopefully, it could be used on Moles too. He held the little rodent against his chest, face out, and placed a fist under his rib cage, feeling for the hollow place just under his ribs. Then placing his other hand over the fist, he pushed inward and upward in small thrusting movements. After three thrusts water gushed from Mole's mouth. Obie laid him on his back on the sand and checked his breathing. There was no breath. Pulling Mole's tiny chin upward and opening his mouth, he placed his mouth over Mole's nose and mouth and began gently breathing air into him. Thirty seconds passed and Mole was still not breathing. As Obie leaned down to try again Mole's eyes snapped open and he started breathing.

"Are you going to kiss me?" he asked between deep breaths.

Obie sat back on his heels with a laugh.

"Mole lives," Tau announced elatedly.

Obie picked him up. "I guess we've grown attached to you, even if you are flea bitten."

His eyes glittering, Mole looked up at his friends. "I know. I'm irresistibly cute."

"I'm sorry to cut this short, but we'd better get out of here while we can." Obie handed Mole to Tau. "Those red muks we teased earlier may have decided to come after us too."

Beat-up and weak from his ordeal, Mole lacked the strength to hold on while riding on Tau's shoulder, so the lion-man carried him in his arms as they hurried upriver. The deepening night made them anxious as it would be difficult to find the path leading up the canyon wall in the dark.

A short distance from the bridge Obie grabbed Tau's arm and pointed to a spot twelve feet above them. "Something's up there watching us."

Tau grunted. "I see its eyes." The creature hooted. It was only an owl. "Follow me," Tau said. Backtracking some twenty feet, he found the path entrance. "The owl is perched on the edge of the path."

They started up and heard the flapping of wings ahead as the owl abandoned its roost. The shrill howl of wolves echoed through the gorge from the canyon rim while Obie and Tau climbed the narrow trail in the darkness. The starless sky seemed devoid of all light for the moon had not yet risen. As Obie had discovered while running through the Vale of Nepenthe, he no longer had to rely on the lion-man to lead him through the dark. All of his senses were growing keener and the changes in him were already proving useful. He recalled something he'd read about people becoming like those they associate with. Maybe this was what happened when you hung out with lions. Would he soon grow thick golden hair over his body? The thought was amusing.

As they reached the top of the cliff the moon drifted above the horizon and spread its thin light over the strip of land between the gorge and the forest. A wolf howled off to their left and was answered by a chilling howl to their right. They moved towards the cover of the trees. Only yards from the forest, Tau growled low and pulled Obie to the ground. Then Obie saw them: two huge hawks were flying by. They bore riders and were heading south. Crawling into the trees, Obie and Tau watched them turn west.

"Torolf must be using big hawks for more than his personal use," Obie whispered. "Who were those riders?"

"Raks," Tau said. "I caught their scent. I wonder where they're going."

Mole poked his head up and squinted to see the rapidly disappearing figures. "Wherever they're going, we can be sure it's nasty business."

The woodland here was younger, comprised mostly of oak, poplar, elm, and a few pepper trees. The canopy was not as high here as it had been in Gnarlwood Forest. During the day sunlight was able to filter through the trees in many spots, allowing bushes, vines and other vegetation to grow. The land was also rockier, with frequent granite outcroppings in the hillsides, and scattered boulders.

A few miles from the gorge they again heard howling nearby. They stopped to listen and Tau's nostrils widened. "The wolves are tracking us. You two stay here. I will return soon." Handing Mole over to Obie, Tau drew his sword and disappeared into the trees before Obie could protest. He stared after the lion-man, thinking of all the reasons he should have remained. Although Obie didn't relish the idea of facing a hungry wolf pack alone, it took him only seconds to realize this was no time to be staring into the darkness wishing Tau was there.

Gabrielle's face flashed through his mind and his resolve hardened. He set Mole in the crook of a high branch and drew his sword. Then he backed against the tree trunk and thrust the blade tip into the ground before him while he loaded his Raptor with his largest steel shot. The wolves howled steadily now. Obie's eyes darted from tree to tree. He wouldn't go down easy, though he didn't intend to let it come to that.

Tau roared at the same time Obie heard loud growls, snapping jaws, and wolf cries. The sounds lasted only a few seconds and then stopped. Trembling, he tried to see into the darkness, praying Tau was the victor. If only his brother, Scottie, was with him now, or Will. A man who could drive mountain lions away with a stick could drive off a few wolves. Obie pressed his back into the tree. Off to his left a small branch snapped. Drawing himself up, he spotted a dark form moving towards him. He raised his Raptor and took aim. It was Tau and he was limping. Obie lowered his weapon. "Welcome back." He could see Tau was bleeding just below his right knee.

Tau was stone-faced, but a smile gleamed in his eyes. When he drew near he raised his right paw-hand. "I give you five."

"Hey, dude." Obie grinned and slapped Tau's paw-hand.

"Dude?"

"That's a friendly name the guys back home call each other."

Mole raised his head from his perch in the tree. "Well, *dudes*, now that the excitement is over, can we find a quiet place to sleep?"

"That is next, little one. I slew the alpha wolf and I do not think we will be bothered again tonight. However, we must stand watch. I do not know whether they are Torolf's wolves. Maybe they are just hungry and like the taste of man-flesh."

"Yeah, if we're lucky they only want to eat us," Obie said. He sheathed Roar and glanced at Tau's leg. "How bad is your wound?"

Tau examined his leg. "Not bad enough to slow me down. I will spread some of the herbs on it that the river sprites packed for us and it will heal in a few days. Now we both limp."

"Yes, we certainly are an impressive lot," Mole said, faking a limp along the tree limb. Obie chuckled. It was good having Mole's humor to lighten their mood.

They found a broad-leafed tree with long branches that drooped to the ground forming a tent-like enclosure within. It would hide them and give shelter from the weather for the few hours they needed to sleep. The excitement of his battle left Tau wide awake, so he stood first guard, peering out through small openings he made among the leaves. Several hours later he awakened Obie for his watch and the night passed with no further sign of wolves. Frost lay on the ground when they set out again, ever watchful for signs of the enemy.

The land grew quieter, with few bird or insect sounds the farther north they went. The air began to feel heavy and oppressive, as though disaster was waiting for them at every turn, or over the next hill. Obie was glad when Tau suggested they never leave one another's sight. That afternoon they spotted a large spider web with the headless skeleton of some unlucky man hanging in it. The skull had fallen to the ground and rested a few feet away. Tattered clothing hanging from the bones flapped in the breeze, and one boot still hung on a foot bone while the other had fallen to the ground.

"The poor guy probably starved to death or froze," Obie said.

"Better than the raks getting him," Tau said. "This is one they missed."

"I wonder who he was," Mole said. "No matter. Let's cut him down and give him a proper burial."

Obie and Tau hacked through the remains of the decaying web, and the bones fell to the ground. They were about to dig the grave when Tau reached down and pulled a half-buried object from the soil. "What have we here?" He brushed off the dirt while the others watched. It was a silver flask with slightly raised grape vine ornamentation crafted around it. Tau removed the cap, then sniffed the contents and took a small taste.

"How is it?" Mole asked anxiously.

A smile crept across Tau's furry face as he replaced the cap. "The spirits are still good. I will bring it with us," he said, tucking it into his pack.

They dug a shallow grave in the hard soil and buried the bones, then piled rocks on top. Mole grabbed one of the dead man's boots in his teeth and pulled it atop the rocks to serve as a marker, and Obie brought the other.

"These were once fine boots," Mole remarked. "Perhaps the man who wore them was of equal quality."

After that they resumed their old habit of watching the trees for black spider shapes and webs and they grew more solemn. Obie's growing anxiety caused him to speak less often, and he frequently withdrew into his thoughts. He was haunted by the growing fear that time was running out for Gabrielle and Mara. No matter how quickly they covered ground, it never seemed fast enough. Every second of Gabrielle's captivity was agonizing to him. What indescribable evil would Torolf work upon her once she and Mara were locked away in his tower at Targus Dol? Were they there already? When tortured by these fears at night, he would sometimes get up and splash water in his face and walk around to calm himself. The cold air and physical activity helped a little. At other times he would lie against his pack and stare into the darkness grasping the small, blue swatch of fabric from Gabrielle's dress that he had taken from the thorn bush.

Tau and Mole were quieter too. On the night they buried the skeleton Obie observed Mole staring into the darkness with a sorrowful, faraway look in his eyes. He wondered what deep thoughts moles had. Was he mourning some lost love? In this cheerless atmosphere beneath the dreary sky by day and the starless sky by night, a sky illuminated only by the fading sun and moon, small bits of occasional humor acted as therapy that helped to hold them together.

Early on the third morning out from Witch River, they were approaching a low hill when Tau halted. Obie came up beside him. "What's up?"

Tau was growling low and his nose twitched oddly. "I smell goblin," he whispered, setting Mole on the ground. "Wait here."

Obie squatted beside Mole as they watched Tau steal to the crest of the hill and look over. Glancing back, he put a finger to his lips for silence and motioned for them to join him.

"A band of goblins," Tau whispered when they arrived.

Obie and Mole peeked over the edge. The hill dropped off sharply into a sandstone slide area. At the bottom, eight goblins sat in a circle, grunting, slurping, and slobbering while gnawing meat from animal bones. When each goblin stripped his bone clean he tossed it behind him and reached for another from the pile in the center of their circle.

"Not all of them feed like pigs," Tau whispered. "These are low-class goblins."

Obie watched in fascination. The creatures' wrinkled skin looked greenish and leathery. They had short, muscular bodies and legs, round baglike heads with only a few hairs on top, bulbous eyes, noses that resembled yams, and sharp teeth. They wore only loincloths, but piles of clothing, metal breastplates, clubs, swords and bows lay off to the side.

"They're late risers when they can get away with it," Tau whispered. "Judging by their tracks, they came from the north and are moving south. We are in goblin country."

At that moment the loose soil beneath Mole gave way and he started sliding down the hill. Obie and Tau grabbed for him, but too late. Clawing in vain at the loose hillside, Mole slid slowly down. The goblins looked up and continued chomping on their bones while they watched Mole sliding towards them, as though he was mealtime entertainment.

"Hrunchhh bolly aggatuch," one of the goblins said. Something resembling a smile formed on the slit of his mouth as he patted his fat belly.

"Naaawww, naaawww, bolly rubba awwga suth," another answered.

Then the first goblin snorted and threw his stripped bone at the second, hitting him in the head. "Awagagaga hisstta," he said, then got up and trotted to the foot of the hill. While the others laughed and continued eating, he waited with outstretched hands to catch Mole.

"What are the goblins saying?" Obie whispered.

"The one at the bottom of the hill thinks Mole will make a sweet desert for his meal." Tau's nostrils flared in anger. "And the other one said moles taste like warm buffalo dung."

Mole was no more than a foot beyond the goblin's reach when he finally came to a stop. Obie peeked over the ridge just in time to see Mole regain his footing and shoot away horizontally along the hill with the goblin following behind.

"Go, Mole, go," Obie whispered. Tau took a quick look.

The other goblins were laughing at their comrade and talking excitedly among themselves.

"What're they saying now?" Obie asked.

"They're placing bets on whether their friend will catch Mole." Tau peeked back over the hill for an instant and then ducked down. "Let's go! Mole's circling the bottom of the hill. He'll be coming this way."

Obie and Tau ran down the slope and stopped behind a boulder to keep watch. Sooner than they expected, Mole's small brown body appeared. He was running with his ears down and the goblin a few steps behind.

"I didn't know moles could run so fast," Obie said.

"Doesn't like goblins." Tau calmly weighed a couple of big rocks in his hands. He selected one and set the other down.

Obie knelt down and waited. As Mole raced by the boulder Obie's hands darted out and snatched up his furry little friend. A second later there was a loud thud.

"Never knew what hit him," Tau said. He was holding the large rock and grinning over the flattened goblin.

Mole laughed between hard pants. "C . . . can we g . . . go now?" he finally managed to say.

They ran east along the base of the hill, then around another low hill, widely circling the group of goblins.

"Hopefully the goblin will think he hit his head on the boulder and they will not pursue us," Tau said.

Obie grinned and said, "If the one you clobbered has any idea of what *did* happen, it may reflect so badly on his goblinhood that he'll be afraid to admit it to his buddies."

Tau barked a quick laugh and glanced at Obie. "An astute assessment of the goblin ego."

For the rest of the day Tau sniffed the air frequently, but detected no sign of pursuing goblins.

The next morning dark storm clouds rolled in and by mid-morning it started raining. They stopped only long enough to turn their cloaks fur-side out to help repel the rain and pull up their hoods. When they hurried on, Mole was snuggled inside Tau's hood. The rain grew heavier in the afternoon and they watched for a place to camp that would provide shelter. The land gently rose and the air grew cold. Oak, poplar, elm and birch gave way to tall firs and pines. By mid-afternoon the rain turned briefly to sleet, then back to rain. They stopped to rest under the thick branches of a tall fir tree. While Tau reclined against the tree with Mole curled up next to him, Obie managed to shoot a rabbit.

"The rabbit favors us with meat today. That is good . . ." Tau's voice trailed off as his eyelids closed for a catnap.

"I'm going to have a look at that rocky area on the hill over there," Obie said. His words were wasted. Mole and Tau were sound asleep. When he returned a short time later, Tau was sitting up.

"How can one who looks so miserable, cold, and wet also look happy?" Tau asked.

"Because this miserable, cold, wet one knows that in a little while he's going to be cozy, warm, and dry. I found a cave in those rocks up there." With a slight jerk of his head Obie motioned up the hill. "And it'll be safe for a fire."

Mole opened one eye and said, "Cave . . . warm . . . fire?"

The cavern was roomy, dry, and well hidden in the rocks. They found a fire pit with a spit and a stack of dry wood left by previous travelers. By the look of things it had not been occupied in several months. While Obie got a fire going Tau squeezed the rainwater from their cloaks and laid them out to dry. Meanwhile, Mole found a large pile of sweet, dry grass in a recessed area of the cavern and started dragging some of it by his teeth when Obie ran back to help.

"Thanks, Mole. That'll be a luxury tonight."

"The last travelers here likely stored it for their horses. Elves I'd say."

Obie's eyes widened. "Elves? Here?"

"Yes—they sometimes travel through this area."

Tau helped Obie bring more of the grass near the fire and they arranged it into sleeping pallets. Resident beetles, disturbed by all the movement, scrambled out onto the cave floor where Mole eagerly collected them. Tau skinned and cleaned the rabbit and then put it on to roast, setting the pelt aside. Finally, Obie and Tau pulled off their damp clothing and laid the pieces near the fire next to the cloaks. While Tau pulled on a pair of clean pants and a vest from his pack, Obie set his fresh clothing down and went to the cave entrance to have a look.

"The rain's coming down harder now," he said. The firelight cast a reddish glow over his bare skin as he stood looking out. "Be right back," he called over his shoulder and disappeared outside.

Mole looked quizzically at Tau, sitting next to him on his pallet by the fire.

Tau shrugged. "Humans sometimes do strange things."

When Obie returned he was shivering and his hair and body were dripping with rainwater. "That was invigorating—you guys should try it." He shook the water from his hair and squatted near the fire, rubbing his hands together to warm them.

"Only furless creatures can appreciate such pain," Mole said. He was basking lazily on his back with his feet in the air, angled towards the fire.

Tau yawned and stretched out on his back. Obie slipped into his pants and then dropped to his pallet where he lay chest down, chin propped on his hands, facing his friends. "I'm starving," he said glancing at the roasting rabbit. "Mole, do you want to try some rabbit tonight?"

Mole raised his head to look at Obie. "There's an abundance of insects in this cave, but since you offer it, I'll try a small piece." His eyes caught something and flickered as he finished his sentence. He rolled over and sat up on his haunches staring hard at Obie's left shoulder. He was squeaking and his whiskers twitched.

Obie was alarmed. "What's wrong? Mole, are you all right?"

"That mark on your shoulder. Where did you get it?"

Obie automatically touched his birthmark. "This? I've always had it." He felt relieved that what had disturbed Mole amounted to nothing.

"You were born with it?"

"Yeah." Already tired of the conversation, Obie rolled over on his back.

"Wait. Let me have a better look."

Obie groaned and turned back onto his stomach. "Look, Mole, it's nothing to get excited over. It's just a stupid birthmark with an odd shape that I've been kidded about all my life."

Tau raised his head in mild interest.

Mole came closer and studied the mark. When he was finished, he sat back on his haunches again and stared at Obie with solemn eyes.

"What is it?" Obie was visibly shaken now.

"Oberon, that's an elf rune. You have the mark of the elves."

"What?" Obie said sharply, bolting to his knees to face Mole.

"Humans who bear this mark have elven blood in their veins. Quite simply, you're a halfling."

Obie stared at Mole in disbelief. His lips parted to form words, but stopped. Then a look of comprehension entered his eyes and he grinned. "Okay, I get it now. This is a joke." He relaxed and changed to a cross-legged position.

"This is no joke."

"But, how can I be part elf? We don't have any elves where I come from, so where did the elf blood come from?"

"There may be elves among your people and you simply don't recognize them because you choose not to believe in their existence. But it's from far back in your lineage. One of your ancestors must have been a High Elf. The wondrous thing about elven blood, Oberon, is that it does not die out. The magic in it causes it to remain as strong in future generations as in the first child begotten from a human and elf union. Have you ever noticed that things seem to come more easily for you than for other humans?"

"I guess it *has* seemed that way at times, except for this freakin' limp I have. I've never really thought much about it, not until lately anyway."

"What has made you think about it lately?"

"For one thing, my limp goes away after I run for a while, as you've seen. And sometimes it goes away immediately. I have no idea why it's happening. It began when I arrived in Windermere— or maybe even the day I left home. Another thing, after I started following the raks my night vision improved, and my hearing and sense of smell are getting stronger. I've sometimes wondered if I was just imagining it."

"You're not *imagining* these changes. It's the magic working in your blood. As you mature it strives to manifest itself more strongly. The fact that you need keen senses right now may be speeding up the process. As to the mystery of your limp, I venture to guess that your elven powers are struggling against something within you for dominance. Whatever is causing your limp is strongly resisting the side of you that wants to bring you good health. If what I am suggesting is true, we must hope your elven blood will win the battle.

Obie felt confused. He needed time to digest all of this. Resting his hands palms up on his crossed legs, he stared at them as if for the first time, half expecting to see something non-human. *Me, an elf? Dad won't believe it. And what's Scottie going to think? But . . . he and Dad must also be . . . It doesn't matter, they'll never believe it. They'll think Ghostrise Valley drove me insane.* Then something occurred to him. "Wait a minute, Mole, my dad and brother don't have this mark. If elf blood never dies out, then they should have the mark too, shouldn't they?"

"No, they wouldn't." Mole lay down again. "The mark only shows up once every few generations. One of your great grand-parents must have had it. The important thing for you to under-stand is the magic in your blood gives you powers and abilities you probably aren't even aware of yet."

"Well if this is true, and I'm not saying I believe it, but *if* it's true, what should I do?"

"You need do nothing beyond what you're already doing. I suspect you already stretch yourself a little beyond your human limitations without realizing it. I would tell you only to continue to explore your abilities, for that is how you will grow into your elven powers. And, above all, trust the voice deep within you. Do you know what I'm speaking of?"

"Maybe. Once in a while, I just know something. I don't know why or how I know . . . I just do. I guess it *is* like a voice inside and, so far anyway, it's never been wrong."

"And it won't be, Oberon. It will never lead you astray."

"I had no idea Moles were so wise," Obie said, staring in amazement at him.

Mole responded with a molish chuckle that made his whisk-ers twitch.

Obie gazed quietly into the fire for a time, thinking of every-thing Mole had said. It was mind-boggling. He wanted to know more about the elves. Turning again to Mole, he asked in a quiet voice, "Can you tell me about the High Elves?"

"I can tell you a little. They live in the Elven Isles of Eluthien, a place of such beauty it will make your heart ache if ever you should see it."

Obie tried to imagine a place like that. "I've heard they live there. Where are the isles?

"By horse it's about seven days northwest of Windermere. Few have ever seen it, though, except from a distance."

"Why?"

"Elves aren't fond of the outside world and have always kept to themselves. They allow very few others into their kingdom."

"Have you ever been there?"

"Once when I was young." A dreamy look came into Mole's eyes, and then he ended the conversation by lowering his head and closing his eyelids, apparently to take a short nap before their evening meal. Though he was curious about Mole's visit to the Elven Isles, Obie decided not to press him. He would reveal things in his own good time. Maybe at this moment Mole was basking in his memories of that fair place.

Tau lay on his back listening, his paw-hands clasped behind his head. He had shown only mild surprise when Mole revealed to Obie that he was a halfling. Smiling, he got up and checked the rabbit, then reported in a mellow voice, "It's done to a juicy tenderness." Mole roused himself. Tau cut savory pieces off the rabbit and handed them to his comrades before cutting his own and joining them for the meal. "Eat well, brothers, for the rabbit may not always favor us so."

When they finished, Obie lay back on his pallet and his thoughts reached out to Gabrielle. He knew with all of his being that he must rescue her and Mara. And he hoped it was true that elven powers were growing within him. He might need them.

***

After Obie and Mole fell asleep, Tau sat working with the rabbit pelt. He scraped the inner flesh side with his knife to smooth it, and then took some cedar oil he carried in his pack for tanning and rubbed it in well. When he finished he put it with the other rabbit pelts he had been saving. Then with a yawn, he got up and put more wood on the fire and lay down to sleep.

CHAPTER SIXTEEN

WOLVES

THE TEMPERATURE DROPPED below freezing during the night and snow was falling when Obie awoke. Flinging his cloak around his shoulders he went outside and around the boulders near the cave entrance. Snowflakes fell on his hair as he looked out at an icy, white world. It seemed as though the Earth and sky were one, the dividing line erased by whiteness, leaving only dark tree trunks and the undersides of branches spread like arms cradling their icy burden. Did the trees revel in the quiet solitude of winter, forgetting for a time the noisy burst of spring? They seemed made for winter; there was perfection in their silent, snow-laden boughs. Lingering a little, he wondered if Gabrielle was somewhere out in this snowstorm. The thought of her among the raks burned in him. He turned and reentered the cave. There was much to do, and time was growing short.

The storm would make travel slow and difficult, so they decided to wait it out. In the meantime, Tau suggested they make snowshoes for traversing the deep, powdery snow. He had learned the secrets of snowshoe making by watching Torolf's worker muks in Targus Dol. The muks had learned the craft from goblins that traversed the land in caravans, and they in turn had learned from aboriginal tribesmen who were masters at it.

After pulling on the boots and winter gloves Zelda had given them, they donned their cloaks and went out to collect some saplings to use as snowshoe frames. It did not take long to find them, and soon they were back warming themselves by the fire and eating nearly the last of their flat bread, nuts and dried fruit. Mole was chewing insects he had found in the cave when he noticed his friends' food supply was almost gone. He laid down the large beetle he was about to consume. "If you have trouble finding food, I'll be pleased to share my insects with you. I'll collect a good supply before we leave."

"Very considerate of you Mole," Tau said.

Obie agreed. *When times get tough, the tough eat bugs.*

Mole started hunting for insects along the cave walls and in the grass piled at the back of the cavern. Meanwhile Tau rummaged through his supply pack and pulled out some river-sprite rope. He cut off a length of the rope and, carefully separating the strands, formed strong cords to serve as the cross-strings for their snow-shoes. "We could use rabbit hide, but these cords are strong and will make construction faster," he said. He instructed Obie on bending the saplings into frames, tying the ends together, winding the strings tightly around the frames, lacing the webbing, and finally on tying two pieces of wood across the frame, spaced to match their boot sizes. They would tie their feet to these cross bars. Then, with a glint in his eye, he sat down to work on his own pair, saying to Obie, "And now, my furless friend, let us see who can finish first."

"You're on, fuzzy one."

They immersed themselves in their task, each occasionally tracking the other's progress from the corners of their eyes.

"Done," Obie was first to say a little under two hours later. He held his snowshoes up and Tau inspected them.

"Crude, but adequate." Tau then tied the last knot on his own pair. "I am finished also, but you won. Your reward is that we will go hunting."

"But . . . you get the same reward."

"Would you prefer to go alone?"

"Good point," Obie said with a half-grin. He got up and pulled his cloak on.

"Me too." Mole ran from the rear of the cave to join them. "I've grown weary of chasing bugs."

The white rabbits were almost invisible against the snow and when they finally spotted one it disappeared down a hole. But soon afterwards they saw a small turkey. Obie shot at it with his Raptor just as Tau threw his knife. Both hit their mark and the bird keeled over sideways. The hunters hooted and hollered and Obie carried it back. Roast turkey would be a welcome change in their menu. They ate a good portion of it that evening and kept the rest for the next day.

Mole was asleep when Tau pulled out several of his rabbit pelts and sat up late working on them again. Obie lay resting against his pack watching. Tau was probably making himself a new vest or something, Obie thought. Whatever he was making, the work was evidently going well because Tau appeared pleased when he put it away. As to why he hid it among some rocks, Obie couldn't guess. When Tau returned he dropped to his pallet and purred himself to sleep in the warmth of the fire.

By the next morning it had stopped snowing, though the dark storm clouds remained and threatened more snow. After finishing a small meal they packed what little food they had left, a little turkey and a supply of dead insects, and prepared to leave. Mole stood ready for Tau to lift him to his shoulder, but Tau hesitated. "Wait," he said, and reentered the cave. He returned with the little hooded rabbit skin coat he had made. "This is for you, Mole. You will need it."

Mole squeaked and his whiskers twitched excitedly. "A gift for me? I'm speechless, Tau. It's beautiful." He sat up on his haunches and Tau helped him slip his arms through the sleeves and pull the hood up. It fit perfectly. Mole looked down at the coat, admiring himself. Suddenly his expression changed. He stood up straight, paws on his hips, and fixed Tau with a narrowed eye. "Does accepting this gift from you mean I'm a pet?"

Tau made a low throaty chuckle. "No. It only means you're a mole in a bunny skin."

"A *warm* mole in a bunny skin," Mole corrected, apparently satisfied with Tau's explanation.

Obie had been watching the exchange while leaning over to put on his snowshoes. "You look ducky in your new coat, Mole." He grinned and stood up.

"Yes, we're a merry looking lot," Mole said with a wink. "I've always admired you in your cloak, Obie, and of course Tau . . ."

Before Mole could get another word out, Tau reached down and lifted him to his shoulder. "I think we had best go now, before the dung rises above our knees."

They continued north moving steadily up the long, slow grade in the evergreen forest. By midday snow started falling again, and traveling became more difficult. They no longer worried about being spotted by Torolf's spies or patrols as the weather made it impossible to see very far, and it seemed unlikely the enemy would even venture out in this storm.

The greatest threats facing them now was the bitter cold and hungry wolves. Sometimes, they saw gray shapes pacing them, awaiting their chance to attack. Other times the wolves simply stood and watched Obie and Tau pass by. Even when they could not see the wolves they heard their frequent, shrill howls. Twice Obie drove them away with his Raptor, yet they always returned, keeping their distance, waiting.

On and on they plodded over the now sparsely forested terrain, hoods pulled low over icy faces and snow blanketing their heads and shoulders. When they stopped to rest, the cold pierced their bones. Movement kept them warm, so they rested only briefly. Mole stayed warm by snuggling against Tau's mane inside his hood. Although they watched for game and fowl, the land appeared lifeless except for the wolves. The thought of eating wolf meat was repulsive, but if starvation became an issue

Obie knew the hunted would become the hunters. By late afternoon round white humps appeared on the ground as the terrain became rockier. Then the somber gray light of day began to fade.

"Tau," Obie called.

The wind prevented Tau from hearing, so Obie whistled his loudest. Tau stopped and hobbled around in his snowshoes to face his young friend, his round eyes glowing out from the darkness under his hood. Obie pointed to the right. Tau made a half-turn, then nodded that he understood. They moved towards a boulder with a tall fir tree growing next to it that was barely visible through the driving snow. Not the shelter they had hoped for, but it would have to do, for it was nearly dark and there was no other.

Obie ran an eye around the area. "Not enough dry wood for a fire."

Mole's snout poked out of Tau's hood and a moment later his two beady eyes appeared. They were standing in the angle of the tree and a boulder.

"We need to build a snow shelter. We can use the tree and the boulder as part of the wall," Obie shouted over the howling wind.

Tau nodded in agreement. Necessity made them work fast, and the movement raised their body heat. They were careful not to work up a sweat though, for as outdoorsmen well know, in subzero weather sweat would make their bodies freeze. They filled the narrow space between the tree and boulder with snow and packed it down hard to form the back and one side of the upper shelter wall. This cut much of the wind chill coming from behind the tree. Then they dug several feet down, creating an area with a flat floor, large enough for them to sit comfortably. The snow they removed was piled and packed to form the rest of the above-ground wall, with a small door. From a nearby tree they broke off small pine branches with plenty of needles to line the floor. Across the top of the walls they laid larger branches, also with thick needles, and packed snow over them to form the roof. When it was finished they crawled in and spread their blankets over the floor and laid their swords beside them in case of wolf attack. The shelter was crude, but efficient. At least they would not freeze to death this night.

Tau piled up a snow wall in the entrance, leaving a small window at the top. No wind came through since it blew from behind the shelter. Obie pulled a handful of partially frozen insects from his pack. "Sorry, Mole. Your food's cold tonight."

"I'm so hungry I don't care how cold it is." Mole stuffed a couple of plump brown beetles in his mouth.

Obie took the partially frozen leftover turkey from his pack and shared it with Tau; and when that was gone they sat staring out at the swirling snow. They were tired, still hungry, and too cold to talk. Mole came out from between them and sat back on his haunches looking up at his two companions. "If we are to survive this night in any condition for traveling tomorrow, we must huddle together and layer your cloaks over and around us to conserve heat."

Obie and Tau agreed. Sitting back-to-back with knees drawn up close to their chests, they spread both of their cloaks over their heads in a double layer like a small tent. Then Mole crawled in under the cloaks and threatened to wreak havoc if anyone farted.

"Have pity, Mole, we're too miserable to laugh," Obie pleaded.

Tau lifted his end of the cloak a little and began digging around in his pack. "Tau, what are you doing? You're letting the freezing air in," Obie growled.

"Relax . . . I have something for us," Tau said, dropping the cloak back down. Mole chortled and brushed against Obie's knee as he moved closer to Tau. Obie heard a glug, glug sound coming from Tau's throat followed by a deep sigh of satisfaction.

"Must be good," Mole said.

"Must be," Obie agreed.

"Judge for yourselves," Tau said, passing the silver flask to Obie. Then Tau added, "Tonight we drink to the dead man whose liquor warms us in our time of need."

"You drink first, Mole," Obie offered, holding the flask out to him.

"You're a true gentleman, Oberon. Don't mind if I do. Just help me hold it up, will you?" Mole sat up on his haunches.

"How's this?"

"Perfect." Obie could hear the liquor gurgling down Mole's throat. "Ahhhh, how it doth warm my innards," Mole said when he finished. "May the dead man's bones rest peacefully. Your turn, Obie."

"Thanks, Mole. May the dead man's bones rest peacefully." Obie took a healthy swallow. Immediately he felt a warm sensation radiate through his body and down his limbs. With a smile on his face, he passed the flask back to Tau.

"There's enough left for another night," Tau said. "Perhaps we should save it."

Mole belched. "Yes, we probably should."

"Yeah, we probably ought to save it," Obie agreed.

"On the otherhand . . ." Tau started to say.

"Yeah, we should always consider the other hand," Obie confirmed.

"My other hand just informed me it's a very cold night and it would like another drink," Mole announced.

"Mine is in agreement," Tau added energetically.

"Mine too," Obie said.

Soon the three basked in the warmth of camaraderie while the storm howled outside their shelter. Then Mole began to wax poetic. "Lads, I feel a song coming on."

"We could do with some entertainment, Mole. What's your song about?" Obie asked.

"In honor of the dead man, I'm inspired to sing about those scurrilous insults to nature, the raks." Mole sat up on his haunches and in a surprisingly melodic voice, began singing:

Beware the nasty raks, boys
They'll ruin your best day,
They'll jump you from the trees
If you look the other way.

They'll chase you over hill,
They'll chase you through the dale,
They're big ugly lugs,
And their breath is always stale.

If they catch you in their web,
It'll surely cook your goose,
You'll struggle and you'll scream,
But you won't be gettin' loose.

They're the worst, they're cursed,
They thirst for your blood,
They'll rip and tear your flesh,
Toss your carcass in the mud.

They'll invite you for dinner,
They're a jolly, jolly crew,
Then they'll throw you in the pot
And cook you up in stew.

Beware the nasty raks, boys,
They'll ruin your best day,
So if ya see 'um coming,
Best you head the other way.

"I didn't know you were so talented, Mole."

Mole belched again. "Nor did I. It just came over me."

"Can you sing us one about the muks?" Tau asked.

"Sorry, that's all I've got in me tonight," Mole said apologetically as he curled up next to his companions. "The muks will have to wait for another night."

They grew quiet then, for it had been a long, hard day and they were weary. Outside the wind gusted higher, and at times Obie wondered whether it was the wind or the wolves he heard howling. It was cold and uncomfortable sitting up to sleep, but they survived the night. Obie awakened first and peeked out from under the cloaks. His movement woke Tau, who pulled the cloaks aside and peered out glumly. Dawn had come and it was still snowing, though the wind was calmer. A squirrel climbed up and contemplated them with interest through the small window in the door. Slowly Tau raised his arm, trying not to alarm it. An instant later his hand shot out to grab it. The squirrel moved faster. The cold slowed Tau's speed considerably.

Groaning, Obie kicked the snow door down and crawled through, dragging his cloak behind him. His muscles were stiff as he stood up. He threw his cloak around him and pulled up his hood. Then his stomach rumbled. It felt like it was sticking to his backbone. Mole was a little better off as he still had a small supply of insects. Tau came out of the shelter already cloaked and hooded. With his back to the others, he stood silently gazing north. Finally he turned to Obie and Mole and said, "I believe the Hundred Valleys Region is little more than a day from here. But now we must find food."

All that day the snow continued to fall. Finding game or fowl dominated their thoughts and their eyes were ever watchful. At one point, Obie saw the shadowy forms of two large wolves loping along on their left. He shot at one hoping out of hunger to bring it down, but the cold or the wind caused him to miss and the wolves bounded off. As night approached again, the best shelter they could find was a deep southwest-facing snowdrift within a wide crevice in the rock face of a hill. They decided to dig out a snow cabin, as here they would be shielded from the blizzard's northerly winds.

The wolves howled while they worked, and today their cries sounded more urgent, hungrier than before. Obie and Tau worked as fast as they could while Mole stood guard. When the cabin was large enough they crawled inside and built a snow wall to seal the entrance as before, leaving a small opening at the top for air. Then they sat wrapped in their cloaks with hoods pulled up. Tau set the last handful of Mole's insects out for him to eat. When minutes passed and he failed to touch them, Tau asked, "Mole, will you not eat?"

"No. I've been riding and I don't need food. Do you see this fat body of mine? I can go a long time without nourishment." Mole slid a claw through the insect pile and divided it, then shoved half to Obie and the other half to Tau. "Here. This is for you. You both need it."

"But, Mole," Obie protested.

"No, I insist. I will not eat." Mole turned his back on his friends and the food.

"Thank you, little one," Tau said. "I gladly accept your gift, but before long, you shall feast."

Obie looked back and forth from Mole to Tau, then followed Tau's example. "Thank you, Mole. I also gladly accept your gift."

Mole seemed pleased when he turned to face his friends again.

Although the insects provided no more than a tiny snack for Obie and Tau, it was something, and their stomachs welcomed it.

When Obie finished chewing he said, "Zelda mentioned we might find help in the Hundred Valleys Region from the Shadow People."

Tau thought for a moment, then answered, "When I crossed the region after escaping from Targus Dol, I encountered no one. Yet I have heard a hidden people live there."

Mole spoke up, "They are the Otawn, though many call them *the Shadow People*."

"Why are they called that?" Obie asked.

"Because they move like shadows through the forest valleys, soundless and unseen. They're nomadic and can relocate from one valley to another on a moment's notice. That is how they evade Torolf."

"Can *we* find them?" Obie asked.

"Not unless they wish to be found. We can only hope they will find us and take us in. The Hundred Valleys Region is a very big place and our chances of being found by the Shadow People may be slender, especially in a blizzard."

They slept sitting up and huddled back-to-back again, with the two cloaks over their heads. Obie slept with difficulty, dozing and waking to the howling of wolves and wind several times. Finally his head dropped onto his knees and he sank into deep sleep. In a dream, hungry wolves were circling him. He heard a loud snarling growl and, turning towards it, a huge red-eyed wolf leaped at him. Startled awake with a sudden jerk, he ripped the cloaks away. Two feet away, four cold yellow eyes peered in through the small window at the top of the doorway.

"Wolves," Obie yelled, grabbing his sword as he kicked down the snow door.

Tau, awakened by Obie's violent movement, grasped his sword in one hand and yanked the cloaks away with the other. Mole leaped out of the way as they scrambled after the snarling gray beasts. Tau killed one of the wolves while Obie chased the others off.

Afterwards, Tau knelt beside the dead wolf and ran his paw-hand over its coat. "Look at this pitiful creature. He's skin and bone, near starvation, and diseased. See the sores on his hide where the fur has fallen out? We cannot eat him or use his fur. I do not believe these wolves are traveling with the pack. They're probably outcasts."

"Let's hope we don't run into the pack." Obie tried to see through the falling snow, but poor visibility made it impossible to see anything.

Morning was near and they did not sleep after that. It was still snowing when they set out at dawn, but the wind had stopped blowing which enabled them to trot along faster in their snowshoes. They kept a good pace, but it was short-lived. When midday approached the wind whipped up again and the snow increased until they were slowed to a walk.

Nearly exhausted, Obie, Tau, and Mole came to the brink of a high mesa. Below, spreading east and west, was a seemingly endless number of valleys and ridges. It was the Hundred Valleys Region. The valleys intertwined as far as they could see, sandwiched between this mesa and another to the north. The northern mesa was mostly hidden behind boiling gray clouds and snow flurries. The valleys were rich with snow-blanketed pine and fir forests with a sprinkling of bare-branched deciduous trees. Strewn within the valleys were meadows, small frozen lakes, and winding rivers. Tau pointed towards a momentary parting of the clouds far in the distance. "If you look hard you can see the dark wall of the Barren Plateau beyond the valleys. It is the wall bordering Targus Dol."

His voice sounded strange and when Obie turned to look at him, he saw fear in the lion-man's eyes, something he had never seen there before. "It looks menacing," Obie said, turning his eyes back to the dark line of the plateau.

"It is. You will see." Then the gray clouds rolled over and the opening closed.

CHAPTER SEVENTEEN

CAPTIVES

GABRIELLE, IT PAINED ME to see that spider creature throw you down back there. Are you hurt?

No, I think I'm all right, Mara, just a little bruised. What about you? Are you all right—aside from having to tolerate that brute riding you? Gabrielle turned in the saddle to look at Mara running behind her on the gloomy forest path.

"Keep looking ahead, human. Do not turn around or you will be blindfolded," the soldier riding Mara bellowed as he glared at Gabrielle.

"We've never seen creatures like you," Gabrielle protested. "What are you? And where are you taking us? At least tell us that."

"We are called *raks* by our master. And you will learn where we are taking you when we get there. Now turn around and be silent," he growled. Frowning at the sight of leather straps binding Mara's wings, Gabrielle obeyed.

Avoid incurring the wrath of these raks, Gabrielle, for though these creatures appear to be part human, I don't think they feel much compassion. They are surely Torolf's creation.

I think you're right. Gabrielle felt Mara's fear of being taken to Torolf and a chill ran through her. She tried to calm Mara by changing the subject. *We're lucky the raks haven't separated us. And it doesn't appear they can hear our thoughts. They must lack the power of mental speech. They'll never know we're communicating with each other. We must stay alert for an opportunity to escape.*

If only you can free my wings, Mara answered. *But be careful of these fearsome raks—their poison can be deadly. You saw what they did to the queen's horse soldiers at the festival.*

Yes. My heart weeps for those brave men.

Hour after hour the raks pushed hard along the Old Path without stopping to rest, and the forest shadows deepened as the day waned. While they rode, Gabrielle recounted in her mind all that had happened during the attack at the festival. Although some of the horse soldiers had been injured or killed, she knew Queen Olwen would send many more in fast pursuit. But the raks had a head start and traveled swiftly. Were Prince Andor and other eagles flying over the forest canopy searching for them? If so, it would be a difficult task, for their vision could not penetrate the dense trees. Was her family safe? Was Obie safe? How many friends and neighbors had survived this day? Tears flooded her eyes as her thoughts went to her mother.

It was Annwyl's greatest hope that her only daughter would marry a suitable gentleman and bear many children. Gabrielle had often seen her mother's worried, moist-eyed look that said, *I want you to be happy, though I fear you never will be.* In her mother's mind, an unmarried, childless woman could not possibly be happy or content. How many times had she scolded Gabrielle that an eligible young woman must dress properly if she is to find a husband? Her mother never understood and Gabrielle had not the heart to tell her she would never marry— would never bear her any grandchildren. Little wonder, then, that she rejected dressing to please eligible gentleman. In fact she dressed to displease them. The last thing she wanted was suitors on her doorstep. She had become skillful at evading their advances, and there had been a few. It was hard to disappoint her mother, yet in this she was resolved.

Only Mara and Nona understood. It brought an inward smile to think that only a few family members and two or three of the queen's servants ever knew her private name for Queen Olwen was *Nona*, the name she had used since childhood. Wise, kind Nona. On special occasions, such as her royal banquets, or the Festival of the Harvest, the queen would gently ask her to dress fashionably. At no other time did she mention Gabrielle's attire. After Prince Ulrik disappeared, she had never suggested to Gabrielle that she marry another. Nona knew who possessed Gabrielle's heart. Ulrik had been gone so long now. Most people believed him dead, including Gabrielle's mother. That was why Annwyl was anxious for her to marry. But Gabrielle would not lose hope. And if he never returned, then so be it. A lifetime would not be too long to wait for him. Unless she and Mara escaped and rode the Moonpath at the next full moon, though, it would be a very brief lifetime for everyone. She felt a sharp pain in her right leg. Her horse had brushed too close to a thorn bush. It was only a scratch, but a small piece from the bottom of her blue dress had torn off.

When the gloom of late afternoon faded into darkest night, the raks halted and made camp. A soldier pulled Gabrielle from her horse. He checked the ropes on her wrists and then bound her feet. A heavy rope was placed around Mara's neck and the other end tied to a tree. Two guards were posted nearby to keep watch over them. Gabrielle was surprised when they made several campfires. Then she realized the forest canopy was too dense for a fire to be detected from above by a passing windlord or eagle.

Before long another rak soldier brought a small pail of fowl-smelling food and set it before Gabrielle. "Enjoy your meal, human," he said with a sly grin. Lingering momentarily, he watched disbelief creep over Gabrielle's face when she examined the pail's contents. She couldn't tell whether the small, slimy pieces of stringy matter were animal or vegetable. It was like pig slop. When she glared up at him he made a sound deep in his throat like a gurgling laugh and went on his way.

She had a sudden urge to kick the pail over, but stopped her-self. She needed food to keep her strength up if she and Mara hoped to escape. She'd try and force it down quickly. Lifting the pail to her lips, she threw back her head and swallowed some of the slop. Moments later her stomach rebelled and cast the concoction back up.

One of the guards said in a sympathetic voice, "Not very good, ehh? Did the nasty food make the little human girl sick?" Then his voice turned gruff. "Well, I don't like it much either. But it's what we have to put up with when we're in a hurry. I prefer freshly killed meat. That's what a rak needs." His round, yellow eyes began to glow with a strange look as he approached and bent over her, sniffing, and prodding her arms. She hit at him with her bound hands. Mara reared up and whinnied loudly, catching the other guard's attention.

"Rrguck," the second guard shouted. Springing over, he backhanded the offending guard so hard across his face that it knocked him down. "None of that, Rrguck. You know our orders. I won't get into trouble because of you. If I catch you doing this again you will wish I had not." Turning to Gabrielle, he observed the vomited food on the ground. "I will find something better for you to eat. We cannot have a sick human holding us back."

After that Rrguck behaved himself and ignored Gabrielle most of the time. The other guard brought food that was less offensive. It did not have a pleasant odor, but the texture was like oatmeal and it was edible. The night was cold and Gabrielle lay shivering on the damp, hard ground. The raks had stolen her warm fur cloak that had lain over Mara's back. After a while one of the soldiers saw her misery and tossed her a scratchy, dirty blanket. She was glad to get it, though she slept little that night. She kept thinking about her family and Obie, and wondered when the queen's soldiers would arrive to rescue her and Mara.

Certain they would come soon, she finally dozed off. When she awakened sometime later the camp was nearly empty. Where had the raks crept off to so quietly—and why? She heard sounds in the distance. Was it the cries of night predators, or some strange birds? Could it be the queen's men? The possibility gave her a surge of joy. She'd soon know. In the meantime, she could only wait and hope. After a while she saw the raks creep back into camp and her heart sank.

The raks broke camp before daylight and followed the Old Path to a river that Gabrielle heard them refer to as the *Weir*. From there they followed the river upstream. They had not traveled far when the raks split up. A large group set out in the opposite direction, and a smaller band of twenty took Gabrielle and Mara and continued along the river. They were the sturdiest rak soldiers riding the fastest horses, for their focus, Gabrielle realized, was on speed.

The next morning drops of water started falling from the trees and Gabrielle knew it was rain filtering through the canopy. Soon her hair and the blanket around her were soaked. Wearing his perpetual scowl, Rrguck rode up alongside and threw an old rain cloak over her.

She lost track of the days as one blurred into the next on the long trek northward through the seemingly unending Gnarlwood Forest. The raks pushed on relentlessly at an unslackening pace, making only one brief rest stop during the day before hurrying on again until well after dark. They slept a few hours each night and were on their way again before dawn. The long, monotonous hours on horseback with little sleep caused a deep weariness to settle on Gabrielle. Once, she dozed off and fell from her horse. Rrguck called a halt, then dismounted and lifted her back onto her saddle.

"If you fall again you will have to ride with me," he warned. "And I do not think you will like that very much."

"I won't fall again."

Gabrielle, are you all right?

Yes. Only my pride is hurt.

Better your pride than your bones. Please talk to me when you feel yourself growing sleepy and I'll help you stay awake. I couldn't bear to see you forced to ride with Rrguck.

Thanks, Mara, I will—though Rrguck's threat will be enough to keep me awake. He thinks of me as lunch. I cringe to think of him prodding and sniffing me if I had to ride with him. But I worry for you. You're a flyer and you're not used to running long distances. I fear they'll run you until you drop.

Don't worry. My legs were sore at first and I felt exhausted each night, but my muscles have responded quickly. Running long distances each day is easier now.

Gabrielle's fear that they were being taken to King Torolf was confirmed one night when she overheard a rak soldier commenting to a comrade that he hoped they could beat the winter snows to Targus Dol. A few days later the raks turned west until they reached the Long Wadi Road, which stretched from the lower southern valleys into the northern high country and on to Targus Dol. Gabrielle guessed the raks were no longer worried about being seen by pursuers from the sky. Far now from Windermere, they would blend in with Torolf's patrols, known to frequently ride the northern section of this road. Rrguck commanded Gabrielle to keep the hood of her dark rain coat pulled up to hide her light hair. Another soldier covered Mara with a dark blanket and placed a bronze helm on her head, like the ones the rak battle horses wore.

The road climbed steadily upward as they moved farther north. When they finally reached the top of the long grade, storm clouds rolled in and it started raining again. Ignoring the weather, they sped on. Just after nightfall they started down a steep winding path, but in the dark Gabrielle could not see what lay below. It seemed like hours passed before they reached a valley and halted for the night. The air had grown so cold Gabrielle's teeth chattered and she shivered under her blanket and rain cloak. Then it started to snow. Lukvok, the rak leader, had Gabrielle brought under a protective tarp next to the campfire and gave her an additional, heavier blanket. She felt thankful sitting among the burly rak soldiers close to the warming flames. But she did not delude herself that they acted out of kindness or mercy. No doubt they feared for their own safety if they failed to deliver Mara and her to Torolf in reasonably good condition. That was one piece of luck, but what horrors awaited them inside the gates of Torolf's stronghold at Targus Dol?

The raks seemed to be in exceptionally good spirits that night. Gabrielle suspected it was because they were approaching the end of their journey. Rrguck even brought her a leg of roast rabbit to eat, a small kindness she had not thought him capable of. Had he stopped thinking of her as food?

It seemed like she had just closed her eyes when she awoke to dark, hairy arms lifting her onto her horse. Within minutes they set out in the predawn. The road was covered with snow and was discernable only because it ran in a treeless line through the forest valleys. By the end of the second day they passed over a rise and, through the mist and snow flurries, saw a high cliff wall looming before them. When they entered a narrow canyon leading through the plateau it proved a temporary relief from the weather, for the vertical walls on either side blocked the storm-driven winds. Just before they reached the other end of the canyon the raks halted and Gabrielle and Mara were blindfolded.

This is strange. Why are we being blindfolded? What are they hiding from us?

Gabrielle was trembling. *I don't know, Mara, but I think Targus Dol must be near.*

***

King Torolf left his two personal guards in the corridor when he entered the stone dungeon. Gabrielle lay sleeping on a pallet and Mara stood nearby. A chain around the windlord's neck was attached to the wall. Torolf stood tall and silent in his long gold and white cloak, studying Gabrielle, waiting for her to awaken.

Is this the child who used to run laughing through the halls of Windermere Castle? The little girl who frolicked with my brother Ulrik, and barely knew that I existed? Yes, it is she.

***

Gabrielle stirred uneasily in her sleep, then opened her eyes and saw a handsome young man with green eyes and light blond hair watching her. Startled, she sat up quickly. Her eyes opened wide as she looked into his face. Had his eyes been blue and his hair brown she might have mistaken Torolf for his younger brother, the resemblance was so close. But she knew she must not confuse him with Prince Ulrik, for they were like summer and winter. She remembered Ulrik as being everything that was good, while Torolf was black-hearted. She must keep her mind shut to this man and never allow him into her thoughts.

He smiled kindly and spoke to her in a soft voice. "Gabrielle, welcome to Targus Dol. It's been many years since I last saw you. I am King Torolf. May I speak with you for a while?"

She gave a slow nod of assent, and the king seated himself on the pallet beside her.

"I apologize for any discomfort you may have suffered during your trip here. I ordered my soldiers to treat you well, but I fear they lack social graces."

"We were unharmed," Gabrielle answered in a flat voice.

"I'm so glad to hear that." He gazed into her eyes. "Gabrielle, dear lady, I want you to believe that I mean you no harm. In fact I hope to become your friend. I've wished it for such a long time.

I've admired you since childhood." He paused a moment, and then continued, "I know you've heard ill stories about me—and no doubt you see me as some sort of villain."

Gabrielle's eyes hardened as she nodded that she did.

"I feared as much." He lowered his head briefly, and when he lifted it again two tears fell from his tragic eyes. "What you couldn't know, Gabrielle, is how badly I've been wronged, how I was driven from my kingdom because of evil lies spread about me when my brother King Urien died so unexpectedly. I swear to you, I harmed no one—much less my own beloved brother. I pale at the thought. Yet, evil tongues convinced willing ears. Fie! Even my dear mother's mind was poisoned against me. Her fury stabbed like a dagger through my heart." Torolf lowered his head again and when he lifted it his face was filled with pain. "After barely escaping the kingdom with my life I wandered far until, finally, I came to this land. And here I have waited for the time when the great wrong that was done me is righted."

"The great wrong done *you*?" Gabrielle could not contain her anger. "And what happened to your younger brother, Prince Ulrik? Did you murder him after you fled Windermere so he couldn't become king?"

"Never! Where did you get such an idea? No one even knew where he was. He had left the kingdom, as he said, to see far lands."

"Some people believe you tracked him down and killed him."

"Another lie spread by my enemies. You must not listen to them." His eyes were pleading now. "All I've wished for is to regain my rightful throne and rule our people with kindness and wisdom. Surely that cannot be wrong? Truly, Gabrielle, I have suffered during these long years of exile." He reached out to gently touch her cheek, but she recoiled.

"Do not try to play on my sympathies because I am a woman," she warned. "And do not mistake me for being weak minded—for I know the truth about you."

Torolf sighed and stood up to leave. "No, you do not know the truth about me, sweet lady. But, we'll talk again later." He stared forlornly into her icy blue eyes, then turned and silently departed.

He is trying to win you over, Gabrielle, Mara said. *You must remain as strong, as you were just now and keep your thoughts closed to him. You know he will try to rob you of them—you know he wants the Light Crystal.*

Yes. I will fight him, but I may need your help

***

Torolf returned early the next morning while Gabrielle still slept. Again he stood silently watching her, studying her features. *So delicate and innocent she looks lying there. Her face so finely formed, yet strong, and how her ivory throat and chest glow warmly in the torchlight.* His eyes moved to the long, dark lashes resting on her cheeks, and he remembered her eyes, like aquamarine pools in sunlight. *Danger, there is danger of drowning in the depths of Gabrielle's eyes* an inner voice warned him. As Torolf studied her, something foreign stirred in him, a buoyant feeling he had never felt before, and he wanted to reach out and touch her. *She's quite . . .* his mind reached for the word he had all but forgotten . . . *beautiful.*

Mara broke the silence when she kicked the floor with a front hoof and snorted. Gabrielle opened her eyes and, seeing Torolf, sat up quickly, combing her long hair from her face with her fingers. Distrustful of the stirrings within him, he pushed them away. He visited Gabrielle that day and the next, speaking of pleasant things and recalling events of their childhood. But he knew she remained firm in her distrust of him, merely tolerating his presence.

***

On the third day he brought her a book of love poetry and read to her. While he read, she observed the lines of his sensitive face, the way his lips caressed the words, the tenderness in his eyes when they met hers. When he finished the second poem, he laid down the book. Gazing at her, he said in a mellow voice, "Gabrielle, do you remember me telling you I wished to reclaim my throne in Windermere and rule as a good and wise king?

"Yes, I remember."

"Come, Gabrielle." Rising up he gently reached his hand to her. "Come, for there is something wonderful you must see." He smiled and his face was radiant like the sun. She stood, but did not take his hand. Then he spread an arm and, laughing gaily, whirled around. When he stopped, the dreary dungeon cell was gone. They were in the Garden of the Queen of Windermere and it was springtime. Pink, blue, and yellow flowers flourished in the golden light of day and birds sang honey-throated melodies from nearby branches of the trees. Blossoms floated on the fragrant breeze and water bubbled joyfully within the brook that flowed along the garden path. Gabrielle stood in a golden gown and Torolf was in kingly garb of white and gold, and wore a jeweled crown upon his head. It seemed so perfect there. King Torolf seemed so noble, wholesome, and so fair. Gabrielle sighed, then breathed more easily and relaxed. How she did wish that this were true—that Torolf could be kind, and good, and blessed with wisdom too.

Danger! Fight Gabriell—he's bewitching you, she heard Mara calling, though she could not see her.

She felt herself afloat within the magic of his soft and coaxing eyes. He held his hand for her to take and, reaching out as one entranced, she put her hand in his. A radiant vision, Torolf seemed a rival to the sun; and fear she set aside like some bad dream.

Danger! Danger! Fight his enchantment, Gabrielle!

Vaguely did she hear those words from somewhere . . . somewhere far away.

"Look at your reflection in the brook, my dear," he urged.

She obeyed and saw a golden crown upon her head. "Ahhh," she said, and turned to gaze upon the fair young king.

"My love, I want you for my bride and queen, to rule with me in Windermere."

He seemed sincere, yet she held back.

"Soon we shall speak more of this, dearest Gabrielle. For now let's be content to bask within the wonders of this hour. Come stroll with me along the path," so tenderly he bade.

The moment seemed so right and wonderful, yet something in her mind cried out: *It's but a dream. It isn't real and I'll awaken soon.*

Then Gabrielle walked with him. Her hand in his, they strolled and stopped to watch a mother hare tend to her bunnies hopping in the deep green grass. He smiled and stooped to pick red roses for his sweet love's hair. "For you, dear one." And when he laid them on her head a lovely garland they did form around her golden crown. "Look in the brook again," he said. And when she did, she saw once more her radiance in splendid garb. An instant later all was gone, the vision ripped away. They stood within the dungeon cell again and Gabrielle felt sad.

"Dearest Gabrielle. I don't like keeping you down here in this cell. You have but to say the word and all will change. Just tell me that you're mine and I will give you splendor such as you have never seen, everything you ever wanted to possess."

With a bewildered look, Gabrielle started to speak, but stopped.

"You're still hesitant, I see. It's best that I go now. Tomorrow I'll return, although I cannot bear to leave your side for very long, dear one. Til then my heart is in your keeping." Torolf took both her hands in his and gently kissed her forehead. Then with a flurry of his cloak he turned and left.

Gabrielle turned to Mara and saw the sadness in her eyes.

Gabrielle, I fear for you. Please try harder to fight Torolf. He's using his magic to win you over. You must not let him into your mind, dear friend, or all will be lost.

Gabrielle lay down on her pallet and smiled dreamily up at the ceiling of the cell. She could barely hear Mara's mental voice. It seemed to be coming through a fog from a long way off. *You're probably right, Mara, but I'm not as sure as I once was. I'm not sure of anything anymore, but he seems so good and kind. Have we possibly misjudged him? Maybe he . . .* Then Gabrielle drifted into a sleep of lovely dreams, while Mara's urgent voice faded from her hearing.

The following morning the king returned and again swept Gabrielle into the vision of the Queen's Garden at Windermere Castle. This time they both wore splendid wedding garb of pearly white. And as they gazed into each other's eyes, Torolf waved his servant forth, who bore a golden chest. And raising up the lid the king took out a wedding gift: a diamond necklace bright as fire from the stars with one red ruby glowing in their midst.

"It's truly beautiful." Her eyes were filled with tears.

Then Torolf fastened it around her neck and softly said, "Yes, beautiful my love, but not so beautiful as you." His eyes met hers and once again he felt the stirring from within, a fluttering lightness that he did not trust. *Away! Away!* he cried inside his mind, trying to resist, to push away the feeling and be rid of it, but it would not depart. And then Love's Arrow pierced his heart and he succumbed. For even he could lose himself to Love. Yes, he would give her everything when she was his.

"What can I give you in return, my love? What would you ask of me?" she said.

"Come close and give to me your mind, that I may know your tender thoughts."

Like ice that cannot long withstand the sun, so Gabrielle's young heart did melt upon what seemed the first bright morning of the world. And so she gave to him her heart and mind. His mind then prodded hers, so gently, gently did he scan each memory and thought, searching, searching 'til, with surgeon's skill, he extricated from her mind the hidden place, the cave that hid the Light Crystal. Jumping back in horror, Gabrielle awoke, and as she wrenched her hand from his her mind snapped shut to him.

"No, get away from me, deceiver! You've betrayed me," she cried. The vision burst and they stood in the dungeon cell, she in her tattered blue dress. Torolf seemed confused and shocked. A look of rage came on his face and his eyes glowed red. But it passed like a wave and he again appeared guileless. He smiled patiently at her, as to a child.

"I did it for you, Gabrielle, you must believe that," Torolf pleaded. "I'll soon possess the world—thanks to you. And if you'll be my bride I'll share it with you."

"I never wanted the world," Gabrielle said bitterly. Turning away with tears streaming down her cheeks, she went to the windlord and wrapped her arms round her neck. Abruptly, Torolf turned and left the cell.

Mara, what have I done? Gabrielle reclined her head on Mara's neck and wept.

As long as you do not go to him there is still hope. You must not let him possess your mind or body.

He will never possess either! I weakened and allowed him briefly into my mind, but it won't happen again, I promise.

Then you must not succumb to his bewitchment again, for if you do, all will be lost. Stay strong and do not give up hope.

I will stay strong, Mara . . . and I'll cling to hope.

***

That night an atmosphere of brooding permeated the chamber atop the Serpent's Tower. A bent and wizened form with scraggly white hair stood in the crimson light at his window, watching the snow falling. His appearance would be unrecognizable to any who had known him in years past. Wielding the power of the Serpent had withered Torolf's physical appearance to the same degree it had withered his soul.

Ahhh darkness, darkness, how I long for you. Already the stars no longer shine, and the sun and moon will soon be blotted out forever. Aye, my desires do consume me. Patience . . . I must have patience. The black sorcerer turned and went to his throne. The seat and back were upholstered in black leather, each emblazoned with a large golden serpent, and the legs and arms were a dark wood carved in the likeness of many entwined serpents. There he ruminated, his eyes burning red in the glow of the fire pit in the center of his chamber.

Long have I waited. But soon now, soon I will have my revenge and claim what is mine. Those who drove me away will suffer. Oh yes, they will suffer for what they did to me, I who was their king. They frolic in their victory now, thinking they have won a war against me, but that will change. Oh yes indeed, it will change. Soon they will know I only toyed with them like a cat plays with its prey. When my full powers are unleashed, their world will change beyond anything they can imagine. He laughed a gleeful, high-pitched laugh. *They shall grovel at my feet. And when they see my terrible and deadly queen sitting beside me on her serpent throne, how they will be amazed. Oh, I revel. When all is done and the Star Crystals are destroyed, the mighty Serpent will make me king over all other kings and kingdoms. He said I am his mighty right hand and I will rule with him in sweet darkness. Soon now . . .*

Restless, Torolf went to a table where his military plans were laid out and reviewed them for a time. Finally satisfied, he retired to his bed across the chamber. It was a lavish canopied bed of black velvet and satin draperies, bedcovers, and pillows embroidered with great golden serpents.

When the sickly light of morning entered King Torolf's chamber, he awoke feeling cheered at the general progress of things. Gabrielle was his final challenge and he was wearing her down. Soon she would be his. He climbed out of bed and went to his mirror. *Well now, the handsome suitor must tidy himself up a bit.* In a sudden flash of light the withered form of the black sorcerer was replaced by the handsome fair-haired young man with green eyes and an angelic face. Today he chose black tights, shirt, boots, and a golden cloak emblazoned with a great coiled black serpent. On his head he placed a serpent crown of gold encrusted with diamonds and blood-red rubies. Pleased with his reflection in the mirror, Torolf smiled and said, "A fair enough form and countenance to win the heart of a fair maiden, I should think."

His reflection grinned slyly back and answered, "Torolf, you devil you."

"Thank you," Torolf said.

***

During the next few days Gabrielle felt herself pushed and coaxed and tempted by the black sorcerer. "Just say, *yes,* dear lady, and the world will lie at your feet. You will be my Gabrielle the Great, the most magnificent queen in the history of the world," he urged.

So strong were his mental powers that she grew weary from the constant bombardment of his thoughts upon her mind. The few hours he spent attacking her mind each day seemed like an eternity of battle against a mighty, untiring foe. She was weakening mentally and, unable to eat much, her body suffered as well. But still she would not yield to Torolf's marriage proposal.

Gabrielle felt Mara weeping for her. And then the windlord said, *Gabrielle, when Torolf comes again, I must join my mind with yours to give you added strength—for I know you're on the brink of exhaustion.*

That will be dangerous for you, Mara, if Torolf discovers what you're doing. Yet if it allows me to hold out longer, it must be done.

So when Torolf came again, Mara joined her mind with Gabrielle's. Mara's mind lay low, thinking no thoughts, acting only as a strong, fortifying presence that would not yield. In this way, Torolf did not discover what the windlord was doing. But Gabrielle and Mara knew this barricade to Torolf's mind attacks was only temporary, for soon Mara's mind would also weaken under the immense pressure.

CHAPTER EIGHTEEN

SHADOWS

OBIE'S CLOAK WHIPPED in the wind and the driving snow stung his cheeks as he stood on the mesa gazing north. His eyes moved across the Hundred Valleys Region to the billowing gray clouds shrouding the sheer wall of the Barren Plateau. *The plateau is beyond those clouds and on the other side is Torolf's stronghold, and Gabrielle. We just have to get over the wall.* He drove away the sinking feeling that started to come. *Don't think . . . just keep moving . . . figure it out when we get there . . . time's running out.* He pulled his cloak close around him, then turned and nodded at Tau. They began searching for a path leading down into the valleys.

It was just after noon when they found a narrow trail and Obie started down with Tau and Mole following. A short way down the trail he stopped. "Look, movement," he called over his shoulder. He was pointing toward some dark objects in the second valley over.

Tau cupped his paw-hand over his eyes to shield them from the driving snow. "It looks like a small herd of deer. We may eat tonight." Obie hoped so. At the mention of *eating,* Mole poked his head out and squeaked, then darted it back inside Tau's hood. But too many days of trudging through the storm with little or no food had taken a great toll on them. Obie's energy level had dropped considerably, and he noticed Tau's movements were more labored. All of them had lost weight, and Tau's face was looking a little gaunt. He guessed his own was, too.

By mid-afternoon, near exhaustion, they reached the floor of the first valley and started through the trees heading towards the next valley where they had sighted the deer. Hunger gnawed at Obie with every weary step he took, but the worst was the relentless snow and freezing cold. Chilled to his core, his limbs grew so stiff that he had to will them to keep moving. His hopes of reaching the deer today faded when he realized they must find shelter soon or freeze to death. Surely Tau would suggest that any minute now. Beginning to grow giddy from the cold and exhaustion, Obie laughed out loud a couple of times for no apparent reason. Mole stuck his head out again and began watching his young companion.

"Just need some firewood and shelter, that's all . . . and then we'll be warm again," Obie said. "Tau, we have to rest . . . yeah . . . rest and then go hunting." But his voice did not carry over the wind, and neither Tau nor Mole heard him. Obie staggered and fell to his knees, got up and staggered again. "Just gotta get some . . ." He fell on his face in the snow and lay still.

Mole squeaked and yelled, "Tau, stop! Obie's fallen."

"Uuuhhh?" Tau sounded dazed. He turned, and seeing Obie lying in the snow, plodded back to him. "Wake up, boy. You can't sleep now." Kneeling down, Tau shook him but got no response. He turned Obie over and brushed the snow from his face, then lifted him in his arms and started walking. Obie opened his eyes and smiled up at Tau, and then his lids dropped shut again.

"Tau, what are those white domes over there?" Mole pointed to their right. "They look like huts." Tau grunted and headed towards them. When they reached the first one, Tau laid Obie down and began brushing snow off of it. Mole climbed down from Tau's shoulder and used his burrowing skills to help. Snow flew in all directions and soon a surface of woven branches and earth appeared. "It *is* a hut," Mole exclaimed. He speeded up his efforts.

"A hut," Tau said laughing. He sank to his knees, weaving back and forth unsteadily. "We will find the door and then we shall have shelt . . ." Before he could finish, Tau fell on his side and closed his eyes. A moment later his eyes blinked open. "There is something I must do . . . what is it? I will rest a little . . . and then . . ." His eyes fell shut again and he slept.

Alarmed, Mole stopped digging and started racing back and forth between his two companions, squeaking and calling, "Tau, wake up! Obie, wake up!" Panicked when he got no response, he shook Obie.

Obie opened his eyes and managed to sit up with his legs crossed in front of him. "Tau's napping," he said with a silly grin.

Mole slapped his paw back and forth across Obie's face to keep him awake. Then he raced back to the hut and started furiously kicking snow aside, frantically trying to find the door before Obie and Tau sank deeper into sleep. Just as he was dozing off again, Obie thought he saw something approaching them.

"White buffalo . . . can't kill . . . good luck buffalo . . ." His words faded away as he lay back in the snow and drifted into beautiful sleep.

***

Obie heard voices talking quietly and opened his eyes. He lay under a blanket on a pallet and something that smelled like stew was cooking. He tried sitting up but felt too weak and lay back down. Tau and the two young men he was talking with looked over. The older one appeared to be about eighteen years old and the younger about fourteen. Obie noticed their olive complexions, large dark eyes, and shiny black hair falling in two long braids. They wore buckskin pants and shirts, turquoise necklaces, and thick fur boots.

"Good. You have awakened," Tau said from his pallet. He and the young men were sitting cross-legged.

"Do not try to get up yet," the younger one said to Obie, motioning with his hand to stay down. Obie was surprised to hear him speak English. Then he remembered Andrus telling him that English was the common language spoken by many races in this part of the world in addition to their own tongues. It had been brought to the native peoples long ago by the goblin traders.

"He is right," the older youth said. He got up and came over to Obie. "Mankato, our medicine man, said you must rest and eat to regain your strength." Kneeling, the youth picked up a jug next to Obie's pallet and poured a draught from it into a gourd cup, then handed to his guest. "Mankato left this for you."

"Thanks." Obie lifted himself up on one shaky arm and drank. The liquid had a pleasing herbal flavor. When he was finished, the youth took the cup and set it down.

"I am Takoda, and you are in the village of my people, the Otawn. My father is Chief Shappa."

"I am his brother, Kangi," the younger one eagerly added.

Obie smiled at them. "I'm glad to meet you. I'm Obie."

Kangi darted an anxious look at Takoda, who caught his brother's prod and took the lead.

"We have given Tau the name *Lion Who is a Man,* and you we call *Brother of the Lion,*" Takoda said. "Before we reached you, we saw Lion Who is a Man bearing you in his arms through the snow, as one would do for his fallen brother."

Light flashed in Obie's eyes. "I'm honored to be known as the lion's brother." Then he said to Tau, "Thanks for carrying me, Lion Who is a Man."

"You would do the same for me—if you could," he said with a grin.

"I don't remember much after we reached the valley floor. It's all sort of blurry," Obie said.

"Nor I, but I recall we were looking for deer."

"I think I remember seeing a white buffalo coming towards us. Did you see it, or was I dreaming?"

"It was no dream," Kangi put in with a laugh. "You did see one. Only it was Takoda wearing our father's buffalo robe with the head and horns attached. He likes to wear it because it makes him look like a buffalo. The snow made him look white."

Takoda's face reddened and he shot his brother a scathing look.

Obie smiled inwardly and turned his eyes away, not wanting to embarrass Takoda. Then, in alarm, he remembered something important and ran a quick eye around the room. "Where's Mole?"

Sounds of clattering, barking and loud voices erupted above the underground hut. Next, they heard vigorous scratching at the overhead door near the far wall. Kangi was about to climb up to open the door when it lifted slightly and Mole squeezed through. He raced down the ladder and streaked across the hut, coming to rest in the crook of Obie's arm. Again the door cracked open slightly and a large brown snout pushed through, sniffing and salivating. Kangi picked up a broom and yelled and hit at the intruder. The snout retreated and the door dropped shut again.

"Just had to make a grand entrance," Obie said, grinning down at Mole.

"Dogs. Big dogs." Mole's voice trembled.

"Maybe you'd better stick close to us for a while." Obie gently rubbed Mole's head in an effort to calm him while he turned his attention back to Takoda and Kangi. "How did you find us?"

"Two days ago, Prince Andor and the eagle Silverclaw came streaking over the valleys screeching their cry of alarm and we hailed them. The prince asked if we had seen the three of you. Then he told of your rescue mission to the land of the Necromancer and said he and Silverclaw had been searching, but could not find you in the storm. We told him we would be watching and would find you if you entered our valleys. We spotted you yesterday when you were coming down the southern wall. You are lucky you were not seen by enemy eyes. But the storm gave you some cover. And even we might not have seen you had our eyes not been watching the southern passages into our lands."

"We're grateful to you for finding and bringing us here," Obie said.

"We are honored to have those who dare oppose the Necromancer stay within our lodges," Takoda said, looking from Obie to Tau to Mole. Obie and the others thanked their hosts.

"Are Prince Andor and Silverclaw still here?" Obie asked.

"No. They returned to the village last night to see if we had found you. We told them you were here and were sleeping. The prince said they had things to attend to and would return in a few days when you are strong enough to travel again."

"A few *days*?" Obie looked anxiously at Tau. "We can't stay that long."

Tau grunted softly and shook his head in agreement.

Mole, sufficiently recovered from his ordeal now, squeaked his concurrence.

"As soon as you are strong enough, then," Takoda said. "And if you leave before Andor returns, he can catch up with you. The storm has passed, so your way will be easier if you leave soon. Mankato warns that more storms are coming."

While they talked, Kangi eyed Obie's Raptor, attached to his pack. Responding to his obvious curiosity, Obie took up the Raptor and slipped it on his arm, then pulled the band taut as if to shoot. The brothers appeared pleased when Obie said they could try it out later. When Tau asked about the lodge he and Mole had uncovered, Takoda said his people sometimes used the above-ground huts in the warm months because it was pleasant under the trees and they were hidden from view from the sky. But most of the Otawn dwellings throughout the valleys were underground, like the one they were in now. They also utilized some large caves. Obie asked how they were able to build so many lodges and Takoda explained that most were built by their ancestors and maintained by each new generation. However, each new generation also built new ones. Having so many lodges enabled the Otawn to easily move from valley to valley and still remain hidden from outsiders.

They talked a while longer and then the visit came to an end when, catching his brother's eye, Takoda motioned towards the ladder with a slight jerk of his head. The two youths stood to leave.

"You must eat and rest now. Our father will visit you later, and we will come also," Takoda said. He and Kangi flung their fur capes around their shoulders and climbed the ladder, exiting through the door in the ceiling.

Shortly afterwards, Chief Shappa's wife, Maka, entered the hut with another woman. While Maka dished up bowls of food from the cooking pot near the center of the lodge, the other woman pulled Obie's pack onto his pallet so he could sit up and lean against it while he ate. Maka smiled warmly as she handed the steaming bowls to Obie and Tau, telling them to eat slowly, and not too much today. Obie was pleased to discover he had guessed right about the food that was cooking. It was a nicely seasoned venison stew. Maka's helper brought them flat bread to eat with the stew, and some water. Mole feasted on a bowl of beetles sprinkled with a few sow bugs the Otawn children had gathered for him. The three conversed as they ate and enjoyed the warm comfort of the lodge. Then one by one they fell asleep.

The next day, Takoda brought his father to speak with them. Shappa was an impressive figure, Obie thought. Standing tall in his buffalo robe, his presence was that of a powerful chief, yet his manner was relaxed and friendly.

"Let us sit together and smoke the pipe before talking." Obie joined Takoda in bringing the sitting mats from a pile against a wall of the hut and they placed them in a circle on the earthen floor. Mole, too, had a mat. When all were seated the chief reached under his robe and brought out a red pipe and a small bag from which he took some pleasant smelling leaf. He packed some of it into the bowl and Takoda brought a lighting stick from the fire pit. Small wisps of white smoke curled upward and dissolved in the air as Shappa drew on the pipe. Obie noticed the strong lines of the chief's weathered face and his knowing eyes. They were like Will's eyes. He wished the old man could be there to smoke this pipe with the chief.

Shappa handed the pipe to Obie. He drew on it as the chief had done and started coughing. The hint of a smile crossed Shappa's face. "You are new to the pipe."

In a haze of smoke, Obie nodded and held his mouth shut in a partially successful effort not to cough again. He passed the pipe to Tau. Tau drew deeply on it and a look of contentment spread over his face. Then he passed the pipe to Mole who was sitting on his haunches awaiting his turn. Obie was impressed to see Mole solemnly smoke the pipe. The little rodent was full of surprises.

Meanwhile Kangi had entered quietly and taken a mat beside his brother. No words passed among them during this ritual. After the pipe had been refilled and passed around a second time, Shappa laid it down and addressed his guests.

"My people and I are pleased to share what we have with you, Brother of the Lion, Lion Who is a Man, and you Mole, whom I give the name, Little Warrior."

"Thank you for honoring me with such a name, Great Chief," Mole said.

Now Shappa turned to Tau. "My sons have told me of the great wrong the Necromancer has done to you, yet you resisted him and escaped. The strength of your heart is very great."

A warm glow lit Tau's eyes. "Your words are kind, Chief Shappa."

Next, Shappa looked at Obie and said, "Prince Andor told us you are going to the accursed tower of the Necromancer to rescue the ones called the Moonpath Riders."

"Yes, Chief Shappa."

The chief searched Obie's face for long moments and then gave a nod of approval. "You are all very brave to enter that black land to do such a thing. But be warned of this: Prince Andor flew high over the Serpent's Tower and saw great activity below. He fears the Necromancer is planning another attack against the lands to the south and west."

"Then we need to get the Moonpath Riders out now," Obie said catching Tau's and Mole's eye. "We're leaving tonight."

"Tonight," Mole agreed, rising up on his haunches. "Yes, tonight," Tau added.

Shappa nodded stoically. "It is decided then. My people will help you. But your way will be dangerous. You should not try crossing over the Barren Plateau into Targus Dol. It is too open and you would be captured or killed. The Necromancer's patrols and his winged devils constantly patrol the cliffs and the land above. We will show you a secret way through the plateau that will lead you to a hidden door overlooking the tower. My people will not enter the cliffs while the evil of the Necromancer is upon that place. But if you do as I tell you, you will pass through unharmed."

"We'll do whatever you say," Obie said. He knew he could trust Shappa and his people, for Zelda had said they could be trusted and advised him to seek their help, and they were also friends of Prince Andor.

"Then hear me. When you enter the cliffs you will pass through a tunnel leading to a narrow valley, the Valley of the Spirits. It is dark and hidden from view above, for its walls curve inward forming a dome over the valley, leaving only a narrow crack on the plateau surface. You must not walk through the center of this sacred land as it is the place of our burial grounds. If you step on the graves of our ancestors, they will be angered. Walk only on the path to the left that runs along the canyon wall. Move quickly and do not stop or gaze into the valley. It will not be long before you will see the entrance to a cave. A path inside the cave will lead you upward until you reach the cavern of the U-Shaped Pool. The north exit is an invisible door located in the cavern wall at the top of the U. You must feel the rock wall for the finger depressions to pull it open."

While Shappa finished giving his instructions, Kangi emptied the red pipe, wrapped it in its cloth, and handed it back to his father. Finally, the chief stood up to go. "Sleep now, and when you awaken prepare for your journey. I will give you good horses and two braves to guide you over the best winter trails."

Shappa went up the ladder with Takoda following. Kangi lingered a few moments more to admire Obie's Raptor again and then scrambled up the ladder behind his brother. Just before disappearing through the door he turned his head and flashed a smile at his three new friends.

While Tau and Mole slept through the afternoon, Obie lay wide awake. His mind was racing. If all went well they would soon rescue Gabrielle and Mara from of the tower at Targus Dol. *Hold on Gabrielle, we're coming to take you out of there.* He still didn't know how they would do it, but they would find a way. He wished his thoughts could reach over the miles to give her encouragement. Finally, he dozed off.

Maka woke them in the early evening when she and a helper brought warm food. They thanked her for the kindness and downed the meal. Afterwards, they dressed in the warm buck-skin clothing she had given them the previous day. Their packs were next to the ladder ready to go, and they pulled their cloaks around their shoulders. Obie was wondering if Takoda and Kangi would come to say good-by when he heard the sound of horses' hooves pounding the ground above.

Moments later the door over the ladder opened and Kangi poked his upside down head through. "All is ready," he announced with his youthful grin.

The three climbed up and exited the lodge into the cold night air. Obie's eyes were drawn to the stark black sky. In the east, the pale greenish moon rode low, casting a thin, eerie light over the land and giving the trees a ghostly glow. Glancing around, he was amazed at how well the Otawn had hidden their village. There was no trace of it. All he could see was snow-covered ground and trees. One could walk or ride over the entire village and never know it was there. It was the genius of the Otawn.

Takoda sat tall on his brown and white spotted horse and next to him was an older brave on a gray. "This is Tashunka." Takoda gestured towards the other brave.

Tashunka nodded at each and said, "I am honored to help The Three Who Fight the Necromancer."

"As we are honored to ride with such fearless Otawn braves," Mole said.

The braves wore buckskins and beaver fur, with bows across their backs. Obie didn't mind that they were riding bareback. He'd expected it. Kangi brought him a spotted horse like Takoda's, and gave Tau a big chestnut. Tau set Mole on their horse in preparation for departure.

When all were mounted, Takoda grinned and said, "My father was going to send only the two of us, but Kangi whined like a little girl until he was also allowed to come."

Ignoring his brother's comment, Kangi sat winding his fingers into his sorrel's golden mane, ready to go.

Obie could tell the two brothers enjoyed teasing one another. "How long will it take to reach the opening through the plateau?" he asked Takoda.

"It is two days' journey northwest of here if we ride swiftly and sleep only a little. And always, we must keep our weapons ready for it is likely we will need them."

Obie slipped his Raptor onto his arm.

Takoda turned his spotted horse with a "Hiyaw," and they were on their way. They rode single-file, Takoda followed by Tashunka, Obie, Mole and Tau, and Kangi pulling the supply horse.

All night they rode over the snowy terrain, winding skillfully through the valleys over the winter paths and taking shortcuts known only to the Otawn. Shappa's people had keen night vision and thought nothing of traveling the forests in the dark. At dawn they stopped to sleep, rotating the guard, and a few hours later were on their way again. The sky grew cloudy and the icy wind whistled and whipped at them as they crossed over passes between the valleys. Sometimes, moving like shadows under the trees, they followed the valley floors through low, narrow passageways to the next valley. Once, a high-pitched shriek split the air above them. Tau drew his sword and Obie raised his loaded Raptor seeking a target. His bow bent, Tashunka whispered back to the others, "It is the Necromancer's servants patrolling this valley." They waited until the threat passed and then continued on.

A few hours later, while crossing an opening in the trees, they were spotted by a large raven that dove straight for Tau's eyes. The lion-man ducked and only the raven's wing brushed his head as he grabbed at it a split second too late. Squawking over the heads of the others, the bird headed west, but Tashunka's arrow brought it down. Passing by the black carcass, the brave leaned down to retrieve his arrow and wiped it off in the snow. No use wasting a good arrow on Torolf's vermin, Obie thought.

The day passed and when the wan light of afternoon faded into night, they heard the wolves howling from the distant northern cliffs. They rode all night again, halting in the grey predawn to sleep a few hours before moving on. The Barren Plateau grew steadily larger as they drew closer, though most of the time the cliff walls were obscured by the thick overhead branches of tall firs and oaks. Just before nightfall on the second day, Takoda stopped at the top of a low hill. The plateau rose directly ahead, but was hidden by the trees. Unearthly shrieks echoed off the cliff walls, causing the hair on Obie's neck and arms to stand up. Takoda pointed through the pines to a small meadow and whispered, "Remain hidden in the shadow of the trees when we reach the clearing. You will see something that will turn your blood to ice."

They proceeded quietly and stopped near the clearing. The vertical cliff wall loomed high before them from its base at the bottom of the hill. Fluttering about the cliff and perched on narrow ledges were hundreds of filthy looking creatures with the head and body of a hag, and the wings, tail, legs, beak, and razor sharp talons of a bird of prey. In a state of calm, the creatures were cooing, but those that flew too close to another's ledge were warned away by shrill shrieks.

Obie pulled his horse alongside Takoda and whispered, "What are those hideous things?"

"They are harpies—watchers of the cliffs. They can tear a man to pieces and carry his soul off to a place of eternal chaos." Takoda stared grim-faced at the creatures and Obie saw fear in his eyes. He sensed it was not dying Takoda feared, for he seemed brave enough to face death. It was the fear of eternal damnation—of having his soul carried off by these monsters and being forever separated from his ancestors and loved ones.

"Can they be killed?" Obie asked.

"Yes, but there are too many of them. If we were attacked, the flock would quickly overpower us. If they should see us, we must ride deep into the trees to hide. The Necromancer controls them, and they guard the plateau from outsiders who try to pass over it. Never do they fully sleep. They just rest on the ledges with one eye always open and watching. But they will not expect anyone to pass *through* the plateau."

Obie glanced uneasily back at Tau. Mole was peering out of the lion-man's hood, his eyes wide and his whiskers twitching as he watched the harpies. For once he was not squeaking.

"We will approach the base of the plateau through the trees," Takoda whispered, motioning to their right. "When we get there you must watch for the Necromancer's foot patrols. They pass frequently along the cliff wall."

The air was suddenly filled with loud shrieks as a flock of harpies flew out from the cliff and headed towards the clearing.

"Quick! Into the trees," Takoda whispered, waving his arm and turning his horse sharply along with the others. They dashed back into the deep shadows and waited in rigid silence. Screeching and shrieking, the harpies circled the clearing again and again, their terrible eyes searching until, seeing nothing, they finally returned to their perches on the cliff wall.

"Close call," Obie whispered to Tau. "How did you get through those monsters when you escaped from Targus Dol?

"They recognized me as one of Torolf's personal guard and allowed me passage. There were not so many of them watching the cliffs then."

Tashunka was listening and whispered, "That is true. The harpies' numbers were greatly increased by the Necromancer only last summer."

Takoda interrupted. "We will go now to the opening in the cliff. Darkness comes and we do not wish to stay longer in this evil place."

"Please take the horses back with you," Obie said. It's too risky to leave them. If anything happens to us they'll be stuck inside the cliff. We might be able to steal some horses to ride back."

Takoda smiled and said, "You think like an Otawn. I wish you luck in taking their best horses—it is great sport." He led them quietly down the forested hill to the plateau wall. They turned right and moved silently beneath the trees along the cliff face. Above the forest canopy the harpies continued cooing and occasionally screeching at one another from their perches. It was a good sign, Obie thought, as they didn't sound aroused. He eyed the dark branches overhead, wondering if any harpies sat watching. They sounded so close. He shuddered and squeezed the handle of his Raptor. They'd know soon enough. After riding a short distance Takoda stopped and they all slid from their horses. Then Takoda slipped his fingers into a vertical crack in the cliff and pulled a rock door open, revealing a dark tunnel.

"Enter here and follow my father's instructions," Takoda whispered. "When you get to the valley, remember to take the path along the left wall. We have brought long-burning resin torches so you can find your way."

Tau set Mole on the ground so he could help Kangi unpack the torches and shoulder packs containing supplies and food. He tied the torches to his pack, leaving two out for immediate use.

"Remember that the Necromancer's soldiers patrol this wall—do not linger here," Takoda warned with a look that told Obie he was anxious to depart.

"We won't," Obie whispered. "Ride safely, and thank you for everything."

Takoda grabbed a handful of his horse's mane and threw a leg over his back. "May the spirits protect you," he whispered. Then he lightly kicked his mount and started up the hill pulling Obie's horse behind him. Tashunka and Kangi, each pulling a horse, nodded as they turned and silently followed Takoda. Obie, Tau and Mole watched them vanish into the darkness.

"The horses were faster, but it will be good to use my legs again," Tau whispered.

"He's in agreement," Obie said glancing towards Mole who was running back and forth along the cliff wall stretching his legs.

There was no time to waste. To avoid having the torches spotted, Obie squatted just inside the passageway to light them. He timed the scraping of his utility file against his rock to the screeches and cooing of the harpies. Their constant racquet made the task fairly easy, and the tunnel walls helped muffle the sound. He quickly ignited the first torch and used it to light the second. Tau had already lifted Mole to his shoulder and entered the tunnel when Obie handed him a torch.

Tau took it and whispered, "You go first."

At that moment, hissing voices erupted outside. The reflection of the torchlight on the open door had been spotted by a rak foot-patrol, approaching fast from the west along the cliff wall.

"Go, go, go! I'll follow," Obie said, fearing his limp would hold Tau and Mole back.

They dashed away and Obie pulled the door shut behind them. The rak patrol reached the door moments later, found the vertical crack, and yanked it open again. They streaked into the passageway yelling and hissing threats. Obie and Tau raced for their lives through the winding tunnel while Mole held tightly to Tau's mane and squeaked excitedly.

Obie faltered as he kept forcing his bad leg forward. It was stiff from riding, but phrases from the pursuing raks like *tear you to pieces, roast you alive,* and *suck your bones dry* spurred him to push harder. Still they gained on him. He needed to do something fast, buy himself time for his leg to limber up. They had to run single-file, maybe he could bottle them up. He spun around and hurled his torch at them. Bull's eye. A maddened scream came from the lead rak. His hair was on fire. While his comrades doused the flames with their water rations, Obie slipped his Raptor over his arm and loaded it.

"Suck on this," he yelled with a shot to the lead rak's throat and a second shot between the eyes. Before the rak's knees hit the ground, Obie raced away. He'd gained a little time, but not much. When the fallen rak's comrades discovered he couldn't run, Obie figured they'd plow right over him. He figured right. They were coming again, and now they weren't just taunting him with threats. Now they projected raspy-throated rage. If they caught him, they'd probably tear his limbs off and eat him on the spot. Up ahead, he heard Tau calling him.

"I'm coming. The raks are behind me!"

"Hurry up," Tau yelled.

Feeling his way along the walls, he could see the reflection of the lion-man's torch on the curved wall in front of him. His bad leg was finally limbering up and each step came easier.

Rounding the bend, he saw Tau and Mole waiting. "Okay, go—I can see you now." If they could outrun the raks they had a chance, but it didn't look like that was going to happen. Raks were strong runners. Then they rounded another curve and the valley opened up before them.

"Left. Turn left," Obie shouted when Tau hesitated.

They made the turn and followed the narrow path against the valley wall, as Shappa had instructed. The wall made a quarter turn before straightening out along the valley floor.

Over his shoulder Obie saw the raks burst from the tunnel into the valley, shouting and shaking their swords. They cut across the center of the valley floor in an obvious attempt to head off the fleeing human and lion-man, and they were rapidly gaining ground. Then a blood-curdling cry burst forth. It echoed through the valley and was answered by other cries.

"What is happening?" Tau called, slowing his pace a little and turning to look into the valley.

"Don't look," Obie yelled, waving Tau on. "Turn your eyes ahead and keep running like Shappa said."

Round-eyed and mouths gaping open, the raks came to a stop. Charging down at them through the darkness were brightly glowing, larger-than-life spirits: fierce Otawn warriors, their faces painted and war clubs raised high, riding wild-eyed horses with steaming nostrils and flaming hooves. The raks panicked and fell over one another trying to escape battering clubs while the multitude of horsemen passed over them. Crazed, the raks started slaying one another until the last two fell upon the heap of rak bodies. All grew quiet. Then a sudden, final war cry echoed through the valley. After that the valley was deathly still.

Obie and Tau kept running until they spotted the cave entrance beside the path, just where Shappa said it would be. They raced in and Obie heard sounds of water ahead. After passing through a short tunnel they entered a large cavern. Tau's torch illuminated long, pink and yellow stalactites reaching down from the ceiling and dripping water into aqua pools. The walls and large rocks were covered with crystal and calcium deposits of many shapes. Some resembled bunches of long, white strings, others looked like popcorn, and still others like yellow coral. Here and there, shimmering white in the torchlight, great naturally formed pillars spanned the gap between floor and ceiling.

They did not linger, but followed a path that wound slowly upwards. When they reached a flat, landing-like area overlooking a small cavern they stopped for a short rest. They sat down and Tau propped the torch between some rocks and set Mole on the rocky floor in front of him.

"I do not think we will be troubled further by the raks," Tau said quietly. "Though we could not watch, our ears informed us of what our eyes could not."

Mole sat up on his haunches, the torchlight playing in his eyes. "It appears we had help from the Otawn."

"Yeah, but we wouldn't have if it had been *us* who took the shortcut across the valley," Obie put in.

"Too bad for the raks, though," Tau added with a sardonic grin.

"Yeah . . . too bad they didn't get to suck our bones dry," Obie added with a grim smile.

They drank from their water bags and soon continued up the path. With all the hard riding and little sleep they'd had over the past two days, Obie knew he should feel weary. But, being almost in Torolf's backyard now, he realized he was operating on shear adrenalin. Little wonder that Mole and Tau also seemed wired.

Yet, with all there was to think about, a part of him was awed by the unexpected beauty and variety of the rock formations around them. Along the way they passed limestone shapes that looked like succulent grape clusters, long curved fangs, delicate lace, and horizontal fishtails. He even saw boulders that could pass for great cauliflowers growing upward from the cave floor, and one cavern resembled a pine forest with the *trees* growing upside-down from the ceiling. It seemed like passing through another world. Obie doubted if any human sculpturer could best these natural formations.

The path continued winding around and up and down, and as he immersed himself in thoughts of what lay ahead he soon forgot the beauty around him. Several hours may have passed before they saw light and heard running water ahead. Proceeding cautiously, they rounded a corner and found themselves in a cavern of softly glowing yellow and blue crystals.

Mole made a sweeping glance around and said, "I've never seen anything like this . . . a cavern that gives off its own light."

"Ditto," Obie said.

"Pardon me?" Mole responded.

"Not important." Obie was too busy looking around to explain the meaning of *ditto* right now. The soft shades of blue and yellow light blended in places to produce varying shades of green.

"We will not need our torch in here," Tau said, dousing what remained of it in a puddle.

"Look," Obie said. He pointed towards a clear pool of water on the far side of the cave where the crystals were predominately blue. "It's the U-Shaped Pool. We've arrived."

The top of the U backed up to the cave wall forming an islet inside. They waded through the shallow water to the islet and dropped their packs on the ground. Obie ran his hands over the wall, searching for the finger holds Shappa said would be there. In less than a minute he found the nearly imperceptible depressions. They were curved inward, allowing his fingers to slide in and hook into place. He pulled the door open and they stepped outside into the night air. Obie grimaced as he breathed in sulfurous fumes. Mole started coughing and had to bury his head in Tau's mane to muffle the sound. Obie saw Tau shudder and noticed a glassy look in his eyes. The lion-man had to be remembering terrible things.

Ten feet in front of the hidden door ran a ridge approximately fifteen feet high and a few hundred feet long. While it blocked their view, it also hid them from any watchful eyes below. At each end of the low ridge Obie could see the dim moonlight shining on a rocky slope leading down from the cliff wall to the plain below. He made a mental note of the twisted tree growing beside the invisible door, and also marked the door's location across from a small boulder on the ridge. Then he found the exterior finger holds and pulled the door shut behind them. Tau's glassy-eyed look had been replaced by an expression of pain.

"Let's go see what's below," Obie whispered. With Mole at his side and Tau following, he climbed to the top of the ridge. When he peered over, an icy shiver shot through him.

CHAPTER NINETEEN

THE SERPENT'S TOWER

THE TENTS OF TOROLF'S ARMY, fifty-thousand strong, sprawled over the white wasteland, illuminated in the night by scarlet flashes of fumaroles coughing up foul vapors and smoke from the boiling Earth below. Stunned, Obie's eyes locked onto the tower in the foreground with its four dark metal serpents rising from the top, their glowing red eyes looking out in all directions. The tower rose tall and darker than the night, shrouded in the ghostly light of the pale, wan moon. So sinister did it appear, thrusting upward from the center of a giant anthill, that Obie felt a sudden weakness, as though his limbs were drained of blood. Two small windows part way up in the tower emitted a greenish light while a window at the top glowed crimson. From the tower his gaze moved to the black outlines of five other giant anthills among the far spread tents. Near many of the fumaroles, dark figures of muk and rak soldiers stood warming themselves. A faint buzzing sound drifted up and Obie realized it was the sound of soldiers snoring in their tents. The three rescuers sat on the hill a few feet from the top, speaking in hushed tones.

"None will be prepared to stave off an army of this magnitude. And it looks like it will march very soon," Mole said. "Torolf will most likely attack Windermere again, and the lands to the west.

"How long will it take them to reach Windermere?" Obie asked.

"Maybe eight or nine days—it is hard to say," Tau answered. "But they cannot ride more than two abreast through the passage in this plateau. That will slow them initially. It will also take time to pass through the Hundred Valleys Region and ascend the southern plateau. But once they reach the Long Wadi Road, beyond the Hundred Valleys, they will gather momentum and move fast. The road is wider there and almost a straight line south to Windermere."

"I pray Gabrielle and Mara are still in the tower," Obie said in a trembling voice. Rising up, he gazed over the ridge again at the dark tower, noting the great entry doors standing open at the top of the ant hill facing the plateau, and the two tall muk guards posted on either side. Then he took note of the two lookout stations atop the anthill, one facing east and the other facing west. He could see the tower was formidable, but he had read enough and seen enough war movies and documentaries to know every fortress had its weakness. This place would not be impossible to enter. They just had to discover how. And time was of the essence. In order to pull off this rescue they needed to get in and out as quickly as possible. He rejoined Tau and Mole.

"There is a staircase winding to the top of the tower where the window glows crimson," Tau said, "and the anthill is riddled with tunnels and chambers used for storage, weapons making, and prison cells among other things. The Moonpath Riders will most likely be imprisoned in the anthill. However the prison cells are not all in one location, so it may be difficult to find them. There are two main tunnels leading down into the ant hill. When you enter the tower one is on the left and one is on the right. I suggest, Mole, that you first explore the tunnel on your right. Most of the cells are on that side."

"I will."

"Do the lookout stations have tunnels leading up to them from the anthill?" Obie asked.

"Yes, a tunnel leads down from each station and connects with one of the main tunnels."

"What if we bring Gabrielle and Mara to a guard station and have them take flight from there?"

"Those were also my thoughts," Tau said. "It would be best to depart from the east guard station since the horses are corralled below it.

"I agree," Obie said. "Mole, can you ride with Gabrielle and guide Mara to the Otawn camp?"

"It sounds like an excellent plan to me," Mole said, "after you get into the citadel and overpower the guards, and assuming Mara's in any condition to fly."

Obie eyed Mole uncertainly. "Yeah . . . we still have some things to figure out."

"Well, if things go wrong, we can resort to the wisdom of the ages," Mole said.

"What wisdom is that?" Tau asked.

"Make it up as we go."

"We are used to that." Tau rubbed his growling stomach. "Let's do the rest of our planning over food. I cannot think when my stomach complains like this."

At the bottom of the ridge, they talked quietly while Tau pulled strips of dried meat, bread, nuts, and a package of dried insects from the packs. As Obie nibbled at his food, a wave of exhilaration passed through him to think that soon Gabrielle and Mara would be free. Then they could ride the Moonpath. He glanced down at Mole and noticed how small and vulnerable he looked. The little fellow was courageous to go into the tower alone. Overcome by a desire to be helpful, Obie asked, "Mole, shall I wrap up some beetles for you to take?"

Mole's eyes hardened as he snapped, "I'm not planning a picnic under The Serpent's Tower, Oberon.

Obie felt his cheeks flush. "Sorry I asked."

Immediately Mole's manner softened. "Forgive me Obie, I'm on edge. I plan to make all haste in finding the Moonpath Riders because I want to return here before the camp awakens. Food will be the last thing on my mind. I will leave as soon as I finish this meal."

"It's a brave plan, Mole," Obie said. "Now we just have to figure out how Tau and I will get inside the anthill without being seen."

"I have already given that much thought," Tau said. "I think we should boldly walk through the front door when Torolf is not at home."

"Boldly walk . . ." Obie repeated with a questioning look.

"With you as my prisoner, of course—wanted for questioning by King Torolf. I will pose as one of his personal guards bringing you in. He and Arend used to leave the tower at night for a few hours. I am hoping he still does that."

"Now *that's* what I call a *brave plan*," Mole said.

"I like it, Tau," Obie said. "Those *antbrains* down there won't expect their enemies to walk through the front door like they own the place."

"Yet, it will be dangerous," Tau said. "Some of those *antbrains* possess high intelligence. We must be convincing so we do not arouse suspicions—and we must move swiftly. The Necromancer could return at any time and trap us like rats in a hole."

Mole scurried down the slope and darted past the tents of sleeping muks and raks. Two raks warming themselves near a fumarole noticed him running by. They threw snowballs at him for sport, but he dodged them and hurried on. The soldiers could not guess the gravity of his mission; just as they could not guess that the future of the world might well depend upon this small creature quietly slipping through their camp. Mole climbed the hill to a spot a little to the right of the guards posted at the two great doors. In the center of each door was carved a large coiled serpent, and around the edges were hundreds of small entwined serpents. Mole ran along the black stone wall of the tower, passed silently behind the nearest guard and through the open doorway.

In the center of the foyer, torchlight shone on the winding stone stairway leading to the black sorcerer's chambers at the top. To the right and left of the stair were the entrances to tunnels leading down into the anthill, just as Tau had described them. A strange looking reptilian creature lingered near the stair as if waiting for someone. To Mole's relief it paid no attention to him. Then two of Tau's people, Torolf's personal guardsmen, entered the tower from outside and hurried up the stairway. Polished bronze breastplates gleamed from under black cloaks emblazoned on the back with a coiled red serpent, and on their heads they wore bronze helms. *Torolf must be in his tower.* Mole's breathing came faster at the thought.

He hurried to the tunnel on the right and darted down the passageway illuminated only by occasional wall torches. Passing by several large store rooms, he saw workers feverishly loading supplies. In another room one of Tau's people barked orders to the workers. Guardedly, Mole approached several small, hair-less, four-legged blue creatures crawling up the passageway. Fish-like heads without necks comprised the front end of their ponderous bodies. As he passed them, they curled their lips and growled, baring sharp teeth. To his relief they did not attack. Before long, he came to a water trough where the tunnel forked. He decided to follow the left passage that wound steeply down-ward. Deeper and deeper he went until he saw red and blue lights flashing on the tunnel wall ahead and heard a rumbling sound. There were no wall torches here, making the tunnel pitch dark between the flashes of colored light.

The air grew heavier and warmer the farther he descended. As he drew closer to the light source, he heard a long, deep-throated growl followed by a shriek that made the fur on his back bristle. He could turn and run back up the tunnel, he thought, but maybe he should find out what Torolf had hidden away down here. Cautiously rounding a corner, Mole came to the end of the tunnel walls. He froze in his tracks. Across the darkness two bright green eyes stared in his direction. Again, he heard the long, low growl. His entire body began to tremble. A jet of molten rock and gas shot upward followed by another and another, sending noxious red and blue vapors billowing upward and illuminating a large cavern. In the flashing subterranean light, Mole saw what the bright green eyes were attached to: a great spiny dragon with glittering red scales and two horns curving out from its forehead. *This must be Torolf's pet.* Strewn around the cavern floor were piles of bones and skulls, some human.

Then he heard fluttering noises and, looking up, was repulsed to see the black cavern ceiling writhing, as though alive. Blinking his small eyes several times, he realized the ceiling was thick with millions of bats hanging upside down. Some were flying about. The molten jets fell back, one by one, until it was pitch-dark again, save for the cold, green eyes now fixed directly on him.

Mole felt weak, as though he would melt into a puddle on the floor. *The dragon's caught my scent.* The jets spewed upward again, flashing the blue and red light on the dragon's raised head. Smoke shot from its nostrils and its forked tongue flickered about. Cowering to make himself as small as possible, Mole began slowly edging backwards, his eyes locked with the great reptile's eyes that had now turned red. Suddenly the dragon shrieked and leaped forward. Mole whipped around and darted up the tunnel, but not quite fast enough. One of the dragon's razor sharp claws crashed down through the tip of his tail and severed it. Luckily, the dragon was too large to enter the passageway and Mole escaped with nothing worse than a shortened tail.

He ran until he reached the water trough he had passed earlier. Tail stinging and throat parched, he climbed up the trough and lapped the oily, sour tasting water, ignoring the wormy creatures swimming in it. At least it was wet.

This time he followed the right fork and found it had smaller tunnels branching off. After trying three of the passageways and discovering they led to large supply rooms, he tried a fourth and came upon some empty prison cells. The doors stood wide open revealing chains and manacles attached to the walls, and instruments of torture lying about on the floor. *Torolf must be preparing to march his army. That's why he's emptied the prison cells and his workers are hurrying to load supplies.* He hoped he wouldn't find Gabrielle in manacles—*if* he found her that was. Rounding a corner, he was encouraged to see two drowsy looking guards posted outside a room. Mole continued along the wall and was thankful the first guard wasn't looking down at his boots as he darted past.

When he scurried into the cell his heart leaped with excitement. Gabrielle lay sleeping on a pallet of straw in the center of the chamber. Her blue dress was torn and soiled and her feet were bare. Mara stood nearby, watching Mole's every move. He saw that she was chained to the wall and her wings were strapped down. His whiskers twitched vigorously and he had to restrain himself from squeaking. He ran across the floor and climbed atop the pallet, then sat back on his haunches beside Gabrielle and whispered her name. Mara's keen ears pricked up.

"Ohhh," Gabrielle said weakly when she awoke, startled to see Mole. Sad, luminous eyes peered from her weary face.

"Shhhh," Mole whispered. "We've come to rescue you."

A gleam of hope flickered in her eyes and she smiled. "Who . . . who's come?" she whispered, rising up on her elbow.

"Obie and another called Tau, and me. I am Mole. Take heart, dear lady. You and Mara will soon be free. I'll soon return with the others."

Gabrielle glanced nervously towards the dungeon entrance, then turned back to Mole and said, "Your words seem true . . . yet I have been deceived so much by Torolf that I would ask you to tell me something so I can believe you."

Compassion shone in Mole's eyes as he said, "I would expect nothing less, my lady, as I can see you've been mistreated. Obie confided in me that he came from the township of Garrett, in a land called Wyoming. He said Queen Olwen of Windermere was keeping this information secret."

Gabrielle's face brightened. "Yes, only she and my family know where he came from. And did he tell you the other part of the secret . . . how he got to Windermere?"

"Indeed, he did. The Spirit Comet brought him. And the queen thinks he was brought to help fulfill a prophecy."

"Thank you, dear Mole," Gabrielle said with a smile. "Now I know this is no trick of Torolf's, for he has learned nothing from me about Obie. You have given me hope."

"Giving you hope is my great pleasure, my lady," Mole said with a bow.

"Please call me Gabrielle."

Mole lowered his head politely and said, "You honor me."

Gabrielle glanced nervously at the entrance again, then whispered, "Mole, what time of day is it right now?"

"A little before midnight, I believe."

"Then you must come for us around this time tomorrow night. Torolf's going to attack Windermere. He told me he's setting out early with his army the day after tomorrow, and he's taking Mara and me with him."

"We'll come for you. Do not worry, Gabrielle."

"Torolf may sense your presence if he's here. But I've heard the guards say he leaves the tower each night for a time. Watch for his departure and please be careful."

"We will." Mole pulled his gaze from hers and turned to go.

"Before you leave . . ." she whispered.

Mole made a half-turn and looked back. "Yes?"

"Tell me, how do the sun and moon look now? And what phase is the moon in?"

"I wish I could say otherwise, but they grow fainter and sicklier each day. The moon is waxing and should reach its fullness in seven or eight days."

"I thank the gods for that. It means there's still time." She sighed and lay back down.

"Farewell, Gabrielle, until midnight tomorrow." Mole jumped down and scurried towards the cell door.

"Farewell, my friend," Gabrielle whispered.

Mole hurried up the passageway. Since he now knew where he was going, leaving the stronghold was much quicker than when he came. As he made his way up the main tunnel, he encountered two muk guards approaching, but they passed by and paid him no mind. Seeing no creature in sight when he arrived back at the foyer, he slipped out of the tower.

***

Obie was on watch when Mole raced up the slope. "Did you find them?" he asked the moment the little rodent climbed over the ridge. Obie's face was tense as he awaited Mole's answer.

"Y . . . yes," Mole said, out-of-breath from running.

A look of shear joy spread over Obie's face. "How are they? How did Gabrielle look? Are they okay? Did she ask about . . ."

"They're fine," Mole interrupted. He was sprawling flat on his belly, his back rising up and down as his lungs labored for air.

"Well, have they been mistreated? Did you tell Gabrielle we're here to rescue her? C'mon, Mole, spit it out. What'd you see? What'd she say?"

"They're just . . . little . . . weak. Tell you . . . all in . . . minute . . . I'm winded."

"All right—go ahead and catch your breath." Beaming, Obie whispered down to Tau, napping below, "Tau, wake up." Turning back to Mole, he finally noticed his severed tail and did a double-take. "What happened to your tail?"

His breathing coming more regularly now, Mole raised his head.

"Dragon got it—hazards of war."

"Sorry about that, Mole," Obie said sympathetically, then added, "Think of it as a battlescar you'll be able to brag about to your grandchildren."

"Grandchildren? That seems a million miles and a hundred years away."

"Does your tail hurt? Shall I pack it in ice?"

"No, it's all right, it doesn't hurt much now."

Tau had joined them and was eyeing Mole's tail.

"Here, let me clean it up while you tell Tau and me all that happened." Obie poured a little water over Mole's tail and washed off the dried blood, careful not to dislodge the scab that had formed on the end.

"I had heard Torolf got himself a fire-dragon," Tau said apologetically. "*Smoker* he calls him. Forgive me for not remembering that. You were very lucky to lose only the end of your tail, little one."

"Let's just hope he doesn't send Smoker into battle," Mole said with a look of dismay that made his whiskers wilt. They all shared a look.

Tau broke the brief silence. "It is no good to worry about something that has not happened yet." He opened his pack and pulled out a blanket from which he tore a small piece of fabric and began wrapping it around Mole's tail. While Tau worked, Mole recited what Gabrielle had said and all he had seen, including the two lion-man guards hurrying up the tower stairway.

Obie wished they could attempt the rescue immediately, but he heeded Gabrielle's warning that Torolf might be able to sense their presence in his stronghold if he was in his tower. The rescue was far too important to blow it through impatience. But would the black sorcerer leave? As Obie's anxiety grew, he thought of Will's admonition not to let his fears overcome him. It helped a little. It was nearly dawn and Torolf and his army would not move out until the following morning. It should be enough time.

It was too risky to remain outside during the day where they could easily be spotted from above, so they covered their tracks in the snow and reentered the cave to get some sleep. Obie had more bad dreams. He saw his mother's face inside the burning car while he stood nearby. Then Gabrielle was there and he saw the silent, dark pursuer above, stretching its long tentacles towards her. When she turned her head to look at him, he awoke gasping for air and soaked in cold sweat. He sat up and took some deep breaths, then pulled his shirt off. From the corner of his eye he noticed Tau leaning against the cave wall watching him.

"Bad dreams?" Tau asked quietly.

"Yeah." He felt Tau's eyes follow him to the pool where he splashed water over his face and chest.

"You've had bad dreams before. Do you want to talk about it?"

"No . . . not now . . . maybe some other time." What Obie really wanted right now was to forget the dreams. There was enough to worry about besides his nightmares.

Darkness had fallen when they exited the cave, but something was wrong. It was too quiet. Hurrying to the top of the ridge they looked over and their faces dropped. Most of the tents were gone. Torolf's army had already moved out, heading west along the base of the Barren Plateau.

"We blew it." Obie stared at the last of the soldiers departing on their war horses, their metal helms and long spears silhouetted against the crimson light of the fumaroles. His chest ached and he felt wobbly, like someone had unscrewed a cap on his body and drained all his energy away. He wanted to protest the cruelty, the unfairness of it, wanted to cry it out at the top of his lungs, but dared not. Sinking to the slope, he lay back on the snow, breathing hard, hating himself. *You've done it, you idiot! You've failed her—like you failed mom—and now Torolf's taken her away.*

Tau stared down at Obie for a long moment, but when Mole climbed the few steps down the slope to his side, the lion-man turned back to watch the commotion below.

"I am also grieved, Oberon," Mole said in a heavy voice. "Torolf must have changed his mind. But we must not give up. We'll think of something. I promise you we'll catch up with . . ."

"Shhhh," Tau whispered, "Torolf and Arend are returning to the tower." Grinning, he added, "Something tells me the Moon-path Riders may still be here."

Filled with new hope, Obie got up so fast he slipped and fell on his face in the snow. When he reached the top and peered over, he saw Arend sitting on a wide ledge extending out from Torolf's chamber window.

"He just went in," Tau whispered. "He is probably waiting until his army has made its slow passage through the pass in the plateau before joining them with the Moonpath Riders."

"As soon as he leaves, let's go in," Obie said, looking anxiously from Tau to Mole. "And if he doesn't leave by midnight we're going in anyway—even if we have to sneak up the hill to the east guard station." He got no argument.

About four hundred soldiers were left to guard the tower, stationed in front and to the west of it. But something new had been added: two mounted guards were riding circuit around the tower at the foot of the anthill, passing one another regularly on the east and west sides below the guard stations.

"Hmmmm, this complicates things a little," Tau said, furrowing his brow. "We must time our approach to avoid being stopped and questioned by one of them. The less attention we draw the better."

"On a more positive note," Mole said, peering over the ridge, "I notice some fine looking horses left in Torolf's corral."

"We couldn't ask for them to be in a better place, either," Obie said.

The hours passed until it was almost midnight. Obie nervously fidgeted about on the slope, unable to sit still. "We can't wait any longer. We're running out of time," he complained. He glanced up for the hundredth time at the crimson glow in Torolf's window.

Mole checked the moon's position in the sky for the umpty-umth time and said, "We agreed to wait until midnight and it's nearly that time. I say we go. Whether or not Torolf feels our presence, we must take that risk."

"Very well then," Tau said. "We cannot knock at the front door if Torolf is there. But we *can* climb the anthill to the east guard station and overtake the guards, as you suggested, Oberon."

"We'll need some camouflage," Obie said. Pulling his cloak around him, he dropped to the ground and began rolling in the snow. Tau stared curiously and then chuckled when Obie stood up. He was covered with snow from the top of his hood to the tip of his cloak, making him hard to see against the white terrain. Mole was already rolling on the ground Tau joined him.

A couple of minutes later a cloud passed before the moon and the night turned black except for a few intermittent flashes from the fumaroles.

"Let's go," Obie said. A second later they were over the top of the ridge and starting down the slope with Mole at their heels.

CHAPTER TWENTY

TUNNELS AND TRICKS

"HIT THE GROUND!" Obie dropped down as he spoke. Tau saw it too and fell to his belly next to him.

"What is it?" Mole said after banging into them from behind.

"Movement in Torolf's window," Obie whispered.

Arend was silhouetted against the crimson glow of Torolf's chamber window. The huge black hawk fanned his wings and then hopped from the window ledge into the chamber. Obie, Tau, and Mole scrambled back over the ridge and lay on their stomachs peeking over the top. Soon Arend hopped back onto the ledge bearing the black sorcerer on his back.

Breathlessly the three watched him open his wings and glide from the tower window towards the cliff, then turn and head southwest.

"Torolf must be checking on his troops," Mole said excitedly.

Arend disappeared into the black distance and the three turned back to the business at hand.

"Back to plan A," Obie whispered.

They shook the snow from their cloaks and then Tau pulled some rope from his pack. He cut a short piece off and wrapped it around Obie's wrists, hiding the untied ends in his hands in case they had to make a run for it. The long piece of rope Tau tied around Obie's neck so he could walk him like a dog on a leash. Obie left his Raptor hidden under his cloak, but gave his sword to Tau who stuck it through his belt next to his own. Finally, Tau lifted Mole to his shoulder and pulled his hood up. Mole hid in the lion-man's shaggy mane.

"Ready?" Obie asked.

Tau grunted and nodded, his yellow-green eyes aglow.

"Ready," came a muffled reply from inside Tau's hood.

They started down the cliff foot, Obie limping at the end of the leash and Tau following. Beneath his cloak, Obie slipped his hand into his ammo pouch and felt the blue swatch. *We're coming, Gabrielle.*

Near the base of the slope they waited behind a boulder while one of the circuit guards passed in front of the citadel and continued towards the west guard station.

"I hope you can act," Tau whispered to Obie when they started out again. "Try to look unhappy."

"I'm looking as miserable as I can. And how about keeping up with me, you're choking me half to death."

"Stop grumbling and slow down then," Tau growled. "You should not seem in a hurry to be imprisoned beneath the Serpent's Tower."

Obie slowed his pace. Tau was right—he must not allow his body language to give him away.

"And let us hope we don't run into any of my kinsmen," Tau added. "They know I escaped and may feel compelled to report me to Torolf."

"Great time to think of that."

"Shhhh," Tau said. They were approaching the tents of the remaining troops.

Passing through them, they aroused a few curious stares from those still awake. When one of the muk soldiers eyed them sharply Obie held his breath. He kept his head down to avoid the muk's gaze. From the corner of his eye Obie saw the soldier finally turn away. Was he one of the muks they had encountered along the way? If so, he didn't give them away, not yet anyway.

Obie's tension increased as they drew nearer the black tower and he glanced upward. A person would have to be mindless not to be frightened by this place.

At the foot of the huge anthill they entered the path leading up the slope to the great serpent doors. As they approached Tau gave the guards a raised fist salute, but the two muks ignored it and stepped towards one another, crossing their sword blades to block entry. Obie continued staring at the ground with his head down.

"Halt, lion-man," the guards said simultaneously.

The glint of a bronze helm within the tower caught the torchlight. It was one of Tau's people coming from the left tunnel. His eyes were fixed on Obie and Tau as he approached and stopped just inside the doorway.

"You are not dressed properly," the first guard said, looking Tau over from head to foot. "Where have you come from and what is your business?"

"I have been south on a special mission for King Torolf to bring this human in for questioning. My clothing is designed to fool the enemy and is unimportant." Tau sounded annoyed and his nostrils flared slightly.

Careful Tau, don't show too much emotion, Obie thought.

Tau's kinsman, stone-faced and steely-eyed, moved closer until he was directly behind the guards. He stood listening and observing.

"King Torolf said nothing of your coming," the guard snapped.

"Our King did not know when I would return. As you well know, he has been busy with other matters. Let us pass." Retaining eye contact with the guard Tau stood to his full height. "I outrank you muk. Let us pass, I say! You would be unwise to trifle with King Torolf's business."

"He is not here now. You must wait." The guard appeared to back down a little, but continued to block the door. The other guard stared sullenly at Tau and Obie.

Finally speaking up, Torolf's personal guardsman growled, "Sentry, you are being disrespectful to your superior. Let him pass so he can take the human to a cell and refresh himself while awaiting our king."

The guards parted instantly.

"I am sorry. I did not know this one," the guard who had been speaking said nervously.

"King Torolf will be back soon," the personal guardsman said to Tau. "You have arrived just in time. We will leave to join our army soon after he returns. In addition to our other duties, our king needs us to help with two captives he is taking on the march. You would be wise to ready yourself for departure with us. I will take this prisoner off your hands while you do so."

His heart sinking to his boots at the guardsman's words, Obie raised his head slightly and stole a glance at Tau.

"Thank you for your thoughtfulness," Tau said to his kinsman, "but this one is more dangerous than he appears and I know his tricks. I will take him myself and then change into a uniform."

"As you wish," the personal guardsman said. "But make haste. King Torolf will return soon."

Don't worry—we'll make haste, all right, Obie thought.

Tau and his kinsman gave one another a raised fist salute. Then the entry guards parted and allowed Tau and Obie to pass into the tower. As they entered the tunnel on the right, the personal guardsman turned and left the citadel to complete whatever errand he was on.

"Good acting, Tau. But how'd we get past your kinsman so easily?" Obie whispered as they rushed down the passageway. His adrenalin was flowing and his limp was gone.

"We were fortunate. He is new since I escaped and did not know me. And, you might have noticed, he disliked the attitude of the sentries towards our kind."

While they sped on, Mole poked his head out and guided them to the correct passageways. Meanwhile, Obie and Tau continued the masquerade in case they met other guards along the way. Obie's fear of discovery if Torolf should return too soon was diminished by his elation at hearing Tau's kinsman mention the two captives. *They have to be Gabrielle and Mara—they have to be.*

Tau pointed out the tunnel leading to the lookout station as they passed by, for it would be their escape route. Finally, they turned down the passageway leading to the prison cells.

"Quick, duck in here," Mole whispered, pointing to an empty cell. "Gabrielle and Mara are in a cell around the next turn."

They entered and Obie began unwinding the rope from his wrists. He was disgusted to see the clubs, pinchers, knives, branding irons and other torture instruments lying about. When his hands were free he loaded his Raptor and hid it beneath his cloak again.

Tau tucked a club under his cloak and they reentered the passageway. Obie hung his head as he walked on the leash—all the while squeezing the handle of his loaded Raptor. Rounding the curve in the passageway they saw two, seven-foot-tall guards standing at attention. Their metal breastplates and helms reflected the torchlight, and their swords hung at their sides.

"Who comes?" the first guard demanded.

"King Torolf's personal guard," Tau said in a commanding voice. He gave them the raised fist salute as he and Obie came near and stopped before them. "I have brought this new prisoner, and I am taking the human female and the windlord to our king."

"You are taking them by yourself?" the second guard asked in surprise. The first guard was looking Obie up and down.

"No. I will need one of you to bring the windlord. I will take the human."

"As you command," the second guard said, relaxing. "We will prepare the prisoners and then I will accompany you with the windlord." Obie and Tau followed the guards into the cell and waited while one of them unlocked the chain from Mara's neck. Had the guards been watching, they might have been troubled by the momentary flicker of joy in Gabrielle's eyes when she saw Obie. But they didn't see it, and Gabrielle quickly resumed her unhappy countenance. Obie noticed how pale she was. She stood up unsteadily and he realized she was also weak. But when the guard led Mara across the room, Obie was relieved. She appeared stronger. Hopefully she was strong enough to fly, and Gabrielle would just have to hold on.

The other guard picked up a neck manacle and gave Obie a twisted grin. "Come over here, dog, and get your new collar. You and I are going to have some fun later."

"Not this time, buddy." With a single movement, Obie threw back his cloak, aimed his Raptor and shot the guard between the eyes. He hit the floor like a two-ton brick.

With cat speed, Tau simultaneously drew the club from under his cloak and bashed the first guard's head. Moving quickly, Obie and Tau removed the leather straps from Mara's wings and then put the two guards in manacles, gagging them with pieces of ripped blanket from the pallet. Obie paused a moment to look into Gabrielle's face. *Are you all right?* He asked her mentally.

Yes . . . just a little weak. In the next instant he was hugging her. She felt so fragile in his arms. He yearned to talk with her, but time was precious and he knew they were already taking too long.

"Obie, take your sword," Tau called and tossed it over.

Half turning, Obie grabbed the sheathed sword mid-air and slipped it in his belt, then turned back to Gabrielle. "Can you run?" he asked, reverting back to speech.

"I'll try." She reached up and began untying his leash.

"I almost forgot," he said smiling at her as it dropped to the floor. "Let's get out of this awful place, Gabrielle." He liked saying her name out loud. Hand-in-hand they raced from the cell and up the tunnel with the others close behind. When they turned up the passageway leading to the lookout station Obie heard the sound of heavy footsteps coming towards them.

"Guards coming. Go back," he whispered, turning and waving his arm at the others.

"Obie, I'm feeling strange . . . lightheaded . . ." Gabrielle's knees buckled and he caught her as she fell. There was no time for anything. Lifting her in his arms, he was surprised at how light she was as he carried her down to the main tunnel. The foot steps were only moments behind and there was no place to hide. Tau pulled the only torch in sight from its wall holder and shoved it into a crack in the tunnel wall, extinguishing it. The tunnel went pitch-black except for Mole's and Tau's eyes glowing like two sets of light bulbs.

"Hey, close your eyes. I can see you guys," Obie whispered frantically.

The lights blinked out. Hardly daring to breath they stood against the tunnel wall. Within seconds two rak soldiers burst from the upper tunnel and stopped.

"Thought I, hssst, heard noises down here," the first rak said to the other.

"Hssst, it just muks moving, hssst, captives. Maybe they bring food," the other said.

The first rak turned in the direction where, only yards away, Obie stood holding Gabrielle. "How come, hssst, it so dark?"

"Ahhhh, da torch, hssst, jus burn out. I not waiting, hssst, while you fart around, hssst, I want meat now," the other said, pushing past his comrade.

"Awwright. Hssst, we go then. I, hssst, starving too."

Sweat lay on Obie's brow as he watched them feel their way in the darkness along the tunnel wall. He could see their outlines, but they hadn't seen him or the others standing against the wall. Then he realized his night vision was not only improving, but he was acquiring the ability to see in total darkness. That was supposed to be scientifically impossible. He'd learned on the science channel that not even owls could do that.

Obie felt Mara's velvet nose on the back of his neck. *Lead on Obie. W're right behind you.*

Glancing back, he saw Mole's and Tau's eyes glowing brightly again behind Mara. "Okay, let's move."

They passed silently up the tunnel towards the lookout station, and even Mara stepped noiselessly, an ability windlords were known for. Not far from the lookout door, Obie set Gabrielle down gently. Opening her eyes, she looked up at him and whispered, "I'm sorry, I'm weaker than I thought."

"Don't be sorry. You did great, Gabrielle. I should have known you were in no condition to run. Just rest here and I'll be back for you in a couple of minutes."

She used all her strength resisting Torolf, Mara said. A pained look came into Obie's eyes as he exchanged glances with the windlord.

Gabrielle touched Obie's arm. "Please be careful."

"Don't worry, Tau and I take care of each other," he whispered with a weak smile. As he stood up his face hardened. He loaded his Raptor and nodded at Tau.

Mole waited with the Moonpath Riders while Obie and Tau crept up the tunnel. When they reached the lookout station Tau darted a quick look around the doorway. "There are two guards and one is facing the door looking down. But that is not the worst part," he whispered with a worried look. "The guards are black widow females. They are big—and they are deadly."

Obie felt sick. "I knew this was too easy," he said under his breath. He remembered how ill he'd been a few years back from a normal black widow bite. The thought of facing a giant black widow, part human or not, made him tremble so badly he had to lean against the tunnel wall for support. He peered back down the passageway at Gabrielle and Mara. *Get hold of yourself, you can't let them down. Everything's riding on this.* He set his jaw and turned back to see Tau staring at him. "Okay, I'll get the one facing the door first," he whispered.

"If the other one sees you, you may not have time to shoot a second time. Draw your blade quickly and be ready, for she can spring at you in an instant."

Obie nodded. *They're only raks.* Clamping his teeth down, he stepped into the open doorway. In the pale green moonlight the great ruby-red mark on the she-widow's underside gleamed through her open cloak. A look of surprise came to her face an instant before Obie's steel shot hit her between the eyes. She faltered and he shot her again before darting out of sight. The other guard turned to see her comrade hit the ground, unconscious.

"The she-widow hissed. Jerking her head up, she glared towards the door. "Hhhrrrrrrrrrrraaaaa," she uttered and sprang into the tunnel. She directed her anger at Tau and they clashed blade against blade. Towering over the lion-man, she quickly proved to be the stronger fighter, pushing him back until he lost his footing and fell. Her sword blade flashed in the torchlight while, with two hands, she raised it high to plunge into him. Obie shot her hard in the head and she dropped her weapon but did not fall. Enraged, she wheeled to face her new challenger, her bright yellow eyes glowing murderously. She sprang at him with all six long, black arms reaching out. He whirled Roar's blade in an upward arc as the angry red mark on her underside came down over him. The force of the she-widow's body pushed him backward with her on top, furiously screeching, coiling and uncoiling her hairy black arms around him. Tau beat at her back with his club until he saw her severed head, still screeching a little, where it lay in a pool of green blood on the tunnel floor. He realized she was dead about the same time he heard muffled shouts.

"Uggggh, get this thing off me," Obie yelled.

Tau grabbed an arm and leg of the rak-woman carcass and pulled it off. Obie rolled over and stood up, grimacing and swearing under his breath.

"Did she . . . ?" Tau started to ask.

"No, she didn't bite me—she lost her head, and it threw her aim off."

Tau and Obie stared soberly into one another's eyes for a moment, then burst out laughing and had to cover their mouths to muffle the sound. But when he noticed the small purple pool of deadly poison on the tunnel floor just past the door, Obie stopped laughing. It was enough to force his mind back to business. Time was wasting. Torolf could be on his way back. Maybe he was already in his tower chamber. He wiped Roar's blade on the she-widow's cloak and sheathed it. Then he and Tau pulled her carcass through the door to the lookout area and left it in a corner, out of the way. Tau set the she-widow's head on her chest and pulled her cloak up to hide the gruesome sight. Working fast they dragged the unconscious guard alongside her dead comrade and Obie shot her in the head again. They could neither take the time to bind her, nor risk her waking up any time soon. The lookout station was a large terrace, the back half dug into the mound creating a partial roof, and the front half bordered by a waist-high stone wall.

Obie heard Mole's squeak just before he came through the door onto the terrace. Then Gabrielle rode Mara through the doorway. The windlord stretched her wings, loosening them for flight. Obie noticed wisps of Gabrielle's flaxen hair streaming out, caught up in the breeze, and her slender arms exposed to the freezing air from under her tattered blue dress.

"Take this, Gabrielle—you'll need it." He removed his cloak and pulled it around her shoulders.

Her eyes widened with concern. "But what about you?"

Mole squeaked to get Obie's attention. He pointed to the unconscious she-widow in the corner.

"I'll, uhhh . . . borrow hers," Obie said, motioning towards the guard.

"Not a style I would select," Mole said with a wink to Obie, "but it will keep you warm." He turned and scurried over to Tau, keeping watch by the wall.

"Tau's keeping an eye out for the roving guards," Obie explained to Gabrielle. "As soon as they pass around the anthill you and Mara can take off with less chance of being seen. The Otawn are helping us—Mole will show you the way to their village. A couple of their braves will be watching for you from the trees, so fly low when you reach the valley and listen for their call of the night loon."

Gabrielle smiled gratefully. "The Shadow People are valuable friends to have."

Obie saw the weariness in her eyes and noticed she leaned forward a little with her hands resting on Mara's back for support. She was riding bareback because the raks had taken Mara's saddle. He opened his thoughts for Gabrielle to hear as he asked Mara, *What if Gabrielle faints again on the way?* A smile came into Gabrielle's eyes, though she remained silent while Mara answered.

I won't let her fall. If she feels herself growing faint, she knows to lie against my neck and wrap her arms around me.

All right. But, what about you? Are you strong enough to fly very far?

Mara opened her wings again to stretch them. *My wings are stiff from being bound for so long, but I will fly to the Otawn village. I would also carry you, Obie, though I sense you would not be willing to leave Tau behind.*

You're right. I wouldn't leave Tau alone after all we've been through. We keep each other out of trouble. You'll fly faster without the added weight anyway. Tau and I will catch up with you in a few . . . Obie stopped speaking when Tau, wild-eyed, rushed over carrying Mole.

"We must flee, Torolf has returned to the tower!" Tau's voice was shaking. He set Mole down in front of Gabrielle and darted to the doorway to listen for the sound of guards coming up the tunnel.

Mara stretched her wings, and Obie ran to the wall to have a look. *Is someone running up Torolf's stairs at this moment with news of the escape?* He peered to his right, around the tower. *Good, his window's facing away from us. Maybe he won't see, but the roving guards aren't out of sight yet . . . almost . . . another few seconds . . . that's it, keep moving.* His trembling hand was raised, signaling Mara to stay back. *Just a little more . . . okay, okay . . . now!* Vigorously, he waved Mara forward.

Tau joined Obie at the wall while Mara took several steps forward fanning her wings. A cloud passed over the moon and blackened the sky. Obie silently cheered.

For a few parting moments Gabrielle's eyes met Obie's. *Farewell my brave friend—we'll watch for you,* she said.

Mara lifted skyward. *Make haste, Oberon.*

And you, also. Fly, Mara, fly!

Mole squeaked a farewell to Obie and Tau. And though Obie could not see the look in his small eyes, he knew Mole was sorry to leave them behind.

Mara wobbled a little as she rose and then, lifting higher on the wind, seemed to find new energy. Steeply and silently she climbed into the black sky and headed east. When she was out of sight, Obie knew she would turn south and cross over the Barren Plateau to the Hundred Valleys Region and the Otawn camp.

Tau handed Obie the unconscious she-widow's cloak, minus the coiled serpent emblem he had just ripped off of it. "Thanks, my friend," Obie said. He threw it around his shoulders and fastened it at the neck. Dropping to the lookout floor they rolled in the snow for camouflage. They were about to leap over the wall, but stopped. The scattering clouds had just parted again and pale moonlight shone over the plateau and on the slope beneath them. Mara was far enough away now that she could pass for a bird in the night sky. A large bird glided past the moon, and Obie nearly jumped out of his skin. He pulled Tau down with him into a crouching position and pointed. "Is it Torolf?" he whispered, then answered his own question, "No, I see now, the bird is riderless."

"Let us hope it's a friend and not a foe," Tau whispered.

Fear clutched Obie's heart as he watched the bird fly northeast, gathering speed, slowly overtaking the fleeing windlord. The sky darkened again as another cloud blanketed the moon and cut off their vision.

CHAPTER TWENTY-ONE

ESCAPE
FROM TARGUS DOL

OBIE AND TAU SLIPPED OVER the low wall and moved stealthily down the hill. Passing to the side of the sleeping troops they climbed over the corral fence and crept among the horses. Obie had his Raptor ready and Tau still carried the club. A horse whinnied and before they could duck behind the parting horses one of the two muk corral guards spotted them over the fence. He opened his mouth to yell an alert, but Obie stopped him with a Raptor shot. Tau took down the second guard. They pulled the unconscious muks out of sight among the horses and left them. Obie knew every second counted. At any moment an alarm could sound and Torolf would burst from his window and hunt them down. They had to pick their horses quickly. Tau chose a big gray and Obie a sturdy looking bay. As he followed Tau towards the gate at the north end of the corral Obie heard a familiar low neigh and a wave of joy shot through him. *Can it be?*

I'd choose another if I were you, Obie heard a mental voice say at the same time he felt a warm breath on his neck.

Obie chuckled. *Where have I heard those words before?* He turned and Shadow rubbed his nose on Obie's cheek in greeting. Obie dropped the bay's rope. *You have a wonderful knack for finding me. Let's get out of here my friend.* He climbed on Shadow's back and leaned low to avoid being seen while they moved quietly through the horses towards the gate.

When I saw you and Tau enter the tower a while ago I was joyous. I always believed you would make it here—I've been waiting for you.

Thanks for your confidence in me, Shadow.

My compliments on your ruse to enter the tower.

Tau gets credit for that one.

Most important . . . did Gabrielle and Mara escape? I thought I saw something fly from the guard station, but it was so dark I wasn't sure.

Yes, they flew with Mole from the guard station just after Torolf returned. I pray they make it to the Otawn camp in the Hundred Valleys Region.

I join you in your prayer. Who are the Otawn?

A native tribe that helped us. That's where we're headed now. Obie kept darting looks towards Torolf's chamber window. He wanted to race away now, but moving too fast would stir up the other horses and bring soldiers running.

Well, Shadow, I hope you haven't grown tired of the exciting life you wished for back in that pasture in Windermere, because we're going to see some real excitement around here starting any time now.

May the gods of men and beasts smile on us tonight, Shadow answered.

At the gate Tau was waiting on the gray. He gave Shadow a quick nod and "glad you're back" smile, then turned and heeled his horse through the narrow gate with Obie and Shadow following. Once outside the corral they rode east a short distance, keeping the corral between them and the sleeping camp to avoid being spotted, then turned south towards the cliff foot. Obie hoped their luck would hold just a little longer—it had to. If Torolf flew from his tower now they'd be sitting ducks.

The clouds parted again and the pale, green moon shone down from behind the cliff, creating a narrow strip of shadow along the top of the slope where it joined the vertical wall of the plateau. Upon reaching the slope, Obie and Shadow started upward with Tau and the gray close behind. Obie leaned forward and touched the dark stallion's neck. *How fast can you climb a hill, my friend? If we can make it to that shaded strip before we're seen we may have a chance.*

Shadow's nostrils flared and, with a low snort, he leaped forward with the gray breathing hard at his heels. Agonizing minutes seemed like hours, yet all remained quiet around them. Could they be so lucky as to make it all the way to the cavern door before the alarm was sounded? Knowing they were fleeing on borrowed time, Obie's heart was racing. Seconds below the strip of moon-shadow the silence exploded with screams of rage issuing from Torolf's tower window. The awakened troops rushed from their tents in a state of confusion. Exerting furious bursts of energy, Shadow and the gray bounded forward and passed into the cover of the moon-shaded area. They turned west along the slope and raced towards the twisted tree by the cave door.

Torolf stood in his window, scanning the land for any movement. Obie held his breath and when the black sorcerer's gaze passed by them he sighed in relief. But it was short lived. Moments later Arend's screech ripped through the night as he shot from the tower bearing his master on his back. *If he flies this way he'll see us for sure, even in the shadow of the cliff.*

Arend flew high and disappeared over the top of the plateau. Obie heard him screeching as he buzzed its flat surface stirring up the harpies until the sounds of shrieking and screeching filled the air. Had Will's prayers won them this reprieve? Obie wondered. If so it was guaranteed to be short. When Torolf failed to find the escapees on the plateau he would return. Chances were, he was only instructing the harpies to be on the lookout.

Below, a large mounted patrol rode east and a second rode west, while three smaller patrols sped towards the slope, branching out to climb it at different spots. A rak patrol rode up the slope, a little east of the low ridge that ran in front of the cavern door. Gripping his Raptor, Obie glanced back at Tau. He was riding hard with his sword drawn. As they approached a receding section of the cliff, where there was no moon shadow for a short distance, Obie almost stopped breathing. *Keep going Shadow. We have to cross that moonlit area. We can't stop now.* The dark stallion and the gray ran into the pale moonlight and seconds later reentered the moon-shaded strip.

But one of the mounted raks saw them and yelled to his comrades as he pointed up the slope. Putting their heels to their horses, the soldiers raced towards the spot. Shadow and the gray reached the ridge in front of the cliff wall and pushed on through the narrow track towards the hidden door. Obie's heart was pounding. It would be close. At the tree he slid from Shadow's back. The raks' shouts grew louder while he frantically felt for the finger depressions. Tau jumped down, ready to bring the horses through the door. Obie's fingers found the depressions and he pushed the door open. Arend screeched from the plateau above as Tau pulled the horses inside. Up the far side of the ridge the raks rode. They were mere seconds from the top, seconds from discovering the hidden door. Obie rushed into the cavern behind the gray and pushed the door closed. It snapped shut just as the raks cleared the top of the ridge. Down they rode towards the door, slipping and sliding in the snow as they came. At the bottom some veered east while the others turned west, continuing the search. From the top of the plateau Torolf swooped down on Arend and veered east, scanning the slope.

Obie's breath came in ragged pants as he sank to the cave floor and leaned his head against the rock wall. "Close call," he said as his breathing steadied.

"Yes, close," Tau said. He was lying on his back with his knees bent upward, laughing to himself. Obie smiled. He knew

Tau was elated at taking the Moonpath Riders from under Torolf's nose and getting away with it. But the thought of Torolf made his smile vanish. When the black sorcerer's present search failed he would realize Mara had been strong enough to fly away with Gabrielle. Soon now, he would rush after them like a heat-seeking missile.

They rested a couple of minutes longer and then wiped the horses down with the blankets. While he worked Obie inspected Shadow closely for signs of abuse. When he lifted a front leg to survey his hoof, Shadow nickered.

I'm still in top condition, Oberon. The soldiers value horses and treated me well.

Obie released Shadow's leg. *Well, I respect them for that at least.*

Tau stood with his arms folded over his chest studying the gray. "I think I shall call you *Gamba*. In my homeland it means *warrior*. A good name for one such as you. You proved your worth out there." He pulled a few pieces of Otawn corn cake out of his pack and began hand-feeding it to Gamba and Shadow. "Torolf's patrols will be searching for us on both sides of the plateau."

"And in the forests of the Hundred Valleys," Obie responded. "I don't think they saw us enter the cave . . . but I don't want to wait it out in here."

"Nor I. The longer we stay the more dangerous it will be for us—until they give up searching that is."

"I'll be ready in thirty seconds," Obie said. Knowing he wouldn't have a moment's peace until he found Gabrielle and Mara safe at the Otawn Village, Obie had counted on Tau not wanting to wait around. They lit the torches and started down the winding cavern trail with Shadow following Obie and Tau leading Gamba. Sometimes the path was steep and a little difficult for the horses, but they finally made it down safely to the

Valley of the Spirits where they silently retraced their steps along the valley wall and then entered the narrow passageway leading to the Hundred Valleys Region. Along the way they encountered the body of the rak Obie had shot when they had first entered.

"I guess he didn't make it," Obie said, stopping to look down at him.

Tau came up to have a look. "I wondered what you were doing behind me when the rak patrol was chasing us. We had better move him aside so the horses won't have to step on his putrid carcass." They pushed the rak body against the tunnel wall and brought the horses through. It was almost dawn when they exited the hidden door. The harpies were still stirred up and clamoring above, frequently flying from the cliff wall and circling over the forest or the top of the plateau.

They mounted the horses and stole up the wooded slope in the darkness. On a distant hill they stopped a few moments and gazed back. In the early morning light they saw scores of hawks on the wing, scouring the land for signs of the Moonpath Riders and their rescuers.

Snow had not fallen since the storm that raged when they first arrived in the Hundred Valleys Region. Obie hoped the weather would hold a while longer, though the clouds had grown heavy and gray and he could feel the temperature dropping. With cloaks pulled close they moved on. All that day, they rode the same paths they had come on. That night while they slept beneath the thick branches of a fir tree the snow storm started. In the morning they pushed on again. A few hours later it stopped snowing, but dark clouds threatened to bring more. As they rode they frequently glanced up when screams of enemy birds sounded over the forest. "The birds fly low searching for movement through open spots in the trees," Tau whispered to Obie.

As before, they rode in the shadows of the trees and kept their weapons ready. By early morning of the third day they entered the forest valley of the Otawn camp. Shadow made a low, nervous neigh when an owl hooted and was answered by another.

Don't worry Shadow, we're among friends now. Except for the look of relief in his eyes, Obie's face remained expressionless.

Stopping, Shadow said, *They're directly above us.*

Tau, chuckling almost inaudibly, pulled Gamba alongside.

Grinning now, Obie asked, "Shall we hunt some owl?"

Tau darted a quick look upward. "Yes, I think I have a taste for owl this morning."

Sudden laughter came from the dark branches overhead and a moment later Takoda and another young brave dropped from the tree, landing on their feet in front of the horses.

"Ho, Brother of the Lion and Lion Who is a Man. My friend Kohana and I have been waiting for you."

"Ho, Takoda and Kohana," Obie answered.

"Ho, Takoda and Kohana," Tau responded.

Kohana wiped the smile from his face though it lingered in his eyes. "I am honored to meet those who fight the Necromancer."

"We're honored by your friendship," Obie said. Then he asked the question so urgent on his mind, "Did the Moonpath Riders arrive safely in your camp?"

"Yes, they are safe," Takoda answered. A feeling of relief flooded through Obie.

"Prince Andor brought them with Little Warrior three nights ago. Mankato is tending to the one we call *Woman with Stars in Her Hair*, and the windlord we call *Moon Dancer* is eating and regaining her strength."

The exact appropriateness of those names was one of several thoughts that passed through Obie's mind at that moment. The tension now gone from his face, he turned to Tau. "So it was *Andor* we saw following them—I should have known." He smiled, remembering Gabrielle's words that the prince was a remarkably dependable friend to have. He had proven that twice now.

Tau chuckled. "I had hoped it was he."

"Is he still here?" Obie asked Takoda.

"He is waiting to accompany the Moonpath Riders back to Windermere as soon as Woman with Stars in Her Hair is able to travel."

Obie had mixed feelings at the news. He was glad the warrior prince would escort Gabrielle and Mara back to Windermere, but they'd be heading straight into danger. More than anything, he wished he could go with them to lend his help if need be. But the distance was too great to burden Mara with the extra weight. It would slow her down when speed was of utmost importance. Nor could he ask Andor to carry him. He had learned from Sword Master Ull that eagles did not carry men on their backs, although they had been known to do so for short distances in emergency situations. The incident over Witch River had obviously qualified. This situation did not.

The braves whistled and when their horses trotted out of the trees they mounted and all headed for the village. On the way Takoda told them that soon after Andor and the Moonpath Riders arrived in camp Torolf and Arend had soared over this valley and others. Two braves hiding in the trees said he had lit the night sky with fire bolts and burned the tops of a few trees. Since then his ground patrols had been combing the valleys. One had passed right over the Otawn Village. He went on to say that the news of Torolf's march against Windermere and the lands to the west was very bad, and they should ask Prince Andor to fill them in.

Upon arriving at the village, Kangi climbed down from his look-out post in a nearby tree and greeted them. Then his eyes fixed on Shadow. "You stole a very fine horse, Brother of the Lion," he said with a big smile.

"Kangi, this is Shadow," Obie said. He's the horse I paired with in Windermere but lost when the muks chased us over a cliff."

"Ahhhh, that is all the better. You stole your own horse back. He is such a fine animal. If I ever see one like him, I will steal him for sure."

"Just don't get any ideas, my friend," Obie said with a quick laugh and a friendly pat on the shoulder.

Kangi threw his head back and laughed too. "If you allow me to tend to him, I promise I will never steal him from you."

Go and check on Gabrielle, Oberon, and let the boy take care of me. We'll be fine.

Alright. Have a good time. "You've got a deal, Kangi, thanks.

Then Tau said, "I will go with you to the Cave of the Horses, Kangi, as I wish to tend to my horse Gamba."

After Tau and Kangi took the horses, Obie turned to Takoda. Judging from the sparkle in his eyes, Obie knew he must be an open book.

"Woman with Stars in Her Hair is in the lodge just beyond the broken tree." He pointed towards a tree that had been destroyed by lightning. "But you will not find it so I will take you there."

When they arrived a woman told them Mankato was tending to Gabrielle, so Obie left a message that he would visit Mara and return shortly. Takoda gave him directions to the Cave of the Horses and then departed. Obie hurried over and found Mara standing under a tree outside the cave. At his approach she neighed a quiet greeting.

It's good to see you safe, Oberon. Shadow told me you would come before long and I came out to wait for you.

Thanks Mara. I was glad when I learned Andor accompanied you here.

Yes, it was a joyous surprise when our old friend appeared alongside us in the sky, as he has done so many times in the past.

They were filling each other in on events since the escape from Torolf's stronghold when Obie heard a familiar screech above. Glancing up he saw the eagle prince descend into the trees a short distance away. Anxious to get news of the war, he excused himself and hurried through the forest to find him.

Andor stood watching and listening at the top of a boulder beneath a tall pine. When Obie came Andor lowered his head and cocked an eye at him. "So we have finally caught up with one another."

"Hello, Andor," Obie said. Andor's emerald and bronze battle helm glistened softly in the gray light of morning. "Wait, I'm come up." Obie climbed the boulder and sat next to the prince, who continued gazing out at the trees. "Nice battle helm."

"Ah, yes, thank you. It was a gift from Zelda and the river sprites. They do fine work."

"I want to thank you for alerting the Otawn to look for us during the blizzard."

"You need not thank me," Andor said. "We each did our part. Your task was to rescue the Moonpath Riders, and it was up to Silverclaw and me to help you do it. I have a lot to tell you, for much has happened since you left Windermere."

Obie sighed. "It seems like a year ago."

"You probably did not know that *The War of the Necromancer*, as it is called, began weeks ago, shortly after Gabrielle and Mara were taken captive."

Obie shot an alarmed look at Andor. "No, I *didn't* know."

"Word of it reached Zelda's caverns while I lay recovering, but you had gone by that time. Not even the Shadow People knew of it. Their scouts no longer travel as far west as the Long Wadi Road. Torolf first sent a small advance army down that road to attack Windermere. It happened so fast that the forces of the Triple Alliance had only two days to assemble for the attack. Queen Olwen's armies, King Konur and the windlords, my father,

King Ymir, and the eagles fought valiantly in the meadows north of Windermere. We lost many, but our combined forces succeeded in driving Torolf's army back. Our hearts were gladdened, for we thought the war might end there. We did not guess the black sorcerer had a vast second army."

"I wish I'd known."

"It is just as well. You needed no distractions during your mission to rescue the Moonpath Riders. And now their retrieval of the Dark Crystal may be our only hope, though we are uncertain about its power." Andor shuffled his wings and when he continued his voice had grown solemn. "All we can do is trust in an ancient prophecy. But without it, our options are bleak: we can either fight Torolf to our deaths, or surrender and become his slaves in a world devoid of all light, though it is doubtful the world will survive very long in total darkness."

Unable to sit still any longer, Obie slid down and began pacing and muttering under his breath as he limped back and forth in front of the boulder. He stopped to pick up a rock and then hurled it as hard as he could.

"Are you all right, Oberon?" Andor asked.

"Yeah. I'm just blowing off steam." He climbed back up the boulder and sat beside Andor again. "Where's Silverclaw?"

"On the night you and your friends rescued Gabrielle and Mara, Silverclaw and I came looking for you. It was then we discovered Torolf's army. Silverclaw flew south to warn those of the Triple Alliance and I hid at the edge of the plateau waiting for you. Shappa had informed me you were taking a secret passageway through the plateau, and I guessed you were hiding within, awaiting your chance. I watched when you entered the tower, and waited until Gabrielle and Mara flew from the guard station. Then I caught up with them and brought them to the Otawn. It was a difficult flight for Mara. We had to fly hard and fast in a straight line to the village for we knew Torolf would soon be after us."

Then the eagle prince told what he had heard about the battle with Torolf's advance army. He recited how bravely the Windermerian ground forces had fought, and of sky battles of Windermerian warriors on windlords fighting muks and raks riding giant hawks. Few of the Windermerian sky warriors had perished, though they had slain many of the enemy. Torolf's hawk-riders were less skilled than the battle-seasoned Windermerians, and the windlords were greatly skilled at using their armored, spiked hooves and the unicorn-like horns on their battle helms against the sharp beaks and talons of the giant hawks. My kind, also, sent many plummeting from the sky, for the eagles are fierce fighters, and well-matched against the slightly larger hawks.

The stories of valor cheered Obie. The War of the Necromancer wasn't lost yet.

CHAPTER TWENTY-TWO

PLANS AND DEPARTURES

GABRIELLE WAS SITTING on a buffalo blanket talking with Shappa's daughter, Zonta, and another young woman when Obie returned. She had made several friends among the Otawn who were attracted to her gentle ways. Two small, glittering eyes stared up at Obie from the blanket, and then he heard Mole's familiar squeak. His brown fur against the buffalo hair rendered him nearly invisible. "Hello Mole," Obie said with a grin, then turned his attention to Gabrielle.

Her tattered blue dress had been replaced by one of soft doeskin, and her hair was pulled back in a single braid that fell down her back. Zonta and the other young woman politely rose to go when they saw Obie. He nodded and smiled gratefully at them as he was anxious to speak with Gabrielle. Her eyes filled with tears as he limped over and dropped down next to her on the floor. She reached out and took both of his hands in hers. "My dear friend, I'm so happy you've finally come. We've been so worried about you escaping from Targus Dol. And I thank you from the depths of my heart for rescuing Mara and me."

"You don't need to thank me, Gabrielle." He noticed an odd smile on her face. "What?"

"Remember the prophecy? You had a hard time believing you were the one it spoke of."

"Yeah," he said lowering his eyes. "It seems like maybe I am the one." Then lifting them again to meet hers, he said, "But I would have come to your rescue anyway, regardless of any prophecy. I want you to know that."

"I do know." She put her hands on his shoulders and kissed his cheek. "I'm glad you're safe now," she said softly.

"I told you, Tau and I watch out for each other."

While listening to Gabrielle and Obie, Mole was flopping his head from side to side and rolling his eyes. When she released Obie and rested her hands on the blanket at her sides, Mole crawled over and lay with his furry neck stretched across her left hand. Obie saw his bright little eyes staring up at him.

"Good to see you back, Oberon. I've, uhhh, missed you terribly."

Ignoring Mole's comment, Obie's eyes went back to Gabrielle. "How are you feeling, Gabrielle, I mean, how are you *really* feeling?" While speaking, he casually reached down and flipped Mole over on his back.

Mole wriggled back over on his feet again and lay quietly back down.

"Much better, truly, Obie." She smiled and scratched her head. Then she told him how the journey with the raks now seemed like a blurred dream. And though the raks were a rough and rowdy lot they had not been abusive. She confided to him how Torolf had used his sorcery to try and win her over so he could control her mind, and how resisting his will had weakened her. The moment she had flown from the Serpent's Tower and breathed fresh air again she had started feeling better. Mankato had been using all of his healing and spiritual skills to strengthen her and rid her mind of Torolf's influence. She had eaten nourishing food and walked each day to rebuild her physical strength.

Obie noticed a pink tinge had already returned to her cheeks. It seemed to him she was almost as vibrant as she had been on the day of the festival.

There was a knock and when the door lifted Tau peered through the opening.

"Tau, please come down and join us," Gabrielle called.

Tau came down the ladder and sat with them. Now they began speaking of the heavy matters regarding Torolf's war against the southern and western lands. Obie recounted what Andor had said regarding Torolf's advance attack on Windermere.

"Yes," Gabrielle said, lowering her head while listening. When she looked up her eyes were clear and filled with resolve. "Mara and I are leaving soon for Windermere so we can be there to ride the Moonpath when it opens. We'll return with the Dark Crystal if Phoebe will give it to us." Gabrielle's face grew tense. "No one's ever seen the Dark Crystal. We must pray it isn't just a legend. Prince Andor believes Torolf's endless supply of muks and raks will spread over the land like a dark tide, winning battles by sheer brute numbers. Not even the elf warriors of the Isles of Eluthien can hope to hold out for long against the onslaught of such an army."

Mole sat up and said, "You know Torolf will do anything to prevent you from joining together the Star Crystals—he'll try to stop you from riding the Moonpath."

"I know. It will be difficult if he tries to block us from entering it. The Moonpath remains open for only a few minutes when the full moon reaches its zenith. But Mara has amazing flying skills, and if any windlord can get past him it will be her."

"If you succeed in bringing the Dark Crystal back, how will you keep Torolf from taking it from you and destroying it?" Obie asked.

"That may be the greatest challenge of all, for I know he will try. He knows now that the Moonpath opens just above the Lonely Oak Tree that grows on top of Mount Iluva. He stole that information from my mind when I lowered my guard. And worse, he also learned that the Light Crystal is hidden in a cave within the mountain. But the cave has an extensive network of tunnels, and I was able to close my mind before he discovered its exact location. I've sent an eagle to Windermere with a message to Grandfather Andras. He's the elder who knows where the Light Crystal is. I've asked him to take it from the cave and hide it in a hollow place in the Lonely Oak. The moment Mara and I return, before Torolf has time to do anything, I'll take it out and join it with the Dark Crystal. Then we'll see."

"Your plan could work," Obie said. "If Torolf believes the Light Crystal is still hidden in the mountain he might not realize what you're doing."

"It must work," Gabrielle said.

"It will help if we can distract Torolf at the moment you return from the Moonpath," Mole said, "since we know he'll be there waiting for you."

Gabrielle nodded in agreement as she reached under the neckline of her dress and scratched her shoulder.

"I want to be there when you return, Gabrielle," Obie said, his deep blue eyes burning with determination.

"And I," Tau added spiritedly.

"And I," Mole said in his biggest voice, sitting up as tall as he could. As usual, he would not be left out.

"Yes, you too Little Warrior," Tau said, looking down at Mole.

"Good. It's settled." Mole lay back down.

"But, you're safe here among the Otawn," Gabrielle objected, scratching her shoulder again. "It may serve no purpose to put you all in danger again of being captured or even killed. You've already performed a great service in rescuing Mara and me. Please stay here and remain safe."

Gabrielle seemed so concerned about their safety that Obie fought his desire to protest. After exchanging quick glances with

Mole and Tau, he changed the subject by asking her when she planned to leave for Windermere.

"Late tonight. We're hoping Torolf's scouts won't be watching closely then and we can ascend into the clouds undetected."

"Are you feeling well enough to leave so soon?" he asked in a troubled voice.

She smiled patiently. "Time is growing short. The Moonpath will open in just five days, at the full moon, and who knows what obstacles we may encounter between here and Windermere."

He drew up a knee and leaned on it resignedly. "I'm glad Andor will be flying with you."

"Yes, I'm thankful for that, and Shappa has given me a bow in case I need it."

"I've seen how well you handle a bow . . . though I hope you won't need it."

Mole squeaked as he often did when he was about to say something. "And I hope, dear Woman with Stars in Her Hair, that should the need arise your arrows fly swift and true." His beady eyes shone with pride as he gazed up at Gabrielle's fair face.

"Thank you, Mole."

The visit ended soon after that so Gabrielle could get some rest before her departure that night.

Mole accompanied Obie and Tau to their lodge and before long two young women brought them warm food and drink. They thanked the women for their kindness and when they left Obie hungrily devoured the best meal he had had in days while Mole enjoyed a small bowl of brown beetles. Although Tau had eaten a little earlier, he made a heroic effort to appreciate this second meal, belching with satisfaction and rubbing his belly when he finished. The three sat talking quietly for a time, and then Mole scurried up the ladder and squeezed through the door. He returned shortly with Takoda and Kangi and they all sat in a circle speaking in low voices. Ten minutes later the two young braves left hurriedly. Obie put more wood in the fire pit and then lay down to rest from the long trip back to the village. Tau was already asleep. Around ten o'clock that night Mole woke his two companions. Maka had brought them warm buckskin clothing and water which she poured into a large bowl for washing. Obie quickly washed up while Tau licked at his fur. When they were dressed and starting up the ladder, Maka brought in stew and bread, and insisted there was time to eat. Although anxious to leave, Obie realized it would be impolite to refuse the food. Tau also reminded him that it might be a long time before they would eat so well again. After thanking Maka they downed the hardy meal. Then they hurried out to look for Gabrielle and Prince Andor.

They found Andor perched on a boulder with his beak lifted high testing the wind and watching the dark sky. They said their good-byes to the eagle prince and were about to leave when Andor asked Obie to stay a moment. When the others had gone he said, "I know your heart, Oberon. I know you will try to reach Windermere to protect Gabrielle and Mara when they ride the Moonpath."

"I guess I'm not hard to read."

"No, not hard. Your eyes reveal what your heart would hide. But time is short and the way will be difficult for you. When we reach Windermere I will have two windlords sent back for you. Are you riding the Long Wadi Road?"

"Yes, by night. By day we'll ride beneath the trees."

"Good. Following behind the Necromancer's army is the fastest way. Begin watching for the windlords in two days."

"We will. And if we see them from the trees I'll signal them with a loud whistle."

"I will tell them."

"Thanks Andor. It would be better if you don't mention this to Gabrielle."

The prince's eyes flickered. "It shall be as you wish, Oberon."

"Good luck my friend. I'll see you in Windermere," Obie said.

The villagers were gathered to send their good wishes with the Moonpath Riders and Prince Andor. Two young braves watched the sky from the treetops, ready to signal if they sighted the enemy. Gabrielle stood waiting in a white fox fur cloak and high doeskin boots, special gifts to her from the Otawn.

As he drew near Obie noticed his own cloak lying over Mara's back.

"It looks like we're the last ones to arrive," he said apologetically to Gabrielle.

"I would have waited. I knew you'd come."

Although Gabrielle appeared glad to see him and the others, he knew her mind must be occupied with her flight to Windermere. Mole was on the ground squeaking and twitching his whiskers at her.

"All right, Mole." Lifting him into her arms Gabrielle peered into his face and whispered, "Thank you little friend for all you've done and for keeping me company while I recovered." As she looked playfully into his eyes glowing yellow in the darkness, she added, "But I do think you've given me fleas."

"Dear lady, I am your servant," Mole said with a troubled look, "and the thought of giving you fleas so mortifies me that I blush beneath my fur. I pray you aren't deeply offended. But I charge you with the greater offense, lady, of being a thief. For surely you've stolen the hearts of those fleas with your beauty, just as you've stolen mine, and they deserted me for you."

"But truly, I'm not offended, Mole," Gabrielle said laughing. "You're a noble little fellow, a king among Moles—fleas and all. And a case of fleas is but a small price to pay for your sweet friendship." Smiling, she kissed Mole on the top of his head.

"I think I wanna barf," Obie whispered to Tau. Tau chuckled quietly.

"Thank you, Gabrielle," Mole said. "May fair winds carry you swiftly to Windermere."

She kissed the top of his head once more, and then set him on the ground. Next, she hugged Tau and thanked him for his friendship. When a hurt expression came onto his face, Gabrielle responded with wide, questioning eyes. In answer, Tau lowered his great head and, smiling mischievously, pointed to his forehead.

Gabrielle let go a small laugh and kissed Tau's forehead.

When she came to Obie she reached up and unfastened the she-widow's black cloak and let it fall in a heap to the ground. Then she took his cloak from Mara's back and placed it around his shoulders. "Thank you again, dearest friend, for all you've done. May we meet again in better days," she said, looking warmly into his eyes.

Unable to speak because his throat had suddenly gone dry, Obie swallowed hard trying to replace the moisture. Gabrielle seemed to understand his awkward silence and, reaching up, fastened his cloak for him.

"Now you can burn that black thing you've been wearing," she said.

From his perch on the boulder Andor flapped his wings impatiently, drawing a glance from Gabrielle.

"I guess it's time to go, huh?" Obie managed in a weak voice.

Gabrielle kissed his cheek and gave him a hug, then turned and mounted Mara. Andor spread his wings and took to the air, circling above while Mara lifted upward.

"Good-bye Woman with Stars in Her Hair;" "Good-bye Moon Dancer;" "Farewell Prince Andor," "May the gods favor you;" "Journey safely," the people simultaneously called out in hushed voices as they waved.

Gabrielle waved and quietly called back, "Stay safe, my friends."

Tau waved while Mole sat on his shoulder staring sadly after her, his whiskers drooping.

"Fly swiftly Moonpath Riders," Obie said quietly. Had he ever seen anything more beautiful? He stood watching until their outlines were swallowed up by the night.

"I'm in love," Mole said, his eyes still glued to the sky.

Obie cast a sidelong look at Mole. "Anyone I know?"

"Uh-huh."

"Well, there could be a tiny problem, I mean, you being a mole an' all," Obie said gently.

Mole sighed deeply. "Don't remind me."

Obie scruffed up the fur on Mole's head. "It's not surprising, Mole. Everyone loves Gabrielle."

Mole shook his head vigorously, as though trying to waken himself and remember the task at hand. Then the three conspirators gave one another sly grins and raced to the lodge where they grabbed their things and headed for the corral in the cave. Takoda and Kangi were waiting outside with the horses.

With an economy of words, they mounted and were ready to ride. Takoda clicked his tongue, lightly kicking his spotted horse forward.

"To Windermere," Obie said as their horses leaped forth.

To Windermere and more adventure, Shadow said to Obie.

Count on it, my friend, Obie said.

When the five warriors rode over the village, Shappa stood tall and motionless in his buffalo robe, stone-faced save for the pride in his eyes. But Maka's sad brown eyes betrayed her fears. "Be safe my brave ones," she murmured.

CHAPTER TWENTY-THREE

FLIGHT TO WINDERMERE

ANDOR AND MARA CLIMBED steeply through the heavy cloud layer, breaking through at last into clear night where the pale moon floated, high enough that a small sprinkle of dim stars were still visible. Although the nature of the journey weighed heavily on Gabrielle, there was a place in her heart that remained free of Torolf's dark oppression, a place that felt deep joy in soaring through the heavens through this quiet realm of the eternal where cares were temporarily left behind and the only sound was the wind. And it felt safe flying alongside the eagle prince, for he was not only a trusted friend to Gabrielle, but a formidable warrior whose fighting prowess was widely known.

We may avoid detection by flying high, Andor said mentally to Gabrielle and Mara, *but if we are seen dive into the clouds and I will follow if I can.*

All right, Andor, Gabrielle responded, laying her hand on the bow strapped at Mara's side. She did not argue for she knew his willingness to fight to the death to protect her and Mara was as much a part of Andor as his love for life. So she simply appreciated her noble warrior friend and loved him for his valor.

They flew east in an attempt to put distance between themselves and Torolf's advancing army to the west, where his sky scouts would be patrolling. After an hour they turned south. When the first signs of dawn came into the east they descended through the clouds and made a dash for the forest. There, under the thick cover of the woods they found a place to rest and the eagle prince stood watch. Perched silent and motionless on a tree branch high above his sleeping companions, his keen eyes continually scanned the dark canopy above and the shadows below for movement. Several times when screaming hawks flew low over the trees Andor raised his wings tensing for battle. But each time the danger passed and he folded his wings again.

After a few hours Gabrielle stood watch while Andor slept. Upon awakening in the early afternoon he flew to the top of a tree and then returned to the ground where Gabrielle waited astride Mara.

All seems quiet at the moment, he said. *I detected no movement within eyesight.*

Let's make a dash for it then, Gabrielle said as Mara unfolded her wings.

They followed Andor upward through an opening in the branches. Then drawing on all their power, eagle and windlord rose in a swift, nearly vertical climb to the safety of the clouds. But as they disappeared within the gray cover a small hawk flew out from the treetops and sped away westward.

Andor and Mara burst from the clouds into the pale gray sky where the sun hovered like a dying, green flame casting a greenish glow over the sea of clouds. They flew south for several hours and, except for passing a large flock of friendly snow geese, they saw nothing. Then a sudden screech ended the tranquility as three giant hawks rose up from the clouds on their right.

Hawks in the west! Dive! Andor called.

Mara dove into the gray cloud floor with Andor right behind and the hawks in close pursuit.

Bank left and we'll try to lose them in this cloud cover, Andor said. *If that fails, dive to the safety of the forest.*

Their hopes of losing the hawks were dashed when, seconds later, a huge, dark form approached through the churning, gray billows to their right and they heard high-pitched laughter. It was Arend bearing a dark hooded rider.

It's Torolf! Flee to the forest! Andor entreated.

Breaking through the bottom of the clouds Mara plunged towards the trees. Prince Andor pulled up to block enemy pursuit of the Moonpath Riders. There, wild-eyed with wings treading air and talons spread, Andor screeched his fierce challenge to Arend and the other hawks. The three hawks answered by circling Andor while Torolf and Arend veered around them and dove like a rocket after Gabrielle and Mara. Flesh and feathers flew as beaks and talons clashed in mortal combat. The eagle prince was smaller but quicker than his foes. Within seconds he sent one of the hawks crashing to Earth, leaving but two against him. He tried breaking away to follow Gabrielle and Mara, but the two hawks kept cutting him off.

Streaking earthward like a meteor, Torolf cackled gleefully, his eyes glowing like hot coals from under his black hood. Gabrielle's arms were locked around Mara's neck and her hair streamed out behind. The treetops loomed near. Arend shrieked behind them. Mara pulled up and swerved sharply just before hitting the trees, a maneuver she excelled at. Arend pulled up too, though Mara gained crucial seconds while he recovered and turned to follow. By that time Mara was gone.

Down she fluttered through an opening in the thick branches, down, down towards the dim forest floor. Her hooves touched ground and she galloped off into the deep gloom half running and half flying through the obstacle course of ancient tree trunks. Arend found the opening and descended swiftly, his large wings snapping small branches.

Her heart squeezed by fear, Gabrielle turned her head and saw Torolf whipping Arend to greater speed, his red eyes blazing in the darkness. She spotted another small hole in the canopy. *Up Mara, through that opening.*

Upward and out Mara went, changing direction, gliding fast and low over the trees until, spotting another small parting in the branches, she dove back under the green mantle just before Arend broke through the treetops in pursuit. Gabrielle heard the great hawk screeching above the canopy. She knew Torolf had not seen them dive, that he must be confused as to where she and Mara had gone, for the vast forest spread endlessly in all directions. Maybe they had a brief reprieve.

Torolf will not stop searching for us, Mara said.

I know. His hawk riders will soon be combing the forest. We must find a place to hide.

Yes . . . I fear it won't be safe for me to fly even at night for a time.

As they fled their eyes darted about searching vainly for a hiding place. The gloom began to deepen as night started to close in. Earlier, they had heard birds singing in the trees, but the woods had become deathly still. And now the quiet gave way to shrieks, yells, and the unmistakable hissing of raks not far off.

Gabrielle shuddered to think she and Mara would soon be hunted down. And if the raks were hawk riders they would come swiftly. Perhaps hearing Gabrielle's thoughts, Mara displayed a new burst of energy. When her legs folded beneath her and she began sailing through and around the trees, Gabrielle knew she was operating on sheer instinct, will, and sense perception; flying so fast through the trees, there was no time for thought, only for action. It was an ability that distinguished her as one of the truly great flyers.

Enemy sounds came from all directions now. They were surrounded and the prospect of escape was fading. There was no place to hide. Then a wood thrush fluttered down from the trees and flew alongside Gabrielle and Mara.

"Follow me," it called excitedly. "I will take you to a safe place."

"Lead the way, friend," Gabrielle called back.

Mara followed the bird as it veered left and flew down into a gully. A hawk rider flew overhead, but did not see them. When they came up on the other side the wood thrush told Mara to land and run over the ground so she would leave hoof prints to fool the pursuers. Folding her wings and lowering her legs she followed the bird through the trees to a rocky hill and turned left along its base. The forest was alive with the shouts and squawking sounds of their pursuers and it was nearly dark. Rounding the hill, Gabrielle heard water lapping a nearby shore.

"Here, here," the wood thrush called, fluttering next to a stone outcropping in the hill. "The hiding place is within these rocks. You must run to the lake so your scent trail and hoof prints will end at the water's edge. Then fly back here and I will open the door for you to enter." Again, Mara did as the thrush bid her and followed the sound of the water to the lake a hundred feet away.

The hawk squalls and soldiers' shouts to one another were so loud now that Gabrielle feared the hawk riders would burst through the trees at any moment. *Fly swiftly back, Mara*, she entreated. The windlord turned and flew back towards the hill. While she moved through the trees a dark shadow passed above the treetops. Over the faint flapping of Mara's wings Gabrielle heard a tapping sound against rock. The thrush had timed it right; just as Mara fluttered to a landing before the rock wall and folded her wings, a door swung inward. Gabrielle slid from her back and after Mara passed through the entrance, brushed away her new hoof prints. Then she followed Mara through the door and pushed it shut behind them. Just inside, they stood listening. Half a minute later she heard the hawk riders outside the door. They paused briefly, and then she heard them fly away. Sighing, she turned to Mara and the thrush.

"I think the trick worked. The hawk riders are probably searching for us in the fog over the lake. We thank you for helping us friend wood thrush."

"You are more than welcome, my lady. You will always be welcome in this wood, although the creatures pursuing you are not."

His words brought a smile to her face and then she glanced around the cave. "What place is this?"

"An elf bower, my lady. You will be safe here as it is well-hidden. I hope it will be to your liking."

"We like it," Gabrielle said without hesitation. She was surprised to see the warm glow that lit the cave did not come from torches, but from a natural rosy luminescence of the rock. Along the left wall were beds almost seven feet in length with deep mattresses and fragrant woven blankets folded at the foot of each. In the center of the cavern was a stone fire pit with a chimney suspended above, and a pile of wood lay neatly stacked nearby.

"You must light a fire to keep warm tonight," the thrush said to Gabrielle.

"I would, friend thrush, but won't smoke rising from the top of the hill bring our enemies down upon us?"

The wood thrush chirped a small sound like laughter. "Forgive me, my lady, I should have told you about the wonderful chimney above this fire pit. No smoke will escape for the chimney spirals up through the hill, and the elves planted a special fungus within it that eats the smoke so well, not even the odor of smoke escapes from cracks on the hilltop. You are perfectly safe."

Against the right wall he pointed out stores of sweet grasses kept for the elf horses, and shelves containing dried fruit, honey, grains, and wrapped loaves of *emui,* an elven honey-bread that was still fresh enough to eat and provided much nourishment. At the back of the cavern a tunnel wound upward to another secret door at the top of the hill. Next to that passageway, he took them down ten stone stairs that led to two clear pools of water; they were fed by an underground spring bubbling in through and opening in the rocks above the first pool. The water from that pool spilled into the second, which was a foot lower, and the water from the lower pool finally drained out through a small opening at its far side.

The wood thrush alighted on the rock floor beside the first pool. "This pool is for drinking, my lady, and the second is for bathing. You must be very thirsty. Please drink and be refreshed."

Before he finished speaking Mara was already lapping the water. Gabrielle joined her, cupping the cool, clear water to her mouth. When their thirst was quenched they went back up the stairs. The thrush perched on Mara's head and continued speaking to them while Gabrielle took a brush from her riding bag and began currying Mara.

"The river sprites passed a message to the free birds remaining in this forest. The message asked us to watch for and give assistance to a young, fair-haired woman riding a white windlord and a young man traveling with a mole and a lion-man."

"Truly?" Gabrielle said, looking up at him in surprise. "It's good to know we have such support."

"You have much support, my lady. I was alerted by other birds shortly after you were chased into the forest, and I came to find you as fast as I could fly. This bower is claimed by the High Elves of the Isles of Eluthien. On their behalf I welcome you to use anything you see within to make your stay comfortable. I am called *Ambiel* by the elves."

Gabrielle stopped brushing for a few moments and looked at him. "Thank you, Ambiel. We are in your debt. I am Gabrielle of the House of Brynnen and this is Mara. My people have long been friendly with the High Elves of Eluthien, for their blood runs in the veins of the Kings and Queens of the House of Gruffydd, the Royal House of Windermere."

"So I have heard it said. I have also heard your names before. Are you not the ones called the Moonpath Riders?"

"Yes," she said, scratching her neck.

"So that is why the Necromancer is chasing you."

"It's urgent that we get to Windermere by the night of the full moon, for on that night when the moon reaches its zenith we must ride the Moonpath."

Ambiel's eyes grew large at learning this. "It is a great task before you, my lady. I will do everything I can to assist you."

"You have already been of great help to us, Ambiel. Will you stay with us and share a meal?"

"I will be honored to do so."

While Gabrielle continued brushing Mara, Ambiel began singing a night-song. It was a sweet melody tinged with sadness that touched her heart. Knowing a little of the elven tongue, she understood why the elves named him *Ambiel,* as it meant *heart song.*

When Gabrielle finished with Mara she lit a fire, set out mats for Ambiel and herself, and brought a bunch of sweet grass for Mara to eat and a small bit of grain for Ambiel. Finally she took a loaf of the emui, broke off pieces for each of them, and sat down to dine with her companions. The emui had a delicate honey flavor and was itself a satisfying meal.

While they ate Ambiel counseled Gabrielle and Mara to remain in the cave and periodically crack the door open to listen. When they could hear the forest birds sing, they would know it was safe to leave the cave and resume their flight to Windermere. For the free birds, those not under Torolf's power, would not sing when his soldiers and spies were near. He then gave them the tapping code to open the lower and upper doors.

After that they spoke of pleasant things and happier days. Ambiel told stories of the elves, and Gabrielle told tales of humans and windlords, and for a time they shared the warmth of friendship. Gabrielle's frequent scratching had apparently not eluded Ambiel. This fact was demonstrated when, near the end of his visit, he fluttered up from his mat to her shoulder.

"Fair lady, did you know you have fleas?" he said, pecking one off.

"I *have* stronly suspected it," she said with a small laugh.

"For myself I think nothing of having fleas, as I am only a bird and it cannot be helped. But it will not do to have a flea-bitten Moonpath Rider. In the morning I shall fly to the far side of the lake and gather herbs that will drive these pests away when sprinkled in your bathwater and clothing."

"Dear, Ambiel, thank you for yet another kindness. But I must correct you. You're not *only* a bird. You're a very *special* bird. For such pure, sweet song could only come from a noble and tender heart."

"That is a very great compliment to end this evening with, my lady." Ambiel fluttered up and hovered before her. "The hour is late and you and Mara must rest. When I visit again I will come and depart by the upper door so I will not be seen.

Gabrielle accompanied Ambiel up the passageway to the upper door. She tapped out the code Ambiel had taught her, and when the door cracked open she smelled rain in the air.

"Until morning I wish you golden dreams in elven glades," Ambiel said, hovering by the open door.

"Until tomorrow," Gabrielle whispered.

"A rainstorm is moving in fast," he said as he flew out.

The Celestial Dimming brought a colder than usual winter to this low country. Although the temperature here rarely dropped to freezing the recent storm had brought snow, and patches of it still lay on the ground. Unless the temperature dropped again, the coming rain promised to melt what was left of it.

Returning down the passageway into the cave, Gabrielle went to Mara and draped an arm over her. Mara neighed. *Ambiel is a good friend.*

And a delightful one—like Mole. We've been very fortunate to have such friends. Then a cloud came over Gabrielle's face and she bit her lip. She had worried about Prince Andor all evening, but had not allowed her feelings to surface while Ambiel was there. *Do you think Andor is all right?*

I fear for him. We can only pray he escaped the hawks.

They were silent for a time, and finally Gabrielle went to put more wood on the fire. When the fire was built up again she sat down and gazed into the flames thinking about their teachers, Ariana and Gandora. They had been such an inspiration the first time she had seen them, gliding overhead with Gandora's beautiful golden wings outstretched on the wind, and Ariana's long red hair streaming out behind.

Mara, do you recall what our teachers told us about riding the Moonpath?

Yes, I remember Ariana saying the Moonpath will be beautiful and perilous—like nothing we have known. And when we ride it, we must not let our minds drift into sleep.

We're fortunate our teachers are among the very few who have ridden the path themselves.

Yet . . . Phoebe did not show herself to them.

No, Gabrielle said with a worried look. *I hope Ariana was right in her belief that she didn't reveal herself because there was no need to retrieve the Dark Crystal. We must believe the Moon Maiden will not fail us in our mission.*

I do believe.

Gabrielle got up and gave Mara a hug. *Thank you for being my dear friend, Mara.*

It will always be so, Mara said. She touched her velvety nose to Gabrielle's cheek.

And on my part also, Gabrielle said as she stroked Mara's muzzle. *We'd better try and get some sleep now. We'll need to be rested for the long journey ahead.*

She lay down on one of the elf beds and pulled the blanket over her. But thoughts of home held sleep at bay and she lay staring into the semi-darkness. It had been a relief to learn from Andor that her family was unharmed during the raid on the festival, but it was troubling that her mother and also Nona might not know she was alive. She hoped they had received the message of her rescue and were spared more grief. Had the eagle she sent with the urgent message to Grandfather Andras arrived yet? But most important, had Grandfather followed her instructions? He wouldn't fail. He was strong. Had he ever failed at anything? Nothing that she could remember. So there was nothing to worry about. Still, she wasn't quite comforted. Something else was amiss, something deep within—a sadness she could not name. She lay awake a while longer and then sweet sleep came to her.

She slept soundly and awoke the next morning more rested than she had felt in a long time. When Mara confirmed the same thing Gabrielle wondered if it was the magic of the elf bower.

She went to the lower door and cracked it open. There was no birdsong this morning, only the steady patter of rain on leaves and the pelting of raindrops on the ground. Lightning flashed and a few seconds later thunder crashed over the land. Were the hawk riders still about? The birds weren't singing, but then, *would* they sing in a storm? There was still time. They would wait and see. Anyway, it would be too dangerous to fly in this weather. She pushed the door shut.

Soon, Ambiel arrived with fresh fragrant herbs dripping with rainwater. He dropped them into Gabrielle's hands and departed saying he would return later. Some of the herbs she set aside, to be sprinkled in her bed and clothing. The rest she dropped in her bathwater. The pleasant herb-scented water felt luxurious against her skin while she bathed and washed her hair. When she stepped from her bath she was free of fleas. An image of Mole passed through her mind and she smiled.

That night Ambiel returned through the upper door in a flurry of excitement.

"Great danger has arrived! Flocks of harpies have flown into the forest and are watching from the trees. Please do not leave the cave or they will be upon you before you know it."

The news was disheartening. Gabrielle and Mara had seen the harpies when they entered the passageway leading through the plateau into Targus Dol, and Rrguck had warned that they could tear creatures to pieces.

"What about your safety, Ambiel?"

"Do not worry. Harpies take no notice of small birds. They seek larger prey."

"Torolf must suspect we're hiding in this area. He must be very worried if he's willing to have us torn to pieces," Gabrielle said.

"Perhaps so, or he may have ordered them merely to frighten you and Mara into remaining in hiding so you will miss your chance to ride the Moonpath. Either way, you must not risk leaving this cave now. Trust that I will find a way to get you safely to Windermere."

"We can wait only a day or two at most, and then we *must* go."

"I understand," Ambiel said. "Will you remain here until I return?"

"We will wait as long as possible for you, Ambiel. But we must leave here in time to reach Windermere before the Moonpath opens."

"Be assured, I will return before you must leave."

The night passed and when morning came Mara stood behind Gabrielle while she slowly cracked open the lower door. A few feet away, his back to the door, a big rak soldier stood in the rain looking towards the lake. Gabrielle gasped and silently pushed the door shut.

That was too close for comfort, Mara said. *Their tents are pitched almost at our door.*

"They must have set up camp in the night. We can't risk opening this door again," Gabrielle whispered.

They waited and waited, periodically listening at the lower door. Each time they heard the harpies, squawking from the trees, and sometimes they heard the raks talking or shouting. Night came, and then morning, yet Ambiel did not come. Gabrielle began pacing anxiously about, wondering where he was. The moon would be full tomorrow night and they estimated it might take ten hours flying time to reach Windermere. The situation was growing critical. The night passed into morning again and, still, Ambiel did not come. Now they feared that something bad might have befallen him.

Gabrielle crept to the lower door and listened, then turned back to Mara. *The raks are still camped outside. We'll have to leave by the upper door and pray we aren't spotted.*

Mara nickered and stretched open her wings, then folded them to her sides again. *When the sun is high overhead we must leave. We dare not wait longer.*

Gabrielle nodded and sat down by the fire. The morning wore on and she peeked out from the upper door twice. The rain had stopped and the sky was clearing. And still, there was no sign of Ambiel. Worse, no birds were singing. The clearing sky was not good either as they needed clouds to hide in during their flight. Without them they would be forced to fly dangerously high.

In preparation to go Gabrielle bathed, dressed in her doeskin clothing, tied her hair back with a cord, and pulled her cloak over her shoulders. She packed a little of the emui and was fastening her riding bag shut when she heard excited chirps and the sound of fluttering wings. Moments later Ambiel flew from the upper tunnel entrance. "Come quickly. I have brought a flock of snow geese to fly with you. They wait atop the hill."

Gabrielle was much relieved at his return, but wondered about the geese. She mounted Mara and they hurried up the tunnel towards the upper door.

"When I open the door the flock will rise up and flutter about, shielding you from sight. Try to ignore their presence, Mara. Just rise up and fly as you normally do and the geese will fill in around you. Keep your eyes on the geese directly in front of you so you do not become disoriented. Soon, it will become easier. Trust them. They will take you all the way to Windermere and you will arrive in time. Fair winds my friends."

"Thank you, good friend," Gabrielle said. "I hope we meet again some day."

The door opened and there was a sudden great flapping of wings. Gabrielle and Mara stepped out and everywhere around and above them white snow geese fluttered. Mara fanned her wings and lifted upward while the birds moved in below, sealing that space also. The geese gathered in tight formation around the Moonpath Riders making them invisible to view from all directions.

As the great white mass glided up and over the hill the bottommost geese dumped their brown gifts on the camp below. The raks sprang for cover, but not fast enough. Shaking their many fists, they hurled insults at the snow geese, but dared not leave their post to chase a flock of impudent geese. A few harpies that witnessed the scene squawked and caterwauled something akin to laughter, though most of them disregarded the flock entirely. The snow geese ascended high over the lake and headed south, their whiteness contrasted against the somber sky.

At first Mara kept her eyes on the snow geese in front of her as Ambiel had instructed. But as she learned to anticipate and feel their movement as a single unit, she became more comfortable with flying in tight formation and was able to glance around at the others. They flew all afternoon and when night came they stopped at a forest lake for a rest.

Gabrielle, do you hear that? Mara asked when her hooves touched down on the grassy shore.

The corners of Gabrielle's mouth turned up in a smile as she listened. *The song of a night bird. We're safe here.*

They refreshed themselves with a long drink of cool, pure, mountain lake water and then rested among the snow geese for half an hour. When they resumed their flight south, the pale full-moon rose and began climbing the sky. After a time they made a ninety-degree turn to approach Windermere from the east. They were still a couple of hours away and flying against a headwind.

I think it's going to be close, Mara. The moon will be nearly at its zenith before we reach Mount Iluva.

Don't worry. I can tell the snow geese are gauging their speed by the moon's upward progress. I sense they want us to arrive at just the right time.

There were no lights below, only hazy moonlight shining dimly on the treetops and an occasional forest lake. When the front geese started honking, Gabrielle and Mara understood it as their message that the lights of Windermere were visible in the distance.

We're almost there, Mara.

Yes, dear friend. Steel your mind for the task ahead.

When they were close the geese opened a crack in their formation for a few moments, allowing Gabrielle and Mara to see the campfires of the Necromancer's great army filling the entire valley of Windermere and beyond.

It's as we feared Mara. Torolf is already in Windermere and he'll surely be waiting for us at the Moonpath entrance.

I'm ready to face that challenge.

You may have to fly as you've never flown before to save us from Torolf's wrath and Arend's talons.

We knew it might be this way, Gabrielle. But once we enter the Moonpath we'll be safe, for he knows he can't follow us onto it.

Yes, the path would dissolve beneath him.

Just hold on tight . . . it's going to be a rough ride.

I promise I will.

They were flying over the valley now, fast approaching Mount Iluva. A few hawk riders spotted the geese and raced up to have a look. Circling the flock and seeing nothing threatening they veered off and headed back to the mountain top. Beside the Lonely Oak Tree Torolf sat waiting on Arend. And with him was a battalion of muk and rak hawk riders. Several large campfires burned, lighting a large area around the oak tree. When the snow geese were close to the mountain they split formation and released Mara and Gabrielle, then closed ranks again and veered away south. The moon was only minutes from its zenith.

The pale lunar light shone on the Moonpath Riders, exposing them to view as they neared the mountain. Spotting them, Torolf's face turned purple with rage. He gave Arend a hard kick and they darted up after the riders. Gabrielle gasped when she saw Torolf for the first time as he truly was: not the handsome young king, but the bent and wizened, straggly-haired creature he had become. His luminous, red eyes glowered at her from sunken, purple eye sockets, and he shrieked hideous sounding words in some unknown tongue. Screeching as he neared, Arend stretched open his sharp talons. Mara's nostrils flared and she spun round kicking at Arend's talons with her hooves as he buzzed by. He whipped round to attack again. Mara swerved sharply to evade him but he was right behind. Again and again she turned and dived, but Arend stayed in relentless pursuit. Torolf hurled a fire bolt at the fleeing Moonpath Riders, then another, both barely missing them. Then Gabrielle drew back her bow and when Mara turned about, unleashed an arrow at him. His high-pitched cackle resounded through the sky as simultaneously he raised his hand and hurled another bolt. The flaming orb intercepted the arrow and burned it to a cinder. Still another fiery bolt whizzed by, singeing Mara's long white tail and burning Gabrielle's right leg. Gabrielle shot again hoping to draw the next bolt away from her and Mara. It worked, and the fire bolt angled off towards the arrow.

Mara, it's time. The Moonpath.

The wan moon shone directly overhead and the air above the Lonely Oak was glowing, though the Moonpath itself was invisible unless one stood at its entrance. Mara arced steeply upward, briefly throwing Arend off, but Arend wheeled and followed. Torolf hurled another flaming bolt, but missed again.

Hold on with all your strength, Gabriel . . . we're going down.

Gabrielle leaned forward locking her arms around Mara's neck, and Mara swooped straight down towards the Lonely Oak. Arend dove after her, seconds behind. Below, the soldiers saw the riders coming towards them and moved back, for it appeared they might crash on top of them.

Can see . . . path's angle . . . from glow . . . ready now. Mara streaked down, not daring to slow her speed. Never had Gabrielle seen Mara fly like this. Bracing for the upward snap, she closed her eyes and laid her head firmly on Mara's neck. With deadly aim Torolf hurled another fiery missile at Gabrielle. Like a red-hot dagger it stabbed through her white fox cloak, doeskin clothing, and deep into her back.

Just before crashing into the Lonely Oak, Mara arced steeply upward and disappeared into the Moonpath. Arend shot off sideways and did not follow.

CHAPTER TWENTY-FOUR

THE MOONPATH

GABRIELLE, LOOK, Mara said.

Gabrielle opened her eyes and saw the beauty of the Moonpath. A little more than the width of Mara's wingspan, it wound in a silvery white mist through black space towards Phoebe, the Moon. Over the path shimmering flecks of stardust floated like a microcosm of stars. Some landed on Gabrielle and Mara and then blew away again into the mist. Mara's white wings rose and fell in a gentle rhythm while a current like a super tailwind carried them along at great speed.

As she fought the agony of her burning wound, sweat beaded on Gabrielle's brow. Looking down she saw the blue and green Earth cloaked in gray haze, receding behind them. Her vision grew fuzzy. With effort she raised her head from Mara's neck and gazed towards the moon, no longer a small greenish orb, but large and bright now. As she looked, it transformed into an ethereal white light more beautiful than anything she had ever imagined, and for a time she forgot her pain. Her heart reached out to the light and it drew her in like the arms of a loving parent, bathing her in an ecstasy of lightness and well-being in a place beyond time; and in that eternal moment she knew the joy of feeling infinitely loved and she knew she would never truly fear anything again. Then the light was gone and the solid white surface of the Moon shone brightly like before, and Gabrielle marveled at what she had just experienced.

But as they flew on and on along the rising and falling Moonpath her wound began to burn again. Tuned mentally to Gabrielle's suffering, Mara pleaded, *Hold on Gabrielle, I'll get you to Phoebe in time. She'll help you—I know she will.*

Drowsiness came upon them. At first Gabrielle welcomed the lulling effect that lessened her pain. But in her groggy state an inner voice warned it was dangerous to sleep, that she *must not* sleep, though she could no longer remember why. So her mind hovered on butterfly wings in that foggy realm between sleep and wakefulness.

Meanwhile, Mara's eyelids began to droop. Then her head dropped and the rhythm of her wings faltered as she drifted into sleep. Each time she awoke quickly and lifted her head, and each time the weight of drowsiness pulled her head back down and forced her eyes shut.

Like a paralyzed dreamer unable to cry out, Gabrielle watched Mara's wings stop flapping, watched as Mara slid off the Moonpath with only the tip of her right wing extending into it. With great effort she succeeded in calling the windlord, *Mara, wake up, we're falling, open your eyes, Mara!*

Mara's eyelids opened onto the starry black cosmos around her. The thin air in the narrow zone alongside the Moonpath caused her lungs to convulse, and she expelled a sound between a gasp and a neigh. The sound startled Gabrielle from her half-sleep.

Shaken free of grogginess and peering into the depths of space, Gabrielle's oxygen deprived lungs made her gasp also. *Mara, Mara,* she pleaded. Mara fluttered back onto the path. Sucking in great breaths of air, they forced their lungs to work again. But the effort had exhausted Gabrielle and she reclined her head on Mara's neck again.

Forgive me, Mara, for not helping you, Gabrielle said feebly. *I should not have forgotten Ariana's warning not to fall asleep lest we stray from the path.*

In your weakened condition, Gabrielle, there's no fault upon you. I'm to blame if blame is to be meted out.

We survived—that's the important thing. Now we must try and understand what Ariana meant when she told us to use the natural joy in our hearts to stay awake. Do you remember?

It was at the end of a lesson and someone interrupted us. We didn't question her about it later. How could we have forgotten so important a thing? Let me think. They grew quiet as they worked at remembering. Then, as though struck by lightning, Mara exclaimed, *Singing, Gabrielle! She had to have meant that natural joy fills our hearts with song.*

Gabrielle made a small laugh. *Mara, you're so brilliant. That has to be right.*

Sing every song you ever learned, Gabrielle. It will ease your pain and keep us both awake.

I'm feeling so weak, Mara. I don't know if . . . Gabrielle stopped herself mid-sentence, knowing this was no time to give in to her pain and weakened condition. As long as she could still think and act she must do what was needed. *Of course* she would sing. At first her voice was small and shaky, little more than a whisper. But as she continued her voice grew stronger and she forgot her pain. She sang all the songs she could remember and when she forgot the words she made them up, to a background of snorts and mental laughter from Mara.

While they were immersed in song, the misty path rose over the face of the Moon partially obscuring it. They did not notice how near they were drawing to it until the path abruptly dipped before them. Gabrielle stared in awestruck silence: Phoebe loomed enormous and bright before them.

The Moonpath descended into the twilight area, a narrow band where the Moon's eternal night side meets its eternal day side. Balanced between the light and dark, the sky glowed softly like dawn on Earth nearest the light side and like dusk nearest the dark side. Silent and watchful, the Moonpath Riders neared the lunar surface. Then something caught Gabrielle's attention.

Mara, what's that glittering object down there?

Mara squinted to see. *It looks like a crystal dome.* Soon they were close enough to see that it was, indeed, a great crystal-like dome enclosing thousands of acres of green land.

I see a forest inside the dome, and gardens with pools and streams and waterfalls . . . it's wonderful. Do you think Phoebe knows we're coming? Gabrielle asked weakly, having expended the last of her energy in song. Blinded now with fever and pain she clutched Mara's long silky mane tightly in her hands.

Yes, I think she knows, Mara answered nervously, sensing Gabrielle's rapid decline. *Don't let go, Gabrielle, please don't let go now!* Mara spotted the end of the Moonpath just inside the dome. They were approaching fast. *Hold tight, Gabrielle—I can't slow down. We're going to crash into the dome!*

Gabrielle locked her arms around Mara's neck but was too weak to brace for the jolt. Then the current that pushed them along abruptly slowed and they glided through the clear wall of the dome as if they had passed through a self-sealing water bubble. On the ground below was a path that wound into the forest. Mara fluttered down to the path and came to a dancing stop.

We made it, Mara. Gabrielle's eyelids slowly dropped onto her cheeks and she slipped into unconsciousness.

Gabrielle! Mara said in alarm, for the mental energy bond she always felt with Gabrielle had dissolved. The windlord's eyes frantically swept the immediate area. Seeing no one, she took flight, following the path through the forest towards the center of the crystal dome. She took no notice of the strange and beautiful trees, the multitude of fragrant flowers, or the brilliantly colored songbirds with long streaming tails. Mara came to rest next to a large, white marble gazebo beside a pool fed by a waterfall. Her hooves clicked up the six marble steps leading into the gazebo. Upon reaching the top and seeing no sign of Phoebe, she made a long, loud neigh of alarm.

A sudden light breeze brought the sweet fragrance of night blooming jasmine and a billowing white mist formed in front of Mara. The mist dissolved and where it had been stood a lovely woman with large, dark eyes and long, black hair. Her filmy blue gown flowed out from sandaled feet, and across her back hung a golden bow and quiver filled with golden arrows.

"I've been waiting for you," she said in a rich voice. Without hesitation she approached and placed her hand on the spot where Torolf's fire bolt had entered Gabrielle's back. "There's little life left in her. Quickly, Mara, bring her into the waters of the pool."

They hurried down the stairs to the pool and the woman pulled Gabrielle down into the water.

Can you save her? Mara asked with wide, sad eyes.

The woman did not answer Mara, but held Gabrielle under the water and began softly speaking in an ancient language. Gabrielle's long hair came loose and floated about her pale face beneath the ripples. Soon the woman stopped speaking and raised Gabrielle's head and shoulders above the surface. She opened her eyes and stared blankly at the woman's timeless face. Then memory returned and she whispered, "Phoebe?"

"Yes, child, I am she. Welcome my brave traveler." The goddess gazed down at Gabrielle like a mother at a beloved child. Gabrielle could feel the faint energy field around Phoebe.

"Rise up now, for your wounds are healed," Phoebe said. She took Gabrielle's hands in hers and they stood. Then Mara made a whinny that sounded like pure joy to Gabrielle's ears.

Standing in the knee-deep water, her clothing heavy and wet, Gabrielle felt a light tingling sensation throughout her body. "Phoebe, I saw a beautiful light on the Moonpath, and then again when I fell asleep a little while ago," she said in a mellow, peaceful voice. "I felt such a wondrous joy when it shone on me that I wanted to remain in it forever. But I knew I had to come back to complete my task. Thank you for bringing me."

A slight smile came onto Phoebe's face and for a moment her eyes shone like diamonds. "You're a little ahead of your time, Gabrielle. The Light you speak of has not yet been given to Earth. But if your world survives, it, too, will be given. And it is the greatest Light of all.

"Yes," Gabrielle said, her face radiant.

The goddess then grew translucent and, lightly lifting above the water, drew back to the shore with her gown and hair flowing softly around her. "I'll leave you now. A table of refreshments is set for you within the gazebo. Eat and drink to your content. There is no need to hurry as we're beyond Earth time. When you have finished I'll return."

Gabrielle smiled shyly. "Thank you, Phoebe, we'll look for you soon."

The Moon Maiden lingered briefly at the edge of the pool and when Gabrielle and Mara stepped from the water she passed her open hand in front of her, enveloping them in a white mist. When it cleared Gabrielle stood in a filmy white tunic and beneath it she wore long, slender white pants. Over her hips lay a golden belt and a white cloak draped her shoulders. Upon her feet were golden sandals. Her hair fell long and soft, and atop her head, as well as Mara's, was a molded, gold mesh headpiece with a bright opal that hung on their foreheads. Mara bore a small white saddle studded with opals, and Gabrielle's white fox cloak was fastened behind, clean and undamaged. Mara's coat shone like new fallen snow and her tail, no longer burned, was full and beautiful again. Gabrielle gazed at Mara in admiration, not yet noticing her own transformation.

"Mara, you look so beautiful."

So do you, Gabrielle, and your garments only add to it. Look at yourself.

Realizing now that her clothing no longer felt heavy and wet, Gabrielle looked down at herself and smiled as she felt her headpiece. She looked up to thank Phoebe, but the goddess was gone.

The table within the gazebo was set with ambrosia, honey and bread, berries and sweet cream, green clover, and urns of cool water. Gabrielle and Mara quietly partook of a small meal. When they were finished they left the gazebo and entered Phoebe's lush garden to wait for her.

Gabrielle listened to the water spilling over rocks into the pool and nightingales singing high up in the trees. It was wonderfully peaceful. Her eyes were drawn to the deep green ferns rising out of spongy moss, and leafy vines with delicately scented blue flowers winding up tree trunks and draping down from branches. The sound of gently rustling leaves came to her ears, and she caught the fragrance of night blooming jasmine. Then from seemingly nowhere, Phoebe was there.

She took one of Gabrielle's hands and placed her other hand on Mara's head saying, "Close your eyes, my young ones, and I'll show you something." They shut their eyes and Phoebe allowed their minds to enter the edges of hers. They saw the Star Crystals shooting to Earth, an eagle bearing the Light Crystal to a high mountaintop and another bearing the Dark Crystal to the Moon. Then, like a fast running filmstrip, they saw the passage of the Light Crystal through all the generations of Eagle, Windlord and Human Guardians. And when the vision passed, Gabrielle and Mara were filled with wonder.

Then Gabrielle asked, "Will you tell us about the Crystals, Phoebe?"

"Yes, child. I will reveal the power of the Star Crystals to you because you need to know. You will be the first to learn these things. They were the gift of Enlightenment to your world and their power when joined is very great and very old. The Light Crystal is the Light of Reason. It projects positive energy that stimulates the minds of Earth's creatures to think rationally, causing them to seek order, growth and achievement. The Dark Crystal is the Light of Intuition. It projects negative energy that promotes intuitive and artistic growth. The balance between reason and intuition in your societies is what brings harmony to your lives and brings you into balance with the cosmos."

"But, the sun, moon and stars . . . . Why are they growing dim to us on Earth, yet remain bright beyond our atmosphere? Our royal astronomer says the world will turn to ice within a year if the dimming continues."

"It will be much sooner," Phoebe said gravely. "Come, sit beside me and I'll tell you what you do not wish to hear, but what you *must* hear." They sat down on a garden bench and Gabrielle tried to brace herself for the worst.

"I will begin by telling you that black magic directly opposes the Cosmic Balance and is deadly to your world. The celestial bodies appear to you on Earth to be dimming because your atmosphere is being saturated by black magic. King Torolf and five other sorcerer kings are using black spells to transform millions of innocent creatures into servants of the Serpent."

Gabrielle's face went pale. "But, how can black spells saturate the atmosphere?"

"Each spell sends a small amount of dark residue into the sky. When six black sorcerers are working such vast numbers of dark spells, is it any wonder that your atmosphere continually grows darker?"

A look of devastation came onto Gabrielle's face and she fought to maintain her composure.

"You have little time left before the Earth will be in total darkness—not a year as you had thought."

"How long do we have?" Gabrielle asked, her voice almost a whisper

"A few months at most, for the darkening effect speeds up towards the end. Already it is beginning to happen. When the light is gone and the Earth becomes an icy world, all life will perish."

Tears streamed down Gabrielle's cheeks. She had known the Earth might die but it was words of hope she sought from the goddess, not a death sentence.

Phoebe looked into Gabrielle's eyes and continued, "The Serpent's followers expect rewards of power and wealth for their loyalty, but they have been deceived. The Serpent has ever been The Deceiver, for it hates all living things and seeks only death and destruction."

"But, can't you stop what's happening?" Gabrielle pleaded.

"It isn't up to me. The Cosmos cleanses itself by allowing its diseased parts to self-destruct. That is how the Great Balance is maintained."

Gabrielle lowered her head and covered her face with her hands. Mara stepped close and touched her velvet nose to Gabrielle's shoulder.

Cry for both of us, Gabrielle. Though I can weep only with my heart, I would shed tears with you if I could.

"The truth is harsh," Phoebe said softly, "but do not grieve yet, for all is not lost—not yet."

Gabrielle tried to speak, but only choked. Unable to sit still, she got up and wrapped her arms around Mara's neck and was briefly comforted. Then she stepped out from under the tree into an opening where she could see the sky. As she gazed up at the dim Earth she felt a warm sensation growing in her chest. Pulling herself to her full height and straightening her shoulders, she heard a voice deep within emphatically, unequivocally say, "NO." The "NO" consumed her, driving out all fear, and like a bright flame her spirit soared. With a firm jaw and eyes hard as blue ice, she turned to Mara and said in a controlled voice, "With all that I am I will fight Torolf and his filthy Serpent master."

Mara's nostrils flared and she responded, *We act as one mind and one will, Gabrielle.*

The goddess's eyes shone bright and she said, "Take heart, for your strength and passion to preserve your world are a great force against the Serpent and Its dark servants. Know there are others who feel as strongly as you and will stand firm with you in your effort to restore The Balance." Phoebe stood up and pulled on a golden chain around her neck, producing a small white pouch from beneath the neckline of her gown. She opened it and took out an object. Instantly, a brilliant light burst forth.

Gasping in awe, Gabrielle whispered, "The Dark Crystal."

Mara shied backwards a step, staring at the flaring crystal. Then the light receded back into the crystal and it glowed softly in Phoebe's hand. "Yes, the Dark Crystal, the Light of Intuition." She dropped it back into the pouch and tightened the drawstring, then placed the golden chain around Gabrielle's neck with the pouch resting against her chest. "You know what you must do, Gabrielle."

"Thank you Phoebe," Gabrielle said solemnly. "I don't know what will happen when we return to Windermere. Torolf will be waiting. But you've given us hope."

"Your hope gives you strength. I cannot tell you what will be the final outcome when you and Mara return to Earth, for although certain events were destined to occur, most are the result of choices which allow you to mold your own destiny. But I *can* tell you that the young man, Oberon, has not yet finished his task. He will help you fulfill the Prophecy of Zephyrus—*if* it is to be fulfilled."

Gabrielle's face dropped. "I . . . I hope I haven't prevented that from happening, Phoebe. I practically begged him to remain safely with the Otawn—far from Windermere."

"Did he agree?"

Gabrielle thought for a moment. "I don't remember him saying anything. He was quiet."

"His silence speaks loudly. He has a strong heart, and the flame of such a heart is not easily quenched."

Gabrielle nodded uncertainly, hoping Phoebe was right, hoping Obie had not heeded her request. Suddenly she was anxious to return to Windermere. Would Obie be there? "Thank you, Phoebe, for your help and wise counsel. There are many more questions Mara and I would ask you, but we must save them. If we're able to fulfill our task and join the Crystals, we'll return the Dark Crystal to your keeping upon the next full Moon."

Phoebe did not respond, but removed her golden bow and quiver and placed them over Gabrielle's back. "Take these—you may need them."

Gabrielle felt a tingling in her fingers as she ran them over the golden bowstring. Her eyes glowing, she turned to thank Phoebe. But the goddess softly touched her fingers to Gabrielle's lips to silence her. Gabrielle smiled at her, then turned and mounted Mara.

Phoebe lightly touched Mara's velvet nose and Gabrielle knew she was preparing her for the journey home. When she withdrew her fingers Mara opened her wings and lifted into the air.

"Farewell, Phoebe," Gabrielle called. As they rose above the trees she saw the diaphanous form of the goddess floating in white mist below.

"Farewell, my young ones," she called, her voice fading away.

Mara reentered the Moonpath and glided through the wall of the dome. The path did not wind ahead into the distance as it previously had, but unfolded before them like the crest of a shimmering wave. Nor were they plagued with drowsiness, but were alert and energetic, as if they'd had a long rest.

Gabrielle prayed that Grandfather Andras had successfully hidden the Light Crystal in the Lonely Oak Tree. Everything now depended on it being there and on her retrieving it before Torolf could stop her. And what awesome power the Crystals had—far more than she had guessed. She clasped the white pouch in her right hand and the fingers of her left hand moved to the golden bowstring. No arrows flew truer than Phoebe's.

Gabrielle, do you remember when we were very young, how you would have tea parties for your friends and I would give them rides around the yard? Mara asked.

And we decorated you with beautiful garlands of flowers. How could I ever forget our wonderful childhood days? And later, when we were a little older, the lovely picnics we had. We must do that again, Mara. We're not too old for that . . . are we?

No. We'll never be too old for tea parties and picnics, dear friend. We will do it again soon.

Then they quietly withdrew into their own thoughts. And all the while the gray-shrouded blue and green planet grew steadily larger before them like a slowly inflating balloon. Finally they entered the Earth's gray atmosphere. Gabrielle glanced back and saw the bright white moon begin to turn pale green.

Ready yourself, Gabrielle, Mara said.

Gabrielle could see the lights of Windermere.

CHAPTER TWENTY-FIVE

A RACE AGAINST TIME

HOODS PULLED LOW against the icy wind, Obie and the others headed for the Long Wadi Road, two days to the west. Takoda guided them over trails that wove along the southern border of the Hundred Valleys Region. The trees were heavy with snow and Obie knew more was on the way.

Shortly after midnight Takoda raised his hand in alarm and reined in his horse. His companions also halted, for they too had seen the black shadows in the sky. Off to their right a large patrol of hawk riders glided silently over the treetops. The travelers sat motionless beneath the trees, waiting for the patrol to pass. A pinecone fell from a branch above and made a small noise when it hit the ground. One of the hawk riders immediately broke formation and flew in a circle overhead, searching for the source of the noise. Obie and Tau gripped their sword hilts and the Otawn warriors bent their bows preparing for battle. But the hawk rider returned to formation and the patrol moved on in the night like the passing of a bad dream.

When morning came they saw two more hawk rider patrols off in the distance, racing in a southeast direction. Later in the day storm clouds rolled down from the north and by nightfall it started snowing. Obie glanced back and saw Tau staring ahead, his jaw set firm against the cold and snow. Mole's bright eyes peered out from Tau's hood, two tiny lights in the darkness. He counted himself fortunate to have such friends.

All night they rode without stopping and when the somber dawn broke in the east their snow covered forms resembled apparitions passing over the white land. At a place where the steep slope forming the foot of the plateau receded into a small bay, Takoda came to a stop.

"What is it?" Obie asked, pulling up alongside.

"There is a cave up there." Takoda motioned towards an elevated spot within the bay. "We will have shelter to rest, and there is firewood stored inside."

He led them to a narrow trail leading up the slope. Here the party dismounted and walked their horses along the path. At the top they squeezed through a narrow opening in the plateau wall and continued another hundred feet where the path ended at the cave entrance.

While the others unpacked blankets and food and Kangi fed the horses, Obie carried logs to the fire pit and dropped them in. Turning, he saw Mole slowly dragging kindling over. "I see you're pulling your own weight, Mole." Obie squatted down and blew on his cold hands.

"My weight is my own concern, thank you. However I could use a hand with this load of twigs."

Obie reached for the twigs. "Maybe a little food will improve your mood. How about some juicy black beetles?"

Mole's eyes flashed. "That could do it. Would you mind roasting them, please?"

"And shall I heat some water for your royal bath while I'm at it, your majesty?"

Mole frowned. "Cold beetles will be fine. Just hurry and get a fire going so we can warm up."

Obie grinned. "I'm on it." He opened his leather pouch and got his rock and utility knife out, then pulled open the metal file component. Mole curled up sleepily and watched Obie ignite the kindling and get the fire blazing. When his eyes dropped shut, Obie set out a few beetles to roast on a flat stone next to the flames.

Soon the others joined them and they shared a simple meal around the fire. Mole brightened when Obie handed him the roasted beetles.

They finished eating and, although he was tired from riding all night, Obie looked across the fire and said, "Kangi, Takoda . . . how about that Raptor lesson I promised you? This seems like a good time."

"It is a good time," Takoda confirmed with a grin.

Kangi jumped up. "I am ready, Brother of the Lion . . . where shall we have our lesson?"

Obie took them just outside the cave entrance where the light was better and they could select targets on the cliff wall along the path. Taking turns with Obie's Raptor, the youths' skill with a bow helped them catch on quickly and with little instruction.

"See, Brothers! I am good at this . . . I love this weapon," Kangi said excitedly. After just three attempts he had hit his target, a small rock in the path fifty-feet away.

"I think you're a natural, Kangi," Obie confirmed.

Takoda also shot well. He almost brought down a small bird perched higher on the cliff, but the shot succeeded only in ruffling its tail feathers, and sent it flying off.

"That was very close, Takoda!" Obie said. "For a first lesson, you guys are doing great."

Takoda looked pleased as he responded, "This Raptor is a good weapon. I would trade you a horse for it, but I already know you will not part with it."

Obie decided that if he ever got the chance, he would have some Raptors sent to Takoda and Kangi from Windermere.

The youths practiced a while longer and then they all returned to the cave and slept a few hours before setting out again.

Obie wondered when the snow storm would let up. In just four nights the moon would be full. Would the windlords come in time? Maybe they would pass by unseen. Or maybe they wouldn't come at all. Tsking at himself for worrying about *maybes*, he switched his attention to the terrain and sky.

In the early afternoon while making their way under the trees at the edge of a clearing they saw a huge flock of fast flying birds approaching. When a sudden clamor passed through the flock the riders knew they'd been spotted. Takoda's horse reared up in terror. "Harpies! Into the trees," he yelled, waving his companions back.

"Aaaiiieee," Kangi yelled turning and kicking his horse.

Steel rang as Obie and Tau unsheathed their blades and followed Takoda and Kangi into the forest. Bringing up the rear, Obie heard a rushing of wings.

"They're coming," he yelled. The flapping sounds grew louder. Obie heard a blood-curdling screech behind him. Turning his head, he saw the hideous, yellow hag-face of a harpy diving at him, its razor sharp talons extended. Its screeches sounded like an old woman's shrill laughter echoing through the forest. Leaning to Shadow's side to dodge the flesh ripping claws, Obie slashed at the swooping creature, but missed. It turned sharply and flew at Takoda. Frozen in horror the young brave stared into the face of the approaching monster. Shadow leaped forward and Obie slid from his back, pulling Takoda to the ground with him as the harpy screamed by. Kangi shot an arrow as it retreated, but it was too late. The harpy flew up through the branches and raced to rejoin its flock, flying fast towards the southeast.

Kangi and Tau wheeled their horses round and leaped down to aid Takoda and Obie who were getting to their feet.

"Close call," Tau said quietly to Obie.

Mole squeaked from his place on Tau's shoulder, his whiskers still twitching from the excitement.

"Horrible things," Obie said. His face white and drawn, a convulsive shiver passed through him.

Takoda was withdrawn for several hours after that. He wore the colorless, melancholy countenance of one who has just looked into the face of eternal despair.

When Kangi found his voice, it was shaky. "It is strange. The harpy flock knew we were here and could have torn us to pieces and dragged all our souls off, but instead of attacking they sent only one to taunt us."

Obie frowned and reflected for a moment. "They must be after more important prey." He feared to think what it might be.

Late that night they reached the Long Wadi Road and decided to follow it up the plateau wall before making camp. It was apparent that a great army had recently passed over the road, for there were many horse, wagon and boot prints, and the shrubbery alongside the road was trampled and broken. In the thin light of the waxing moon they saw part of a wagon wheel protruding above the snow in one place, and a little farther on the outline of a damaged supply wagon lying on its side. Weary when they reached the top of the high mesa, they found a place to sleep under some trees in a gully below the road.

In the early morning a light snow was falling when Obie awakened to Shadow's warm nose nudging his face. *We should leave soon, Oberon. This place does not feel safe.*

Obie sat up and looked around. *I agree. It's too quiet.*

A bird call pierced the stillness. It was Kangi on guard nearby, sounding the alarm. Leaping to their feet, everyone grabbed their weapons and dove into the bushes next to the bank. Almost immediately they heard hooves thudding softly through the snow on the road above. The riders stopped at the side of the road and dismounted. Obie could hear the soldiers talking quietly to one another. Through a tiny opening in the bushes he could see them peering into the gully. Tense moments passed. Finally they remounted their horses and continued on.

Kangi crept down from the bushes near the top of the slope and spoke in a hushed voice. "That was a rak patrol, but don't worry, the falling snow covered our tracks."

"What were they doing up there?" Tau asked.

"Leaving purple pee holes in the snow," Kangi said with a chuckle.

"I don't like the feel of this place," Tau said.

"Agreed," Obie said. "So let's get out of here."

On their horses and ready to ride, the three travelers said their good-byes to Takoda and Kangi as it was time for their Otawn friends to return to their village. The Long Wadi Road should be easy to follow and if all went well Obie, Tau and Mole would soon meet up with the windlords Andor was sending for them. After friendly good-byes and well wishes, Takoda and Kangi headed down the slope and into the trees.

Obie and Tau turned their horses and set out through the high forest flatland following the road at a distance. Too risky to use by day, they traveled the road only at night. The windlords were badly needed for they had just three days to reach Windermere and it would take four or five on horseback. As the tension mounted they spoke little. Moving south they watched the sky through gaps in the trees and listened for the fluttering of wings hoping to spot the windlords.

By midmorning they came to the place where the high plateau began its long descent into the southern lowlands. Below lay the Long Wadi, a valley stretching south towards Windermere. The road ran along its western border. Obie gazed through the falling snow over the slopes of dark pines and firs blanketed in white, and far down the valley to the gray fog in the distance. Then his eyes scanned the icy sky. He hoped to see the windlords but there was no sign of them. They began the long ride downward. The snow let up for a few hours, but started falling again by mid-afternoon.

Night came and they stopped under the trees near a meadow to rest and eat a cold meal. Obie walked to the edge of the clearing and, leaning against a tree, stared quietly up at the sky. Tau soon joined him. "It is a perilous journey for the windlords— yet they are not strangers to danger."

"You must be reading my thoughts," Obie said.

"I don't have the gift, but I know you."

Obie heard a squeak. Mole was sitting on the ground looking up at him from under the hood of his rabbit coat. "The windlords will likely come tonight or tomorrow, Oberon."

"Yeah, let's hope so, Mole. Otherwise we may have to take some drastic measures."

"What drastic meas . . ." Mole started to say, but stopped abruptly, startled by the sound of whipping wind. Looking up they saw two large, glowing red embers with black centers moving towards them above the trees. The darkness deepened as a huge black form glided overhead and moved slowly over the meadow, blocking the falling snow like a giant umbrella. Mole's nose and whiskers twitched and Tau held his nose high, sniffing the air.

"Dragon," Tau whispered, dropping to the ground and pulling Obie down with him.

"Big dragon," Mole whispered. His fur bristled as he lay flat on the snow between Obie and Tau.

"Shhhhh," Obie said in a barely audible whisper.

He lifted his head and saw the dragon's dark, massive hulk silhouetted against the lighter background of falling snow. It was turning around. The dragon's red eyes stared in their direction and its head was cocked slightly, as though listening. They heard loud hissing and a rush of air, and the dragon spewed forth a great stream of fire into the nearby treetops. The mantle of snow instantly evaporated and the branches burst into flames. The dragon's scales glistened like rubies in the light of the burning trees and Obie saw that it was a red fire-dragon. It circled the meadow again and as it came towards them its mouth opened and it began sucking in a great quantity of air.

"Run," Obie yelled, jumping up and grabbing Mole. Obie and Tau bounded away as the dragon expelled its torch-breath and the trees around them erupted into a crackling furnace of flames. Tau's cloak caught fire and he roared and threw himself into a snowdrift at the edge of the burning trees. Hearing Tau's roar, Obie turned back and saw the lion-man on fire, rolling in the snow. Obie and Mole scooped more snow over him and doused the flames. Tau's mane was singed slightly, but he was otherwise unharmed. His fur cloak was damaged in spots but still wearable. Obie glanced up and saw the dragon flying away south over the burning trees. Sighing, he lay back in the snowdrift with Tau and Mole and scooped a handful of snow over his sweating face.

Tau's nose was twitching disagreeably. "It had the foul odor of Torolf's dragon, Smoker. I can still smell the beast."

A disgusted look came over Mole's face. "The beast that maimed my tail."

"And it's headed for Windermere," Obie said angrily. "With the huge army he's got, why does Torolf have to bring a dragon into the battle?"

"Yet it appears he is planning to use Smoker for something," Tau said.

"To terrorize Queen Olwen and her army I'll wager—or maybe worse," Mole said.

Obie's face darkened. "Or Gabrielle," he said quietly.

Mole and Tau had a small meal warmed by a burning tree while Obie sat in silent thought. He didn't know exactly how he was going to help Gabrielle when he got to Windermere, but he'd raise his sword against Torolf himself to protect her if it came to that. Not getting to Windermere in time was not an option. Reason told him the odds of being much help were slim, but something else told him he must be there to protect Gabrielle and Mara when they returned from the Moonpath. It was the voice inside that Mole had spoken of, the voice that had never been wrong.

After an hour's rest they were on their way again, riding all night in the beaten tracks of patrols that passed during the day. The trees began to thin and the snow turned to sleet and finally to rain when they reached the valley floor. Obie was glad to see snow hadn't fallen this far south yet. But Mole had said winter's grasp would soon bring howling blizzards to these lowlands also, like the one they had experienced on the way to the Hundred Valleys Region.

The dawn revealed that the Long Wadi was scantily forested for many miles ahead, while a dark line of trees marked its eastern and western borders. Since the valley floor would provide them no cover they retreated into the forest hills to the west of the road, planning to follow it at a distance. When the terrain proved too broken and rocky to traverse they decided to risk riding the road by day. Obie and Tau kept a sharp eye out for hawk riders and other enemies approaching from the south, while Mole rode behind Tau watching their rear as he had often done from Tau's shoulder. Twice they had to dash into the woods when dark specks appeared in the distance. Obie had hoped it was the windlords coming, but was disappointed when first it was a small patrol of hawk riders from the south, and then two vultures from the north. The day passed and the windlords did not come. Time was running out and, still far from Windermere, Obie's anxiety grew.

All night Shadow and Gamba pressed on through the rain over the muddy road, uncomplaining and resting little. The early hours of the morning brought a break in the weather and it stopped raining. When the gray-green dawn came the ragged clouds were breaking up and blowing southeast. To the south was the beginning of the forest that blanketed the southern part of the Long Wadi. Nearby on the valley side of the road they were glad to find a copse of oak trees where they could rest.

"Oberon, after we get a little sleep," Mole said, his eyelids drooping wearily, "I want to hear about your *drastic measures* for getting to Windermere. It appears we're going to need them."

Obie nodded glumly. They were still at least two days ride from Windermere and Gabrielle and Mara would ride the Moonpath tonight. There seemed only one answer to their transportation problem: they would have to commandeer someone else's sky steeds—and that someone else was the enemy. It would simply be a matter of attracting the attention of a few hawk riders. Too restless to sleep, Obie volunteered to take first watch. While the others slept he strolled to the edge of the copse and leaned against a tree, cracking his knuckles nervously. He'd let Mole and Tau get a couple of hours sleep before waking them and putting his plan into action. He wouldn't take the time to sleep—as keyed up as he was, he doubted that he could anyway. To pass the time he slipped his Raptor on for some target practice. He took aim at a knob on a tree stump, then hesitated and lowered his arm. It was unmistakable. Hissing sounds and low murmuring voices were coming from the far side of a group of boulders just beyond the bottom of the hill. His heart leaping with excitement, he sprang from the trees, climbed the boulders, and peered over. Hawk riders. Four raks with four healthy looking hawks were camped below. And the hawk rider raks were smaller than the huge ground raks he'd encountered. These were a little bigger than him, but a little smaller than Tau. Torolf must have created them from ordinary house spiders. Obie's hopes soared as he scrambled down the boulders and raced back to camp to awaken Tau and Mole. This seemed the perfect solution.

CHAPTER TWENTY-SIX

FOES AND FRIENDS

SWORD IN HAND, Tau bolted up and spun around scanning the bushes for the enemy. "Where are they?"

Mole, too, was on his feet squeaking and looking around nervously.

"Shhhhh, relax. Nobody's here but me," Obie said in a low voice. He squatted next to Mole.

Tau lowered his weapon. "What are you so excited about that you had to wake us?" He dropped down next to his companions.

"It's just that I don't think the windlords are coming. Something must have happened."

Tau threw Obie an exasperated look. "And that's what you woke us up to say?"

"No. I've found a way to get us to Windermere—tonight."

Mole sat back on his haunches and looked Obie in the eye. "Is this the *drastic action* we've been waiting to hear about?"

"Yeah." Obie grinned slyly. "An opportunity's fallen in our laps."

Mole's eyes widened. "All right, I can't stand the suspense any longer. Let's have it."

"I just discovered four hawk-riding raks camping on the other side of a boulder cluster out on the meadow. And they're smaller than any raks we've seen. If we take them by surprise we can overpower them and ride their hawks to Windermere."

"Why, Oberon, that sounds absolutely diabolical," Mole said with a glint in his eyes.

"Yeah, I know." Obie flashed Mole a devilish grin.

"Two against four sounds like good odds to me," Tau said, his face now beaming.

"*Three* against four," Mole corrected, putting his hands on his hips indignantly.

"Sorry Mole. *Three* against four."

Shadow stabbed a hoof in the ground, catching Obie's eye. *Gamba and I are coming also. You may need our help.*

"Five against four. The horses are joining in too," Obie said, standing up. "Let's go."

The raks were immersed in conversation when Obie and Tau climbed the rocks and peeked over.

Obie loaded his Raptor and whispered, "I'll take down the two biggest raks before they know what's hit them." Tau nodded. He looked ready for a good fight. In a flash the burliest of the raks toppled backward and hit the ground. When his surprised companions looked at him, a second slumped over on his face. Shocked at seeing their comrades falling, the two remaining raks glanced up at the boulder pile and then sprang for cover behind large rocks.

Obie and Tau leaped down from the boulders and drew their swords. They had to stop the raks before they could escape with the hawks. The raks saw them coming and stood up ready to fight. As the sound of clashing blades resounded through the meadow, Shadow appeared from around the boulders followed by Mole riding Gamba.

It did not take long for Obie to realize the smaller raks were tougher than he'd thought. They fought hard and had great endurance. Worse yet, the two raks he had stunned woke up and, though they appeared a little groggy, were at that moment hurrying over to help their comrades. Obie heard Shadow neigh behind him. When he glanced over his shoulder the dark stallion was attacking the newcomers. Rearing up and kicking savagely he was driving them back. *What a horse!*

Mole whispered something in Gamba's ear and he shot forward kicking and biting at one of the raks while Shadow held off the other. Losing his balance, Mole tumbled from Gamba's back to the ground but recovered quickly. With a wicked glint in his eye he pounced on the foot of Gamba's opponent, sinking his teeth and claws deeply into the rak's hairy brown ankle.

"Aaaiiieee," the rak screamed in pain. He knocked Mole off and fell to the ground clutching his bleeding ankle. Mole moved in for the kill but fled when Gamba reared up to trample the rak. The rak rolled over and regained his footing. Meanwhile, Obie's and Tau's opponents appeared to be wearing down. The fight seemed near an end when Obie knocked the brown rak to the ground and stood over him with the point of his sword at his throat.

"Spare me, master," the rak cried woefully, peering up with pleading yellow eyes.

"Run then. And don't stop until you're far away from here."

"Yes, master, I'll do as you say."

A shadow passed over them forcing Obie's attention upward. "Uh-oh. Tau, look."

Tau glanced skyward. "I see it."

Four new hawk riding muks with scimitars were joining the fight. And at that moment two of them dove at Obie and Tau. Utilizing his attacker's momentum, Tau drove his blade deeply into the muk's chest. The mortally wounded rider slumped over his hawk as it carried him away. Simultaneously, his comrade swooped past and knocked Obie to the ground. Now the tables were turned. The rak that Obie had knocked down sprang up and pointed his blade at Obie's throat, pinning him to the ground.

Obie looked up nervously. "Hey, we had a deal."

"The deal's cancelled." The rak threw out an ugly laugh and raised his sword to plunge into Obie.

With a quick roll Obie got to his feet and the blade plunged into the ground. The rak's initial look of surprise turned to a wry grin. He calmly leaned forward on his sword with two of his claw-hands resting on the hilt and a third hand waving slowly at Obie. "Bye-bye, human."

"What?" Obie glanced over his right shoulder. A hawk rider was diving straight at him, his scimitar braced to relieve Obie of his head. Looking on in horror, everything seemed to move in slow motion. *No time to run, no time.*

An instant later the rider fell dead at Obie's feet and the riderless hawk flew on. A white-feathered arrow protruded from the rak's neck. Something else dropped from the sky and thumped heavily on the ground nearby. It was another rak wearing a white-feathered arrow through his chest. The brown rak stood gaping upward, his entire body shaking. Obie looked up and his heart leaped for joy. Two silver-helmed warriors clad in glistening silver mail and riding white windlords circled above. Then his breath caught, for the two remaining hawk riders spun round and dove at the larger of the warriors. Windlord and rider whirled to meet the challengers. The warrior's sword blade flashed as with one deft stroke he sent the first hawk rider's head spinning earthward with his body following. Another flash and the last hawk rider fell dead. The two white windlords fluttered to the ground and the silver riders silently waited for the ground fight to end.

Inspired by such fighting skill, Obie delivered an aggressive stroke that severed the rak's sword arm at the elbow and sent him running for his life. Tau also appeared invigorated, and he made short work of his own multi-armed opponent. Mole and the horses joined Obie and Tau to share in the moment of victory, for they had successfully sent the other two wounded and bruised raks running towards the eastern forest. After wiping his blade on an enemy cloak and sheathing it, Obie turned towards the two warriors and smiled as they cantered over on their steeds.

"Hail, human. We thought we would even up the odds, though we did not wish to interfere with your victory," the larger warrior said. They removed their helms and Obie did a double take when the smaller warrior's deep chestnut hair fell long and full to her waist.

Held by her gaze, he said, "Thanks for your help. We're glad you happened by when you did."

The male warrior was looking doubtfully at Tau and gripping his sword. "Is this other one friend or foe?"

"Friend," Obie said, pulling his eyes away from the female to the male warrior.

"Friend, master elf," Mole said as loud as he could from his place on the ground. "He is a lion transformed by the Necromancer into a lion-man, though his mind never succumbed to that dark power. He escaped and now fights the black sorcerer."

The male warrior eyed Tau curiously. "We have seen your kind in service to King Torolf. That you were able to resist his dark magic shows great strength."

"Your words are kind. We are in your debt." Tau bowed courteously.

Obie observed the noble manner and graceful movements of the two warriors. So these were High Elves. The larger one was over six feet tall, a handsome, fair-haired young man whose gray eyes shone with a wisdom that seemed unusual in one who looked so youthful. The elf maiden was fair of face, slender of build, and her eyes made him think of a deep green sea. Was it really possible he could be related to these beautiful beings?

"I am Aristeil and this is my sister, Eleri. We have come from the Isles of Eluthien."

Eleri smiled at Obie, and he wondered if she had heard his thoughts.

Obie forced his gaze away from her to respond to Aristeil. "I'm Obie Griffin. My two companions and I are in the service of Queen Olwen of Windermere."

"I am called Tau."

"And I am Mole."

"We are pleased to meet you, Obie, Tau, and Mole," Eleri said. "These are dark and dangerous times to be traveling in this land. May we inquire where you are going?"

"We're on our way to Windermere. We have to get there tonight. What about you?" Obie asked.

"We are pursuing a dragon that is flying towards Windermere," Aristeil said. "We have been sent to slay it before it wreaks devastation there. We mean no insult to the valor of the Windermerian warriors, but we know they are unskilled at dragon slaying and many would die trying."

"Are you able to send warriors to help Queen Olwen against the forces of King Torolf?" Mole piped up.

"Our king regrets that we cannot send more help, for our own land is also on the brink of attack by Torolf's dark army. Two large divisions are now camped across the water from our isles, and his soldiers are quickly building many boats. We fear they will soon crash like a tidal wave upon our shores and it will take all we have to repel them. The dragon is but one more grievance in these times when black sorcery grows so strong in the world that even the sun and moon pale at the sight and threaten to desert us. Still, we thought to do what little we could and at least relieve Windermere of the terror of the dragon."

"It is still far ahead of us," Eleri said, "but the beast flies slowly, and we hope to overtake it before it reaches that kingdom. At first we thought it might be our Joy Dragon, the Blue Dragon of Ellowan, known for his healing powers. He was lost to us three summers ago. But when we saw the devastation along the way we realized this is a fire-dragon, not the Joy Dragon."

"We saw the dragon joyfully setting the forest ablaze two nights ago," Tau said. "It had the stench of Torolf's dragon, Smoker."

"Yes, we have been following the burned patches of trees," Aristeil said grimly. "We suspected Torolf possessed a dragon, and now we think this one is his. If so, then it surely has a black heart and my sister and I will slay it. But first we must catch up with the beast."

Obie turned a troubled gaze to Eleri. When she returned a meaningful look he knew she'd heard his thoughts.

"Have no fear for me, Obie, for my brother and I possess the ancient skill of dragon slaying. We know how to make the creatures expose their weak spot, and our arrows do not miss."

"So I've seen. But what if you run into more of Torolf's hawk riders, or worse?"

"We are also skilled at eluding the eyes of men and beasts," Eleri said.

"We must be off now—time grows short," Aristeil said. I am sorry we cannot bear you with us to Windermere, but your added weight will slow us and we require speed."

"We'd rather ride with you, but if you can't take us it's okay. We plan to ride a couple of those hawks over there to Windermere." Obie motioned towards the tethered hawks.

Eleri glanced at them and then looked gravely at Obie. "Ahhh, but that would be great folly. It is very fortunate we happened upon you this day, for in truth the hawks fear Torolf more than they fear you. If you try to ride them they will bear you straight to him."

"Then you've *got* to take us with you to Windermere . . . our mission is important," Obie pleaded.

Aristeil's eyes grew stern. "I am sorry, we cannot."

Obie's face reddened with anger as he stared silently up at the dragon slayer sitting tall on his windlord. Eleri spoke softly to her brother in the Elven language, but he only shook his head and began turning his windlord away. Mole screamed out something that was incomprehensible to Obie.

Aristeil stopped abruptly, listening. "What is this?" he said, turning his windlord back and looking down into Mole's smoldering eyes. "A mole that hurls insults in the Elven tongue?" His brow was raised in surprise.

"Oberon, please lift me up. I wish to speak privately with Aristeil," Mole said.

Glancing quizzically at Tau, Obie shrugged his shoulders, then reached down and lifted Mole onto the windlord in front of the dragon slayer. Obie and Tau moved away to allow Mole the privacy he requested. Mole spoke quietly and the elf warrior appeared to question him several times.

By the time Mole finished, Aristeil's stern look had vanished. Looking down at Obie now, a warm, though curious, look shone in his eyes. "We will bear you with us to Windermere, Oberon of Griffin, for we gladly help those who aid the Moonpath Riders in their quest to retrieve the Dark Crystal."

"Thanks," Obie said.

Aristeil nodded slightly and turned his eyes to Tau. "You may ride behind me."

"Thank you. I'll only be a minute," Tau said, then glancing at Obie, "Will you turn Gamba out for me while I retrieve the packs?" Obie nodded and Tau bounded off around the boulders.

"Oberon, you may ride behind Eleri," Aristeil said.

"Give me a minute to see to the horses." Obie quickly removed Gamba's bridle and Shadow's halter.

I'll see you in Windermere, Oberon.

I'll watch for you everyday, Shadow—try not to get captured again.

Gamba and I will run beneath the trees by day and use the road by night.

Good. Stay safe.

And you also, my friend.

Obie patted his flank and the dark stallion leaped forward heading south towards the forest. Neighing, Gamba sprang after him. Obie stood watching the horses for a few moments. Then he shouldered the pack Tau had just dropped at his feet and pulled himself up behind Eleri.

"Have you ridden the sky before?" Aristeil asked, extending an arm to Tau.

Tau took his arm and swung up behind him.

"No, I have not," he answered with an uncomfortable look.

Aristeil rolled his eyes. Then to Obie, "And you. Have you ridden the sky, Oberon?"

"I've ridden some windlords."

"Good. Then you will not hold on to my sister too tightly."

"I promise I won't." Catching Aristeil's meaning, Obie's eyes flickered with amusement.

"And try not to hold on to me too tightly, Tau. We will not let you fall, not very far, anyway. That is my promise to you."

Tau breathed deeply and shut his eyes. The two white wind-lords stepped forward, their great wings treading air, and lifted skyward. Obie felt a pang of sadness as he watched Shadow galloping away below, his head held high and his long black mane and tail flowing in the wind. Would they ever meet again? The dark stallion raised his head and whinnied.

I understand your sadness. It would be very hard for me to leave my windlord behind, Eleri said mentally to Obie.

Thanks. Shadow and I have been through a lot together. He fell silent after that and so did Eleri. Though he hoped for an opportunity in the future to enjoy a conversation with this lovely elf maiden, too many things pressed on his mind right now. He appreciated her sensitivity in allowing him to be alone with his thoughts.

After a time he looked over at Mole riding in front of Aristeil. He was sitting up with his hood thrown back and his beady nose high in the wind. Tau was looking down and appeared a little sick.

"Look ahead and breathe deeply, Tau, it'll help," Obie called.

Tau nodded and waved. Apparently he didn't feel much like talking at the moment. Aristeil responded by pulling a flask from under his cloak and handing it back to the lion-man. "Drink two swallows of this, but no more, or it will work too well."

Tau took the two swallows of the elf draught and handed it back to Aristeil. Almost immediately a smile came to his face and he pulled himself up straight, his color and physical appearance improved considerably. "Good stuff," he said with a contented grunt. "Where can I get some of that?"

"*You* can't. But I am happy to share mine," Aristeil said.

The windlords flew just high enough within the scattering clouds so they could see below, yet go undetected by hawk riders flying over the Long Wadi Road. Sometimes they had to dart through small open spaces between the clouds. And once when they approached an area of open sky, they were forced to hover within the cloud while a hawk rider patrol passed below.

On and on the great white windlords flew without stopping. Everyone kept an eye out for the dragon. But all they saw were signs of its recent passage: burned spots in the forest marking its path towards Windermere like a trail of breadcrumbs. The clouds grew thinner the farther south they flew. By dusk the sky was nearly clear and they gained altitude to avoid being spotted by the enemy. When night came they were able to fly lower again. The pale green moon rose over the horizon and began its trek around the empty black sky. Without warning a huge goshawk swooped down from above flying straight at Eleri and Obie. Eleri stretched her bow and sent an arrow at the bird before Obie's blade cleared the scabbard. But Aristeil's arrow was swiftest, and sent the creature in an earthbound spiral.

Obie kept checking the progress of the rising moon. Before long it would reach its zenith. Where was Gabrielle at this moment? Was she in Windermere? Would she and Mara make it to the Moonpath?

When he saw campfires dotting the land and enemy infantry and cavalry soldiers carrying torches, he knew they were drawing near. And still they did not see the dragon. Soon a multitude of lights appeared in the distance. It was Windermere. When they were close enough to see Windermere Castle, Obie felt like someone had slammed a sledgehammer into his chest. The keep was surrounded by Torolf's troops standing in full battle gear. No doubt they were awaiting their king's signal to attack. So great was the army that its campfires covered the valley floor and beyond, extending west and south and even into the eastern fringes of Gnarlwood. Several large campfires atop Mount Iluva drew his attention and he knew Torolf was there.

Eleri called to Aristeil and pointed at the West Meadow where enemy fires encircled a large, dark area. Hardly had they focused their gaze on the spot when fire flashed and smoke curled upward from the center, and a sound like a great roaring furnace blasted forth. Obie had wondered why no hawk riders challenged them when they neared Windermere Castle. Now he understood. The dragon's spiny red wings flapped powerfully and flames spewed from its mouth as it flew up from the dark circle and sped towards them.

CHAPTER TWENTY-SEVEN

THE STAR CRYSTALS

SMOKER CAME FAST, screeching and lighting the night sky with streams of fire.

"Hold on," Aristeil yelled to Obie, Tau and Mole. "We'll take you to the keep before we battle this beast."

Bracing himself for the rough ride, Obie saw that the moon was riding near its zenith. The windlords dove towards the keep with Smoker almost upon them. The beast swooped by on their right and looked them over while his red wings fanned great torrents of air heated by his fiery breath. Then he made a loop and dove after them. Battle horns sounded along the castle walls as hundreds of archers bent their bows in readiness for the dragon. The windlords sailed over the bowmen and fluttered down to a landing in the main courtyard. Bowstrings sang and scores of arrows sailed towards the oncoming beast. But when the arrows bounced off his armored hide like toothpicks and the terrible reptile's mouth opened, valor ebbed. Some of the bowmen dropped down and leaned against the wall for cover while others ran for safety into the towers as the dragon passed over spewing a river of fire. A hay wagon ignited in the courtyard below, and a man in flames leaped into a water trough.

Shouts that the dragon was returning to his camp came from the men resuming their battle stations at the wall. Among the voices, Obie heard a familiar one shouting down to him.

"Oberon, Oberon! And is that you, Gabrielle?"

Obie saw a man waving. "Andras," he called back. "Are you all right?"

"Yes, the dragon heated things up a bit, but did little damage up here."

"I'm coming up." Obie raced for the stone stairway leading up the wall with the others following.

"Obie, lad." Smiling hopefully, Andras embraced him. Then his eyes fell upon Eleri at the top of the stairs and his smile vanished. He pulled back and held Obie at arms length. Suddenly he appeared old and frightened. "Where's Gabrielle and Mara? We heard you'd rescued them and she was returning with Prince Andor."

Stunned by his words, Obie stared into Andras' face. He'd known the flight home would be dangerous for Gabrielle and Mara, but he wasn't prepared to hear that they never made it. He had to do something . . . get help and go look for them . . . they must be out there somewhere, he thought. "They left the Otawn Village with Andor. They should have gotten here days ago," Obie answered.

Andras looked devastated. "When I saw you coming just now, I hoped they were with you. It's almost time for the Moonpath to open. Gabrielle and Mara are our last hope, Oberon."

"What about our armies? Where are they?"

"Ull and twenty-five hundred men rode out a few days ago with Cadwallen and his army of two thousand. They were going to try and stop Torolf. Gerallt followed a day later with twenty-seven hundred warriors, but he was cut off and sustained heavy losses. He and his men fell back to the North Field, and when they could no longer hold it they retreated into the keep."

"Where are Ull and Cadwallen?"

"The eagles reported both were driven west into the hills. The queen had but a thousand fighting men here at the keep. Including what's left of Gerallt's army, we have maybe twenty-five hundred men to defend Windermere Castle." Sighing wearily, he leaned against a tower on the crenellated wall and closed his eyes.

Obie went to the wall and looked over. Below and far into the distance the muks and raks stood at silent attention. It was an eerie scene. The ghostly moonlight shone dully on their armor and reflected off the cold metal tips of their spears. Soon the silence would break and they would swarm over the high stone walls in a great wave. They would need no ladders. According to Tau, their insect-like feet and hands could easily climb walls. They only awaited Torolf's command to attack. His eyes turned towards the moon and his thoughts went to Gabrielle.

Nearly choking on his words, he asked Andras, "Do you think Torolf captured Gabrielle and Mara?" While he spoke he became aware of something moving in the eastern sky. Illuminated in the dull moonlight, a great flock of white geese was flying towards Mount Iluva. Somehow it seemed odd, out of place. He remained vaguely aware of its movement while listening to Andras.

"No, he hasn't captured them—not yet at least. He thinks she's here at the keep and we haven't told him otherwise. Torolf arrived at the gate today and demanded we send her out to him. But Queen Olwen came to the wall and, with old Marduk beside her, sent curses down to him instead. It so infuriated him, he hurled a fire bolt that sent Marduk flying and wounded the queen slightly. Both she and the old wizard are recovering now. Torolf's turned into a monster, Oberon. I saw him. And now he's on top of the mountain waiting for Gabrielle and Mara to try and enter the Moonpath. He intends to capture them. It'll be a miracle now if . . ."

"Andras, look!" Obie was pointing to a spot high above Mount Iluva. Fireballs and lightning bolts were shooting through the night sky over the mountain. In the light from the fireworks Obie made out two riders: one on a huge hawk and the other on a windlord. "The geese must have brought them!"

"Brought who?" Andras asked excitedly, squinting to see. "All I can see is fire and lightning. Is it Gabrielle?"

"Yes, it's Gabrielle and Mara. Torolf's chasing them. He's hurling fire bolts!"

"Oh my, oh my, it's them, they've made it." Andras' face filled with emotion and he shuffled about excitedly, trying hard to see, unable to contain himself. "Fly, fly my lassies," Andras shouted waving his fists in the air. "Don't let the villain catch you! You can do it! I know you can my lassies!"

Excited talk passed among the warriors manning the wall and some shouted down to men in the courtyard and pointed towards the spectacle in the sky.

Obie watched helplessly, wishing he was up there riding alongside Gabrielle and lending a hand. His pulse raced as he watched Mara evade Arend. Down she dived, then pulled up and swerved sharply while Gabrielle drew back on her bow and shot at Torolf. They flew across the face of the moon and Obie saw that it was at its zenith. The Moonpath must have opened, but Gabrielle and Mara were high above the mountaintop. Then they dived almost straight down with Torolf and Arend close on Mara's heels. *They'll crash into the mountain!* Obie gripped the wall, his palms sweating and his muscles as tight as a drawn bowstring. He held his breath when Torolf hurled another lightning bolt. Did it hit them? He couldn't tell. But they were still flying so they must be okay. Then Mara arced upward and disappeared just above the Lonely Oak Tree. Instantly Arend veered away from the tree. He circled once and then bore Torolf to a landing near the oak.

Obie and Andrus were suddenly hugging, laughing, crying, and dancing around for joy, shouting, "They made it! They made it!" A throng of cheers erupted on the keep wall and spread to the people in the courtyard below. Eleri and Aristeil were smiling hopefully and their eyes shone brightly. Tau laughed uncontrollably as tears streamed down his cheeks and Mole squealed joyously from his shoulder.

Then Obie remembered something and his smile faded.

"What is it, Oberon?" Andras asked.

"Andras, did you get Gabrielle's message to hide the Light Crystal in the Lonely Oak Tree?"

Andras' face went white. "The eagle messenger was attacked by Torolf's hawks and lay helpless in the forest a few days before he could fly again. By the time I got the message a large company of hawk riders was guarding the Cave of the Light Crystal at Mt. Iluva. Our warriors went to do battle with them, but then the dragon came and shot flames everywhere. The bloody beast was too much for our men—they barely escaped with their lives. Torolf arrived soon afterward with his army. Gabrielle and Mara will have to make a run for it when they return with the Dark Crystal."

"How soon will they be back?" Obie asked.

"Very soon. Time stands nearly still on the Moonpath and in Phoebe's realm. Although it may seem to Gabrielle and Mara like they've been gone a long time when they return, hardly any time will have passed here on Earth."

"Then I have to go to her. I have to tell Gabrielle."

"Take Magnus, he's in the courtyard."

"Thanks," Obie answered, then turned to Aristeil and Eleri. "I'm going to try and help Gabrielle and Mara escape from Torolf when they return from the Moonpath. A distraction might turn his attention away for a while."

"You will have your distraction," Aristeil said. "The dragon will come after you when you leave the keep, but Eleri and I will draw it to us. Our battle will attract much attention."

"I'll call all available sky warriors to follow you, Oberon," Andras said. "Tell Gabrielle and Mara to fly up quickly from the mountaintop and our warriors will swoop down and shield them from the hawk-riders."

"I will," Obie said. "Can you lend me your white muffler and a spear?"

"Take it." Andras pulled the muffler from his neck and handed it to Obie. "I wish I were still young enough to go with you."

"Here, take my spear, lad," a nearby soldier said, holding it out to Obie.

"Thanks," Obie said, taking it. He ran the spear's point through the muffler to make a white flag, then turned and raced down the steps to the courtyard. There were no moments to spare. Eleri and Aristeil hurried down behind Obie.

"We're coming too." Tau bounded down the stairs with Mole clinging to his mane.

Andras whistled and Magnus galloped over from the far side of the courtyard, his golden coat aglow in the light of the burning wagon. Obie grabbed the pommel and threw himself into the saddle.

"A windlord, we need a windlord," Tau's voice boomed. He spotted a big black one nearby and mounted.

The warrior paired with the windlord came running up, but when he saw Obie, he nodded and waved Tau on. "His name's *Thor* and he'll serve ya well." Tau acknowledged with a wave while Thor snorted and danced about.

Aristeil rode over on his windlord. "Here, two swallows," he said, handing his flask of elven draught to Tau. Tau took the swallows and handed the flask back. "I owe you."

Ivor, the royal archer, joined them on his windlord, Rune. "I ride with you also, Oberon," the warrior called in his deep voice.

"And I, if you'll have me," a man's voice shouted, as Magnus shuffled his wings preparing for flight. Obie turned and was surprised to see Jasper ride up on a chestnut windlord.

"I admit I was wrong, Obie. Will ya let a man make amends by fighting at your side?"

"Come on then. I'm glad to have you, Jasper." Addressing all the men, Obie said, "Torolf may allow four windlords in, but we don't want to appear threatening. Don't draw your weapons at first or they'll make mincemeat of us. My plan is to peacefully surround the Moonpath Riders and escape with them when Torolf and his troops are distracted by the dragon slayers battling Smoker. It may sound like a desperate plan—but it's all we've got."

"Aye, we're with you lad," Ivor said.

"Lead the way, Oberon," Jasper said.

Within moments six windlords bearing seven warriors, including Mole, rose up and over the castle walls heading for Mount Iluva. From his dark resting place, Smoker flew up swiftly and darted after them.

May the gods of men be with you, Oberon, Eleri said to him mentally.

And may the gods of elves be with you during your battle with the dragon, Eleri, Obie answered.

Then Eleri and Aristeil streaked ahead on their battle steeds, drawing the dragon away from the others.

Meanwhile Andras had sent two messengers to muster the men. Within minutes, twenty-eight seasoned warriors and their windlord war steeds passed over the walls heading towards the mountain with instructions to circle high and watch for the Moonpath Riders to fly up from the oak tree.

***

Nearing the top of Mount Iluva, Gabrielle saw Torolf waiting below on Arend at the Lonely Oak, accompanied by hundreds of heavily armed hawk-riders. His black hood was pulled back exposing his withered face, and straggly strands of his white hair were stirring in the breeze. With trembling hand Gabrielle grasped the white pouch around her neck.

Mara exited the Moonpath and fluttered to the ground while Torolf silently watched, his thin lips twisted in a malevolent grin. Instantly Gabrielle slid from Mara's back and took the few steps to the tree trunk. As she reached her hand into the small opening, she wondered why Torolf wasn't trying to stop her. Then she knew.

"Aaahhh, hah, hah," he laughed, seeing the shocked expression on her face when she withdrew her hand. "Not there? Ohhhh, too bad. Oh well," he sighed. "Now perhaps you and your windlord will come to your senses. How could you think you were any match for the powers of the Serpent? Gabrielle, it would be so much better if you chose to join me. You *will* become my queen, you know. You will be the *Queen of Chaos*, beautiful and terrible sitting on your serpent throne. How do you like that name, my dear?"

The blood drained from Gabrielle's face. She mounted Mara and sat clutching the white pouch.

Torolf's eyes moved to the pouch. "Come now, be a good girl and give me the Dark Crystal, so I don't have to come and take it from you. Anyway, it's useless to you now that I've . . . oh, silly me. I forgot to tell you about the little joke I've played on you. Since you hid the Light Crystal so well inside the mountain, I had to permanently seal the entrance to the cave. So, you see my love, you'll

never be able to join the Star Crystals. Eehhh, hee, hee."

Mara, fly us away now to save the Dark Crystal, Gabrielle urged.

Yes . . . wait, what's that? Mara was looking at something moving in the sky a little to the north of them.

Gabrielle turned her head to see what it was.

Torolf must have noticed as he also turned to look. Smoker had taken to the air and was spurting flames at two sky riders that were circling him. The black sorcerer laughed long and hideously.

"Well, little Guardians, we're in for some entertainment. Wait until you see how my dragon can incinerate his opponents. Do watch closely now."

All eyes and ears turned towards the red dragon as its reptilian shrieks echoed through the sky. Mara's muscles tensed in readiness to fly away, when from the side she saw another movement in the eastern sky and turned slightly to look. Four windlords glided noiselessly on the air, approaching Torolf from behind. Gabrielle also saw it and her heart skipped a beat when she recognized Obie's silhouette against the sky.

He's come, Obie's come to help us, Gabrielle said to Mara. She wanted to cry out, but dared not. Magnus and the other windlords descended slowly while Obie waved his white muffler flag for a truce. He wondered if Torolf would honor a white flag. The black sorcerer king jerked his head around, startled at the sudden intrusion.

"What . . . ?" he uttered, sitting up straight.

The hawk riders drew their bows and pointed arrows at the four intruders. Obie and Tau landed at the left side of Gabrielle and Mara, while Ivor and Jasper landed on their right.

"We've come peacefully," Obie asserted, trying to make his quivering voice sound confident. In truth, his whole body quaked at close sight of Torolf. The black sorcerer was the most frightening human being he had ever seen, if human being he could be called. It was his eyes that seemed inhuman; nor did they appear to be animal, because no animal could harbor such malevolence as projected from the sorcerer king's red eyes.

Torolf raised his arm. "Stay," he called to his troops. The archers relaxed their weapons. "We'll see what these simple-minded idiots want, my lads. And then I may let you use them for target practice. So," he said eyeing them more closely, "a youth and a runaway servant with a pet accompanied by two witless guards. No, wait . . . . You're the thieves who stole into my citadel like rats in the dead of night and ran off with the cheese, aren't you. Ahahaha, the fun increases. Do I detect that Gabrielle has a young champion vying for her heart? Hmmmm? Speak," Torolf demanded, his eyes narrowing to red slits.

"We . . . we've come to stand with Gabrielle and Mara," Obie forced his voice to say, though his throat was so dry it was difficult to speak.

The black sorcerer impaled Obie with his glare. "Well, of course you may stand with Gabrielle and Mara—where I can keep an eye on you. The price will be high, though. After my dragon's main event I might let him burn you to cinders for rudely interrupting his show. But if you want to live that long, be still and watch."

Torolf's words were more encouraging than frightening, for Obie believed the dragon would soon be dead. And if Torolf killed him at least it wouldn't be while he sat idly by. The windlords were swift and skilled in battle flight and evasive maneuvers. Then his spirits lifted on a wave of hope, for he knew—as he had always known—that he was *supposed* to be here with Gabrielle at this moment in time.

The furnace-like sound of Smoker's fiery breath blasted the air as the battle between dragon and elf warriors neared the mountaintop. The fire dragon was flying in loops around his challengers. Skillfully dodging the flames, Eleri's windlord dove past the dragon's face so he would lower his head, causing the red armor-like scales at the base of his skull to part and expose his soft vulnerable spot. The ploy worked. Smoker lowered his head and Aristeil drew back his bow. At that moment Eleri looked into the dragon's eyes and screamed, "No! Aristeil, don't shoot!"

As he released his bowstring Aristeil jerked his arm to knock the arrow off course. The deadly arrow zipped past the dragon's soft spot, hit an armory scale, and bounced off. Seconds later, Eleri passed close to her brother above the dragon. "Pretend to battle Smoker with me, Aristeil, but do not kill him," she called. He nodded and continued fighting a mock battle, shooting only at the dragon's tough outer scales. Round and round the light show twirled in the sky, the dragon spewing streams of fire and the elf steeds skillfully evading them.

Atop Mount Iluva Gabrielle's eyes flickered in acknowledgment of the mental instructions Obie was sending her and Mara. *We're taking you away. Fly up quickly Mara while Torolf and his hawk riders are distracted, and we'll surround you.*

Barely noticeable, Mara loosened her wings, ready to spread them quickly for flight. Obie nodded a signal to Tau and the others. They were a second away from flight when something happened. White smoke began seeping out from beneath Obie's cloak. He saw it at the same time Tau did. Instantly, Tau slid from Thor's back. "What the . . .?" Obie said pulling at his cloak to see what was burning.

He felt Tau's strong paw-hands pulling him to the ground. Torolf's attention was drawn from the dragon battle to Obie and Tau, fumbling on the ground and coughing amidst the engulfing smoke. Torolf responded with hearty laughter, and his hawk riders joined in.

"Blundering buffoons," he said slapping his thigh. "Ehhh, heee, heee. I may not kill you after all, but keep you as my fools. Yaaahhh, haaa, haaa."

Obie pulled his cloak off and discovered the smoke was coming from his ammo pouch. Tau yanked the strap over Obie's head and threw the pouch down, then stamped out the smoldering cloak. Torolf and his hawk riders were still laughing when the pouch burst into flame and burned away, leaving only Obie's rock glowing red-hot.

Gabrielle felt heat against her chest and then saw smoke issuing from the white pouch. Now she understood what was happening. Ripping the smoking pouch from her neck, she slid to the ground and placed it next to the other. The white pouch started burning. Obie's rock crumbled and in its place was the Light Crystal sending forth bright rays of light. Not laughing now, Torolf stared in amazed disbelief. The burning white pouch fell away and the Dark Crystal flared equally bright. Dropping to her knees Gabrielle reached out and joined the Star Crystals.

Tremendous blasts of energy and light flared up from the two Crystals while onlookers cowered in awe, shielding their eyes from the brilliant emanations. Riding upon the light came spirit warriors: eagles, men, and windlords. Passing over the heads of all present they moved down the mountain, gaining speed. Like wind from a nuclear blast they passed over Torolf's entire army and continued outward. At tremendous speed they passed around the Earth in a matter of seconds. Upon their return the light and energy of the spirit warriors drew back into the Star Crystals. And all was calm.

CHAPTER TWENTY-EIGHT

METAMORPHOSIS

OBIE OPENED HIS EYES and saw Torolf looking dazed astride a tall, black windlord, for the spell that had transformed Arend from a windlord into a hawk was broken. Hundreds of normal sized hawks fluttered away in all directions and everywhere on the ground lay weapons and heaps of battle garb.

Gabrielle was staring at the ground and smiling when Obie asked her, "Where's the muks and raks?"

"There." She pointed to streams of small ants and spiders speeding away towards the edge of the mountain as fast as their tiny legs would carry them.

Ivor and Jasper were surveying the scene in stunned silence.

A roar startled Obie and he turned towards Tau, but the lion-man was gone. In his place stood a magnificent lion with a great, golden-brown mane.

"Tau?" Obie said softly.

Instead of answering Tau made a quiet growl and Obie knew he could no longer speak. As a lion he had not possessed the gift of speech. But his eyes were the same as before, and as Obie gazed into them he believed that Tau was pleased with the transformation. Then he remembered Tau saying a while back that he and his brothers wanted the spell over them broken, that creatures ought to be what they were intended to be.

His thoughts were interrupted by the sound of many fluttering wings. Looking up he saw the twenty-eight windlords and warriors that had been circling high above. They were coming down and landing among the numerous piles of war-gear. The men raised their weapons signaling their readiness to help. For even though Torolf's army was no more, his presence among them was still menacing.

Torolf had recovered from his dazed state and sat cursing. Beneath him, Arend had developed a dangerous look in his eyes. Snorting and stabbing his front hooves into the ground, his agitation appeared to grow by the second until suddenly the black windlord leaped up and threw the sorcerer king from his back.

Torolf hit the ground and lay still as Arend raced away.

Obie quietly said to Gabrielle, "Torolf's broken. It's all over now."

"I'm not so sure," she whispered. In silence they watched Torolf pull himself to his feet, his emaciated face purple with fury.

"Not broken yet, you fools," he hissed. "You think you've won the battle—but the victory is mine." Gasps went up as he raised himself to twice his full height and swept a menacing eye over the gathering.

"I will build another army. I am as powerful as ever while you have grown weaker. Weep for yourselves that the power of the Star Crystals could be used *only once*. Now you have only your own strength to rely on, and it is no match against mine. The future belongs to the Serpent and to me." His face darkened as he pointed a long bony finger in Thor's direction.

Obie and Gabrielle turned to look. Torolf was not pointing at the windlord, but to one who had escaped their notice, one who sat quietly observing. A handsome man, with brown hair and beard slightly streaked with gray sat tall on Thor where Mole had been, and Mole was nowhere to be seen. The man's demeanor was noble, his face strong and a little weatherworn. He was dressed in hunters' clothing with a bow across his back and a sword with a golden pommel crafted into a lion's head at his belt. Returning Torolf's gaze, his violet-blue eyes looked sad, but wise.

"You should have died long ago," Torolf yelled. An instant later he thrust out his chest and shocked onlookers by transforming into a large, black, red-eyed wolf. The beast threw back his head and howled hideously. Then, opening his jaw to expose large, sharp teeth, he leaped towards the man on Thor's back. In a flurry of movement the archers drew their bows to shoot, but moving swifter Gabrielle unleashed a golden arrow from Phoebe's bow. The arrow tore into the creature's ribcage, pierced through flesh and bone, and stabbed into the center of the wolf's black heart. The wolf screamed, twisted round in mid-air and fell limp to the ground. Smoke rose from the carcass and then it burst into flames. Soon, nothing remained but a small pile of gray ashes. Then a gust of wind came and blew the ashes away.

"*Now* it's over," Gabrielle said to Obie. She turned towards the man astride Thor and their eyes met, and then she went and stood before him. He smiled down at her and a flicker of recognition came into her eyes. "Prince Ulrik," she softly said.

"Yes. It is I, Gabrielle. The black spell Torolf cast upon me many years ago is broken. Mole is no more."

Gabrielle's breath caught and her eyes filled with tears. "You've come back to us."

A murmur of awe passed through the assembly of warriors. Dismounting, they sank down on one knee to their prince, their faces filled with wonder and joy. Obie, too, bent a knee to Prince Ulrik, and Tau sat down on all four legs. Finally, the enigma of Mole made sense to Obie.

"Three cheers for Prince Ulrik, the Crown Prince of Windermere," Ivor shouted. He drew his sword and held out the blade in his two hands, offering his allegiance to Ulrik. The other warriors did the same and shouted three times, "Hooray for Prince Ulrik, Crown Prince of Windermere." Tau joined in and roared in salute to his friend.

"Thank you," Prince Ulrik said to all. "I could not have wished for a more joyous return or a warmer welcome." Then he looked at Gabrielle again and saw her tears, and she lowered her head.

A look of distress came onto Ulrik's face. He slid from Thor's back and gently lifted her chin in his hand. "Bravest of maidens, will you tell me the cause of your tears?"

"They're tears of happiness at your return, my Liege. But . . . I fear you may be angered that it was my hand that slew your brother."

"Gabrielle, Torolf ceased to be my brother long ago when he gave up his humanity and grew mad for power. He had to be slain, and I think only *you* could have done it. He had become so powerful that I suspect ordinary weapons would have been useless against him. Your bow must be great," he said, looking at the golden bow in her hand.

"It's Phoebe's Bow. She said I might need it."

The light of a smile came into Ulrik's eyes. "She knew." He gently brushed his fingers over Gabrielle's cheeks and wiped away her tears. Then taking her hand in his he said to all present, "Please rise up my friends."

Gabrielle was so well-loved by the Windermerians that the warriors watched in approval while Ulrik's eyes fixed searchingly on hers. Looking into his deep blue eyes brought back a rush of childhood memories. In the space of a few seconds she remembered their laughter when the young prince had swung her around in the air, and how he had decorated her hair with bright flowers. He had chased her, giggling, through the gardens and when he tagged her, she chased him back, and he was stung by a bee and she had cried over his ouhie. Then Mole's dear image came into her mind and she smiled, for she and Ulrik were not strangers.

A gentle smile came over Ulrik's face and, releasing Gabrielle from his gaze, he turned again to his subjects and friends. "The kingdom, nay, *the world* is restored to health. It appears that all black spells are broken, thanks in no small part to the stout hearts of all of you. And I tell you all, when the sun rises this day it will be the dawn of a new time. You have only to lift your eyes to the heavens to know the truth of my words."

All eyes turned upward and murmurings of joy passed among them, for a billion stars now twinkled down on the Earth. "The celestial bodies are restored!" a warrior shouted. "And look," another called out, pointing at a shooting star crossing the sky as if in response to Ulrik's words, "The Spirit Comet!" And when a third voice called out, "Haldor and Allegra ride the sky this night, hail to Haldor and Allegra!" all joined in with a "Hail to Haldor and Allegra!"

Bright colors burst from the comet's tail while it streaked like fireworks across the sky. And amidst it all the moon loomed huge and bright. It seemed there would be no end to the wonders of that night when Eleri and Aristeil came out of the sky on their white windlords. Between them flew an iridescent blue dragon with blue and green gossamer wings tinged with pink, and surrounding him was the scent of honeysuckle. He was the lost Joy Dragon. For Smoker, the fire-breathing red dragon had been the product of Torolf's black spell upon this creature, the Blue Dragon of Ellowan. And now that the spell was broken he would return home to the Elven Isles of Eluthien.

Prince Ulrik gave Eleri and Aristeil a warm greeting and praised their valor. Placing a hand on the shoulder of each, he said, "Friends, will you remain as our guests for a time? I and my people wish to honor you."

"It would please us greatly to stay," Aristeil said, "but there will be many festivities at home in Eluthien now that Torolf is gone, and we are anxious to share in the great joy of our people."

"We are also anxious to return the Joy Dragon to them," Eleri said. Then she looked at Aristeil and added, "But, perhaps my brother would agree to stay for a day?"

Aristeil gave his sister a momentary searching look, then smiled and turned back to Ulrik. "We will be honored to be your guests this day and night and join in your celebration, Prince Ulrik, though we must leave early the following morning." Now, he turned a curious look upon Eleri. "Tell me, sister, when you stayed my arrow from slaying the red dragon, how did you know he was the Joy Dragon?"

Eleri smiled shyly. "He told me himself. When I flew before Smoker's eyes and he looked fully upon me, the Joy Dragon trapped deep within must have remembered me and the sweet days he had spent with us in the Isles of Eluthien. And though he could not get out, he shed a tear. When I saw it, I knew this dragon had been enchanted and was not truly evil. I knew he must be The Blue Dragon of Ellowan—our Joy Dragon." By now everyone was crowding around this wonderful creature.

Meanwhile, Gabrielle quietly put the Star Crystals away, the Dark Crystal in a small bag on Mara's saddle and the Light Crystal in a bag on Magnus' saddle. Afterwards, she joined Ulrik and Tau the lion. Obie was standing at the edge of the crowd admiring the dragon when he had an uneasy feeling. Turning, he saw Prince Ulrik, Gabrielle and Tau staring strangely at him.

"I know . . . you're all wondering how I got the Light Crystal. Right?"

"We're mystified, Obie. How ever did you get it?" Gabrielle asked. "Torolf said he sealed it under the mountain."

"May you never cease to amaze me, Oberon. How *did* you do it, my friend?" Ulrik walked over and, putting his arm around Obie's shoulder, drew him into the group.

"It surprised me as much as it did you," Obie said. "The Light Crystal was encased in a rock I found back home about a week before the Spirit Comet brought me to Windermere. I've been using it to start campfires. I didn't know the Crystal was inside. The odd thing was . . . the rock had my name on it. I thought my friend Will Gray Eagle might have been playing a joke on me, but he said he wouldn't do that. He said spirits in the valley were summoning me on the night of the full moon. I went, and that's when Haldor and Allegra brought me here."

"Is Will Gray Eagle an eagle?" Gabrielle asked.

"No, he's just a very wise man I've known most of my life."

"Hmmmm," Gabrielle said thoughtfully. "Where did you find the rock?"

He flashed her a knowing smile. "It was in a cave under Watcher Mountain in Ghostrise Valley. I've always wondered if Watcher Mountain was the same as Mount Iluva and Ghostrise Valley was the same as the Valley of Windermere. The valley and the mountain look pretty much the same except that back home they aren't green anymore and the valley's deserted. That has to be it."

Gabrielle shook her head in agreement. "The Light Crystal was encased in rock to prevent it from being found and stolen. When Torolf searched for it he expected to find the bare crystal. He may have passed by it without knowing what it was. When he couldn't find it, he sealed the entrance to the cave. Haldor and Allegra knew when it would be found again, and they brought you to us just when we needed it."

"And it just happened to be me who brought it," Obie said.

Ulrik gave Obie a doubtful smile. "Somehow, Obie, I can't quite believe it just *happened* to be you. It seems to me there's been something more at work here, something even beyond Haldor and Allegra. And I suspect some consciousness operating deep within caused you to help things along."

Obie fell silent for a few moments, remembering the conversation in the cave when Mole told him he was a halfling and that halflings had magic in their blood. "Maybe," he said, and shrugged it off. Then something else came to mind. "Gabrielle, you once told me 'the universe is a wonderful place full of unimagined possibilities.' Do you remember?"

"Yes, though I don't think you believed it. How do you feel now?"

"I believe."

***

While everyone was talking, Arend returned and stood at the edge of the group, his head lowered. Ulrik had been listening to Gabrielle and Obie, but when he saw Arend he was filled with compassion for the windlord he had known and admired so many years ago. He walked over and placed his arm over the windlord's long black neck and began speaking with him mentally, for, being of the House of Gruffydd, Prince Ulrik had the gift of mental speech, though he had not possessed it when he was Mole.

Torolf did you great injury in bending you to his uses, Arend. But you mustn't be so hard on yourself. Remember, as a windlord he could never have forced you to serve him. It was the black spell.

I know it was the spell that twisted me. It is the memory of my cruel deeds as Arend the hawk that brings me grief.

I was also under his spell, though I suffered in a different way. But it's over now, my friend. And in time our wounds will heal. You and I will heal together. Will you stay with me?

I would like that, Arend answered, raising his tortured eyes to Ulrik. While standing with Arend, Ulrik became aware of something large moving at the edge of his vision. Half turning, he saw the Blue Dragon of Ellowan approaching, floating a foot above the ground. The dragon stopped before Ulrik and Arend and the air around them was rich with his sweet scent. Ulrik caught Eleri's eye. She smiled and nodded encouragingly. The Joy Dragon touched his spotted nose to Arend's nose, gazing at the windlord with one eye and at Ulrik with the other.

Touch your hand to my nose, the dragon said mentally to the prince.

Upon touching the spotted nose Ulrik was drawn deeply into the creature's timeless eye; and in that higher dimension of the Joy Dragon's vision, he beheld pure, indescribable beauty beyond anything he had ever known. A buoyant feeling came over him and a wave of sublime joy flowed through his body.

Then the dragon spoke to them. *Seek to find in the eyes of all you meet what you see in my eyes, and know that the great joy you are feeling now has always resided within you.*

The dragon pulled his nose away and the blissful feeling passed. But Ulrik wasn't disappointed, for he felt the power of the experience etched indelibly in his heart. The knowledge that he was capable of experiencing unspeakable joy tempered the feelings of loneliness and sorrow he had suffered for so many years in the forest and made the memory of those lost years bearable. When he looked at Arend he was touched by the change in the windlord's eyes and the two shared a few moments of renewal.

Then Ulrik went to Gabrielle's side. He knew all that had happened to her while imprisoned in the Serpent's Tower, as she had confided in Mole while she lay recovering in the Otawn Village. Although she, too, had suffered at Torolf's hands, he recalled how even in childhood her eyes had shone with the deep light of joy. Only now did he understand the source of that light. She had tapped into the great joy of her being long ago, without help from the Joy Dragon. The strength she drew from her knowledge of the eternal goodness must have been what enabled her to resist Torolf's power as long as she did. And when he finally did bewitch her and she discovered his treachery, it had enabled her to snap back to herself again. These thoughts passed swiftly through his mind while the dragon moved on towards Obie and Tau.

Obie backed away as the Joy Dragon approached, but Tau remained. All watched in fascination as Tau reached his paw up, touched the dragon's nose, and gazed into his eyes. Tau's eyes began glowing like yellow-green fire and he purred so loudly it brought smiles to the warriors' faces. When it was over and Tau pulled his paw away, Eleri took the Joy Dragon away from the crowd to rest. Obie felt a light hand on his shoulder and turned. It was Gabrielle and Prince Ulrik.

"Oberon, the Joy Dragon wanted to give you his gift," she said gently. "Why didn't you take it? I know there's something that's been hurting you for a long time. I've seen it in your eyes. The dragon can help."

A look of pain came onto Obie's face. "I try not to think about it, Gabrielle. The thing is . . . I don't deserve anything from the Joy Dragon . . . not like the others." His voice cracked and he looked away for a few moments, then turned back to her and continued. "But everything's worked out—better than we ever thought it would. I'm content with that, really." He glanced at Ulrik, then turned and limped away while they stood watching.

"But . . ." Gabrielle started to say to him.

"Let him go. He needs some time," Ulrik whispered.

"You've seen it in his eyes too?"

"Yes, he doesn't hide it well. When I was Mole, I used to watch him toss and turn in his sleep at night, and I wondered what demons possessed his dreams. He would never speak of them."

"I'll talk to him soon."

Ulrik smiled. "I'm counting on it. But for now, it's time for some lightness and gaiety. Get Mara and let's leave this mountaintop." Turning to the warriors he said, "Let us go to Windermere Castle. This will be a day, nay, *a week,* of celebration beyond all celebrations." Ulrik mounted Arend and the black windlord stepped forth bearing the prince amidst cheers of the men who were ready to follow him on their battle steeds.

Tau stood at the edge of the mountaintop, gazing down as though ready to descend. Hesitating, he turned his great head towards Prince Ulrik.

Prince Ulrik smiled down regretfully at Tau. "My good friend, I would be honored to run down the mountain at your side. We've traveled far together and you've borne me many miles on your shoulder. But I would only hold you back. I know those great legs of yours must be crying out for a good run."

"We could keep up with Tau if we run-fly down the mountain on the windlords—if the windlords are willing," Obie called over from Magnus' back.

The prince lifted his brow in surprise. "Run-fly? That's something new. Quite imaginative, Obie. Are the windlords agreeable?" Ulrik called to them. The windlords answered mentally that it sounded exciting and they would like to give it a go. "All right then," he laughed, "the windlords say they are agreeable. We'll run-fly down the mountain with Tau. All who wish to join us are welcome."

"A new sport? Include me," someone yelled. Then, in a flurry of voices, the other warriors shouted that they also wished to join in.

"My Prince," Gabrielle said, "with your leave, Eleri and I will take the Joy Dragon to Windermere Castle and tell the queen you're coming home."

"Thank you for thinking of it, Gabrielle. It would be unwise to shock my mother with a sudden appearance after all these years. It's best that you go ahead with news of my coming.

"Thank you, my Liege."

"I'll see you at the keep then?"

"Yes."

"Will you promise me you'll sit by my side at our celebration table tonight?"

She smiled radiantly. "I promise."

Then, swathed in the light of the full-moon, Ulrik, Obie, Aristeil and all the warriors began run-flying down the mountain, keeping pace with Tau who was bounding easily along. Down steep grassy slopes, up and over rocky ridges he loped, leaping down on boulders, then jumping off and racing on through tall pines, springing from low rock faces, exhilarated, stretching the muscles of his lion legs as he had not done for many a year. The warriors laughed and whooped alongside, bellowing like boys at play, while their windlords swooped from ridges making galloping touch downs on green slopes; then, leaping from sheer ledges, expert wings caught wind 'til hooves touched ground and on the windlords thundered, tails flying and nostrils spread.

***

Queen Olwen was beside herself with joy when she embraced Gabrielle and learned that her son Ulrik was alive and on his way from the mountain. The keep sprang to life with excitement as the news rapidly spread that Torolf was no more, and Prince Ulrik was finally coming home. Horns blew when he rode through the castle gate with Tau running on his left and Obie riding on his right, followed by Aristeil and the sky warriors. Every person at the keep turned out for the momentous event of Prince Ulrik's return, and the people cheered wildly at sight of him.

A little later, Prince Ulrik led Queen Olwen, Gabrielle, Obie, Tau, Andras, Eleri, and Aristeil up the stairway to the east wall of the castle. Below them in the meadow crowds of people from the keep and also from town stood waiting in the predawn with eyes turned eastward, the only sound an occasional trilling of a meadowlark. Soon the black sky over the forest melted into deep purple, pushing night from the edge of the world, making way for horizontal streaks of vermillion, orange, and pink; and over this palette of color, golden rays shot out in all directions as the sun rose over Gnarlwood Forest, like a great golden ball buoyed up from a dark green sea, spreading its bright promise over the Valley of Windermere.

CHAPTER TWENTY-NINE

THE NEW DAWN

THE PEOPLE WHO HAD FLED to the western hills during the siege returned to their homes over the next few days and the Valley of Windermere exploded with activity. Much of it involved clearing away and piling into huge heaps the war gear the muks and raks left on the ground throughout the valley. The metal would be melted down by the blacksmiths and recast into new battle gear and farm implements, and the leather and clothing would be recycled.

Eleri and Aristeil were honored at the first royal banquet, and then departed the next morning with the Joy Dragon for the Isles of Eluthien. Ull and Cadwallen arrived at Windermere Castle with their men, though some of Cadwallen's troops had already been dismissed to return to their homes in Wesley. Gerallt and his men remained at the keep for a time, camping on the North Field and the West Meadow along with Cadwallen's men. After enjoying the festivities the warriors participated in the clean-up and were allotted shares of the enemy battle gear to take back to their homes for their own uses. Those warriors who fell in battle were honored by a formal service held in the Chapel of Phoebe, and later many toasts and words of praise were said for them.

Prince Andor's body was brought in by eagles that had scouted the forest below the place where Gabrielle and Mara had last seen him. His wounds revealed that he had fought well, but the enemy had been too many. Gabrielle and Mara believed more hawks must have joined the fight. He had been much loved, and sorrow over his death was widespread. Queen Olwen had his body wrapped in royal robes of red velvet, and the next morning he was borne on a bier carried by four white windlords, two on each side, to his father, King Konur, in the Lofty Mountains to the south. Queen Olwen, Prince Ulrik, Gabrielle, Obie, and Andras flew alongside followed by thirty Windermerian sky warriors. Ymir, the Windlord King, and many of his followers also joined the group to honor Prince Andor.

At dusk, when the last golden fingers of the sun touched the highest mountain peaks, Andor was given a warrior's departure on the craggy mountaintop of his birth. Upon the funeral bier Prince Ulrik and others laid rich gifts befitting a great warrior prince. And when the last light of the sun blinked out the bier was set aflame while a hundred eagle warriors circled high above.

***

It was after midnight when the Windermerians arrived back at the keep from the funeral. Feeling heavy of heart over the loss of Prince Andor, it lifted Obie's spirits to find Shadow there waiting for him. They talked for well over an hour about all that had happened since their separation. Finally, overtaken by weariness, Obie returned to his room and collapsed in bed.

Midweek, eagle messengers began bringing reports from other parts of the world that Torolf's counterparts, the other servants of the Serpent who had also sent out conquering armies, had been killed. After the power of the Star Crystals broke all dark spells and the invading armies collapsed back into small insects, the people had risen up against the black sorcerer kings. When the reports finally numbered five, Gabrielle breathed easily. But it was not until word came that the practice of black magic was banned in all lands that she knew the danger was truly past.

At Windermere Castle a banquet was held every night for a week. Although the war had reduced the food stores, there was still much flour and grain for baking, and the hunters and fishermen busied themselves daily bringing in game, meat, and fish. Reserves of wine and mead were opened too, for there was no better time to use them and they could be replaced in the future. So the feasting abounded, wine and mead flowed, and the halls resounded with the music as in the old days.

During a banquet held later in the week, Queen Olwen announced she was retiring, and the coronation of her son, Prince Ulrik, would take place the following week. There was great gladness at the news, as now the people would have both a king and a queen mother. Lord Cadwallen of Wesley proposed a toast to the long and wise rule of the future king, and his fine words were followed by toasts from Lord Gerallt of Barrington, and Ull (soon to become Lord Ull) of Gruffhaven.

Tau had gone into the forest to be with his kind who had retreated there once the spell over them was broken. Knowing Tau would not want to miss the Coronation of King Ulrik, Obie and Shadow went searching for him in Gnarlwood and brought him back in time.

All eyes were fixed upon Ulrik as he walked up the aisle of the great Throne Room in his white satin clothing and sable coronation robe. And when the newly crowned King of Windermere turned to face his people, the quiet room exploded in wild cheers and exclamations of "Long live the King." That morning not even the sturdiest warrior was dry-eyed.

Following his coronation King Ulrik honored Gabrielle, Obie and Tau for their parts in the victory over Torolf, and presented them with royal gifts. Gabrielle was given land and a small estate on a pristine lake in the forested hills a few miles west of Windermere Castle. In future years it would be used as a pleasant summer retreat. Obie was speechless when King Ulrik gave him the official title of *Lord Oberon of the House of Gruffydd*. He had not expected the honor, or that he would be adopted by the Royal House of Windermere. He was also given a new Raptor made of hard leather with the House of Gruffydd Coat-of-Arms inlaid in gold on the arm brace, a golden ring with the Coat-of-Arms inlaid with rubies, and he was paired with a peregrine falcon of noble lineage whose name was *Lord Perault*. Obie discovered it was a talking falcon when the bird gave him permission to simply call him *Perault*.

Obie did not forget the Otawn. When he told the king about Kangi's and Takoda's great interest in his Raptor, Ulrik had special new Raptor sling shots made up for them and Chief Shappa. They were made with skillfully hand-tooled handles depicting scenes of their parts in recent events. An additional thirty were made for Chief Shappa to distribute among the braves as he saw fit, but these had plain handles, hand-toolable as each new owner desired. Silverclaw enlisted the help of several other eagles and they delivered them.

***

On his next visit to the castle Tau brought two friendly lions with him. It was then that King Ulrik decided to protect them. He issued an edict proclaiming a pact of friendship between the Windermerians and the Lions of Gnarlwood, and ordered that no person shall ever hunt them. After the edict was formally read to the people in Tau's presence, he made a low roar, and the pleased look in his eyes was unmistakable. Although Tau lived in the forest, he would become a frequent and welcome guest at the keep and his close friendship with the royal family would remain strong. In future days he and some of his kin would often serve as royal trackers, which earned them high respect among the Windermerians.

During the next few weeks, King Ulrik, Obie and Ull spent many pleasant mornings in the meadows with their falcons. Obie always brought Lord Perault, perched on his shoulder. The close friendship developing between Obie and Ulrik was different in quality than the friendship between Obie and Mole, for Ulrik was all that Mole had been and more. Obie couldn't exactly explain it. Maybe it was because Ulrik was happy now.

Particularly enjoyable were the evenings Obie spent at the Brynnen estate with Gabrielle and her family. Although his limp still bothered him, he looked forward to the after dinner walks with Andras. During such a walk one evening Andras questioned him as to why he had grown quiet of late.

There was a noticeable sadness in his voice when he responded. "I guess I've just been thinking a lot about going home. I'm looking forward to it, but it'll be hard to leave all of you. We've been through so much together."

A frown passed over Andras' face. "Well, you shouldn't be surprised to hear your presence will be greatly missed, Oberon," he said softly. "I wish—and so do many others—that it was possible for you to remain in Windermere."

"Thanks, Andras."

"By the way, have you talked to Gabrielle yet about going flying?"

"No, I've wanted to, but she's been pretty busy."

"I know she intends to fly with you, she said so."

"She did?"

"Absolutely. And I'm sure she hasn't forgotten. That wouldn't be like her. There's still time yet—and Magnus wants to take you."

"I'd like that." Obie's eyes shone as they walked quietly on, listening to the songs of night birds.

After a time Andras broke the silence. "I spoke with the king today."

Obie wondered what he was working up to.

"He mentioned that you have a unique birthmark, and I should have a look at it." Andras stopped and turned to Obie. "That was all he'd say. Just that I should look at it. May I?"

Obie hesitated, then reached up and pulled his shirt away from his left shoulder, exposing it.

Andras' eyes widened when he saw it. "Elf runes, I knew it!" he said with a gleeful chuckle. "The Queen Mother suspected it too."

"Suspected that I'm a halfling? Mole told me that. But how did you and the Queen Mother know when you hadn't seen my birthmark yet?"

Andras' eyes twinkled. "Haven't you figured things out yet, Oberon?"

Obie blinked at him. "I'm not exactly sure what you mean."

"Well, well," he said with a smile. "I will not say more. You should have a talk with King Ulrik, for I don't think Mole told you quite everything."

***

A different mystery was cleared up a few days later when the entrance to the Cave of the Light Crystal was unsealed. On that day Gabrielle took Obie with her into the cavern where the original crystal was hidden. When she found the rock containing the Light Crystal she held it up for him to see. "Wait a minute," she said. She handed Obie the torch and turned her back on him. He watched her pull something small from a pocket in her dress and then heard a scraping sound on the surface of the stone. A minute passed and finally she turned around smiling mischievously. "Just to be safe," she said, holding the rock in her outstretched hand for him to see. She had scratched his name on it. The printing was exactly the same as on the rock he had found under Watcher Mountain. "So the mystery is solved," he said with a grin.

"Yes . . . I think that should do it. And when we leave here the cave will be resealed. I no longer need access to the Light Crystal, but I must still protect it. Sealing it in the mountain seems a natural solution."

"So I can find it again in some other lifetime?"

"If need be." Gabrielle's smile was almost apologetic.

"Does this go on forever?"

"I don't know . . . maybe. But if it does, we won't remember."

***

Obie, Gabrielle and Tau frequently spent afternoons at the keep with King Ulrik and the Queen Mother. On the day before the full-moon, when Obie was to try returning home again, Andras joined the group in King Ulrik's drawing room. Tau lay on the floor next to the fire crackling in the great hearth with Rae and Asta curled up next to him. The others were seated in comfortable chairs enjoying cups of hot spiced cider and small honey cakes. It was an afternoon of pleasant conversation, a bit of playfulness, and some laughter.

"There's something Tau and I have wondered about, Your Majesty," Obie said.

"What is that?" Ulrik lifted a silver jug from the table beside him and refilled his cup. Tau raised his head to listen.

"Remember when you were Mole?"

"Ahhh yes . . . my cute, furry days."

Obie chuckled to himself, fondly remembering Mole. "Why didn't you tell us you were a prince?"

Ulrik leaned back in his chair and swallowed some cider while the others awaited his answer. "I didn't tell you for a couple of reasons. It would have been dangerous for you to know who I was in the event you were captured by Torolf. He would have forced that information from you and then hunted me down. As it was, he must have thought I'd died in the forest. Only I didn't die. Although I left the kingdom in my mother's capable hands, I was to be crowned King of Windermere when I returned from my travels. Torolf knew this. Turning me into a mole was his way of preventing it. I couldn't come home to Windermere after that—not as Mole, anyway. Think of it. A *mole* king. I thought it best that no one learn my fate. Only Zelda, the river witch, knew."

"So you were content to suffer alone all that time?" Andras asked, a touch of sadness in his voice.

"Content? No. Not by any stretch of the imagination. Just resigned to it. But I kept in touch with what was happening outside the forest. Zelda tried to break the spell upon me, but the black magic was beyond even her powers. So I waited and the River Sprites regularly brought me news of the outside world. I lived from day-to-day and year-to-year hopeful that someday something would happen to change things. And then when you and Tau came and I learned you were going to rescue Gabrielle, I knew I must join you."

Obie stared in admiration at Ulrik while Gabrielle and the Queen Mother wiped tears from their eyes. When two servants brought in more refreshments the conversation turned light again, and then the Queen Mother invited everyone to dine with her and a few other guests that evening. The afternoon was almost spent and soon the gathering broke up so everyone could dress for dinner. Obie got up to leave, but Ulrik stopped him.

"Oberon, will you walk with me in the garden?"

Andras caught Obie's eye and smiled, then turned and left.

"I'd enjoy that, Your Majesty," Obie said.

The two walked quietly along the garden path. A whippoor-will sang down at them from the branch of a fir tree and the fragrance of the pines and wood burning in nearby fireplaces floated in the crisp air. After a time Ulrik said, "Obie, you've become a cherished friend to me."

"Thank you, Your Majesty. I feel the same way."

Ulrik laughed softly and Obie turned a questioning look at him. "Sorry," the king said. "I just thought about the time I told you I was in love with Gabrielle. Do you remember telling me it could be a bit of a problem because I was a mole?"

"I remember," Obie said with a quick laugh.

A joyous expression came onto Ulrik's face and he looked as though he could barely contain his excitement. "Well, Oberon, what I didn't tell you was that I've always loved Gabrielle. It wasn't just a molish fancy. Today I asked her to be my bride and she accepted." Stopping, he placed his hands on Obie's shoulders and looked into his eyes. "Your blessing is important to us, Obie. Will you give it?"

Obie swallowed hard, fighting back the waves of emotion flooding through him. He'd known a marriage was in the making, but he wasn't ready to hear Ulrik's words.

"Say something, Obie. This *can't* be a surprise to you."

Turning away, Obie stuffed his hands in his jacket pockets and sat down dejectedly on a garden bench.

The king studied him for a few moments. "I see," he finally said. "I suppose I've always known that you love her too. I'm sorry, Obie. Hurting you is the last thing we want."

"I'll be all right. Just give me a few minutes."

Ulrik sank down next to Obie, a barrier of silence between them. A couple of minutes passed and finally Ulrik said softly, "Do you remember telling me *everyone loves Gabrielle*?"

"Yes."

"Well then, of course you love her. And you *should* love her. But be realistic man! Haven't you realized there could never be anything more between you and Gabrielle than this love you bear for her? I mean, haven't you figured it out yet?"

Obie's cheeks reddened. He bolted to his feet and stood glaring at Ulrik. "What's *that* supposed to mean? Figured *what* out? That I'm not a *king*?"

"Such fire, Oberon," Ulrik shot back with a look of surprise. He stood up and took Obie forcefully by the shoulders. "Listen to me now. Take a good look into my eyes. They're very unusual eyes, wouldn't you say? Where have you seen them before?" Obie stared into Ulrik's deep blue eyes and something stirred in his consciousness. "Yes, I can see you're starting to think now, yes, that's it. You *know* what I'm talking about don't you, Oberon. Tell me where you've seen my eyes before," Ulrik demanded.

Obie sank back down on the bench and, looking up at Ulrik, answered, "I've seen your eyes in the mirror every day of my life."

"That's right! And if that's not enough for you, then have a look at this." Ulrik rolled his left sleeve up revealing the elf runes on the underside of his forearm.

Obie's mouth dropped open: the runes were exactly like the ones on his shoulder. "I . . . I already knew the children of the House of Gruffydd are halflings—Andras told me." His voice was shaking, his eyes unsure.

"And did you never make the connection about our similarities: that we're both halflings, that we have the same unusual eye color, and finally that your surname *Griffin* is somewhat similar to *Gruffydd*?"

"Yes . . . but I thought they had to be coincidences."

"Coincidences? Coincidences?" Ulrik said sharply. He paced back and forth impatiently, then wheeled around and looked at Obie. "Wait. Are you assuming all halflings have the *same* elf rune birthmarks?"

"Yes . . . I guess that's what I've thought."

Ulrik heaved a sigh and sat down next to Obie again. "Then it's my fault for never clarifying that rather important point for you, though in the beginning I had my reasons for not telling you. The fact is, Obie, elf rune birthmarks are *not* the same on all halflings. They're only the same within a family line. You and I happen to have the exact same birthmarks because we're both descended from the House of Gruffydd."

Ulrik's words hit Obie like a twenty-pound hammer. The thought had occurred to him in the past, but he'd pushed it away as wishful thinking, sheer daydreaming. He'd even laughed at himself for imagining he might be descended from kings. A light came into his eyes and he smiled. It seemed the universe had played with him. But it had also given him a wonderful gift. "Are you telling me you're my distant grandfather and Gabrielle . . . ?"

"Is your distant grandmother? Yes, Oberon. That's what I'm telling you."

"So, when you gave me the title *Lord Oberon of the House of Gruffydd*—you weren't adopting me?"

"Of course not. You were already a member of the House of Gruffydd. Forgive me, Obie, for not speaking with you about this sooner."

Obie studied Ulrik's face, searching every resemblance.

"I can see this has all been a shock to you. The question is . . . does it disturb you?"

"No—how could it?" Obie locked eyes with Ulrik. "You and Gabrielle are the two people I admire most in the world. I love you both. And even if we *weren't* related, I'd want you to be happy. Maybe . . . do you think maybe our kinship was part of what drew me to Gabrielle?"

A look of compassion came into Ulrik's eyes. "I'm sure of it. The magic in our blood works to preserve itself. If you hadn't been drawn to her . . . you might not have rescued her. Things might have turned out far differently, and if that had been the case, Oberon, you would never have been born."

Obie knitted his brow. "That's a pretty mind blowing thought. Time is hard to comprehend. In fact, I don't see how any of this could even have happened."

Ulrik smiled and nodded understandingly. "On the other hand, I don't suppose the universe would be such an exciting place if it revealed all its mysteries to us. Who can say what strange criss-crossings and convolutions time might take?"

"Well, it all *did* happen—so it has to be possible."

"Gabrielle thinks *anything's* possible."

"I know," Obie said, sharing a smile with Ulrik.

Ulrik stood up. "Why don't we go and dress for dinner now so we don't arrive late."

Getting to their feet, Obie hesitated a moment. "I want to give you and Gabrielle my blessing, Your Majesty. And I hope you have many children and grandchildren."

Ulrik smiled warmly and put his arm around Obie's shoulders as they walked back along the garden path. "Thank you, Obie. I trust we shall."

Dinner was a merry affair, though Obie was a little subdued. The king surprised no one when he announced that he and Gabrielle would be married in the spring. Gabrielle's face was radiant with happiness and the Queen Mother beamed. Everyone cheered and drank toasts to the future marriage. When the gathering was finally breaking up and the guests were leaving, Gabrielle waved Obie over to where she stood with Ulrik. "Will you go riding with me tonight, Obie—just the two of us? There's something special I want to share with you."

Obie shot a glance at Ulrik who smiled and said, "You should feel honored, Obie, Gabrielle rarely takes anyone with her when she and Mara ride the sky at night."

"I'd like that a lot, Gabrielle," Obie said.

Minutes later they arrived in the courtyard where the windlords were waiting. Ulrik stood below waving when Mara and Magnus bore them into the night sky.

"Where are we going?" Obie called.

"Higher than you've ever been," she said, turning her head and smiling at him. "I want you to keep your mind open to my thoughts, Obie, will you do that?"

"Okay," he said with a puzzled look.

The air was filled with the gentle promise of an early spring and the huge, yellow moon floated in the clear night sky. The riders climbed until the ground faded to a memory far below and it seemed to Obie they had entered a dream realm where they glided on a cosmic sea. Gabrielle's flowing hair and gown made her look like an angel soaring across the star-strewn heavens on the wings of a snow-white windlord. And he remembered the angelic woman, many years before, singing him to sleep . . . something about fishing for a dream in the night sky. This night had a magical quality like that night, only now Gabrielle was the angel. Then the memory of his mother and the accident so many years ago came crashing down on him, filling him with the old pain and remorse.

Gabrielle heard his grieving thoughts and gazed at him with sorrow in her eyes. *Let it go, Oberon, let it go. It wasn't your fault. Close your eyes with me and see into the universe within you. The answer you so desperately need is there.*

He gave her an agonized look and nodded slightly. Closing his eyes, he willed himself to remain open to her thoughts. For a few moments he saw nothingness in his mind's eye. Then he heard her praising the One whose hand created the cosmos and set it all in balance, and he felt her deep humility and awe. And the more she praised the wider he felt her heart opening in gratitude and love. Sharing in her experience, his own heart opened so wide he thought it would burst. Suddenly it seemed he was thrust onto another plane of existence where he beheld a sublime white light that drew him close. The light washed over him, bathing him in the energy of pure boundless love, a hundred times greater than he had thought possible. And the guilt and anguish he had lived with for so long melted away. For the first time he knew with a certainty that he was loved, had always been loved, and always would be. Then he was aware of a multitude of jubilant voices singing; and though he could not see the singers and his ears could not make out the words, his heart heard pure joy; and it seemed to him the voices and the joy were inseparable, existing in this eternal moment outside of time. And somehow he knew his mother's voice was among them.

Then the light and the singing voices were gone and, his heart filled, he returned to himself. Gabrielle looked over and smiled at him and he thanked her for the gift she had given him.

CHAPTER THIRTY

HOME

THE FOLLOWING NIGHT when the full moon rose, King Ulrik, Gabrielle, the Queen Mother, Tau, Andras and Obie's many other friends stood with him in a meadow just east of the Old Frog Pond. Even Rae and Asta were there frolicking among the crowd that watched and waited for the Spirit Comet to appear over Mount Iluva. Still, no one knew for sure whether Haldor and Allegra would take Obie home. He carried the Light Crystal he had brought with him, encased in stone again in a new ammo bag the royal tailor had made for him. When he arrived home he would hide the stone deep in the cave where he found it.

But Obie was not the only one planning to take a trip that night. Gabrielle was wearing Phoebe's Bow across her back and the Dark Crystal hung from her neck in a new white bag. When the moon reached its zenith she and Mara would again ride the Moonpath and return these things to the Moon Maiden.

It was difficult enough for Obie to leave his friends, but the difficulty was magnified with the knowledge that some of them were his kin. And there was the matter of Shadow. Obie knew he would never again find such a horse. Lord Perault said he was going to try and return home with Obie by hitching a ride with him on the Spirit Comet. In a private conversation with the falcon, unknown to Obie, King Ulrik had asked him to remain with Obie and watch over him.

The hours passed while Obie and his friends talked quietly among themselves. Finally, at nearly ten o'clock, a bright light appeared over the mountain and a voice in the crowd yelled, "The Spirit Comet comes!" Cheers went up as it began streaking on its counter-clockwise course around the Valley of Windermere. In a state of excitement people called out final good wishes to Obie.

Tau looked up from Obie's side, his eyes ablaze with the yellow-green fire Obie had come to know so well.

"Maybe I can return and run with you and your kin some night through Gnarlwood Forest."

Tau made the sound between a purr and a low roar that Obie knew meant *yes*. Then he lifted one of his great paws, and when Obie stretched out his open palm he gently slapped it. Kneeling, Obie wrapped his arms around his friend's neck and great golden-brown mane. "Good-bye, my friend." Obie's voice cracked on the final words.

When he stood up Andras was there. After exchanging a quick hug, Andras held him at arms length and with a fond smile said, "This peacock will miss you, Oberon . . . you've been like a son to me."

"Ahhh, Andras, will you ever forgive me for that?"

"There was never anything to forgive, lad," Andras said with a twinkle in his eye.

Obie felt a warm hand on his shoulder and turned. King Ulrik embraced him and said, "Fair winds, Lord Oberon of House Gruffydd. We had quite an adventure together."

"Thank you, Sire." Obie's moist eyes mirrored Ulrik's. Then Gabrielle was embracing him and he could no longer hold back his tears.

"You'll always be in my heart, Lord Oberon," Gabrielle whispered and kissed his damp cheek.

"Good-bye, Woman with Stars in Her Hair. I'll always remember you. Always."

"The Spirit Comet is finishing its second circle, Oberon," Andras quietly advised.

Obie nodded and took one last look at Gabrielle, then turned and ran to the center of the meadow. Lord Perault fluttered behind and landed on his shoulder when he came to a stop. Standing tall in his long cloak Obie waited in the moonlit meadow a safe distance from the others.

Haldor and Allegra had completed most of their third circuit around the valley and were starting back towards the mountain. Everyone expected the comet to fly overhead and swoop Obie up, but Haldor and Allegra passed by and continued on towards the mountain. The crowd stirred with worried murmurings. Obie stared after the departing Spirit Comet, his hopes sinking. Could it be they really wouldn't take him home?

Suddenly a golden arrow zipped forth from Phoebe's bow. Swiftly it flew, and as it crossed Haldor's and Allegra's path it burst into flames.

The Spirit Comet immediately turned back, dipped low over the meadow, and flew straight towards Obie. He could hear his friends cheering behind him at the approaching spirits of the eagle wizard and the windlord. Tau roared and Shadow whinnied and the last thing Obie was aware of before he was swept up by the comet was the sound of galloping hooves. Once again Obie was pulled onto the comet's tail and his sky steeds shot upward. He was glad to hear Perault's screeches behind him, which meant he'd made it too.

Soon he saw the vortex of blue and purple mist and upon reentering it they began an upward spiral amidst bursts of white light. Obie was relieved that he didn't feel sick this time, maybe because he was mentally prepared. Finally, the Spirit Comet finally exited the vortex and sped downward towards home. It seemed like he had been gone a long time. Haldor and Allegra dipped almost to the ground and dropped him on his back with a soft bump. He heard Perault's wings flutter shut about the same time he felt something warm and velvety touch his forehead.

Are you all right, Oberon? A mental voice asked.

A smile spread over Obie's face. It was Shadow. Laughing, he got to his feet and put his arm over the dark stallion's neck. *So you also hitched a ride with me on the comet, huh?*

What else? Did you really think I would let you slip away without me? We made a pairing, remember?

It was still night and they were standing at the base of The Boulders in Ghostrise Valley. Glancing at the moon, Obie noticed it was in nearly the same position in the sky as it had been when he was first picked up by the Spirit Comet. A dog started barking and he realized it was Hudson. Then he heard Josh calling him from the other side of the boulder pile. "Obie? Obie, is that you laughing?"

"Josh, I'm over here. Hold on."

"Thank goodness, dude! You really had me scared."

Obie pulled himself onto Shadow's back and they headed around the boulders. The fire was burning low when they approached camp. Hudson was yelping and wagging his tail, and Josh was just plain stunned when he saw Obie ride up on a horse with a falcon on his shoulder.

"What the . . ." Josh rubbed his eyes. "I'm really asleep and dreaming this, right Obie?"

Obie smiled down at him. "Lord Oberon to you, Josh."

"Sure. Why don't we make it *King* Oberon. You'd probably like that even better."

Chuckling to himself, Obie dismounted.

"You must have hidden the horse, hawk, and that Halloween costume nearby and you're just playing a stupid trick on me, right?"

"Nope, and nope. And if you think this is a Halloween costume, Josh, come and take a closer look." Obie removed his sable cloak and threw it around Josh's shoulders.

Josh grasped the soft fur in his hand. "Wow, this is real fur."

Obie unbuckled his sword and fastened it around Josh's hips, then showed him his new Raptor and golden ring with the Gruffydd Coat of Arms on them. After examining everything Josh eyed Obie uncertainly for a few moments. "How . . . how'd you get all this stuff? Did you find a treasure in the mountain when I wasn't looking?" He glanced again at the stallion and the falcon and his face contorted into a look of confused dismay.

Obie grinned sympathetically. "I know this is a lot to lay on you at one time. But will you just try and keep an open mind?"

Josh nodded slowly.

"Okay, then. I want you to meet my friends, Shadow and Lord Perault. Shadow, Lord Perault, this is my friend Josh."

Shadow raised his muzzle and neighed a greeting. But when the falcon said, "It's a pleasure to make your acquaintance, Josh. You may call me *Perault*," Josh's face paled and he began to shake.

"I can't take any more of this, Obie. I mean it, man. I've never heard of a talking falcon. I don't know what's going on— has this valley gotten to me? Has my hair turned white like that guy last year?" He pulled a couple of hairs from his head and examined them.

"No, your hair is as red as ever. "Trust me, Josh, nothing's wrong with you—everything's fine. I'm going to build up the fire and then we'll sit down and I'll explain everything."

Josh sat down on his sleeping bag and watched Obie walk to the wood pile and pick up some pieces. "Hey, what happened to your limp?" he demanded.

"I lost it on a moonlight ride," Obie said as he carried the wood to the fire.

"Dude, you've got a *lot* of explaining to do."

"Yeah . . . but you have to swear on your life to keep what I tell you a secret. All right?" Obie dropped down on his sleeping bag and sat cross-legged facing Josh.

"Haven't I always kept our secrets? But if it makes you happy, okay. I swear. As long as you promise me we're getting out of this valley early in the morning."

"First I have to make a quick trip to the mountain to replace the rock I found. It's important. You can wait here if you want."

"No, you already disappeared on me once tonight. From now on I'm sticking by your side like peanut butter sticks to your teeth." Hudson came over and curled up next to Josh.

"Alright then," Obie said, the firelight reflecting in his eyes. "Josh, you're not going to believe this but . . ."

Obie talked until the sun rose above the forested eastern plateau.

"Geez, Obie, what an adventure you had," Josh finally said. "And with all this stuff you brought back, I guess I have to believe you. I just wish I'd been there. If you ever go back, can I go too?" Without waiting for an answer Josh got up and drew Obie's sword and swished it about in the crisp morning air. "I'd have given those raks and hob-goblins something to think about—you'd better believe it!" He stopped and turned towards Obie. "Do you think the ghosts in this valley could be good ghosts who just wanna keep people away?"

"I don't know, Josh . . . maybe there's good and bad ones here." An odd smile crept over Obie's face. How much had Will really known about the stone containing the Light Crystal? Obie strongly suspected Will had withheld some information before sending him off to Ghostrise. He needed to have a serious talk with him.

***

When Obie arrived home that afternoon, he found a note from Will asking him to come by the cabin as soon as he was rested. Josh and Hudson went home, and Obie grabbed a couple of hours sleep before heading over to Will's place.

When Obie's dad returned home from his business trip the next day, Obie told him Shadow and Lord Perault were gifts from a friend for some work he had done, which he reasoned was more or less true. The thing that amazed his dad—and everyone else—was that Obie was no longer limping. His only explanation was, "Whatever was causing it must have healed." Some people thought that losing his limp was the reason he was able to control his anger now. But Obie knew it was the other way around, and so did Will Gray Eagle.

A few days later Obie let his brother take Shadow out for a ride. It was then that Scottie made the startling discovery that he could communicate mentally with the stallion. When Scottie started asking questions, Shadow said it would be better if he talked to Obie about it. So Obie told him all that had happened and about their elven blood. At first Scottie laughed and told Obie his imagination was running away with him, but when Obie started speaking to him telepathically and Lord Perault engaged him in a conversation he changed his mind.

Obie and Scottie tried unsuccessfully to communicate telepathically with their dad. Obie knew his dad had the magic in him, but maybe it had gotten repressed somehow. If so, he wondered if he might someday discover it. Obie decided to wait until the time seemed right to tell his dad the story of his trip to Windermere. He hoped it wouldn't be too long. In the meantime he began to see something reassuring and comforting in his father's eyes when their gaze met. Had it always been there and he'd just missed it?

Obie tried out for the track team at school. When he crossed the finish line well ahead of the other guys Coach Webber slapped him on the back. "Good work, Griffin. Looks like there's going to be two star players in your family. Practice starts tomorrow at 8:00 a.m. sharp."

Things changed for the better with Shannon Piper too. A few days after he returned she stopped him in the school hallway and apologized for the way Jabo and his friends had acted the morning they met him and Josh on the road.

"I didn't believe you were a part of it, Shannon. Jabo and the guys were just acting dumb and so was I."

Shannon laughed. "We all do dumb things sometimes." Her soft brown eyes met his, and she added, "I also wanted to tell you, well . . . I'm not seeing Jabo anymore."

"You're not?" Obie beamed. "Well then—what are you doing Friday night?"

When he and Shannon started seeing each other Jabo skulked for a while, but he and his friends kept their distance. Obie figured it was partly because his brother was on the school football team, and partly because he was gaining in popularity and had a lot of friends on the track team.

Something else happened. And it was something of the greatest importance. He learned about it on the evening of the day he arrived back home, when he went to see Will Gray Eagle. The old man sat waiting for him on his cabin porch, and as Obie approached he could feel his eyes boring into him. He knew what Will was observing.

"I see you've decided to walk straight now, Oberon." The old man's eyes were sparkling.

Obie grinned at him. "I have a lot to tell you." They went inside and Will brought a pot of hot tea from the stove while Obie got two cups out and sat down on a floor mat across from Will. Sitting near the fire in the hearth, Obie began his tale again. Will listened silently, nodding occasionally while Obie talked.

". . . and then Haldor and Allegra dropped me, Shadow, and Perault back in the Valley by The Boulders. And that's the end of the story."

"Not quite the end," Will responded in a mellow voice.

"What do you mean?" Obie was startled.

"Do you have the stone containing the Light Crystal with you?"

"No, I returned it to the cave this morning when the sun came up."

"Good. It will be safe there."

"What I'd like to know is, how much did you know before you sent me to Ghostrise Valley?"

"There was much I could not tell you, Oberon, because you would not have understood. Only now . . ." Will spread his arms wide and his eyes glowed yellow. "Only now will you understand as I reveal to you that . . . I am Haldor's descendant." Obie's mouth dropped open as Will transformed into a large gray eagle.

Startled, Obie pushed backward off the mat to avoid his fanning wings. He wondered how, after all he had seen and experienced, he could still be surprised. Then as quickly as the eagle had appeared it faded away and Will was there again, calmly sitting on his mat.

Obie expelled a deep breath. "Nice intro." He fought to appear calm as he crawled back onto his mat. "So . . . my second dad's an eagle."

"I'm glad you finally know my secret, son. I assumed human form and came here almost twenty-five years ago to wait for you. As for my introduction just now, it's been said many times that *one picture is worth a thousand words.*"

"It did explain things quickly. So, you're also a wizard?"

"Yes. I am skilled in the old magic, handed down to me from a forgotten time. Like Haldor I have the ability to assume other forms, though my powers are not as great as his were."

"Then you must have known about the prophecy and the Light Crystal."

"I have been the Guardian of the Crystal for over three hundred years."

Obie's head was swimming in the revelations about this man he had thought he knew.

"And now," Will continued, "it is time for you to take that responsibility, for the Crystal must always be protected."

Obie was taken back. "Me? The Guardian?"

"Do you remember the riddles in the prophecy, Oberon?"

"Yes. But I've only been able to figure out the one about the fiery breath burning the frozen trees. I'm sure that referred to Smoker, burning the frozen forest on his way to join the battle at Windermere. The *two is three* lines I never really understood."

"The exact words are, *When skies are dark and two is three.*"

"What does it mean?"

"*Two* is a reference to the two Guardians, Gabrielle and Mara. When you arrived with the Light Crystal, although you didn't know it, you became the third Guardian. Thus, that part of the prophecy was fulfilled: two Guardians became three. You're already a Guardian, Oberon."

Obie was silent while the significance of Will's words sank in and his heart accepted the awesome responsibility.

Finally, Will said, "I'll remain here with you for a while to help you come fully into your elven powers."

"Thank you, Will." In the back of his mind Obie wondered if the Lonely Oak still stood on top the mountain and if the Moonpath still opened on nights of the full moon. He had much to learn.

ABOUT THE AUTHOR

G. A. Hesse developed an early appreciation of folklore, fantasy and science fiction and recalls writing her first fairy tale during recess in second grade. She has worked for Corporate America and taught High School English. Her curiosity about the world and other cultures has sent her on travels through the U.S., Europe, Mexico, and South America. Ms. Hesse earned a Bachelor of Arts Degree in English and American Literature with a minor in philosophy from California State University at Long Beach, and a Juris Doctor Degree from Western State University College of Law in Fullerton, California. Choosing to pursue writing rather than practice law, she now lives and writes in Aliso Viejo, California.